The Swordmaker

KATIE CROSS

KCW

Author's Note

THE SWORDMAKER was a story that I once dreaded to write, simply because I knew it would be gargantuan in magic. The depth of power that I'd need to dive into alarmed me.

How to organize it?

It's a story about *two* magicks converging into one witch. That witch must decide to whom he belongs.

If to anyone at all.

It's also a story of friendship. The power of the other witch that holds space for you without expectation.

Greater than all that, however, Andrei's tale is one of knowing. Knowing oneself. Knowing the powers that we can't explain. The world, life, magic, and ability that unfolds on the paths we trod.

All of us have a knowing deep inside.

A voice.

A Guide.

In the end, Andrei's story is one that begs the question: *do we trust the knowing?*

—Katie Cross

PS—Swordmaking is a culture unto itself, so I've included a List of Clannish Words at the front of the book, as well as a map, and pictures of swords that you'll meet throughout the story.

At the back, you'll find a guide to help you understand the different parts (pommel, tang, blade, it all blurs together!) as you read.

List Of Clannish And Southern Network Words

Blad—Yazikan swear word similar to *damn*.

Buschey—A cement-like paste used to create hearths that withstand great heat.

Calavander—A type of mushroom in the Southern Network. Very fragrant. They're mostly olive green and grow along tree trunks, even in winter.

Calphia—An iridescent mushroom that glows a bright aqua and purple. A well-known hallucinogenic amongst the clans.

Chthu—The name of the clan god known to be a trouble-maker. He's selfish, and blamed when bad things happen.

Chudo—Miracle.

Falfalla—Bright red flowers that bloom in the spring. They have tulip-like petals that form cups. Inside, a honey-suckle-like fluid can be extracted. Many clan witches harvest it, dry it, crush it, and sprinkle it in tea as a sweetener.

Fere-fil—Almost son. Typically given to a male fiancé before the handfasting has completed.

Fil—Son.

Haniye—The inability to breathe. A word used when

something has taken your breath—used akin as a deep surprise, one that *takes the breath* or *stirs the soul.*

Hulu—The name of the clan god known for kindness and compassion. He is invoked when blessings are desired.

Ira—An exclamation, like 'Ah!' or 'Hey!'

Maman—Mother.

Mizziya—A time when a Southern Network witch (non-clannish) will go into the great white tundra to prove their ability to live off the land, their connection with the snow.

Nelos—Nephew.

Pana—Thin slices of meat stuffed with marrow and herbs, then rolled together.

Praznick—Annual celebration dedicated to the Sirilas magic and the lives of the *maleesa.*

Privet—A greeting, equal to *hello.*

Saltov—A cheers for good health and warm fires to all present, usually done with drinks in a social setting.

Sirilas—The name of the grimoire that sets out all the magic the clans use to create and run the silk trade.

Tanta—Aunt.

Teriteria—The third eye. A belief in the clans around the 'insight to the soul' that is manifested through the *teriteria.* In other explanations, a subconscious.

Vyzov Bitvay—The official challenge to a High Priest that may come from any witch. The battle is to the surrender. If the current High Priest surrenders, he loses his title.

Yakuza—Oil made from seeds native to the Southern Network. Often used for polishing or high heat cooking.

Zamuk—Leaves from a crawling bush typically dried, crushed, and smoked in a pipe for a relaxing effect.

Zavok—A type of bush that produces the leaves that *maleesa* require to spin threads.

Zandelia—A perfumed flower that grows along the riverbanks in the spring.

Sarasam

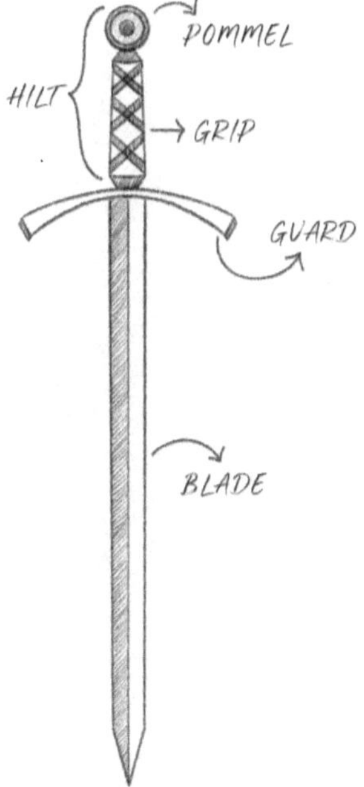

Map of Clannish Lands

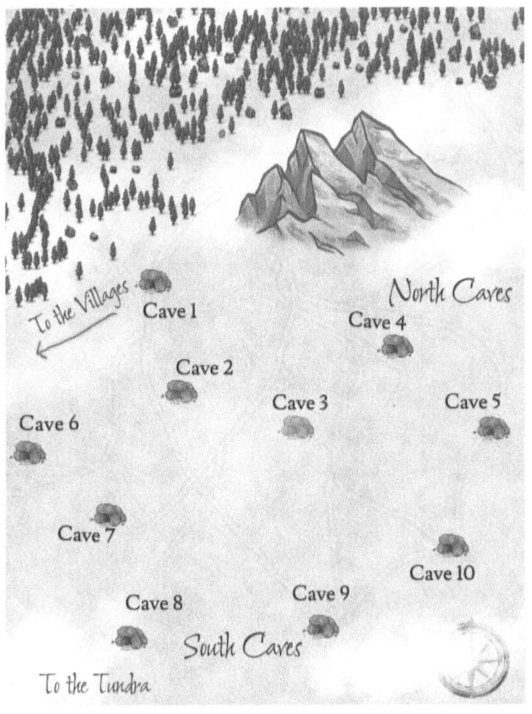

Introduction

WINTER, YEAR 1447

Far away, days of walking from any desirable land, lay a quiet tundra topped by a glacier. The glacier was hidden from those who wanted to see it and revealed to those chosen to see it.

Near it lurked a family.

Nay, a clan.

Andrei's clan.

Chapter One

Fickle, hideous things.

The maleesa are creatures of magic. Cheeky clan
members call them the winter butterflies, *but this is an
incorrect, offensive phrase. It should be stricken from our
culture.*

In fact, the maleesa are more.
Non-clannish witches expect them to be worms, but they
are not. Neither arachnid, for they spin no web, only
threads of silk.

Magic.

The maleesa were sent by our kind god, Hulu, to provide
for the clan. There is no other justification for such
powerful magic, nor is any justification needed. Long
ago, the clan found favor in Hulu's graces and we
received the magic.

Hulu provides.

We consume.

The magic works, so long as we are obedient to it.

This is the cycle of our life. Clan members remain indebted to the god and taken at his will. The Sirilas magic that was left on our glacier demands much. Nay, the maleesa demand much.

They are worth it.

—Odessa, Reeler
Year 1289

A silver sparkle drew Andrei's eye.

He glanced down, then paused. Stuck in the snow, tip down, lay a metal sword. It was about the length of his forearm, with absolutely nothing to adorn it. No leather wrap around the handle. No gems. No sheath, or whatever that was called.

The sword stood in the middle of the cave walkway that he'd just exited, as if such a tiny weapon could arrogantly hold him back. Barely the width of his palm, the sword had little prayer of doing anything mighty. It was little more than a bland hunk of metal.

Odd.

He nudged it aside with a toe and a grunt. The Guards would need to gather it. Who in the clan had a sword, anyway? Magic was their greatest defense here. Specific spells protected the clan in unusual ways. Physical violence wasn't allowed. Such barbarity might knock the Sirilas magic out of balance and the clan would suffer.

Andrei stepped further into the cool, brisk air. The sun, a white circle so far away he could cover it with the tip of his pinky finger, shone from the distant sky. Frost bristled off the cave wall, as if it reached for the retreating warmth.

Maman shuffled out behind him.

He turned to face her. "Everything will be fine, *Maman*. Thank you for telling me. I'll note it in the scrolls just in case, though I think there's no problem."

The hunched, shriveled figure of his mother grinned from right next to him. She always kept herself one or two steps away so she could whack him in the arm if he did something she disagreed with.

Though bitty, the woman moved faster than an arctic baer.

"Don't sass me." Her deep-set eyes, lined with wrinkles from the bold sun this far south in Alkarra, glared at him. She wagged a finger close to his nose. "I'm telling you, something is wrong with the *maleesa*. This batch . . . it . . . feels different. The magic is out of balance."

"Stacia—"

"Call me by my first name again, you clod, and I'll box your ears. You might be the Guide for this cave, but you're still my *fil*!"

"Forgive me, *Maman*."

She grunted. "I have cared for the *maleesa* all my life, Andrei. I know when something is wrong. Their reproductive cycle is off by three days. Eventually, the color of the silk will be impacted, and that affects orders. If we do not deliver exact amounts—"

"The only thing that is wrong with the creatures," Andrei murmured, "is going to be when they lose you as Caretaker because you fall ill while standing outside. I understand, *Maman*. Something feels wrong with the *maleesa*, and their reproductive cycle skewed late this time. Everything in the scrolls, the reports, appears fine. We'll watch, *Maman,* and wait."

She snorted, but gently.

"Fine."

He lowered his brow in a silent suggestion of firmness. "Go back inside, please."

She waved a hand, ignoring the silent rebuff in his gesture. A deepening scowl manifested, but he sensed her quiet capitulation when she blew a raspberry.

"I am noting my concerns in the record," she snapped, but little force lay behind it. Even she would admit her tendency to fuss over the creatures too much. After decades of giving her soul to the work, how could she not?

An affectionate chuckle rolled through Andrei. "Note it in your records. I'm meeting with Sergei in a few minutes. As always, he will guide us to the right path. For now, continue on."

With a grumble, she spun on her heel.

"Oh, *Maman?*"

She paused, glanced back.

"You will have the *maleesa* picked out for the *Praznick,* correct? The celebration begins in less than three months. We must report to Sergei that we have chosen the creature and set it aside by tomorrow."

"I know about the *Praznick,*" she growled. "I've already selected ten creatures to winnow to the final one. I'm just waiting to confirm their transformation cycle is on track."

"Thank you."

"The correct one will be in its glass jar by the morning. Sergei is welcome to see it himself."

Her peeved tone continued as she turned, muttered under her breath, and disappeared into darker chambers.

Andrei shuffled to the side several paces, chuckling to himself as he cast his eyes around. Nothing but a quiet tundra stretched ahead. White space as far as the horizon, represented in a thin line below the giant blue sky. Slivers of unbroken snow. No trees. Only openness. A barren terror that seeped into the soul when one stared at it for too long.

The tricky tundra, however, hid much.

The Sirilas magic—or the magic of the silkmakers—hid cave entrances like Cave Three where *Maman* worked. Incantations from the grimoire prevented any witch without clan blood from seeing an entrance.

A non-clannish member could accidentally stumble into a cave, perhaps grope their way inside, but such an event had never happened within recorded history. Non-clannish witches never crossed the magical, invisible boundary that hid this part of the tundra.

The underground caves cached the *maleesa*, precious silk creatures, away from jealous eyes. The Sirilas magic protected the caves, which brimmed full of the secrets of the silkmakers.

Behind him?

Well, that was a different story.

A hulking glacier lurked at his back, emanating cold. It soared overhead, several stories high, and long as a run of forest. Brilliant facets glimmered in the bitterly cold light. Edges of sapphire, cyanic depths that glittered like a soul.

At the bottom of the frozen mass, where glacier met ground, stood several doors. They glinted, carved from the ice itself. Interior hinges hid them from outside eyes. The entrance for Cave Three disappeared entirely as he walked away. Relief washed through him, as it always did, when the magic issued its protection.

He spun toward the glacier, mind shuffling ahead. Middle-meal with *Maman* complete. Next, meetings with Sergei, his future father-in-law and direct superior, awaited.

The *maleesa* in the North Caves fared fine right now, but if something—

A *ting* stopped him.

Shocked, Andrei peered down. The simple sword stood in his path yet again. Tip down, buried into the snow, as if someone had fisted it in their palm and shoved it into the ground.

He stared at it with a tilted head.

"What are you doing here?"

Hadn't the sword appeared several paces back there? He scoured the land to find it empty again. No one had moved the sword ahead of him. He would have heard. No clan member would touch a weapon unless they were a Guard, just to be safe.

Which meant . . .

Face scrunched in annoyance, he reached for the handle. Better take it to the Guards so other clan members wouldn't tread on it. A child might hurt themselves. His fingers wrapped around the warm hilt.

Everything went black.

Chapter Two

The maleesa bond with the Caretaker of their cave. This is a fact that none refute.

Such a bond comes from consistency. Hulu knew this, which is why the Sirilas magic requires the Caretaker to be loyal to that cave, that batch, for four years, until the maleesa die.

We receive a new batch. We care for it for four years. The maleesa will slowly drop off, one at a time, after year three, until they are all gone. Rarely do they see the dawning of the first day of their fourth year of life.

Like the mother ducks with their ducklings that dot the rivers in the spring, the Caretakers watch their flock until the final maleesa, old and shriveled, gives its life to the creation of the silk so that we might live.

When that happens, I weep.

Oh, how I weep.

Bogdan, Overseer
Year 1319

A groan woke Andrei.

Several seconds passed before he realized the sound came from his own throat. He blinked away snowflakes that cluttered his lashes, and opened his eyes to view the understory of a forest.

Green boughs reached overhead, prickly with sharp needles. Snow burdened the pinpoint tops of trees, coating them in latticed layers of white. Bitter cold penetrated through his fur coat, black silk shirt, and onto his back.

With a jerk, Andrei sat up.

He lay beneath a towering tree, partially sheltered from drifts of snow by the branches. Was this the same forest that cluttered the river to the north?

Clan members occasionally lived with villagers there. They sent fish and metal they harvested from the river for the clan. Andrei had never ventured to the villages. As the future Guide to the Clan, he could not leave clannish lands unless it was to protect the clan and the *maleesa*.

Dazed, he shoved to his feet and waded through snow into a clearing between trees. Clumps dropped from above to land on the back of his neck with a slushy *plop*. He shivered.

Muttering under his breath, he scooped the snow free, shuddering as remnants skittered down his spine. He wore a thinner coat than usual, because he needed little when walking back and forth between *Maman*'s cave and the glacier.

Where was he, anyway?

Clouds marred the sky in between the treetops and hid the position of the sun so he couldn't determine the time. With broken recollections, he recalled the sword in the snow.

Maman. He had an impending meeting with Sergei to discuss the Southern Network High Priest and begin planning for the *Praznick.* A clan member who worked with the trade partners in the Network had a question about currency exchange.

Everything restored to his mind with crystal-clear clarity, then funneled back to that sword. As if a voice called to him, he sensed a presence.

Andrei whirled around.

The sword stood upright, embedded in the snow several paces away. As before, it pointed tip down. There were no sparkling gems or decorations in which it could boast. It was, perhaps, the plainest sword he had ever seen.

Vaguely, he recalled the warmth of it against his hand before it brought him . . . here.

Stuck in the snow, yet still warm?

The questions compounded.

Hesitantly, he approached it again. Each step closed the space between them. At every pace, his mind grew increasingly fuzzy. As if someone reached into his head, smeared his thoughts.

Andrei paused just short of being able to reach the sword.

"What are you?"

The sword gave no sound. His mind stirred with vague shadows that felt foreign, but could be shock. His fast breath fractured the strange air.

"Did I hit my head?"

A quick glance showed no rocks on the snow where his body imprinted the ground beneath the tree. Several long moments of consideration followed before he determined he didn't imagine this.

Whatever that sword was, it clearly held dark magic. Nothing to mess with, particularly not for the future Guide. If he dabbled in other magic systems outside the Sirilas, it would compromise the integrity of the magic. The protections could fall, the secrets of the silkmakers revealed, and all physical and economic safety for the clan lost.

He hissed the clannish noise through his front teeth. "Pft. Not for me."

Andrei turned away and braced himself. After a moment of pause, he called for the Sirilas magic to help.

"Back to the glacier, please."

Nothing happened.

He blinked.

Andrei whirled around. The sword hadn't budged. No stir of snow indicated the Sirilas magic could hear the plea. Louder, he cried, "To the glacier, please!"

Nothing.

Panic swelled inside. Calmly, he repeated a final time.

"Will you please return me to the glacier?"

Nothing stirred.

He tossed a hand in the air with a growl to the sword. "This is your fault!"

The sword said nothing.

Other requests to conjure paper and ink failed. In fact, the usual playful response of the Sirilas—twirling wind, puffs of snowflakes—had dropped like dead air. Terror struck him.

How far outside clan lands had this . . . thing . . . taken him?

Could the Sirilas not find him?

Stumbling back, he put distance between himself and the hexed weapon. Perhaps if he stood far away the Sirilas would sense him? The sword might emit a dangerous aura that prevented magic.

He put five paces between them.

More magical requests still didn't work. Not at ten paces. Not twenty. Frantic now, he raced deeper into the trees.

Fifty?

Still no.

As he swung around to continue running, the sword appeared in front of him. Tip down, buried in the snow. The gleaming metallic hilt echoed the stormy clouds. He skidded to a stop and shrieked.

A sheet of ice hidden below the top layer of snow caught his big toe. He flailed forward, arms wheeling, until he landed with a *thud* on his stomach. The impact rocked through his jaw, clanging his teeth together painfully. When his eyes blinked open, the sword lingered a breath away.

In the reflection, his own slanted eyes peered back.

Mental stirrings rumbled through his mind like oil on water. An otherworldly blurriness spread, viscous and unclear. Was it trying to communicate in a whisper?

No.

An . . . image.

"I've lost my mind," Andrei whispered. His breath fogged up the exposed part of the blade. "Did I eat a *calphia* mushroom by accident at middlemeal?"

Also no.

Middlemeal was hours ago.

This was no hallucination. This had to be nefarious magic. A hexed charm that followed him. A way for the clannish gods to tell him he'd done something wrong, or perhaps discover his loyalty to the Sirilas magic.

At that, Andrei frowned.

Impossible.

What wrath might he have incurred? He lived the exact path set out for him. The one which Sergei chose for him years ago. He never strayed. He had dedicated the last thirty years of his life to the *maleesa*, to his clan, to the silkmaker trade by which they survived. Predictable, routine action. Such rote work sustained them in the harshest deserts of Alkarra.

"What do you want?" he asked the sword. "Please, tell me so you can take me back. I shouldn't be here!"

Desperation must have unlocked his mind, lessening a wall he didn't know existed, because a flood overcame him. Thoughts that were not his own crept into his mind like smoke. Intruders and foreign, none of them made sense.

He could only breathe.

Listen.

Finally, amidst the swirls of strangeness and the infiltration of something outside his mind, the vapor-like sensation settled on one thought.

Yours.

* * *

The word created an explosion in his chest.

Yours.

Again and again it repeated until Andrei shoved out of the snow. Standing, he looked down on the pathetic sword with utter disbelief. This far away, the murky thoughts weren't so troublesome.

"You're not mine. I don't . . . I don't hold weapons."

He could have sworn a sensation like irritation followed, but surely that was his own. Swords, even enchanted ones, had no ability to feel.

"I belong to my clan. As a Guide, and as a future Guide to the clan, all that I have I give to them. I am not a Guard that would hold a sword. You cannot be mine. It's . . . it's not done."

The sword issued no further thoughts.

Andrei glanced overhead. Between thick branches, the hidden sun faded behind a restless gray sky. Darkness thickened the air. Somewhere in the distance, the sun would set soon. Night would fall. Andrei rubbed his arms, quivering. If he didn't return to the clan, he'd die before middlenight.

The sense that one thing held him back rippled through

him. He couldn't *quite* put his finger on it, but had the idea that it related back to the sword. The sword had brought him here.

Would it return him?

He didn't want to touch it again, because what if the sword took him *farther* away? He had no other magic to use except the Sirilas, and clearly that would only work on dedicated clannish lands. The sword had obviously taken him outside of those.

A gentle nudge came to him. An undeniable urge to reach for the sword.

He crouched down.

"What if I don't want you?"

No thoughts stirred back up. He reached a shaking hand out, but stopped a finger's-breadth away. If he touched it, would other magic—more sinister in nature—overcome him?

As terrifying as this had been, he felt no capturing of his soul, the way the old ones spoke of. No darkness in his mind to cloud his judgment. The more his initial terror abated, the more he saw the sword.

With a sigh, Andrei sat down.

Cold seeped through his pants, wrinkling his nose. He forced himself to set the discomfort aside and focus on what stood between him, a warm fire, his favorite dinner, and a predictable schedule.

This sword.

A final push of annoyance urged him to just touch it already. The tips of his fingers closed around the hilt. He sucked in a breath, screwed one eye shut, and anticipated a sweeping sensation to take him away.

No such thing came.

He remained in the same spot and held the warm metal. Heat flowed all the way to his fingers, his wrist, through his arm. He withdrew the sword from the snow. It gleamed with a muted luster.

Though not apparently beautiful, it appeared sturdy. Precise, if nothing else, with a whetted edge. Nor did it weigh as heavily as he expected. The blade had no splotching or brittleness. He pressed on the metal with a thumb and it yielded nothing. Light, too, for so thick a thing.

Flummoxed, he could only stare.

His mind emptied more and more the longer he held the sword. The frustrating, agitated perception ebbed into . . . thoughts. These ruminations were less tangled, more ready. As if they'd presented themselves to him before, and knowing the path could go more easily.

A flutter of movement in the snow just beyond his feet drew his gaze. A hammer appeared, along with a wooden bucket. Inside lay a linen bag, the top tied together. Four additional linen bags followed.

"What's this?"

Andrei leaned forward. When the tips of his fingers grazed the top of the first linen bag, he knew what was inside. Not physically—the bag remained closed—but with the sight that lived in the *teriteria*. The third eye.

Tiny pieces of pure metal lay inside.

He felt it with a deep certainty that didn't require sight. His hand wandered to the next linen bag. Gems. The varying bumps beneath his touch meant loads of them, and in various sizes. Colors followed. Sapphire. Crimson. Yellow. Deepest emerald.

A rolled leather case showed up next. He undid a bone clasp and flung it open. Carving instruments of varying types, all with the same metal construction as the sword, lay inside.

"What have you given me?"

Glowing blue runes appeared in the snow, illuminating in a circle around the tools. Andrei slipped back, dropped the sword. The runes instantly faded. Clearly, a connection existed between the tools, the sword, and the runes.

With another tentative touch, he reached for the sword again. Toasty in his palm, a dizzying rush of thoughts followed. Calmer, this time. The runes scrawled again in the snow, scripted with a clannish slant.

But not his clan.

Ancient clannish, perhaps. He didn't recognize these. With his finger, he traced them. Canted his head, studied the swirls and swoops. They faded after his touch. An urging compelled him to speak before he knew what he wanted to say.

"I'm supposed to take all of this and . . . do something?"

Nothing.

The lack of response shouldn't have been a surprise, but after the strange ripples in his mind, it was.

"Ah . . . something with the metal rocks?"

This conclusion, at least, relied on logic. Clearly, the sword wanted something from him, and it seemed to stem from the tools he'd been given. Andrei glanced down and studied the strange collection of *things* again.

"Another sword?"

A current slipped from the sword into his hand, so fast it startled him. With a shout, he dropped it and leaped to his feet, heart pounding. The sword lay inert in the snow. Once he released it, his thoughts cleared. He stood there for several moments, catching his breath, before he shook his head.

"I've lost my mind."

Grudgingly, he picked up the linen bags, rolled the leather back together, secured the end, and gathered the sword. Nothing else manifested. No runes, tools, or thoughts that made little sense.

What was he thinking?

None of this made sense.

Another compulsion—or a hunch—followed. The moment the tools lay in his arms, he held them close. Another request for the magic to take him away issued from his mind, but nothing happened.

"I'll make a sword with these supplies," he said in a rush of inspiration. "You have my promise, but return me to my dwelling. They're probably worried and waiting. Sergei is sick and I need to discuss the *Praznick* with him while he has the energy and I have meetings to attend, thank you very much. There is no room for mysteries in my life!"

At his agreement, the magic whisked him away.

Chapter Three

What would we do without the maleesa?

Can you ask a question that I might understand?

—Viktoriya, Spinner
Year 1354

An indrawn breath, filled with the deep scent of nutmeg, and a firm reminder that *I'm safe at home, where I belong with my clan,* repeated through Andrei's mind for the thousandth time the next day.

He opened his eyes.

The familiar comfort of his dwelling still surrounded him. Freshly washed sheets stretched tight. Dust-free shelves scattered with artistic renditions of the most vibrant *maleesa.*

Ah.

Ease.

Morning sunlight slanted through the windowpanes and fell on top of his head, warming the dark black strands. He shuffled his fingers through his braided hair. It swung all the way down his back when loosened from the braid, which he only did once a week.

Thankfully, no dreams had interrupted his sleep. They would have been nightmares with the sword mucking up yesterday in such an uncomfortable, intrusive way.

Though it had seemed like he spent hours grappling with that sword and whatever magic had been involved, when he returned, only minutes had passed.

Perhaps two, at that.

The sword had returned him to his dwelling, where he hid the tools under the bed and hurried to the glacier. His meeting with Sergei had been completed without a hitch, confirming the High Priest's visit today. Details of what they'd decided eluded him now, but he'd remember them later.

Filled with new resolve for a far more routine day, Andrei swung his legs off the mattress. Despite the bitter cold radiating from his window panes, the floor warmed his feet. He smiled.

"Thank you, Sirilas magic, for the comforts of my life."

A gentle shift of air followed. An acknowledgment. The magic thrived in the air of the clannish lands like a breathing thing. They gave their life to the magic, and the magic protected them from violence, danger, and made their life more comfortable.

His gaze caught on the sword. The affable air dropped as he frowned. An even darker thought occurred.

Would the presence of the sword interrupt the Sirilas magic?

So far, the Sirilas magic had issued no complaints, and he knew when the magic wasn't pleased. Any shift of imbalance in the Sirilas magic would create a palpable sensation in his chest, like standing on unstable ground.

No such feeling came now.

The sword lay in the same place he dropped it in his haste yesterday, on top of the chest of drawers.

"Well, you haven't taken yourself to some other part of my dwelling, or attempted to kill me in the night, or brought anyone else here through dark magic. At least that's something."

The sword said nothing.

Andrei walked past.

As he moved through his ritual ablutions—wash the face, freshen the arms, scour the teeth with a dense rag—he considered the fact he might have imagined it all.

No.

He couldn't fathom the fact that the sword, accompanying linen bags, and leather pouch sat in his room. The tools had no eyes, but he felt as if they did. Pressure stared at him from all angles.

Unfortunately, he'd agreed under duress to make a sword. Clan members never went back on their word.

A *sword*, of all things.

Well, he would have agreed to stranger requests just to get out of the peculiar forest and back to safety, at any rate. There had been no time frame given, so he'd . . . figure it out later when the High Priest of the Southern Network wasn't visiting.

Gratefully, he turned his mind to pleasanter things. A pair of freshly laundered clothes lay across the bottom of his bed— a gift from the magic. He drew in a deep breath, appreciating the bright smell of cotton, finished dressing, and found himself outside in the blinding sunshine minutes later. He soaked in the light, eager for a bland day.

"Andrei?"

The delicate peak of a female voice drew his gaze.

He smiled. "Anastasia."

His petite fiancée bustled to his side, arm extended. He accepted her plump hand, pressed a kiss to it. She touched her fist to her chin in reciprocal greeting.

A fur-lined coat, taken from a wild fox and hare that village members traded for silk, fluffed out from her tiny neck. She tightened it with a sash across the middle of her waist. Beneath that, a leather dress fell to her calves, protected by knee-high boots.

Her slight brows rose high, mere pencil-lines against her tawny skin. The exaggerated lift of her brow gave a greater accent to her small eyes. "*Papan* says that you expect a visit with the new High Priest today?"

"Yes."

"Good luck. I came with mushrooms."

Her clipped way of speaking left little room for affection, a trait he didn't mind. Anastasia reached into a pocket, extracted a small, woven case of reeds. He accepted, squeezed the sides. It popped open to reveal a collection of mushrooms, about the size of his thumb, inside. A fragrant smell followed.

"*Calavander.*" He breathed deep. "Thank you, Anastasia. They will bring all the luck the forest has to give."

She had already turned, giving him her profile. A vague nod acknowledged his acceptance as he pushed the case into his pocket. He loathed the *calavander* strain of mushrooms. They populated tree trunks at this time of year, despite it being the depths of winter. Their olive green color made them unattractive, their pungent stench filled his house.

Their betrothal stretched eighteen years, yet he still felt as if they hardly knew each other.

Then again, he expected little.

Anastasia was only twenty-one, after all. Still of the age when romantic fancies overtook the pragmatism that life in the clan required. She longed for romance. He loved routine.

One day, they'd figure it out.

He accepted her gesture of caring for what it was, dismissed the rest.

She fell in step next to him as he walked toward the North Caves area where the open tundra awaited. Most clan members lived in small dwellings made of ice or wood along the edges of the tundra behind the glacier, where the forest met snow. Some lived out in the open, though the Sirilas magic hid them, too.

A river lurked in the northern trees. If one headed west, it would lead toward the river villages—perhaps the area the sword had taken him last night.

The tree line snaked an S curve behind the glacier, filled with homes. It allowed the Suppliers to seek food in the forest, and the woodlands to protect the clan from other witches. Clan members like Anastasia, daughter to the Guide to the Clans, lived within the glacier, where business was conducted.

"Last night I had a strange experience," he said.

"Oh?"

"A sword appeared to me."

Unblemished skin, smooth as ice planes, wrinkled between her brows. "A sword?"

"I touched it, and it took me elsewhere. Prevented me from escaping when I tried to use magic. Other things appeared. Tools. Gems. It . . . finally let me go when I agreed to make another sword."

A curling laugh startled him so much he jumped, turned to face her. Anastasia held a delicate hand to her wide face.

"You jest, Andrei! How unlike you to tell stories."

Her hilarity continued. Andrei opened his mouth, then closed it again. In review, it *sounded* like a joke. A bad dream. Andrei, to whom nothing unplanned and exciting ever happened.

And by design.

They continued until her amusement faded into a gentle hum and intermittent chuckle. Not for the first time, he wondered if it had been a strange dream.

Still impossible.

The proof lay on his chest of drawers at home.

"What a dream to have." She dabbed at the corner of her eyes. "Please, whatever mushroom you ate at lastmeal, eat it again tonight. I'll return in the morning for a report on your dreams. In the meantime, I must go. New silk has arrived at the Creator's Cave and I have a dress to sew."

Without another word, and amusement still bright in her smile, Anastasia peeled away. It had been months—perhaps years—since she'd shown that much vivacity with him.

Andrei paused, watched her go. The leather of her dress flapped around her knees in taut sounds until she disappeared through a cave entrance and into the warmer ground. The Creator's Cave in his collection—the North Caves—wasn't so far into the tundra. All the caves lay underground, but they built them into cooler earth than other areas, due to what the *maleesa* might require.

With no *maleesa* present, the Creator's Cave was warm, held more light, and easier to work within.

Befuddled, he turned to head toward the glacier.

"A joke," he muttered with a shake of his head. "I wish."

Then he resolved to keep his mouth shut.

* * *

"Andrei, are you ready?"

A heavy hand on his shoulder brought Andrei out of strange thoughts. He jerked upright to find Sergei's dark eyes peering at him like flecks of ground peppercorn. Their sharp intelligence glittered.

"Yes, Sergei. I'm ready."

Sergei nodded once, shoved Andrei back a bit with his hand. Andrei braced himself against the push, but it still rocked him more than he would have liked. He'd never been a physically powerful witch, but working as a Guide, whether for caves or the clan, didn't require brawn.

"Good. It's time for you to see a bit more of the world, now that the *Praznick* closes in. You'll take over as Guide to the Clan this year, Andrei. You're ready. The magic has told me."

The words sent a little thrill through Andrei. Relief as well. For years, when the annual *Praznick* celebration approached, Sergei would speak in vague terms of *transferring the clan* and *readiness of magic,* and then told him to *wait until you're told.*

Finally, an end to the wait.

Sergei's failing health certainly contributed to his willingness to resign the position, no doubt. He stooped more readily these days. Coughed so much. Andrei had been peeling away layers and responsibilities for months now, to give the aging man space to heal.

The Sirilas magic had aided Sergei, kept him upright and capable. Every day, however, Sergei became a little weaker.

The quiet wooden walls of the Meeting House opened around the two of them. Thanks to the impending visit from the High Priest, it lay empty.

The Meeting House was a sprawling structure made of wood, set far from clan lands and closer to the towns of the Southern Network. Clan lands lay to the far west of Zamok Castle. The Meeting House was a veritable in-between for the two worlds.

Clan witches came here with Sirilas magic to meet silk buyers, negotiate deals, and speak with tax collectors. On a far-less-frequent schedule were rare meetings with Network leadership, perhaps once every couple of years.

The open main floor held no interior walls. Structural beams ran vertically, thick timbers shaved down, then carved with clannish runes. Horizontal beams of the same construction lay overhead. The runes contained old prayers to Chthu, the god of tricks and selfishness. Timbers on the opposite side dictated blessing chants to Hulu, the clannish god of good graces.

A wise clan balanced their care for both gods.

Fire snapped from each wall, the four different hearths heating the room to a comfortable temperature. A long table ran along the wall to the left, close to the fireplace. Food offerings from the clan burdened bowls and plates, most carved from moose antlers or reindeer skulls. Bowls of melted fat, and slices of frozen meat, sprawled out in ready offering for the High Priest.

Unlikely he'd take it. Most Network witches didn't enjoy the fare of the tundra, but the attempt to provide kept the magic happy. A peace offering, if nothing else.

Another stir of wind, like a sigh, swirled quickly around him. Andrei smiled to acknowledge the blessing of the Sirilas over this meeting. The protection and power of the Sirilas magic extended to the double-story Meeting House—a bubble in an otherwise unsafe world.

Andrei preferred not to be here long, if he could avoid it. Outside the clan lands, all lay in chaos.

Or so he imagined.

Sergei stepped closer to a nearby window and peered out. South Guards had come before the High Priest. Not surprising, as they had their own procedures for checking magical systems and security threats.

They stood on either side of the main entrance, expressions stoic, as Andrei and Sergei bustled around inside. Bare nods encompassed their greetings when they first arrived. The South Guards said nothing in the time that had passed.

Andrei regarded Sergei with concern. He'd retired early from work yesterday, claiming fatigue. Indeed, he didn't seem well. Slightly yellowed skin, a general pallor. Like many clannish witches that worked within the glacier, Sergei was slender. Their work required little physical stamina—unlike the Guards, the Suppliers, and clan members outside the clannish lands that broke and sold ice to make currency.

Andrei saw himself reflected in Sergei, more than anyone else.

"The new High Priest won't stay long," Sergei said. "He's been busy since his recent appointment to power, but wants to introduce himself. It's a token of trust, I believe. He would like to form a better relationship than we had with the former High Priest."

Bitterness tightened Sergei's tone.

The scathing sound of *former High Priest* and lack of name was issued as an insult. Whatever relationship Sergei had with Leonid, the recently toppled Southern Network High Priest, had always caused him great pain and deep disappointment.

Sergei had never permitted Andrei to meet Leonid, a fact for which Andrei felt gratitude. Network witches.

He shuddered.

Sergei cast him a sidelong glance, as if he could find out his thoughts. The silent command of the glance didn't require a statement or an answer.

You will form a better relationship with the Southern Network.

Angst between clan and Network had never been a desirable thing, but a steady relationship was a hard pill to swallow on either side. The clan held their secrets, while the South held its tax power, and neither would yield.

Well, Andrei would try. If Alek, the new High Priest, would leave them alone, then all would be well.

"I will do most of the speaking this time," Sergei said, "but join if you think of something intelligent to say. You have gone through all my preparation and training for this event. You'll rally just fine."

"Yes, Sergei."

"Anastasia has begun her handfasting tunic. Have you heard?"

The news prickled the back of Andrei's neck. Indeed, he had *not* heard despite their brief discussion this morning. Irritation streaked through him. Such information seemed important enough to merit a mention while they walked together, at least.

Oh, but her amusement with him had been too great.

The annoyance burned deeper.

"I haven't heard this joyous news," Andrei said carefully. "Other topics distracted Anastasia and me this morning. I'm happy to hear that."

"I expect the handfasting might move forward more quickly now." A note of hesitation lingered in his tone that seemed to indicate otherwise. "As you know, we've encouraged her to wait and give herself time to figure out her place in the Creator's Cave."

"Of course."

The awkward topic trailed away. *Maman* and Anastasia's *maman* had arranged the handfasting between Andrei and Anastasia years ago. Sergei and *Papan* had little to say about it, though neither put up a great protest. Sergei acted uneasy whenever the topic surfaced.

The thought of the handfasting made his stomach queasy. Neither he nor Anastasia had given interference to the union. She'd been three when it was announced. They'd grown up more like brother and sister than lovers, which kept things predictable and easy.

Yet, Anastasia had done nothing to move the handfasting along. The power of such a choice lay with her. By clan rules, a woman could marry or leave whomever she wished, whenever she wished it.

Anastasia hadn't seemed to *wish* for much.

With a clearing of his throat, Sergei finished. "Well, let's be done with this discussion. The High Priest will be here soon. Better early than late. Pft, what's that sword doing here, by the way? Have you seen it before?"

The feeling of ice shooting through his veins arrested Andrei. He followed Sergei's gesture and froze.

The sword had returned.

It stuck, tip down, into the floor in the middle of the doorway. Only an idiot wouldn't see it there, and the rest would stub their toes on its sharp edges. Shock rendered Andrei unable to speak.

What in the—

Frantic, he strode over to the sword, yanked it from the wooden boards. It slipped free with no resistance. The warmth returned to his hand when he touched it. Andrei's voice sounded strangled when he responded.

"Not sure, Sergei. I'll take care of it."

The same obscure swirls of thought filled his head, muddying his mind. They made it almost impossible to think. Should he give into them, it would provide more thoughts. He sensed this in the weird way he could understand, but not explain.

Now wasn't the time for peculiar magic.

What was he supposed to do with the weapon? He didn't have a scabbard or a sheath or . . . whatever it was called.

He didn't even know how to hold it safely. The razor-sharp edges gleamed with violent promise.

Sergei's bushy eyebrows surveyed it before he turned away. "Ugly little thing, isn't it? Too light and short to be of much use against an enemy. Made for a woman, perhaps?"

"I wouldn't know."

"Pft. Well, there he is. His Majesty has arrived."

Chapter Four

Life in the clan is almost comical.

The way we live, breathe, exist to support thousands of creatures that, without magical balance, would fade to puffs of dust.

I freeze my feet to fish, scrape my hands across harsh hides as I hunt, and all that I supply is for the support of a thing so small I could crush it without knowing it's there.

There's sense in the absurdity, isn't there?

—Gregor, Supplier
Year 1399

Anxiety tightened Andrei's chest as he stepped away from the doorway, the sword awkwardly clutched in his hand. Sergei stood in the middle of the room, the first thing the High Priest would see when he entered.

Andrei moved to stand just behind him, to the left. He attempted to set the sword on a nearby table. What else was he to do with it? The moment his fingers opened, nothing happened.

The sword stuck to his palm.

Clumps of boots, a bright laugh, filled the porch outside. He was moments away from the High Priest entering!

He couldn't be seen *holding a sword*!

With a shove, Andrei attempted to place it into his belt. The rope could hold it there, for the time being. The belt severed, nearly dropping his pants. With a suppressed cry, he reached for the falling belt. The sword clattered to the ground. Sergei cleared his throat, but didn't look back.

Andrei tightened his belt, then the sword appeared in his hand. With a cry, he attempted to transfer it to his other hand. It wouldn't budge. Each time he opened his fingers, the sword remained stuck to his palm.

Panic billowed inside him.

"What in the—"

"What did you say?" Sergei asked over his shoulder.

Andrei straightened with a snap. He whipped his hand behind his back, shoulders pulled taut.

"Nothing. Nothing, Sergei. Just mumbling to myself."

"What's wrong with you?"

"Nothing."

"Don't tell me you're nervous."

"No."

Andrei shook his hand, hoping to hear the clatter of falling metal. The sword remained glued to his palm.

Along with the sword came a pressing urgency. An inexplicable desire to forgo this meeting, gather the metal-scattered rocks from his dwelling, the leather bag of tools, and go . . . somewhere. Such a desire pressed on him, compelled him to action.

But *where*?

To what end?

Oh, right. The promise to make another sword. Surely, it couldn't mean right now!

Meeting with the new Southern Network High Priest would be one of the most important hours of Andrei's entire life. Years of dedication to the clan had built to this moment. The magic finally felt that Andrei was prepared to become Guide to the Clan and he had a chance to prove it right before the *Praznick*.

That Sergei brought him along would be an affirmation of the transfer of power.

All with this hideous sword he couldn't get rid of!

A pounding came on the door.

Andrei clasped the hilt of the sword in his opposite hand and pulled yet again.

Nothing.

He swore under his breath.

"It is good," Sergei said with a nod, as if to empower himself. "We are ready, always. Remember, my *fere-fil*. Relationships with the Southern Network High Priest are like a tight rope tied between trees. You balance on it one step at a time, and never look back. In the turning to see what has already been, you fall."

Andrei whirled around, issued a peep of shock when he nearly whacked a chair with the blade, and clutched it to his spine. His shoulders heaved.

By Hulu, he'd kill someone with it!

"Come in!" Sergei called.

The door creaked open. Cold air raced inside, stirring against Andrei's cheek. Fur-clad shoulders and a broad chin appeared in the doorway, but didn't venture a toe beyond the threshold.

"Sergei?"

Sergei pasted a firm but clearly strained smile on his face. "Alek Popov, you are welcome here."

Permission granted, the new High Priest crossed inside, two South Guards followed at his back. A small number, historically, when other High Priests had brought entire contingents.

Alek commanded the room with his presence. Though not a tall man, he had the broad face and piercing eyes of a witch that knew his power. Arms like ice cliffs hung by his side. A blonde beard, draped with an opal, hung onto a chest thickened with muscle and fur.

Beyond physical prowess, one had the sense that Alek Popov didn't enjoy losing.

Andrei joined at Sergei's side, hands behind his back, his expression carefully neutral. Sergei and Alek met with an arm clasp. Andrei flicked his fingers—futilely—to get rid of the sword. Sweat beaded along his palm, but the metal went nowhere.

Would the High Priest require an arm clasp?

He'd done so with Sergei's right arm, yet the sword occupied Andrei's right hand. To refuse the arm clasp would be an insult. The worst kind of beginning to their blooming friendship.

"Alek, I would like to introduce you to Andrei, my *fere-fil*. He will take over as Guide at our next *Praznick*, vote willing."

Andrei shoved his left arm forward before the High Priest could even blink.

"An honor, Your Highness."

Alek startled at the unexpected move, dropped his right arm to the side, and reached with his left. The High Priest had a confident, nearly overpowering squeeze in his tight grip.

A statement without words.

His eyes were affable and curious. Their arms fell away.

"Good to meet you, Andrei. I've heard only good things

about the silk coming out of the clan for the last decade or so. May the prosperity continue in your time as well."

Sergei's silent, burning question bore into Andrei's head from the side. Andrei ignored it and hoped they didn't move from this spot. He dropped his arm to his side, held slightly back, where his pant leg hid the relentless sword.

Cursed thing!

Sergei motioned to the table. "Let us have a seat, then. We have much to discuss."

* * *

Alek held both hands open on the table. "Forgive my predecessor, Sergei, for his ignorance. I've heard stories about attempts for South Guards to invade clannish lands and find the secrets of your grimoire under Leonid's rule. When I heard the tales, I was horrified."

Sergei's mask-like expression gave away nothing. Indeed, Leonid had allowed, perhaps funded, several groups' attempts to reveal the clannish lands. All met with failure, of course. The Sirilas magic protected the clan well.

"Horrifying and true," Sergei finally said. "Whatever story was told was unlikely to be embellished by much. We endured much at the hands of the former High Priest. I admit to relief when I heard of his . . . passing."

The last word came a bit more delicate than most. By Southern Network tradition, a High Priest attained such a position by killing the current one. As the High Priest aged, his ability to defend himself typically declined. Young upstarts, such as Alek, ritualistically took whatever chance they had to gain the throne.

Leonid's beheading had been whispered about for several months now. A gory fight, villagers told the Gatherers at the river. Blood-slaked tile floors and final, gasping breaths that ended when his head rolled away. The old High Priest, a devil in his own right, had met a fitting end.

Alek smiled, waving Sergei's comment off with an errant hand.

"He passed legally. I declared the *Vyzov Bitvay*, gave the time, and the place of the fight. We fought in the throne room the following night. Leonid died at my hand, and it was a fitting death for his ill reign."

The calculated violence that lurked beneath such a reply shook Andrei. He hid a shudder.

"You know what the *Vyzov Bitvay* is, Andrei?" Before Andrei could reply in the affirmative, Alek continued. "The challenger to the throne declares the *Vyzov Bitvay*, then states the time and the place. Gaining a Network is as simple as that."

Andrei *had* known as much. Clearly, he thought Andrei a sheltered clannish witch who knew nothing of the outside world.

Well, that was fine.

Alek leaned back in the carved wood chair. His light hair, slicked away from his face in strands that ended near the bottom of his ear, lent a youthful appearance. He had light eyes, a trimmed beard. The fire popped happily behind him, climbing in spurts of yellow and orange that swamped the High Priest in both buttery light and shadows.

Alek had a swallow from a nearby tankard. Mellow ipsum, taken from clannish villages that worked to send food and supplies into the cave workers. Watered down, in Andrei's opinion, but tolerable.

Alek gestured to Sergei, who held rigid shoulders and a prominent chin.

"I came to establish a more realistic relationship between us. To do so, I have one question: what can the Network do to make it right? I understand that there is a concern about—"

"Leave the clan alone."

Alek's lips twitched with a smile that he reluctantly allowed. "I expected that response, believe it or not. As long as you pay your taxes, and allow my auditors to determine that they *are* truthful taxes, I'm happy to give you what space you require."

Something sharp edged his tone now.

Sergei gave a firm nod.

"Anything else?" Alek drawled.

"No."

The rebuttal revealed no surprise on Alek's part. He nodded, twisted the tankard around in circles as he fell into deeper thought.

"I will do as you ask, Sergei, if that's truly what you want." His gaze darted to Andrei. "But I would like to offer another route to you, Andrei, as you and I are more likely to have a working relationship soon. There are Council Members that expressed an interest in . . . building stronger bridges with the clan themselves. Understanding the silk trade more, if you like. I can't help but agree."

All the air left Andrei's lungs at once. Sergei stiffened. The fire crackled.

Understanding the silk trade more, if you like.

"Taking our spells?" Andrei said.

His defensive tone was too tight. Too obvious. Distrust showed up too powerfully and betrayed too much. Already, he felt like a fool. Perhaps he was the bumbling idiot that Alek must believe, for the High Priest chuckled. A note of derision lined it.

"So there are spells," Alek drawled.

Sergei clenched more.

Andrei froze. Not even the sword could warm him now.

"Interesting, but your secret is safe with me. No." Alek leaned over his tankard, staring within and frowning. "No stealing of spells, just a desire to understand your way of life. How you make the silk, what we could do to make it an easier trade for you. There's a growing idea we're trying to promote amongst Southern Network leadership that cooperation and partnership is better than competition."

We? Andrei wanted to ask, but didn't dare open his mouth. Alek moved too fluidly between a singular and plural suggestion. Did he mean himself? The Council? The Network at large?

Something else?

A note of surprise colored Sergei's tone. "How is such an unusually affable sentiment received?"

Alek shrugged. "Well enough. Most are leery of it, like you. Competition drives a better market, but mostly for those already on top. I'm . . . trying different things. At any rate, keep your mind open to the possibility of deeper friendship. If we can educate Southern Network witches about the clan and remove obstacles or difficulties, let me know."

The High Priest pushed to his feet. The heavy chair slid back, groaning against the wooden boards. Both South Guards stepped forward from their positions at nearby windows, hands on their swords.

Andrei stood.

He gasped.

The hiccup of breath went unnoticed, but his frantic scrambling to keep his pants from falling to the ground did *not*. He used his left hand to clutch his trousers at the top, eyes wide as he stared down.

Both pockets, one on either side of his hips, bulged.

"Something wrong with your pants?" Alek asked, amusement lining his voice. Sergei's face hardened as he stared at Andrei, his pants, then back to Andrei's face. His mustache bristled.

"What is this?"

"Nothing," Andrei said. "Just . . . n-n-nothing."

"Hoarding something?"

With one hand, he held his pants up. He could only stare, wide-eyed, at both of them.

Sergei's eyes flashed. "What are you doing, Andrei?"

"Nothing. I . . . these have just arrived."

Sergei reached into Andrei's pocket, extracted a circle of pure metal. One of the miniature ones collected in the linen bags back at his dwelling.

Heat flared in Andrei's cheeks, burned like a punishment from Chthu. The smaller granule of metal flashed in the firelight like a chunk of dulled silver in Sergei's palm. A silent question lived in Sergei's furious stare.

What is this?

Sweet Hulu, what was happening?

Alek tilted his head to the side, then chuckled.

"Strange thing to find in your pants. At least unexpectedly. Clearly, there is magic in the clan. I'm inclined to like you even more for all your oddities, Andrei. It's an actual pleasure to meet you both. Especially you." Alek met Andrei's horrified gaze. "I have a feeling you'll have many funny stories to tell in future dealings. Expect to hear from me soon."

Chapter Five

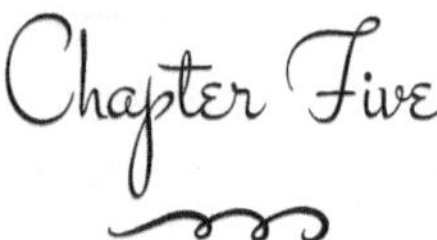

The progression that a maleesa takes from egg to larva to pupa is the most delicate of their simplistic life cycle.

Temperatures in their environment must remain absolutely stable. No wavering.

If the temperature drops too low by four degrees, the maleesa will not develop and it will die. If the temperature is too hot by four degrees, the threads it later produces will be brittle and turn to ash.

Any variation?

Death.

—Alyona, Caretaker
Year 1292

Dozens of metal pieces glittered on his table.

Andrei fumed as he strode past them a third time. The

table trembled with each footfall, sending shivering prisms of light onto his wooden wall. The sword lay in smug satisfaction across the top of the collection.

The moment he'd returned home, the sword had released him.

"What do you want?" he shouted, driving his hands through his hair. "That was the most important meeting of my life, and I left it like a fool because of *you*. The High Priest thinks . . . the sword . . . my pants!"

His sputters died in sheer disbelief.

Sergei would never forget it. Oh, his irate expression after Alek left, the brittle command to *never let me see anything like this again* before he disappeared, still rang in the air.

Andrei hadn't lost his position as Guide of the Clan from this, perhaps, but he'd looked like a fool for the first time in his life. No one expected a Guide to be an idiot.

Certainly not one that almost lost his pants.

Andrei groaned.

"You are not the most important thing!" he shouted, hands in the air. "You're a *sword*. How can you even do this? Who controls you? What is conjuring these . . . these *things* to my pants? To my hand?"

Nothing.

With a growl, he turned around. He couldn't be sure, but he had a feeling the sword felt equally frustrated with him.

A knock on his door followed next, then a bright voice called out, "Andrei?"

His shoulders slumped in relief.

Sacha.

He threw open the door to find his aunt standing there, hand poised to knock a second time. Surprised rippled across her delicately boned face as soon as she saw him.

"You all right?" she asked.

Silky black hair framed her wide, heart-shaped face, the

same as the rest of the clan. A black-fur hood lay on her shoulders. She had mossy eyes, so different from the usual black-or-brown amongst the rest.

Andrei shuffled back, opening the door wider.

"Come in."

The door slammed behind her, rattling on the hinges. She advanced into the room with unrepressed curiosity.

"You look positively rabid, *nelos*. What is wrong with my sister-son?"

He jabbed a hand at the metal mounds on the table, upon which three small piles of bright blue gems glimmered. He did a double-take.

When had they arrived?

"That. *That* is what's wrong with me!"

"Oh."

She bustled closer. Like Anastasia, she wore the leather clothes of the clan with the fur facing inside, near the skin. It rubbed against a shirt meant to keep the occasionally rough hides from chafing. Her skirt flowed to the ankles, where leather boots rose to her mid-calf. Bunches of white fur fluffed from all sides.

"What have you got here, Andrei?"

"Magic. Evil magic."

"Looks more like metal and gems and . . . a sword. Why do you need a sword? Do the Guards know? Sergei won't like it. Better get rid of it."

He could only growl.

She laughed, then calmed when he sent her a sour glare. Only nine years his senior, she was the youngest aunt of his mother's extensive family. *Maman* was the oldest of thirteen, and Sacha the last of those.

If Sacha's stalwart opinions didn't get in her way so much, he'd invite her over more often.

At some point, the package of tools had also reappeared

on the table. He squeaked, turned away. All of them had been resting on his chest of drawers this morning, now they found their way here.

Front and center.

With a shrewd eyebrow, she nodded to the piles.

"Tell me."

Frantically, he gave her everything. The story criss-crossed in too many places. Too much made too little sense. It drove out of him with uncertain regard, barely held into place by so much panic.

"The High Priest, Sacha!"

Annoyance glimmered in her gaze. "You and Sergei shouldn't have been meeting with a new, unproven High Priest on clannish land in the first place," she snapped. "I don't care if you went to the Meeting Place. It's still too close."

"Sacha, it's days away."

She folded her arms across her chest. "Still, Sergei should have taken you to Alek. You need to see the castle, the outside world. What kind of Guide hasn't left the clannish lands?"

"An obedient one."

Sacha quelled his rising irritation with a glare. "A doomed one."

His mouth snapped shut. No point in arguing with her. Sacha and her wild opinions . . .

"Sergei's a fool to entertain Alek's idea. The High Priest is using platitudes to weasel his way into the clan with a goodwill offering. Mark my words, Andrei. Don't be a fool like your *fere-papan*."

"Sergei is not a fool."

"Says you, a student of his. Those of us outside his bubble of approval see a different side of the clan, Andrei. Sergei may not trust me all that much, but I *do* work in the glacier. I see the workings behind the silk production, the pieces that keep the clan fed and supplied and happy."

"Set aside your ridiculous opinions on Sergei. This is not the time or the place for this argument again. I've had too many of your lectures before. What do I do about this sword?"

With a roll of her eyes, she dropped her folded arms. They hung at her side as she studied the pile, this time with renewed interest.

"Well . . . it's certainly strange."

"You believe me?"

She shrugged, waved a hand. "Yes. Where else would you have come across all this? You wouldn't get your hands dirty enough to find these metal pieces, nor do you know anyone in the gem trade. You're far too obedient to harbor a sword willingly."

Of a truth, she knew him well.

"Please, Sacha, help me."

"With what? This magic has come upon you, not me. There must be a reason for it." She leaned closer, put a hand over the metal chunks and wafted, as if bringing the air closer to her face. Eyes closed, she murmured. "It's not evil, Andrei. I smell no signature of Chthu in this magic."

He huffed a breath, though couldn't deny relief.

"Then what?"

"I don't know, but I believe Hulu guides. Trust, Andrei. If we can't trust magic, what do we have left?"

"That's it? That's your advice? What if it doesn't go away?"

She shrugged.

"What else is there to do? See what happens next and fulfill your vow to make the sword. Maybe that will get rid of it." She eyed it, then turned back to him. "Clearly, it's trying to tell you something."

Three steps took her back to his door. There, she hesitated, then half turned. Her wary gaze met his.

"You're more in danger from Alek than this unknown

magic. Be careful, *nelos*. You are my favorite. Don't get wrapped up in saccharine promises from a High Priest who has never had high motives."

How do you know anything about Alek Popov? he almost asked, but the question stalled. Sacha wouldn't answer it.

She strolled back out of his dwelling. The door breezed to a close behind her as he stared at the glimmering metal and gems. Only the issuance of cold air after the door had briefly opened felt real anymore.

A welling of dread swelled from the depths of his chest.

"Is it that easy? Do you really just want me to make a sword?"

Something told him it didn't have to be that hard. A push of assurance. The vague feeling of disturbed water followed the sensation, but with far greater subtlety. As if he'd accustomed himself to the voice of the sword.

"Why do you want me to make another one?"

Nothing.

"Fine. I'll work on it. But . . . *how?* I don't even know how to hold a sword. I'll have to melt the metal, right?"

At the question, his mind activated.

Thoughts, images, emotions flooded him. Elation, relief, hunger swept by in an avalanche. The sensations took his breath away, holding him in a trance, until they faded.

In the aftermath, one clear thought remained.

Fire.

"Fine. I will make this . . . other sword. This *one sword*. It means nothing at all except that I want my life, my routine, and my schedule back. Do you understand? I'm doing this to get rid of you."

No response.

He turned.

Time to find a scorching fire.

Chapter Six

The color of the silk is determined at the final stage.

At such a point, the Caretakers have raised the maleesa. The Gatherers have brought their threads to the Reelers, who place the silk strands on a reel and prepare it for the Spinners, who have woven the threads into a garment.

Then it comes to us.

The Finishers receive the garment. We submerge it in the potions as the Sirilas instructs and turn to magic.

Heat. Time. Patience.

In the end, the color of the silk emerges. A single misplaced thread can destroy this process. One thread of a different color could ruin the entire garment.

We have seen it, because the magic relies on steadiness, trust, and the integrity of the clan.

Without clan integrity to the magic, all power is lost.

—Kiril, Finisher
Year 1312

Borat stared at Andrei with a bristling mustache. He blinked once, twice. Not a change in expression followed. Andrei leaned a little closer.

"I need an enormous fire, Borat."

Beads of condensation gathered at the end of Borat's mustache tip. A heartbeat before a drop would have fallen, Borat reached up, swiped it away with an arm.

"Why?" he asked.

"Ah . . . no reason."

A suspicious eyebrow lifted. "No reason for the Guide to the North Caves to request a huge fire after he's eaten last-meal, and the kitchen is closing?"

"Not a pertinent one."

"Is this clan business?"

"No."

"Will it make a mess?"

"Probably."

Borat's nose twitched, causing his entire mustache to ripple like a wave. He studied Andrei, a giant cleaver in his left hand. The carcass of a young reindeer lay sprawled out on a chopping block in front of him.

At Andrei's back, a bright hearth burned inside the icy walls. Fire danced, sluicing the sides. Water slicked down the edges into a small canal that rushed it away to be used for drinking water.

By the end of the day, the hearth would be large enough to hold an entire arctic baer carcass. Once it stopped, Borat would move to a different hearth, melt it out, and the old one would freeze back over from the Sirilas magic. Through the days, they rotated between four positions in different corners of the room.

Smaller pots and cauldrons sat on racks of varying heights. Whale blubber warmed for firstmeal in the morning. Cast-iron skillets, bone utensils, wooden plates, stacked irregularly along the wall. Dried herb sachets hung overhead, loosening flakes here and there on top of the butchering block. Hints of mint wafted by.

Borat sniffled, turned back to his meat.

"No. You can't use the fire."

"But—"

"We are too busy for such a thing, and I won't let you in here without supervision, just in case the magic becomes unbalanced in the kitchen. We run a tight routine, Andrei. Interruptions burn the food and create shortages. For the past couple of months, it's been more unpredictable. We're cautious, which means all the clan is eating. One break? Pft."

He twiddled his fingers, as if all went up in smoke.

Andrei relented.

"I understand, Borat."

He couldn't battle it out any further lest he draw greater questions. He wouldn't be the one that caused such a shift in magic. And if word returned to Sergei about Andrei putting pressure on Borat, he'd immediately intervene.

After the debacle with the High Priest, Andrei needed as little attention from his *fere-papan* as possible. He needed to duck down, do his work, and disappear into his role.

Apparently, that wouldn't happen until the sword found satisfaction. This was one situation he'd have to figure out without having a path.

Andrei spun. The quick capitulation avoided an argument, and the discomfort of using his authority to get what he wanted. Besides, creating a sword in the kitchen? Extremely unlikely, as it would only draw more questions. He'd have to work at night, after the kitchen closed. Even then, clan members might notice. The risk of the magical balance wasn't worth it.

As he maneuvered around racks of *pana*, round rolls of thinly sliced meat filled with bits of marrow and herbs, he kept his eye trained ahead. Thankfully, Borat let him go without further question.

Out in the dark night, he breathed easier.

Lines cut through the snow, winding from caves to dwellings and everywhere else. Some of them plunged into the forest beyond the glacier, others headed out past the half rings of the North and South Caves and into the wide tundra.

Clannish lands occupied so little of the Southern Network when compared to the sheer amount of land, but still felt too big to understand. The caves, the glacier, the clan members that lived in the wild all encompassed so much.

Andrei shoved his hands into his pockets, pressed his face into his scarf to avoid the chill in his nose, and plowed into the night. He skirted along the edges of the dwellings to avoid questions.

Or Anastasia, to be honest.

As she lived in the glacier, it was unlikely he'd run into her at night. Some evenings had passed when she pretended *not* to see him and avoid talking with him, a fact he rather resented.

Tonight, he would have done the same.

Another weight dropping in his pocket served as a reminder that he couldn't go to his dwelling yet. There was one more potential place to pursue, and more metal shards arrived by the minute. The amount must be beyond a single sword at this point. Perhaps enough for one and a small knife.

The sword moved awkwardly at his right side, tucked under his belt and, thankfully, *not* attached to his hand. It seemed to understand that he was trying to fulfill his vow.

Finally, through the maze of trails barely illuminated by

moonlight, he broke into woodlands. The glacier loomed high at his back—a mastiff against an empty sky—as a reassuring landmark. He always knew where to pivot back to when he stepped into the forest. The Sirilas protection extended this far.

We raise you under the sky and above the snow for a reason, Maman always said. *The magic made you for big places, Andrei.*

Several clan members preferred to live in the trees over the open tundra. Mariya was one of them.

Before long, torchlight broke through the darkness of the forest. He navigated clumsily around snow banks and tree roots, heading toward the dancing yellow fire. The descending cold numbed his face. Such a strange sensation is why he avoided going outside after dark. The clannish lands changed utterly at night, unpacking a whole new world filled with bitter cold and violent predators. A world he'd rather not grapple with.

Several paces away from Mariya's shop, he called out, "Mariya?"

No answer.

Several more calls brought a figure to the front door, which opened. Her feminine figure raised an arm.

"Hallo?"

"It's Andrei."

A pause of astonished silence followed. In it, Andrei felt a lessening of the pressure that had been sitting on his chest all day. A gradual waning of tension that left him feeling light.

This was the right path.

He could *feel* it.

"Andrei?" she called. "The future Guide?"

"Yes."

"The *fete-fil* of Sergei?"

Irritated, he cried, "Yes! You know my voice. May I come

inside for a moment? All is well," he hastily added. "This isn't clannish business."

A quiet exclamation preceded her agreement.

"Pft. Come. Come inside."

* * *

"You're joking."

Mariya clutched a steaming tankard, mouth half open. Andrei reached for his pockets, dumped all the metal chunks on top of her table he could reach. They tumbled free, then formed in a straight line.

She leaned away.

"I'm not joking. I just need to make a sword."

"But . . . why?"

Above all else, *not* telling her everything felt like the right thing to do. Mariya wouldn't likely believe a word he said, and it would be one more clan member to think him crazy.

Besides, the sword didn't want him to say more.

Yet, how to explain this otherwise?

"You don't even know how to use a sword." She set aside her tankard. "Andrei, the most dangerous thing I've ever seen you handle is a quill. Why do you want to make a sword?"

"I have a letter-opener. That's more dangerous than a quill."

She countered with a cocked eyebrow.

"It's a wedding gift for Anastasia," he blurted out. "She's begun the handfasting dress."

The brow lowered ever-so-slightly, buying him just enough space to lean into it. Here, he had some footing. Not much, but enough.

"So," Mariya drawled. "You're making her a sword?"

"I'm making *a* sword."

"For her?"

"I don't know."

"Why?"

"To . . . symbolically show . . . the depth of . . . ahh . . . my sharpness of regard for . . . her."

"Pft."

"I'm doing it, Mariya. I need your fire."

She leaned forward. Her muscular forearms, stout all the way to her shoulders, leaned against the edge of the table.

"Do you know how to make a sword?"

"No, but I know someone who does."

The words felt right the moment he said them, though they made no sense. The magic wasn't a *someone,* and neither was the sword. He didn't know that the magic was going to tell him how to make a blade, though he hoped.

Desperate, he leaned into the hunch as he had all the others that came up. It manifested as a sense of something just beyond certainty, like light down on a path only one step ahead of him.

"Not me," she countered, hand pressed to her chest. "I can't teach you to make a sword."

"No, not you."

"As a gift, it's terrible. The Sirilas magic protects us, not swords."

He gritted his teeth. "I'm aware, thank you."

Mariya sighed.

"Fine, but my hearth is occupied for the night. I have a few joint fittings for Cave One to finish before I leave tomorrow. You use my place then. Some clannish Gatherers need outfitting with fishing baskets on the other side of the river. It'll be several days before I return, so your timing is good, even if your idea stinks."

The ripple of satisfaction that moved through his mind seemed to mean something. Perhaps that the timing of her trip was no accident. The thought disturbed him as much as it seemed to excite the sword, because ribbons of anticipation flowed through him.

"I'll be gentle with your forge, Mariya."

She hooted.

"Shows how much you know."

"Mind if I leave these metal pieces here overnight? I'll return first thing in the morning to get started. With any luck, I'll finish before you return."

How long did a sword require, anyway? A day, maybe two?

Mariya slipped off the stool, cackling.

"Before I return? You're going to kill yourself, Andrei. Please, try not to leave too big of a mess behind when you do."

Chapter Seven

The maleesa are too small to make sense. We don't even figure out what color of silk they spin until their first batch of threads has gone through all the steps.

Without magic, would maleesa exist?

Would any of us?

—Valentin, Cleaner
Year 1432

Andrei stared at the tools.

Hammer. Anvil. Tongs. Post vise. The leather roll filled with chisel-like tools lay open at the top of the table. Well, the magic must trust him, since the tools didn't follow him home for the night.

Fleeting comfort.

The sword adhered itself to his hip, though. Unable to extract it, he'd taken it to his dwelling.

Mariya had left other tools for him. He could feel her pity

in the air once he arrived. They laid out flat, in a neat array, on a wooden table close to her bellows and fire.

His eyes felt like balls of hot sand in his head. There had been no sleep. Dreams disturbed him all night. Frissons of emotions, thoughts, images. He understood it was the sword talking to him, but didn't know what it meant. Nor did he like it.

When he awoke, fully extricated himself from the unknown buzz of too-little sleep, his brain felt like a fuzzy miasma. Rarely did he lose sleep. Through the depths of fatigue, the thought occurred to him that he shouldn't handle heavy tools in this state.

What was he thinking?

This would be filthy, back-breaking work. He'd pushed off three important meetings with other Reelers, Spinners, and Gatherers to forge a sword and he didn't even know *how*.

The anxiety of not knowing the next step left an uncomfortable roiling in his gut. Forced to set that aside, he focused on the tools again. Hammer, anvil, those made sense enough. The tongs and post vise? Those too, on some level. A leather apron dangled off a hook in the wall. He grabbed it, quickly slipped it on.

The rest?

Pft.

Overnight, a bag full of something grainy had appeared. White, like sand, and easy to touch. It emitted no fragrance and remained tucked into a tight pouch. A barrel of water stood next to the anvil.

His gaze drifted higher, to the sword waiting at the top of the table.

"You want a friend? Let's get started, then." He waved to the table. "You have my time until noon today."

The too-familiar sensation in his mind guided him to the bag of metal chunks. He hefted it, grunting at the weight, and dropped them on the table edge. Five paces away, fire sprang to life in the massive hearth. He startled, glanced at the sword, and turned back to the bag.

The metal pieces spilled onto the table in a shimmering rush. All of them were of the same shine, color, consistency, and thumbnail size. *Rock* didn't seem right—but what else to call them? He ran his fingers over the top, enjoying the prick of sharp edges on his palm.

When he counted out fifteen, he stopped.

That felt right.

A glance around confirmed that nothing in the smithy had moved. Shadows still covered the world in a wintry blanket, giving him the sense of being the only witch alive in the world.

He turned to face the fire, all fifteen metal pieces in his palm. He startled. A stone circle sat in the middle of Mariya's wide hearth, built close together. Coals and heat simmered at the very bottom of the circle, stacked several thicknesses high. Flames, oblivious to the new intruder, danced.

"Oh."

A bowl appeared in his hand. Metal? No . . . some sort of stone? The interior was lined, but he didn't recognize the material used to line it.

"What is the name of this metal, anyway?"

No answer.

Did metal *have* a name? Surely, it must. Like minerals or rocks or stones.

The pieces fell inside the bowl when he tipped his palm closer to it. They clacked together, accumulating on the bottom. The fire warmed his arms as he leaned in, set the bowl inside the stone circle, and quickly retracted.

Off to the side, another wide circle had appeared. Thin stone, like pounded river rock, that would just cover the top of the bowl.

"Ah."

A surge of excitement compelled him to tug the stone circle over. His puny arms were no match for the heavy weight. Eventually, he wrestled it on top of the stone circle. Flames singed the hairs on his arm, releasing a noxious smell. He recoiled, brushed the offended spot off, and gave one final push. The cover groaned as it grated across the rock circle and sealed the metal inside.

Flames flared from within, licking through small gaps. Entranced, he could only watch.

Wait.

Wonder what happened inside.

Time inched by. He swept up his mess, cast frequent stares toward the fire. Heat continued to build inside the circle. He didn't feed it, so the magic must. Light rose. His stomach grumbled. He paced. Fretted.

Finally, thick gloves, made of wool sewn into several layers, appeared in front of him.

"Ah!"

Andrei let out a cry, fell on his bottom. The gloves remained. Scowling, he reached up, tugged them on. Still no voice, only an innate propulsion to keep going.

Questions dissipated as he pulled the gloves over his hand, tugged the cover off the circle, and shoved it to the side of the fire. With the tongs, he extracted the hot bowl, setting it carefully on the dirt.

"This much," he murmured brightly, "I can do."

His confidence halted there.

A red liquid bubbled inside. Smoke curled off the top. Gentle seams of darkness floated along the edges.

An image of a small ladle came to mind. He turned to the leather roll of tools, saw the exact one, dipped it inside the liquid. Next to him, on the floor, sat a rectangular mold about half the length of fingertip to elbow.

He blinked.

"And when did *you* get here?"

The moment he reached for the mold, it scooted back. Andrei glanced up, saw no one present to have moved it. He moved for it, again it slipped away.

"What?"

The container of white sand tipped over, dribbling inside.

"Oh."

He set aside the ladle, scattered the white powder over the mold until it seemed sufficient. In some ways, this magic was almost like the Sirilas magic. It made tasks easier, yet revealed no path.

Irritating.

When the white powder covered the inside, he leaned back on his haunches.

"That?" he asked.

A sense of rightness followed. Without question this time, he ladled the hot metal inside the mold. It filled to the brim, but not over.

An unknown amount of time later—after splashes of hot metal beaded on the dirt—the metal cooled. He leaned back, watched the color leach away. The crack of a tree branch, and the call of a bird, drew his attention back.

Andrei blinked, encompassing the room in a glance.

Sunshine filled Mariya's place. Early morning had advanced into day. Heat from the dwindling fire left his back sweaty, but cold radiated from the windows. Dirt caked his leather shoes, sprinkled his arms where sweat left a slight sheen.

Had he ever been this dirty?

Andrei straightened, leaned closer to a window, peered into the sky. Chthu, it was almost middlemeal! He had meetings. How had the entire morning whittled away in what felt like minutes?

Panicked, he shucked the gloves off, stepped over the

molds, and hurried to the table. The tools lay scattered in disarray across the top. White sand scattered on the ground. The stone circle had disappeared in the hearth, so Andrei scattered the fire and rushed out the door.

He'd have to deal with the rest later.

* * *

When he returned late that night, an organized, clean forge awaited.

He'd left Mariya's forge in a mess, but only because he had to and because she was gone. Normally, he would have cleaned it up himself.

No ashes lingered in the fireplace, no metal chunks on the table. The linen bag stood upright, the top tightly tied, as if someone had neatly swept it all back together and set it down. The leather bag was unrolled, each tool in place. Fresh firewood stacked in a pile near the hearth. Stones lay in a heap an arms-length away.

No other signs of Mariya's return were clear. No other footsteps on the path, smell of food, shuffle of sound.

Something had tidied his mess.

He lowered to his knees. The molds filled with the metallic pieces that he poured earlier lay in the same spot on the ground. With the tip of his finger, he touched the metal. The shimmer of something moved through his mind. Not a thought, nor a whisper. A hush, like the sound the moment before one spoke.

He withdrew.

Swirling thoughts of *maleesa*, *maman*, Sergei, and aunt Sacha's warnings about the High Priest stirred through his mind all day. These settled back into recesses where he could more easily forget them.

Here, a different quiet beckoned.

With renewed courage, he touched the metal piece poured from the red-hot liquid earlier. It jostled. Using the tips of his fingers, he pried it away from the mold with surprising ease. It felt heavy in his hands. No imperfections marred the surface, though he didn't know what they might look like.

"A good sign," he said with confidence, though he knew nothing about weapons or forging. "This is an ingot."

Such a response *seemed* true. He'd certainly never used the word *ingot* before. Andrei set the ingot on the table and straightened. A thunk of sound drew his attention back down.

The mold disappeared.

Startled, he turned back to the table. Where had it gone? The sword rested on top of the other tools, as if waiting. Andrei frowned. Earlier apprehension about his agreement to make a sword faded. This morning, the sword—or was it a new magic?—had guided him through each step.

Surely, the same would continue.

He groaned at the thought of the building fire, the anticipation of waiting for the next step to manifest itself.

"So much work!"

A current of annoyance that wasn't his own hurried into his mind, then back out.

"Well? You didn't let me have any sleep." Andrei stacked his hands on his hips. "I woke up so early this morning to start. I'll begin again in the morning. I'm exhausted."

Something prevented him from taking another step.

Hesitantly, he glanced at the empty hearth. The next steps of the process filled his mind. Fire, ingot into the fire, heat it up, anvils and hammers and . . . it blurred. Exhaustion lowered him to a chair. If he didn't have to start a fire, then maybe it would be tolerable.

He was just so *tired* . . .

Flames leaped to life.

He jumped away with a cry, toppled over the chair, and fell

onto his shoulder. Heat rolled out from the hearth and barreled toward him. A blazing burst of light illuminated the room.

When Andrei lowered his arms, a healthy fire snapped in the hearth, bigger than anything he'd ever seen.

"*Ira!*"

The urge to act now renewed.

"You are an impatient little thing, aren't you?" he mumbled.

Resigned, he sighed. Moving more by instinct than knowledge, he set the ingot inside the flames. Minutes passed—he didn't know how many—before the metal shifted to a deep red. Brighter than blood, than the *falfalla* flowers that bloomed in the spring.

Time ticked by. He heaped coals on top, goaded the fire to greater hunger when a bellows appeared at his feet. With his feet, he pumped it. Heat swept through the hearth, curled in the air. The ingot bled to deepest orange. Lemon yellow lightened along one edge, but not at the center . . .

He sat.

Waited.

Presumably, at some point, he'd have to withdraw the metal. He didn't know when. His mind felt like it had fallen into a quiet torpor before a nudge urged him to glance up.

Something about the pomelo tones in the ingot drew him. With gloves and tongs, he stood, extracted the ingot. The burning edges hissed as he withdrew it to cooler air, then set it on the anvil.

There it glowed, brilliant against the darkness.

"I just . . . I hit it?"

Confirmation followed in a surge of anticipation. A heavy hammer lay on the table now, just within reach. He hadn't seen this one before . . .

He reached for the heavy, giant hammer, lifted it, and

slammed it into the metal. It absorbed the blow, creating a slight divot in the hot ingot. Andrei hesitated. How was he supposed to create a sword?

Instinct spurred him on.

He listened.

The crash of hammer against ingot reverberated through his arm as he hit the glowing piece again. His teeth clacked. Bones trembled. The hammer didn't bounce out of his palm, at least, which meant something must be right.

Less tentatively, he swung again.

And again.

He turned it around, smacked it a fifth time, because that felt right.

Rhythm emerged from the *ting* and *bang* of metal on metal, an oddly satisfying sensation. The hammer felt heavy, but each swing came with a little flare of power. Magic, perhaps. Energy and a rush of life and something he'd never felt before. The ache in his shoulder and forearm faded entirely.

In the background of his mind, the original sword murmured.

He listened to whatever inner guidance the magic gifted, because the easiest path was the one with the least resistance. If he must be a vessel, at least something else could do the work of filling him up.

The hammering simplified. He abandoned the gloves. It was easier to feel without them. The flow of the banging sang its own melody. Turn, tap, tap, tap. Turn, tap, tap, tap.

Night edged by in the flicker of shadows tossed against the wall. The fire built itself higher. He set the metal back into the flames, heated it until it made sense to pull it out, and hit again. He felt his way through the hammering.

Sometime near middlenight, when the balance of darkness tipped toward the favor of light, a blade emerged. His entire body thrummed with fatigue as he held up a shaft as long as his arm. Blunted edges. Dark metal. No handle near the bottom, but he'd have to figure that out later.

As he studied it, an image arose. A flashing sword. Straight. True. With a gleaming silver exterior, a crossing leather grip, and a round . . . thing . . . at the very end. Dumbfounded, he could only stare at the black hunk of metal.

"You're jesting. I'm supposed to make *that* sword?"

A cloud of annoyance followed. This time, it came from the metal in his hands. The emerging sword spoke to him now.

"That is what you want to be?"

Affirmation surged, a rolling cloud of joy.

By some miracle, it had at least formed a straight line, but it must have been the magic. His hammering felt clunky, the movements uncoordinated. Whatever failings he suffered, the magic must smooth over.

Chatter filled his mind next, like a seamless transition of words, though he heard no sound. More emotion than audible noise. From it, he understood impatience. Andrei lowered to a chair.

"There's no time."

A metaphorical *humph* followed.

He set the sword down, rubbed his eyes with the heel of his hand. The connection seemed to break, because his mind cleared. He wiped his face off with the back of his arm— grimaced at the char coating it.

Exhaustion swept through him. His entire body ached from the pounding. His jaw had become so tense his teeth ground together. He reached up, pressed a hand to his cheek to clear the tension, to no avail.

Too tired to go home, he lowered to the cooler stones away from the hearth. The fire crackled in an ebbing circle. Sleep reached out, beckoning him. His tired body molded to the ground.

His eyes closed.

A thought bothered him.

"No," he growled.

The thought returned. The original sword called again. A wordless, lonely keen.

"No. I'm sleeping now."

The jittery feeling under his skin wouldn't abate. Forsaken refrains flowed from above where the sword lay on the table.

Andrei rolled his eyes.

Unable to relax, he stared into the dying fire. Minutes later, when he couldn't bear another moment, he sat up, grabbed the original sword, and pulled it onto the floor next to him. It clattered on the dirt, then settled.

The dissonance within dissolved away, like melting dross. He drew a deep, full breath, and let it out. With it, the soreness liquified. The tightness in his jaw abated. Andrei relaxed as if someone had enchanted him.

"Tomorrow," he slurred, vaguely aware that morning lurked only an hour or two away. He'd pounded out the blade overnight.

The new sword issued no protest. The original sword settled happily at his side, gleaming in the firelight. He closed his eyes.

Oblivion awaited.

* * *

A sharp pain in his ribs pulled Andrei from the depths of sleep. He groaned, rolled onto his back, where a second jolt rippled through his spine. A voice spoke just overhead.

"How did you know what to do?"

Mariya.

He cracked an eye open. Bright sunshine silhouetted her from the side. The edge of the hearth loomed nearby. Cold stones pressed into his back—that had been the sharp pain against his spine. Andrei pressed up, one eye screwed shut.

"What?" he croaked.

A long, metal blade lay in Mariya's hands. Awkward, lumpy, uneven, but certainly more blade than ingot. She tapped it with her fingertip.

"The blade. How did you do it?"

Andrei groaned and lowered back down. Flashes of the previous night filtered through his mind. Hot metal. Pounding, pounding, pounding. The reverberation of the hammer rocking him all the way to the teeth. His shoulders ached. He thirsted for more sleep.

"Not entirely sure."

"You know," she drawled. "It's not half-bad? Clearly the work of a first time bladesmith, but you're heading the right direction."

He covered his eyes with an arm.

"Really, Andrei. How did you know what to do? You must have had a mold. It's very nice! Wait, where did you find those stones in the hearth? They haven't even cracked from the heat!"

Her exclamations continued as Andrei sat up, moaning. His mouth watered, ravenous with thirst. Food. He needed a large firstmeal, ten more hours of sleep.

His eyes flew open.

"Ira!"

"What's wrong?"

Greater pains assaulted him as he leaped to his feet, then moaned. "I haven't walked with Anastasia to her cave in days. She's going to ask questions. I meant to wake up early and . . ."

Mariya set the blade down. He rubbed his eyes with a fist, startled to see that, as Mariya pronounced, the blade was better than expected. By morning light, he could see a sword in the shape.

He touched the blade, felt another ripple of pressure. An unfamiliar sensation, altogether different, but the same. It seemed pleased enough.

"You're strong, at least," he murmured.

Mariya swung around to face him again. "What?"

"Oh, nothing."

She eyed him as she stepped back, her gaze roving the place. To his eye, nothing stood differently, no resources used he might need to replace.

The same thought seemed to occur to her because she asked, "Did you only need my hammer and anvil and hearth?"

Further astonishment dropped his gaze to the table, empty entirely except for the smaller sword that started this whole mess. When had it moved from the floor? And where were all the tools?

"Ah . . . I already cleared the rest away."

"When?"

Helpless, he shrugged. Suspicion lined her features as she regarded him, head tipped back.

"How is it, Andrei? It's as if you have done this before, but I know you haven't."

He sighed, rubbed a hand over his face. "You wouldn't believe me even if I told you."

The poor explanation hung in the air for several moments before she sighed.

"Well, Anastasia will . . . appreciate the work that went into it."

Anastasia would hate it. Of course, it wouldn't be hers anyway. Mention of his fiancée moved slowly through his brain, then straightened his spine with a cry. Andrei scrambled for the swords with a cry.

"*Ira!* I must go! Thank you, Mariya. I will bring you something as a recompense later today. Some . . . gems, maybe?"

A dark feeling clouded his mind after he offered. The only gems he had were those the sword had given. Meant for decoration, no doubt. Well, perhaps he shouldn't have offered.

Mariya shouted something at his back as he darted out of her house, requested the Sirilas magic take him back to his dwelling mid-stride, and landed inside with both blades in hand.

The swords clattered as they dropped to his table. The Sirilas magic had already delivered his firstmeal from the kitchen. Sliced mushrooms, gently roasted for a blooming flavor, leaned against a hunk of seal meat no doubt brought from the sea by distant clan members. A good sign, at least. If the magic continued to feed him, it must not be upset.

He ignored it for now, tossed water on his face, scrubbed hastily, found a new pair of clothes, and flung the door open. Anastasia stood on his stoop, arm raised as if to knock.

She blinked.

He stifled a gasp.

"Anastasia."

"Andrei." Her gaze dropped the length of him. Too late, he realized his belt remained untied, and he wore only one shoe. "Are you all right?"

"Fine."

"You're . . . winded."

"Just woke up late."

She sniffed as he snatched the second shoe from inside and hobbled into it. "You smell like . . . ash."

"A smoky fire earlier, that's all."

Not at all untrue, for the hearth had belched flames and smoke all night at Mariya's. Anastasia's gaze slid to the room behind him. She tilted her head to the side, a waterfall of lacy hair cascading over one shoulder. Her eyes locked on something, then widened.

"What are—"

With a little cry, he shut the door behind him. "How are you?"

"What?"

"How are you?

"Fine," she intoned, as if talking to an irate child. She shuffled back a step. "Andrei, you have no coat."

"Oh! Right. I . . . didn't sleep well. The cold will . . . keep me awake."

"Are you *sure* you're well?"

"Shall we go?"

Reluctantly, Anastasia fell into step beside him. His heart hammered in his chest, all soreness and fatigue forgotten in the sheer rush of panic that morning brought with it. Awkward silence stretched between them as they fell wordlessly into the same rhythm as the days before.

"I'm sorry I wasn't here yesterday morning to walk you to your cave."

She recoiled a little, but quickly recovered.

"Oh, that's . . . that's all right."

The fading sounds of her voice seemed to suggest she either hadn't noticed or hadn't minded.

Did Anastasia want their morning walks? It was the only time they interacted, a tradition born out of *Maman's* suggestion that they get to know each other years ago. The pregnant silence that followed made it clear Anastasia hadn't noticed. And why not? The truth bothered him until he pinpointed the exact reason.

Something must have stopped her from noticing.

At the divergence in the path that led to the Creator's Cave, Andrei slowed. Anastasia stalled next to him.

"I hope your day goes better than your morning," she said evenly.

"Thank you. It will." He smoothed his palm down the front of his wrinkled black silk shirt—a dirty one, at that—and realized he'd forgotten to tuck the bottom into his pants.

A right mess, he looked like.

Before he could turn to go, she spoke again. "I wanted to ask you something."

The statement trailed away, as if lost. He said nothing. She picked it back up again without looking up.

"Are you opposed to delaying our handfasting until after *Papan*'s retirement ceremony? After the *Praznick*, I mean. He mentioned that the Sirilas magic feels you are ready to be the Guide this year.

"That way, the handfasting won't lessen your promotion. You will be quite busy afterward and I think it best if you can retreat to the quiet of your dwelling while you acclimate to your new position. Guide to the Clan is important above all other things."

He almost said *it would be easier to have a partner at my side,* but kept his tongue glued to the roof of his mouth.

In fact, would it be easier?

Living with another witch. Hearing her snorts and snuffles and sighs. Giving up his quiet living space and the simplicity in which he existed, thanks to the Sirilas magic. He rather enjoyed the quiet of his dwelling.

Perhaps her request made life easier on him, in fact, now that the sword had shown itself to be a persistent companion. A longer engagement gave him time to puzzle out what the sword desired, and without her asking questions.

Andrei shifted, his shirt uncomfortably stretched between his shoulder blades.

"Andrei?"

He cleared his throat, brought himself out of his thoughts.

"Ah, no. I don't mind. If you feel that is best, then I'm all right with that. Do your parents approve?"

Light flooded her eyes again.

"They will," she said quickly, "now that you have given your blessing to change the date."

"You could have changed it without my permission."

"I know. I try to be fair."

The smallness of her voice surprised him. Her mouth opened, as if to say something else, but doubt clouded her eyes. Her lips closed again. She nodded slightly, gaze averted.

"Thank you, Andrei. I'll let you know soon what date will suffice."

He watched her go, disappearing into the cave and the magic that hid it. His thoughts ran long, strange trails.

The shout of someone nearby, and a rolling laugh in response, brought Andrei back to the moment. All this spacing out. All this inattention couldn't be good for the clan to see, for the balance of the Sirilas.

Chastising himself, he turned away, hesitated for a moment before requesting the Sirilas magic to take him back to his dwelling. Andrei, the future Guide, walking through clan lands like a drunken fool?

That was the last thing the clan needed now.

He landed back in his dwelling with a sigh. A good sign, at any rate, that all this *other* magic hadn't truly affected the Sirilas.

Not yet.

"Thank you," he murmured.

The magic stirred up a little sigh of snow that dissipated in a puff. There, he collapsed to his bed, pressed his forehead to the pillow, and fell to sleep.

Chapter Eight

The maleesa! How ugly are they!

—Fyodor, Guard
Year 1412

"This *maleesa* is the one," *Maman* declared. "It is ready to walk the path of all the other *maleesa*, and to stand as a symbol of magic."

Her confident tone left no room for question. Not that Andrei would have dared, anyway. He studied the tiny *maleesa* creature, so small in the background of glass where it lived.

Maman had given it a long, rectangular atrium in which to live alone. The *maleesa* were, by nature, solitary creatures. They spun their threads, laid eggs, and died. Threads and threads and more threads came from each *maleesa*. For months they spun before dormancy claimed them. When they awoke months later, they would spin all over again.

After three years, they spawned eggs and died.

This fresh *maleesa*, just barely out of the larval stage, would be the symbol of the Sirilas magic at the *Praznick* celebration in three months. The clan celebrated the coldest part of winter, just before the world warmed.

Maman had chosen well. This hideous *maleesa* was a gray, mottled thing with sprouting hairs and large antennae out the front. For the next three months, it would transform slowly. The bumps would smooth out, the wings sprout, the hair fall, until it became an entirely new creature.

Something in the latent potential thrilled Andrei. A zest of life he hadn't felt when regarding the *maleesa* before. Did this *maleesa* know it stood on the cusp of its life? Recently born, edged away from its *maman*, and ready to grow into the beautiful creature it would become.

Did it feel the energy ahead?

These thoughts washed away as Andrei straightened.

"Very good, *Maman*. It will please Sergei to know you have selected the chosen one and settled it. I'm sure it will be happy."

She frowned. "Not happy. I have taken it from everything that it knows and set it aside to be something different. It didn't ask for this. It's young to be alone, though eventually it won't mind. Stages, Andrei. All of life is stages. The transition between them is hard, my *fil*, but there are lessons in the pain."

Andrei nodded, unsure of what to say next.

Maman waved a hand. "Anastasia says you acted funny this morning. You came to work late. You never sleep in. What's wrong with you? Are you sick?"

"I had a difficult time sleeping last night, that's all. Sergei didn't notice, and all my work is complete now."

"Pft."

Maman turned back to her duties within the cave. In the corner, a fire crackled. Smokeless, built of magic and a specific stone. With the incantation and the right stacking of rocks, the temperature in this room would maintain the exact degree these maleesa required for optimal health.

The flames licked around the rocks in hues that alternated between wildest pink and deep magenta. It was a comforting sight to see *Maman*'s profile set against the colors.

Several barren twigs from the *zavok* bush lay across a rock slab in front of *Maman*. She murmured as she ran each stick through clasped fingers. On one side, it went into her grasp entirely barren of life. It sprang out the other side, heavy with leaves, weighted from their burden.

Maman eyed him as she set to work pinching the leaves from the branch. She dropped the fluttering pieces to the table in front of her.

"Well?" she asked. "What are you thinking about? Your thoughts are so loud I can hear them from here."

"Sorry. I have a lot on my mind."

"Have you looked into why things are feeling out of balance?"

The question startled him back to the present moment. "What?"

Maman tilted an eyebrow higher. "I'm telling you, Andrei, the magic is off. I can feel it in these old bones."

"Everything is running fine. My meal arrived this morning, and that's always the first thing to stop working when the magic is off balance."

She tutted.

"You aren't paying attention. Something is wrong. We'll see it soon, in other areas. Mark my warning, Andrei."

"Yes, *Maman*."

"Tell me what present will you offer your fiancée? Word around the clan says that she's started her handfasting dress."

Grateful to dismiss the previous subject, he waved an errant hand. "She has said nothing about it to me."

He opened his mouth to say *I am making her a surprise,* but a block in his throat stopped him. Another attempt to speak of the magic failed. He'd been able to tell Sacha every-thing about the sword, so why not *Maman*?

Or perhaps he promised something he couldn't. To whom would the sword go when he finished, anyway?

Andrei dismissed those questions and turned back to *Maman* before she clapped him on the side of his head.

"Anastasia has asked to delay our handfasting again."

A puzzled expression filled her face. She tilted her head to the side, seemed to think that over, and continued with her work.

"Pft. Perhaps not doing her dress, then."

Stymied, he could only frown at the wall.

"She might be shy," *Maman* ventured.

She might not want to handfast me, he silently countered. The thought startled him, for he'd never before given it space to rise.

Was it possible that Anastasia had delayed their hand-fasting so long simply because . . . she didn't desire to handfast?

Yes.

Also, no.

She had the power to walk away. So why didn't she? If she truly wanted to, wouldn't any woman?

Startled at the dichotomy of questions, he stepped away from the *maleesa*. The cave felt too close, the air too warm. *Maleesa* wings fluttered from where they lay in long burrows in the wall. Soft pillows of willow bark that *Maman* spread around the cave ledges provided an area for them to nest. The crisp leaves left a gritty scent.

"Good to see you, *Maman*. I need to speak with Sergei, and tour the Reeler's cave. There have been some issues with an incantation that I shall check."

She sent him a knowing look, as if to say, *see, I told you?*

Trouble in the magic. He dismissed this with an equally annoyed expression.

Maman laughed.

"Go. I won't bother you about the unbalanced magic until I must. Please, pay attention, Andrei. You are the future Guide to the Clan. The magic will speak to you as it does to me."

* * *

Andrei stood before the new sword the next evening, a rag in one hand, a potion in the other. He dabbed drops of the potion onto his ink-stained fingers and scrubbed at the stains, to no avail.

With a disgusted sigh, he dropped the rag into the fire.

The sword said nothing.

With Mariya back at home, he couldn't return to her forge. No other massive hearths existed that he could use to continue the work. He refused to use the kitchen. Besides, the sword agitated at the thought of him working at either place.

He flopped onto his mattress and willed sleep to come. As before, when he tried to sleep, the restless sword prodded him awake.

With a growl, he shoved off the bed, grabbed it from where it lay on the table, and moved it into his bedroom. The plaintive cry, more clear by the day, quieted.

For a moment.

Minutes later, the sound resurrected, only different. The new sword desired more work. The original sword seemed to just make noise for the joy of it. Unable to bear it, he dragged his exhausted eyes open.

"What can I do? I have nowhere to work on you. I—"

He gasped.

Instead of his bedroom, he stood in the forest. Quiet snow fell around him. His boots protected his feet, and his coat lay across his shoulders—yet he'd put neither of them on. Both swords pierced the snow right in front of him, blades down.

His breath hitched.

Why had the new magic brought him here?

Andrei reached out, touched the snow on a nearby trunk. It crumbled beneath his hand and cold zipped through his skin. He stomped in a circle, collapsing ice at his feet. It was real, at any rate. It had taken him from his dwelling to somewhere utterly unknown.

Exhaustion, perhaps a little fright, leeched all his annoyance. It wouldn't be worth attempting Sirilas magic, either. These certainly weren't clan lands. If he must leave clan lands, at least it wasn't Zamok Castle or somewhere with Network witches.

He hoped.

When this magic wanted something, there was no fighting it.

He sighed.

"Fine! You win. I'll . . . do something. What now?"

Eagerness at his ready capitulation rose in a wave. Snow broke into a trail behind the swords, guiding his way through the closest trees. Moonlight canted through the branches overhead, illuminating a path.

Andrei grasped both swords, jerked them from the snow, and followed.

Not long had passed before the trail stopped. He lifted his head. Ahead of him lay a clearing washed in moonlight. Ripples of snow glowed, unbroken, between copses of trees. They grew tightly packed here, almost to form a jagged, oval wall. Somewhere nearby, he thought he heard the trickle of a stream.

"What is this place?"

The sensation of returning to a familiar home washed through him. It made little sense—must have been the swords

—because he'd certainly never been here before.

He lowered the blades into the snow as an image floated through his mind. A dwelling, not sprawling by any means. Similar to most in the clan, with wooden planks built in alternating weaves and layers that, with sheer tenacity and thick enough mud chinked between, led to a warm house in the winter.

Sharp-sloping eaves, a few window panes. In his mind, the exterior walls bled away, ushering him inside. A table, bed, chairs, tools, and sprawling hearth awaited. The entire space appeared two or three times bigger than the exterior made possible.

Magically altered, somehow? The outside might have been a mere illusion, but he had a feeling something built it.

The sense that he dealt not just with a rambunctious sword or two, but perhaps a far more powerful magic system than he'd first assumed, continued to grow in him.

Affection for the home surprised him. The swords wanted inside this dwelling. They experienced longing. Hope, even.

"Am I to build a dwelling as well?" He threw his arms up in exasperation. "I haven't even finished the sword!"

Rustling in the trees startled him. He whirled around, then shouted. The tip of a blade hovered an eyelash away from his face. At the end of a dark blade, a pair of eyes peered at him.

The tapered ends of each eye ended like a teardrop in a wide-set, flat face. A woman. Her skin reflected the light from the moon. A lock of hair dropped into the space between her eyes.

"Don't move," she whispered.

Andrei obeyed.

When he gave no resistance, she lowered her sword. The tip remained pointed up, a hands-breadth from him, thankfully not within a half-second of slicing his face open. He breathed a little easier as she stepped back.

Suspicion lined her tone.

"Who are you?"

"Andrei."

"Why are you here?"

"I don't know."

She was a lithe witch, like the willow branches that bent in the spring. He used to stick them in the mud, see how far they could stretch before they broke. Furs covered her torso, crossed by leather straps over her chest.

"You're wandering the forest in the middle of the night," she said with amusement, "and you don't know why?"

He swallowed.

"Correct."

She laughed. The delight sounded so off-kilter against the maniacal banging of his heart that he didn't know what to say. The sword she held disappeared from her hands.

He blinked. "Where did it go?"

"That doesn't matter."

"Do you have a sleeve for it?"

"A sleeve?"

"What do you *do* with the sword?" He waved toward her. "When you don't want to carry it. Do you have somewhere it goes?"

Uncertainty slowed her words. "Yes, and I will not tell you where. It's a poor woman that outfits her enemies with her secrets."

"I assure you," he muttered dryly, "I am no danger to you. I'm just tired of carrying mine and want to hide it."

I'm just tired of carrying mine tripped through his head. It was the first he'd stated any kind of ownership of the blade, and a rush of delight issued from the sword.

"You're a clan member." Her eyes flashed. "You are my *greatest* enemy."

Astonishment bound his tongue for several moments. Andrei lowered his hands.

"The clan, an enemy?" he cried. "How?"

She scowled.

"Are you not also clannish?"

"No."

She spat the word so quickly he recoiled, as if her metaphorical venom could harm him.

"But—"

He gestured to her eyes, her appearance. She looked clannish, not Southern, with the svelte frame, dark hair, and low slung eyes of the clan. She lacked the thicker features and wider-set bodies of a Southern Network witch.

"Appearances can deceive. I may have the eyes of a clan member, but my heart isn't good enough. You may ask your leader, Sergei. He'd have more information for you."

A nasty tone like that made him think of Sacha. Her lack of immediate pouncing, and that she still hadn't drawn blood from him, gave him courage. They must not be *that* far from clan lands . . .

"Who are you?" he asked.

"Mila."

"Mila. I'm Andrei."

"I know."

"You know?"

She motioned to the meadow. "Why were you looking at this place?"

"I already told you. I don't know. Can we discuss your sword? I want to know how to carry a sword but not have to carry it in my hands."

Mila scrutinized him. Finally, she motioned to his hips with a wave. "A scabbard would be all you need. Though some witches use sheaths, which you see more with knives. Depends on what magical capability your sword holds. Why do you ask?"

"I've heard of a sheath, but what is a . . . a scabbard?"

She spoke more slowly, as if to a child. "A leather sleeve that hangs off your back or shoulders or waist. You put the sword in it."

Andrei studied her. Should he feel offended? He didn't feel that way. In the dim moonlight, he saw no sign of her wearing a scabbard. He lifted his brow. To his silent question, she chuckled.

"I will *not* show you mine."

"You said your sword has magic?"

"No."

"But it disappeared, and you said—"

"It doesn't."

Her blithe replies irritated him. Silence stretched, during which he couldn't tell if her sword had magic—and she didn't want him to know—or if it truly didn't.

He didn't know how to change the uncomfortable quiet or whether he even should. A shiver ripped through him. He needed to move or start a fire. In this depth of winter, standing on a snowy plain would lead to death.

A decidedly torturous one.

"I'll make you a deal," Mila said, breath billowing out like smoke. "You tell me your truth. I'll tell you mine. You explain why you're looking at this open spot, and I'll tell you what I did with my sword."

He opened his mouth, but hesitated.

Could he?

As if he sought silent permission, the sword ballooned inside him with heat. Was it approval?

He frowned at the blade in his hand.

"What does it mean?"

Too late, he realized he'd spoken the question aloud. Before he could take it back, Mila smacked him in the arm with the back of her hand.

"You're not dumb! You know what that means. I'm making a deal. A—"

"No, I'm not talking to you."

She stilled.

"Oh."

Another rush of something like approval. The idea of telling her about the swords didn't lock his throat, the way it had with *Maman*.

"I'm here because the swords brought me."

He gestured ahead of him, where the two swords stood in the snow. He hadn't set them that way. They seemed to find that position on their own. Mila regarded them, then him.

"Oh."

"It sounds . . . crazy, I admit. But I was in my room, trying to fall asleep, and I made the mistake of asking what they wanted because they wouldn't let me sleep. They responded by bringing me here."

"They wouldn't *let* you sleep?"

He shook his head.

Mila reached out, touched the top of the original sword, then the top of the other. With a skilled hand, she reached for the original, yanked it from the snow. She spun it in circles, then lowered it again.

A rippling sound moved through his mind like music. He put a hand on his ear, realized the sword was . . . singing.

"That's a reliable sword." She lifted it higher, peered at it through tapered eyes. "Balanced, not too heavy."

Another burst of energy soared through him.

Andrei gritted his teeth.

The sword *preened*, like an overconfident bird fluffing its feathers. The maelstrom of emotions that followed ran like a cascade. Though he couldn't be sure of anything anymore, he felt certain the swords adored Mila.

"You are vain and obnoxious," he muttered.

Her head whipped up.

"What?"

"Not you!" he cried.

With deep distrust, she hefted the other sword. Grooves formed above her eyebrows, marring the porcelain precision of her skin.

"That blade is terrible, even unfinished. Who made it?"

Andrei scowled.

"Look, I told you why I'm here. Now it's your turn to tell me. What do you do with your sword? I'm tired of carrying them around. I keep almost killing myself. One of these days, I'm going to maim someone."

"So leave them at home."

"You would think that would work!" he cried, throwing his hands in the air. "But they won't let me!"

Mila drew in a deep breath, then coughed. Arctic air this cold made his insides want to curl away and die like a flower. Clannish he might be, but a cold-lover he was not.

Still, the wild forest, so still and calm, wasn't as frightening as he'd expected. Even in the depths of the darkest night, he found it soothing instead of dangerous.

"There's a spell that my friend taught me." Her palm opened, and the sword reappeared. She held it by the handle, spun it around so the blade faced down, and held it out. As she reached forward, the blade shrank, then faded.

Andrei recoiled.

"Where is it?"

She spun, pointed to her back. A pack lay there, twisted with lines of tied leather, rolled up blankets, pouches of water, some of them frozen like bags of rocks. Nestled in the middle, in between two rolls of furs, lay a smaller version of her sword.

"Oh."

She twirled to face him with another serene smile.

"See? Easy."

"You can hide and summon at will?"

"Sword magic."

"Sword magic is real?"

She gestured to him with a wave. "Obviously."

He shifted his weight to his other foot when the left prickled. How easily she accepted the magic. Like it just . . . made sense.

"How do I learn this spell?"

"Aren't you the future Guide to the Clan?"

"Yes."

"Then you can't."

He scowled at the reminder. Indeed, he shouldn't execute any other magic but the Sirilas magic. A smug expression flattened Mila's lips. She cocked a hip, arms folded across her chest.

"It's against your rules."

"Of course," he muttered.

Delight zipped back through her expression. "Then you will return to your clan with your swords."

"No."

The word came out of him all at once, but he couldn't figure out why it sounded so defensive.

Mila reared back. Clearly, she wasn't used to being refused. "No?"

"Why are you out here?" he asked, motioning around. "This isn't your land. Why can't I be here?"

"I'm looking for a spot to live."

"Maybe I am, too."

She frowned.

So did he.

Recollections of the smithy brightened in his mind again.

Indeed, he *was* looking for a place to live. For the swords, perhaps?

Certainly not himself.

She shrugged. "That's fair."

"Do you live in the forest?"

"No."

"The tundra?"

Her blank expression caught him by surprise.

"You don't live in the rest of the Network?" he said with certainty. A self-assured witch like her had too many supplies on her back to be from the Network towns.

No response.

"Well, I don't know why they brought me here, but I don't understand most of what's happening. Mila, good to meet you."

She tilted her head and left before he could.

With a sigh, Andrei stared at the spot she'd occupied, cognizant that some of the discomfort of the forest had returned without someone else at his side.

A cold shudder later, he found himself back in his house. Teeth chattering, he set several logs on the fire, curled up in a ball, and waited for his frozen fingers to thaw out again.

The swords arrived at the table, snow dusting their hilts. Andrei relaxed, the smithy filling his mind.

All fell quiet.

Chapter Nine

This question has been posed to me many times: which came first, the magic or the clan?

To that I respond: what does it matter?

Whether the clan existed before the Sirilas magic, or the Sirilas magic brought the clan together, doesn't have any significance.

What matters is that we work hard for today, keep the maleesa and the magic safe, and the magic will do the same for us.

Though I am merely a hobby historian, even I know that looking back only benefits us when our focus is truly forward-facing.

Odessa, Reeler
Year 1290

Sergei frowned at the ceiling.

Smoke ringed the top of Sergei's office. It chugged from a long reed pipe pressed to his lips while his bloodshot expression gazed with intent at the ceiling. The skin along his cheeks had flushed a bright red hue as it always did when he smoked the *zamuk* leaves.

Andrei lingered in the doorway. Thanks to Mila's help, he'd concocted a *sort* of scabbage—or whatever she called it.

The sword hung at his side, but tucked into his pants. It gave fewer protests as long as he kept it with him, but freed up his hands to do more work. He walked quite awkwardly, and a few of the younger girls giggled at his stiff gait as they passed him, but at least no blood had spilled.

He'd take the good when he had it.

When Sergei made no move to acknowledge him, Andrei rapped his knuckles on the circular door.

"Guide?"

Sergei's feet dropped from where he propped them on his desk. He leaned forward, shoulders still hunched, as he replied.

"Yes?"

"I've finished the monthly inspections of the North Caves. All is well."

"Good."

Sergei set the pipe aside. Ash tumbled from the top, dribbling to a flat circle on his desk. He picked up a rectangular paper folded into a square, the bent edges folded in like dying spider legs. With a shaky hand, Sergei extended it to Andrei.

"Here."

Andrei accepted, skimming almost impossible to read handwriting in the interior. The slopes were so deep, the lines so closely pressed together, the runes were almost imperceivable.

To His Mighty Guide,

I've spoken with my Council Members about our previous conversation and would love to discuss the results with you in person.

If it's not too bold of me, might I request that Andrei be present? As the Praznick ceremony is on the horizon over the next several months, I would be most grateful to develop a relationship with him as well.

Sincerely,

Alek Popov
High Priest of the Southern Network

If the flourish meant anything, the High Priest had written it himself. The scrawl had as much texture and sense as the rest of the letters.

Andrei set the parchment back down.

"I'm available as you need me, Guide."

Sergei waved a hand. "For this, I shall have you conduct the meeting yourself. There's no need for me to be present. In fact, why don't you manage him from now on?"

"Sergei, it—"

"It's time. We're going to have to do this eventually. Might as well get it done sooner, rather than later. Try not to show up with too much metal in your pants, if you can avoid it."

Heat warmed Andrei's cheeks.

"Yes, Sergei."

Regardless of whether Andrei *could* be the future Guide to the Clan, given a successful vote by clan members at the *Praznick*, he was not yet Guide of the Clan. Sergei doled out a responsibility that wasn't truly safe to give away. A result of his growing fatigue, perhaps.

Andrei fumbled to breathe in the wake of the unexpected

assignment. More than just talking to a silly High Priest lay in the meeting. His *fere-papan* dismissed such a bold assignment too easily. The suspicion that rose within Andrei felt like a betrayal to his mentor, but he couldn't help how he felt.

What about the swords?

Had the thought been his, or the blade?

Was there a difference anymore?

He still didn't understand what his journey to the forest had been for the previous night. He knew only that he stumbled blearily through his day as a result. It seemed to indicate that he was supposed to build his own place to develop the sword, which meant other things he couldn't quite face.

Namely, that there might be more swords in the future, not just one. That this new magic had a bigger expectation than he dreamed and wasn't sure he was ready to execute.

Yet, he didn't want to turn away.

Something elemental in the work drew him closer. A sense of . . . excitement in the work. He kept those revelations tucked into the recesses of his mind. So far away that he couldn't panic over the havoc to his plans, his responsibilities.

"There continues to be no pushback from the clan as we close in on the *Praznick*," Sergei continued, oblivious. "Clan members seem to accept you taking my position. Only Sacha doesn't agree."

His eccentric aunt as a potential opposition surprised Andrei not at all. Sacha was not the topic he wanted to tackle now, however.

"Do you have any idea what the High Priest wants to discuss? Continued friendship, I presume."

Sergei snorted, a guttural sound from deep in his throat. He leaned back in his chair, propped his feet up, and picked up the pipe again. With a gentle tap, he ridded the ash from the top and drew it closer.

"A likely scenario. Though I doubt there'll be much harm

in whatever idea he holds. All we truly know about Alek is that he's a better fighter than the last High Priest. Your guess is as good as mine."

"Do you have any advice for me?"

Sergei tipped his head back. "A good question. Try to have an open mind. If he truly wants to mend bridges, we should embrace the opportunity."

"You trust him?"

Sergei didn't meet his eyes.

"I didn't say that."

"Alek excels at flattery if the greeting of *His Mighty Guide* is any indication."

In the clan, they accepted labels only out of organizational necessity. Hierarchy meant nothing in a clan that sought to share power and magic in equal parts. The Sirilas magic would fail without harmony between clan members. Each cog built a greater wheel, with every piece holding sacred importance.

"Perhaps, but it's not to say that such a title isn't appreciated," Sergei said with a low chuckle. "*His Mighty Guide* has a nice ring to it."

Andrei held back a scoff. "What if he wants more information about our magic?"

"He likely does."

"I'll hold a firm boundary against it. I'll protect the clan at all costs."

The words came to him in rote tones he struggled to feel.

"Good." Sergei puffed out a circle of smoke. "Just remember, Alek won't be that bold. The sneakiest predators trick you into their nest. They don't attack outright. Too much work. Life would be much easier for Alek if he lured you closer bit by bit, convincing you to his path. The question isn't whether he *will* do it." Sergei tapped the pipe against his teeth, his voice a study of bitterness. "The question is whether sharing more information is good for the clan."

"Surely, it isn't."

"Isn't it?"

The question floated in the air, drifting like the smoke from a tobacco pipe, as Sergei fell back into thought.

Without another word, Andrei backed away.

* * *

Alek strolled through the forest at Andrei's side early the next morning, a velvet jacket fitted over wide shoulders. It tapered to mid-forearm, where a pristinely pressed white cuff covered the space from coat end to wrist. Cufflinks—obnoxious opals lined with diamonds in a luminous rim—clasped the fabric at the end of the shirt.

A strange, non-functional fashion.

"Tell me honestly, Andrei. Are you excited to be the Guide of the Clan?"

The High Priest strolled lazily. He carried a sword, walked with his head high, eyes alert. No doubt a witch like him had challengers nipping at his heels, attempting to overtake the throne. Here, he had no tension.

"Excited? No."

"Really?"

The drone in his vowels revealed surprise. Andrei struggled to find the right words in the more popular dialect of the *Yazika* language. The clan spoke it as well, but nuances cluttered the conversation when one didn't choose their words wisely.

"Excitement isn't expected in our line of work. We fulfill responsibilities for the good of the clan."

"Fair."

"Are you excited to wake up as High Priest every day?"

"I'm excited to wake up at all," he said drily. "But that's a topic for a different day. My Council and I have met. I announced my intention to leave the clan alone, with a yearly correspondence between yourself and me where we discuss tax audits and paperwork. Per our standing agreement, we will be free to use any magic to out attempts at concealing tax evasion, etc."

Alek extrapolated other boring details while Andrei's mind sped through the current agreement between Sergei and the former High Priest. Alek required similar terms, if not *less* lenient. The former High Priest demanded meetings every three months. Considering that most Network witches wanted the secrets of the silk trade, such generosity came with a heaping dose of suspicion.

"Would those terms be agreeable to you, Andrei?"

"It could be. I speak on behalf of the clan, not myself. Is that something you're aware of?"

"Yes."

"I also decide based on what's put in writing, not what's discussed without trustworthy witches to act as witnesses, particularly in a discussion of this nature."

A grin split Alek's face. "I knew I'd like you, Andrei. You're funny *and* careful."

Not a single witch had ever found Andrei funny. He wasn't sure what to do with such a statement, so he continued.

"At face value, it sounds like an ideal arrangement. Not once has the clan attempted to lie about our tax status, and we have always paid the amount for our income. Our reporting is as clean as our magic."

"Is it?"

Frost coated the question, sending a bolt of fear through Andrei.

"Do you have information that I don't have, High Priest?"

The sudden chill cleared into a sober mien. "All is well, Andrei. I want a clean relationship. The power in the

Southern Network is mine, and you will work with me directly. I can promise that."

Andrei nodded, though one thing had nothing to do with the other. Nor did Alek's promise lend any reassurance.

"You're a hard witch to impress, I sense," Alek said after several moments' lapse in conversation. He folded his hands behind his back, drawing his shoulders out across the chest. "I can respect that, particularly for someone in an influential position. Clan leader. Required to navigate the nuances of a far more complicated Network. I don't envy you, Andrei.

"While I may be the decision-making power for the Southern Network, that doesn't mean that I'm hungry for more. I'm grateful to have a Council that I share the burden with. There will always be an effort for me to work with my Council Members to keep the peace in the South. If I don't, everyone loses."

Andrei slowed, sensing a truth about to drop. Alek followed suit. They turned, stood face to face. Sweat broke along Andrei's spine. He curled his fingers, then forced them to open again. The discomfort of remaining loose and unbothered burned like a hot cinder in his chest.

"May I speak without holding back?" Alek asked.

"Please."

"My Council Members are distrustful of the clan." Alek shrugged. "Witches out in the Southern Network are scrabbling with their bare hands in the gem mines, attempting to find whatever they can so they can feed their children. Others starve. The economy isn't as powerful as it will be once I'm done turning it around. There's an idea that the silk trade is . . . benefitting while others suffer."

Andrei's hand flattened over the sword handle. The moment he touched it, felt its warmth, he forced himself to slide his palm away.

What was this?

When did he ever reach for a weapon?

"I'm sorry to hear about the state of the Network," Andrei said. "It's unfortunate when witches suffer according to circumstances outside their control."

Alek's gaze tapered. "What are your thoughts on the state of prosperity in the clan, Andrei? Per *your* report, everything sounds clean and perfectly in order."

Inflection in his voice tripled Andrei's tension. Was something *not* in order? Did the High Priest mock him?

"Our prosperity results from our labors. We work steadily, we work smart."

"You have, presumably, a powerful magic that is kept under lock and key, in a civilization that harbors no outsiders—not even half-born clan witches—and you eat plentifully all year long."

"I repeat the same."

The friendliness bled from Alek's face, which Andrei faced with a sense of relief. He'd rather face the truth, not the banal lies of friendship.

"Fortunately, I've been able to talk the Council away from words such as *civil war* and *attack strategy*. We need not take unnecessary measures until an actual threat presents. To assuage their worries, the Council requests something rather small when you consider the bigger picture. Something completely within your capabilities and without another witch setting foot on sacred land."

Again, a subtle mockery.

The sword burned along his thigh. Andrei would have ripped it off his hip to get away from the heat if it wouldn't have revealed his hidden weapon. Instead, he swallowed back the rising nerves. Had the High Priest just hinted at violent measures from the Council?

No.

Those weren't hints.

"What is it they desire?"

"Very little, frankly. They want to see a silkworm, bug, or whatever they are. None of your hidden areas, not even a grimoire or magic. No exchange of incantation needs to come about. They wouldn't even need to talk to a clan witch or leave Zamok Castle. They want only the bug."

Commonplace assumption about the *maleesa*—for which Alkarra had no correct word for—categorized them as worms. Bugs.

"The silkworms are quite fragile."

"There must be millions of them. Surely, you could spare one? It's all the Council asks, Andrei. Nay, it's all that *I* ask in order to preserve peace in the entire Network and safety for your clan. A single silk bug, in a glass jar, delivered to Zamok Castle, as a sign of goodwill. You may deliver it yourself and not let it out of your grasp. A glimpse is all they need."

Alek leaned closer. His breath smelled like old vinegar.

"So little to ask, Andrei, when I am the only thing that holds back a tide of witches who would sever your head from your body in your sleep, then set fire to your precious bugs until no sign of clannish civilization remained."

Andrei's throat gummed up. Heat built in his fingertips, which had found the sword again. He couldn't tear his hand away from the sword. They wrapped around the handle. He pictured jerking the sword free, burying it in the High Priest's belly, and taking the Network for himself.

The bloodthirsty thought brought him out of the strange reverie. He jerked away from the High Priest, startled to see shadows interposed over Alek's face. Alek stood there, unmoving.

Frozen.

Andrei couldn't feel his heart, his breath, his body.

Time had stopped, opening a vision.

A blurry figure crawled free of the ground only two paces

away. Black mist, almost. It morphed into a grayish being with protracted claws and leaped. Slate tones turned white as the driven snow.

An arctic baer.

Gauzy talons and teeth appeared, flashing. They clung to the shoulders of the High Priest. Ivory canines buried themselves in Alek's neck. White haunches, thick shoulders, bunched on the High Priest's back as he toppled.

Blood spilled through the vision, darkening the snow. The clan appeared beyond it as ethereal beings. Witches crying, children screaming. Their wails spiked through Andrei's ears.

The smoky baer dissipated, the vision stopped with a jolt. Time released. Everything sped back up.

At the same moment, the sword came to life at his side. Power bubbled from within Andrei like a welling geyser. He reached for the sword, yanked it free. The hiss of his sword sliding free rang like a scream.

A white, furry thing sprang from a hole in the snow and sprinted toward them with an open-mouthed maw. The roar rippled through the trees. Andrei drove a shoulder into Alek's chest, knocking him to the side with a thud. The High Priest grunted, fell to the side.

Andrei's heart beat a steady tune as he offered his body to the magic of the sword. As if he had done this before, in a different life or time, he clutched the handle and swung.

The magic consumed him. He let it flow, angled the sword high, body braced. The ease of the violent arc flowed through his body in a wave.

He *knew* this dance.

He'd merged with the sword; they had become one. Shared emotions surged as the blade struck the underbelly of a charging arctic baer. The baer screamed, jerked free to skid across the ground.

Blood stained the fur.

It charged again.

Andrei shoved the sword into its neck. Tip glanced off bone. The baer whirled, snarling. Andrei ducked. His muscles tensed as he sprang upward, swinging wide. A final grunt, shriek, and heavy thud passed in seconds.

The baer collapsed.

Andrei toppled to the ground beneath it, sticky liquid gushing down his wrists. His head slammed into a rock.

All turned dark.

* * *

Andrei woke with a moan.

He lifted his head, pointed groggy eyes overhead. Branches criss-crossed in an intricate pattern, braiding a lattice over the blue sky. Silence prevailed in the forest until a *clank* came.

"*Privet?*"

A South Guard?

Dizzy, Andrei let his head drop back. All at once, he noticed a heavy weight on his chest, heat spreading across his abdomen. He let out a cry, and tried to leap to his feet.

"Hold on!" a voice called. "Don't move!"

A second one followed. "Is it dead?"

"I think so?"

His fingers ached. Something heavy lay in the fingers of his right hand, which twisted at an awkward angle. White fur lay across his chest.

An arctic baer.

Memory served.

"*Ira!*"

Two burly South Guards peeled the creature off of his chest. Vermillion dribbled down a burly ribcage, staining the fur shades of crimson and pink. Blood smeared his hands, his arms. The sword broke free of the baer's tangled legs when Andrei pulled, then clunked back to his side.

Annoyance at the unintentionally careless handling surged from the blade.

Andrei ignored it.

With a groan, he struggled to stand. The High Priest hovered several paces back, eyes wide.

"Blad," he cursed. "How did you see it? That sword! So fast. I've never seen a witch move as quickly as you."

Laughing, Alek stepped to his side, clasped Andrei's hand, and yanked him to his feet. Andrei groaned when his head pulsed. An ache ballooned from his left shoulder and right wrist.

"You destroyed a creature three times your size as if you were filleting a steak. Who is your trainer? Is this a clan skill? My goodness, we need more South Guards from the clan. Skillful as Shieldmaidens, I'd wager."

A dark pit of uncertainty grew in Andrei's stomach. Whether it ballooned from the fact that he'd inadvertently given the High Priest an idea that the clan had hidden warriors —which couldn't be a good thing—or the outside-his-body moment with the sword, he couldn't tell.

The overwhelming current of power that ran through him stole those thoughts. He recalled only the sword. Felt the raw, visceral energy that channeled from the sword to him.

By Hulu, but everything had changed.

Andrei braced himself on firmer feet now. He clutched the sword more tightly. Like an appendage, he didn't *want* to let it go. It completed him. Sword and master.

Coated in coagulating blood and still panting, Andrei surveyed the High Priest.

"You're well?"

"Well?" Alek laughed again, clapped him on the shoulder. "I'm alive and happy to be so, thanks to you. Andrei, my

Guide. Thank you for your quick response and reflex. Come, let's head back to the Meeting House and wash that blood off. I have a feeling Sergei will want to hear about this in person. Guards, follow us. Oh, and send the baer home. Might as well have a feast at Zamok Castle tonight."

Chapter Ten

What is more impressive than the silk that the maleesa create? The greatest depth, softness, quality. It is power-ful, yet gentle.

Only the transformation they endure can be compared. The change from larva to pupa to maleesa is one of pain and hellfire. In it, they become an entirely different creature.

I've seen the process thousands of times, and have happily lived in my quiet cave, my gentle, unchanging life, as a result.

—Yury, Caretaker
Year 1313

The overwhelming realization that he'd never be the same swamped Andrei. The magic ebbed through his skin in waves and made concentration difficult.

When Sergei arrived and Alek regaled the story, Andrei

thought of the sword. While Alek spit out question after question regarding their protective training, Sergei forced a smile, said little.

Andrei kept his fingers on the blade.

Once Alek left, he would put it into the fire to burn the blood free. He thought of reinforcing the handle with strips of leather to make it more comfortable. He could fit it to his grip, his palm.

Over time, it would wear down, be just right . . .

Lost in thought, Andrei didn't realize that quiet had fallen over the Meeting House until it lingered too long. He lifted his head to find Sergei standing at the door, peering out. Cold air wafted past him. The jubilant High Priest and his South Guards had left, perhaps long ago.

Still, Sergei waited.

"One never knows," Sergei said by way of idle explanation, "if they've actually gone."

Andrei turned, stuck the sword in the fire, and stared at the flames. The blood bubbled and slid down the tipped blade, filling the air with the scent of char. Weariness infused him. He didn't care if Alek lingered, yet if he never saw Alek again, he'd be fine with that, too.

Would, in fact, prefer not to see the High Priest.

A hunger for something else filled him. The forge in the forest. His own bellows and hearth. Plans flooded his mind to build the dwelling he'd seen only in vision. Ideas for planing boards, places to find the right mud for the pitch to chink the holes between layers. The magic had unleashed, and he let it run wild.

Only Sergei's firm hand on his shoulder drew him from the reveries. Andrei startled, looked up.

"Andrei?"

"Yes, Sergei?"

Andrei pulled the sword from the fire.

"You've done an impressive thing." Sergei's focus flickered from Andrei, to the sword, then back again. "Are you all right?"

"Fine. Thank you."

"The baer . . ."

Sergei trailed away, leaving questions whether he meant it as a question or an unfinished comment. Slowly, Sergei settled on a chair next to him.

"I've brought attention to the clan," Andrei said. "I—"

"It would have been worse if the High Priest had died while here. The next High Priest would have retaliated. Would have shown . . . well, it would have been bad. You did well. Please, tell me about your sword."

A knot welled up in his throat. Not of fear, but of magic. It wouldn't allow him to tell Sergei. Sacha and Mila flashed through his mind, then back out. The magic wouldn't allow *Maman* or Sergei to know.

Why?

"It's a sword, that's all."

As if he had done so thousands of times before, Andrei stood, slipped the sword into the horribly-made scabbard, and kept a tight grip on the end so it didn't bang the table.

"Please, allow me a few moments?"

With a hooded expression, Sergei nodded. Andrei silently begged the Sirilas magic to take him away, and it did.

* * *

Voices called outside his dwelling the next morning.

Andrei tried to ignore them. The thick walls, created by layers of wood and mud, muffled their words. The indistinct chatter distracted him from his breakfast, which steamed on the table. Several attempts to eat later, he choked half of it down, shoved the plate away.

Once finished, the tray disappeared. He sat on a chair, elbows propped on his knees, fisted hands to his lips, and stared at the unfinished sword.

Thoughts occurred to him, given by the magic. Wordless certainties that he understood but didn't hear. More swords awaited. They came to him in images every now and then. He let them flow through his mind, eager to know more.

Guilt that he ignored his clan danced in the back of his mind. He sat tangled in both excitement and dread, paralyzed, unable to move. A rap came on his door. Andrei sucked in a breath and straightened, whisked from the mental standstill. The pause allowed Anastasia to call over the din.

"Andrei?"

Clearly, Sergei already told the clan what happened. No secrets lived amongst the clan lest it upset the daily harmony. Better to air the truth now than let it simmer and create problems with the magic.

Though his meal had arrived this morning as it always had, Andrei thought he sensed something *off* in the air.

A tightness.

Is that what *Maman* warned him about? Changes in the Sirilas that would impact them later?

Andrei shot to his feet and hurried to the door. Despite his inclination to hide, he wouldn't disrespect his betrothed by making her stand in the cold without answers.

"Coming, Anastasia."

Rarely did something this exciting happen in the clan. Their days and life rotated round the *maleesa*. The rhythms and flows and oddities of the silkmaking process dictated the slant of their days, the way they ate, slept, had babies. Such an extraordinary occurrence would draw gossip for weeks.

Right when he didn't want it.

He removed the wooden slat that prevented witches from entering and pulled the door open. Her thin form slipped inside. He shut it quickly, sliding the board back into place, before he spun to face her.

A flush filled her cheeks. Excitement because of those milling around outside? No. She disliked attention as much as him. Beneath the glow he sensed a different radiance. Something else had put such a buoyant expression on her face.

She studied him, the energy faded into something like concern.

"You're all right?" she asked.

She wore the same outfit as before. White leather dress, high boots, fur lined neck and arms. Her hair braided away from her ears, then coiled around the back of her head. In appearance, she remained the same.

Yet *something* had changed.

Perhaps him.

"Fine." Andrei swallowed past the desert of his mouth. "I wasn't harmed."

"You saved the High Priest."

Her unnecessary statement vibrated with shock. That same disbelief must be why the clan congregated outside. *Maman* raised him to become a leader, not a military strategist. He'd never touched a weapon before, yet he protected the strongest witch in the Network. They must think it couldn't be true.

"I'm grateful no one was harmed."

"This will look good for you with the upcoming promotion to Guide of the Clans. No one was contesting your appointment, of course, but this shows Hulu's favor. The clan is quite pleased, I think."

Andrei could only nod.

The question churned him up inside. *Was* this from Hulu? Or was this something else entirely? A system of magic that allowed him to communicate with swords, of all things. A tool that the clan had no history with, no experience over.

Buried amidst all the other questions lay the beating heart. *Why me?*

He sensed, more than knew, that the answer wouldn't come yet.

Anastasia stood on the opposite side of his small dwelling, awkwardly unsure of how to be alone with him. Obligation likely compelled her here. With so much attention on him, her lack of appearance would have fostered questions.

Anastasia cleared her throat.

"Can I help you with anything?"

"No, thank you."

"I'll just be going."

"Thank you for coming by."

"Oh, your *maman* told me to give you a message. She wants you to come and see her when you can." Anastasia motioned outside with a tilt of her head. "She understands it might be awhile."

"Thank you."

After another hesitant beat, Anastasia crossed the floor. He pulled the board up, tugged on the door, and she slipped back out. A renewed surge of questions and voices followed.

Only when Yazkin—the Guide to the South Caves— bellowed in a deep voice for *everybody to go to work!* did the masses begin to disperse. Sunrise fluffed the distant sky.

Another thirty minutes passed before the shuffles of curious feet hiding around his dwelling faded completely.

"Bring my work to me, please?" he asked.

The Sirilas magic obeyed. Parchments, inks, books, unopened messages, scrolls, and more appeared on his desk. With relief, he eyed his locked door, the freshly-replaced firewood, and sank into a chair.

Quiet fell.

Middlemeal came, went. Clan members strolled by, knocked on his door. He ignored them. They departed. Sergei sent messages in response to business inquiries and said nothing of Andrei hiding in his dwelling while conducting work.

Darkness inched closer.

Finally descended.

When all light disappeared from the sky, Andrei requested that the magic return his work back to the glacier. It obeyed.

Did the Sirilas magic know his intent after he finished?

Did it care?

He stood, yanked his boots on, pulled his coat over his shoulders, and reached for the sword. It warmed to his touch.

"Take me there," he whispered.

The sword obeyed.

Chapter Eleven

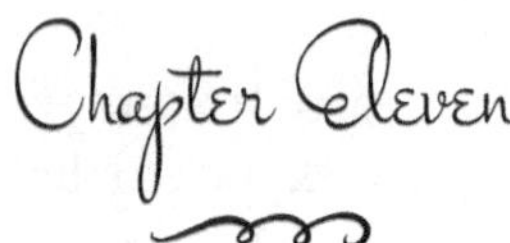

*We live, breathe, speak of magic. It stirs in our veins,
infuses our body, lightens our soul. It creates the maleesa
by which we live. It conducts, changes, transforms.*

Yet, we think nothing of it.

We demand more.

Still, it changes us.

—Blanka, Sewer
Year 1362

Moonlight illuminated the glade. This time, a structure stood there. *The* structure.

Andrei recognized the area immediately. The tight-knit dispersal of trees in an oval-like pattern. The hidden trickle of water over the rocks, tucked into a berm of snow. No prints disturbed this place, not even from wild hares or marks from dropping snow.

As if someone set the structure down and disappeared.

Andrei studied the dilapidated dwelling, filled to the brim with images of what would be inside. This was the home for his swords.

Swords.

Plural.

He had accepted that more would come. Hungrily welcomed the truth, in fact. The full flush of the magic lay open and he wanted nothing more than to work the swords. In his own space, it would be far easier.

Trepidation still rose, however.

Exactly *what* did he strive to undertake here?

Andrei crossed the snow, the squeak of it beneath his boots a comforting sound. The depths of darkness and unknown didn't matter here. The sword sent dizzying whirls of joy and expectation into the air as he approached the outside wall.

Andrei reached out, touched a board on the outside. It cracked. He frowned.

"You provided a failing home?"

The sword gave a *humph.*

"Is it you doing this magic or something else?"

The sheer lack of sensational reply that followed seemed to indicate the latter. The thought didn't comfort Andrei as he circled around the home, about the size of his dwelling. Large enough for a bed, a table and chair, shelves for storage, closet, and a very little open space.

Functional, but not expansive.

The door faced the entrance to the glade where Mila had held her sword between his eyes. The memory of her sent a stirring curiosity through his blood. Where was she? Would she come back? He hoped so.

The swords responded in kind, as if they could call her to them. Such a thing hadn't happened with Anastasia or Sacha or Sergei or *Maman*, and he hated that all weren't included in this secret life.

Andrei ducked inside.

The wooden door creaked to a close behind him, moving on bent hinges that groaned. The inside felt as chilly as the outside. He reached into his coat, pulled out a candle. After several attempts to light it with flint and steel—he had no Sirilas magic to aid him here—the wick caught the spark and flared to brighter light.

A cavernous space unfurled.

Andrei lifted the candle. High shadows lifted overhead, two stories up. Darkness saturated the attic space. A ceiling soared above, barely out of sight.

He turned, lifted the candle along the walls. Sturdy, but would require reinforcement in the true heart of winter, which crawled closer everyday. A hearth with broken stones, moldering wood, lay off to the right.

Slowly, Andrei canvassed each wall, the table in the middle, the pile of wood next to the hearth. Only the trod of his feet on the ground broke the stillness until he heard a breath, a rattle of wood.

Mila's voice called before he had the sword fully in hand.

"Andrei?"

"In here."

Astonishment filled her voice. "Did you . . . how did . . . I know it wasn't . . ."

"Come in, Mila."

A dark figure stumbled into the room, backlit by low light canting from the moon. Mila shut the door behind her, stomped the snow off her boots on the hard-packed dirt floor. Candlelight illuminated her wide-eyed face as she tilted her head back.

"What is this?" she asked reverently.

"It's from the sword. Or the magic of it, I guess. It . . . the magic put this here."

"Tonight?"

"I don't know. I just arrived myself."

He sidestepped to a table. On top lay the leather roll of tools. Hammer. Anvil. Chisel. The names and purposes filled his mind as he ran the tips of his fingers over the top. Could the tools teach the master what needed to be done?

Didn't that happen already?

Mila's rabbit fur hood slipped back, allowing several strands of silky hair to fall forward. She reached up, tucked them behind her ear with an unconscious thought. Her lips remained parted as she turned from side to side, inspecting each nook and cranny.

"It's enchanted to be so big," she said. "Why all this space?"

"For the swords."

The certainty in his voice surprised him. With it came more questions. *How would it be possible? What about the clan? They will not approve.*

"Let me?"

Her fingers opened and closed in a beckoning gesture. She nodded to the candle. He passed it to her. She accepted, then the candle slipped away from her fingers and moved higher. It soared into the rafters, throwing light to the top of the shack.

A hint of jealousy tugged at him. So much magic in the world, and the clan lived confined to a single sliver. Though he appreciated the Sirilas magic, he hadn't realized how little autonomy it offered. The magic conducted the acts.

He wanted his *own* ability.

Mila inspected the north wall. It was the sturdiest of the four, and utterly barren except for the wide hearth at the bottom. The image of glittering swords, stacked one over the other on the wall, slipped through his mind. He blinked the breathtaking image away.

Mila drew the candle farther down the wall, humming to herself as she studied the intricacies of the hearth, the other walls, the floor. Table aside, no other furniture, not even a bed, filled the room.

The sword continued to issue happy warbles, little peals, that journeyed through his mind in stirring sensations. It didn't want to leave and longed to stay. A distant keen, like a tug from without, startled Andrei.

The unfinished sword.

It called to him from afar, wanting to join them.

Mila spoke, breaking the strange silence. "It needs some work, Andrei. Holes in the roof require patching. See those stones in the hearth? They need new cement if you want to make things hot enough to melt metal. You'll need wood, lots of it, to cover the holes, reinforce the walls, and for the fire needed to make swords. Charcoal, too."

"I know."

"Will you be repairing this . . . house? This . . . gift?"

He frowned. How could he find the time to restore it? There was still fallout to deal with after saving the High Priest from the arctic baer, not to mention the *Praznick* to prepare for, and other negotiations to put into place.

He wanted to make swords, not build a smithy.

He had audits and staffing rotations to look through and .

. .

"No."

She turned, looked at him in surprise. "No?"

Assurance filled him.

"You will."

Chapter Twelve

There's a sense of inevitability in the maleesa's transformation. Of course it must happen. What else would become of them?

Yet, I imagine there must be a moment in the process when they decide to survive the unknown.

Or not.

I have attributed too much intelligence to creatures of magic that, for all we know, have little mental faculty.

One can't help but wonder if the maleesa endure because they must, or if they accept what will happen and so live through it, instead of dying.

How would they change it?

Does the tide stop when it tires?

Do the stars extinguish when they weep?

Can witches stand in the way of gods?

—Odessa, Reeler
Year 1291

Mila's candle lowered, nearly dropping all the way to the floor. He caught it, a splash of hot wax dripping on his knuckle.

She stared at him, mouth agape.

"Me?"

"Why else are you here?"

She bobbled wordlessly for a response, but none came. He withdrew the sword from his side, set it on the table to his left, followed by the candle. The light flickered off the blade, brightening the area.

"The sword wants you."

He felt the certainty before he said the words—it was right. Magic, Hulu, or sheer circumstance brought Mila here for this very moment. Her body locked as she regarded the sword, then the dwelling. Her arms remained stiff at her side, thin eyes stilled.

He held the pause.

What to say? The magic might boss him around, but now he had brought other witches into this tangled web.

Was that fair?

Finally, Mila unlocked. She relaxed as if a breath of wind moved through her body, wiping the tension. Her slender fingers reached out, touched the blade. A rush of affection, endearment, swept through him. The sword loved Mila.

She lifted her chin. "You're right. I can . . . there's . . . urgency in the air."

"Does it speak to you?"

She shook her head, hair rippling. Her fingers fell away from the blade, and the sword missed her with an ache he felt.

"Not in words, but . . . there's *something*."

Her hand lifted, as if she wanted to touch something intangible. The magic. The sword. Logic. All of it distant and incomprehensible. Relief weakened him. He opened his mouth to speak, but she continued.

"I'll return in the morning with what I need to get started."

With that, she disappeared.

Andrei extinguished the candle and grabbed the sword. The powerful weapon took him back to his dwelling, where the unfinished blade called restlessly for their return.

* * *

The buggy eyes of the *maleesa* opened, then closed.

Andrei studied the tiny circles, glossy as frozen black water. The fat, squat body had smooth areas in between wrinkled spots, like panes of onion skin. It held to mottled gray and brown shades, bland against the world of color it would one day explode into.

Such a strange creature, with fuzzy hair and long feelers. Endlessly, it crept around the bottom of the glass cage as if it sought something.

Eventually, the *maleesa* would crouch into a corner, spin a gossamer hiding place so transparent a gentle wind could tear it. Within the web, the transformation would occur. The lumpy body would eventually morph into a sleek pearl cylinder. The wings would sprout with a slight sheen of color, like layered opals. Fragile and impossibly soft.

Zavok leaves scattered the bottom of the atrium, near a small clay circle with fresh water. No droppings, because the best Caretakers swept those up immediately. Candles illuminated the space in a gentle glow that eased the almost-blind creatures. An unsuspecting soul plucked from its comfortable life and placed somewhere apart because it was . . . special.

A cage.

But a comfortable one.

Maman coordinated this quiet cave. Her age and experience as a Caretaker left her with the honor every year when *Praznick* prep resumed. Through Sirilas magic and careful control of the environment, *maman* regulated and maintained conditions solely for the *Praznick maleesa*. The symbol of the clan.

"Do you know?" Andrei murmured. "Do you know that you're trapped? That we've taken you from your natural dwelling and put you in this to set you apart? That you're different, which makes you lonely? You're comfortable. Warm. Fed. Is that enough?"

The ruminations wrenched out of him, wholly unexpected. Never had he viewed the *maleesa* as anything but a creature maintained by magic. Supported by forces outside its ken that it didn't understand, but leaned on for survival.

"You have done a good thing, future Guide of the Clan, when you saved the High Priest."

Sacha's voice came from just behind Andrei. He straightened away from the atrium. She was the exact witch he wanted to speak with—and the one he dreaded speaking with.

"It was an accidental good thing."

"Most are."

Sacha slipped into the cave from outside with a cool brush of air, stacks of parchments in her hands. Audit collections. Sacha worked in the glacier, which meant she rarely interacted directly with the *maleesa*. Her position kept the paperwork portion of the business of silk running. Though she never touched the *maleesa*, she knew them as well as anyone.

The door closed firmly behind her. Too much cold air

would alter the room temperature too rapidly, endangering the *maleesa*. Another witch couldn't enter for a small stretch of time. A silk apron wrapped around her waist, the same shade as the kerchief that tied her hair back. She set the paperwork aside, eyed him with a cocked hip.

"You have never picked up a sword in your life, Andrei. Which makes the story of you saving the High Priest from a bloodthirsty arctic baer a little unrealistic. Please, tell me more about this daring feat."

He shrugged.

She studied.

"So you've kept your word to the magic, then? You're making the sword."

"I've tried."

"What does that mean?"

He opened his mouth to explain, but a knot returned. There wasn't much more he'd be able to say. "I cannot stop myself from interacting with the magic. When I'm working with the metal it . . . makes sense."

Puzzlement crossed her features.

"What makes sense?"

"Everything."

After a pause, she lifted a finger to her chin, then nodded. "Yes, I understand. It's the way of clan members."

He scoffed. "*It* is not. We are not a sword-bearing people. The Sirilas magic protects us too well, we know nothing of this art."

She leaned forward, thumped a fist over his heart with her knuckles. "We know of *this*. That is what I sense in you. Also, good for you for learning swordmaking. No reason we shouldn't expand our knowledge base. Now, tell me about the High Priest. Is he as insufferable as I expect him to be?"

"Perhaps."

Her brows lifted. "What did Alek Popov ask of you?"

"How do you know so much about him?" Andrei gestured around them. "When do you find time to learn more about the Network? I work in the glacier, too. I know how busy you are!"

Her prickly tone told him he'd overstepped, but her agitation quickly soothed. With a careless wave, she motioned to the window. "I go to the villages along the river and talk with the villagers."

"Sacha!"

"What?"

"How? They're so far away."

"They're not that far if you go through the forest."

"But—"

"Fine. It's magic."

He stilled a gasp. "We are—"

"Forbidden to use outside magic systems, yes." She clucked carelessly with her tongue. "Chthu hasn't destroyed or banished me yet, as you see. Neither you, for what it's worth, and you meddle in other magic."

"Does Sergei know?"

"Why should I care?"

"Because we have a sacred obligation of obedience to the Sirilas magic."

She whirled around, eyes flashing. "Don't insult me, Andrei. I care about and work for the *maleesa* daily. I fulfill my obligations. Never once have I compromised the safety of our witches or the *maleesa*. Not once. Nor will I ever!"

The low-toned growl in her voice sent him back a step. Such a formidable locked jaw and hardened gaze forced him to drop his eyes.

"Forgive me, *tanta*."

Using her title as his aunt calmed her wrath. The silence rolled out until she broke it.

"Andrei, the Sirilas grimoire gives no rules against other magicks."

"But—"

"Sergei has demanded such a sacrifice of *you* in order to hone your attention to the Sirilas magic, but no such rule applies to *us*. Sergei just doesn't speak about it. It's a control mechanism, that's all."

He opened his mouth, then closed it again.

What to say?

She released a slow breath. "Onto other topics. The villages are eager to discuss how much they hated the old High Priest, but they're not sure about this new one. Some don't like him, but can't tell me why."

Grateful for another topic, he leaned into the change. "Alek has only been in power for weeks, at most."

"That's the most important time to get a measure of his character." Her nose wrinkled. "Based on what I've heard from Zamok Castle servants, he seems oily to me. A witch that is too pretty to trust."

Andrei shifted uncomfortably.

She went all the way to Zamok Castle?

"We're fools if we don't try harder to stay connected with the outside world," she added in a mutter, as if she read his mind.

"For generations, we've steered away from the Network and lived respectfully with the *maleesa*. Why does that need to change?"

"We lived respectfully with the *maleesa*, but not with witches outside of our clan. Is that really serving us?"

When he said nothing, she fluttered a hand. "Pft. Perhaps, as Guide, you'll see."

"What do you mean?"

She turned away, bitterness in her voice. "Ask Sergei if the silk trade has always existed as peacefully as it does now, even under his reign. We will discuss it more then. Now, tell me. What did the High Priest say to you?"

Andrei couldn't dismiss the topic so readily. What secrets lived beneath the ice? What had Sergei hidden that the future Guide to the Clan wouldn't know, but other clan members might?

"Ah . . . there is trouble in Alek's Council. He spoke about his desire to create a friendship between us but they want to dominate."

Sacha swiveled, her fixed gaze pointed right at him as he explained the meeting in generalities. Unburdening himself lent some relief. When he finished, Sacha paced across the floor, arms tight against her middle.

"Fool!"

"Sacha, I—"

"There is no problem with his Council, Andrei. He's using them as a shield. I would be too, if I were him. He knows you won't check his sources. You won't venture out of the clan lands to inquire if he tells the truth. He knows that. He's using the Council as a . . . a means to gain your trust. If he acts favorable, and makes them seem hostile, you might play into his hand."

"No, surely, that cannot . . . I mean . . ."

He trailed away, lost in the thoughts her suggestion brought to life. Sacha could be correct and he never would have known.

"Now he thinks we have armed clan members." She paused, fisted hands on her hips. Her dress swayed over her ankles as she contemplated, then shook her head and kept going. "That may not be the worst thing."

His head jerked up.

"What?"

"So what if he thinks we're armed and prepared? Maybe it will frighten him."

"We aren't."

She shrugged. "We are, but not in the ways of the South Guards. We have the magic to keep us safe."

She reached out, put her fingertips on top of the leather-bound grimoire right next to the *maleesa*. "Have you not read from the Sirilas?"

Andrei's breath caught.

"From the book itself? Of course not."

"Really?"

"Why would I?" he cried. "I am not the Guide to the Clans."

"Pft." She rolled her eyes. "That rubbish is from Sergei. He didn't want the pages of the book harmed, so he made a rule that only the Guide to the Clan could read from it."

Andrei spent his childhood reading the Sirilas spells and directions from long animal hides, the leather stretched as thin as possible, to allow greater space. Clan members touched the grimoire when first assigned their job for the clan, but never opened it.

"It . . . it will imbalance the magic."

She laughed. "Will it? Ask my sister. Your *grandmaman* used to read from the Sirilas as a little girl all the time. You can read it. I do it all the time."

She ran her palm over the top of the grimoire, then flipped it open. Andrei held his breath. Did he expect lightning to descend? To crackle over the top, drop on her, and strike her dead?

Chthu would love such antics.

"When?" he gasped.

"At night, when I couldn't sleep as a little girl. Sometimes I come in during quiet days, just to remember who we are." Her voice distanced. "It's hard to remember."

He nearly choked.

"At night? How is that possible?"

A coy smile followed. "*Maman* and *Papan* slept like the dead. I would steal outside, come here, and read. Anyway, the reason I tell you is that there are spells at the back to protect the clan, Andrei. Powerful spells. We've never had to use them, but we could. Though I doubt Sergei knows *how*, which irritates me. What kind of Guide doesn't know all the intricacies of the Sirilas?"

She shoved a lock of hair out of her face. Sacha had always been bewildering, but never had his heart tried to leap out of his chest at something she said. Today, he could hardly keep it contained.

"No one else must know," he insisted. "Sergei would banish you."

She looked at him coolly.

"I know."

Andrei understood the silent command. Dismissing that topic with another brush of her hand, she closed some of the space between them.

"Don't trust Alek, Andrei. I don't care if Sergei enjoys his flattery, and I don't care if the political world of the Southern Network falls apart because of the clan and our secrets. Saving toxic Network leadership is not our responsibility. We can be good neighbors without approving of barbarians. You understand?"

Carefully, he nodded.

In fact, he wasn't sure.

For years he'd walked a carefully laid-out and proven path. Trod the trials that would impart the wisdom to make powerful decisions under a specific role. He followed established mentors, constructed an efficient routine, and lived to serve the clan. He existed to handfast Anastasia, accept Sergei's position, and Guide the clan.

Until Sacha's gaze bored into him, he'd never questioned it.

Did he fit?

Would he be the Guide the clan needed?

What sort of Guide didn't recognize political machinations amongst brutal enemies? What sort of leader thought more about swordmaking than his own clan?

Andrei let out a shaky breath. "I will consider this," he said carefully. "Thank you, Sacha."

She stood in front of him, arms crossed over her face, lips pulled down. The sour tilt of her lips weakened his stomach.

"Do more than consider it," she snapped. "You're going to guide the clan into a bloody disaster if you don't figure this out on your own first. Go to the villages. Talk to the witches."

He nodded, if only to get rid of her. Cross out of clan lands on purpose? The new magic was one thing—he couldn't get rid of it—but to blatantly seek the villages? The Sirilas would unbalance.

Wouldn't it?

Besides, how could he possibly find said villages?

Sacha softened. She reached up, put a hand on his shoulder.

"You're still young, Andrei, even if you're a man. Thirty is . . . the beginning. No one will expect you to be a perfect Guide. Chthu knows Sergei wasn't, and the clan still supports him. But we expect you to be *safe* as a Guide."

"Thank you, Sacha."

Her ire faded, melting in a calmer expression as she peered past him. She waved toward the lone *maleesa* in the glass atrium. The folds of the rock wells held the glass above their waist, making it easy to peer over the grotesque thing.

"A beauty this year, is it not?" she asked while gathering curled parchments that awaited her in curled cubbies along the wall.

He glanced back.

"It will be."

Chapter Thirteen

Maleesa, maleesa.
Ugly, small, and weak.
We pity the thing,
That changes its wing,
And dies for spinning a thread.

—Children's song
Year 1345

Moonlight led the way to the smithy.

The sword magic had dropped Andrei far from the edge of the glade. He waded through knee-deep snow, attempting to catalog the trees as they stood around him. At some point, he'd need to figure out where in the South it stood.

For tonight, he had other things to focus on.

Gentle rolls of land capped the snowy trails around the smithy. Animal tracks scampered to the right and left. Each breath escaped from his lips in curling tendrils of smoke. The tips of his fingers tingled when he approached the door.

He shoved inside, startled to find the weak, hollow planks

had been reinforced along the bottom and sides of the door. Extra wooden boards, thick as a fist, were nailed into place. They added a sturdy layer of protection against constant coming and going, not to mention the cold.

Along the floor, running from one side of the frame to another, lay a log split in half. It reached high as his ankle, jammed between the doorframes to prevent snow from sweeping in.

"Very wise," he murmured, stepping over it.

When he shut the door, it closed firmly.

No snow twirled in with him.

Andrei kept his hood over his face as he advanced, drawn toward a low light in the hearth. The smithy felt different than his dwelling. Packed with energy. Adventure. A sense of unknown.

He knew nothing of this place. Not the holes in the walls, how much wood it required for heat, nor whether it was truly livable. He had yet to see it by daylight. Regardless, the simmering, brimming possibilities infused his blood.

A huddled figure knelt near the hearth, muttering. The abrasive words were delicately whispered. Fire flickered in a tepid beginning. Cold pressed on the walls, creeping inside. The interior lay marginally warmer than the arctic snows.

"You work quickly."

Mila jumped, whirled around. Her chest heaved twice, sword pointed at him, for five seconds before she lowered it.

Annoyance hardened her features.

"Announce yourself next time, Andrei."

He lifted two hands in apology.

With an exhalation, she returned to the flame. She pressed her right palm down, leaned into it, and blew gently. Flames sprouted along the bottom of a pile of twigs, growing higher.

"I used potions that the villagers suggested and magic to seal up the hearth so you can start making fires."

"Thank you."

"It felt like the right first step. Well, after I fixed the door, that is." She shivered. "It's difficult to lay the potions in crevices while snow blasts your face on the floor."

"I can imagine."

"Now, the seams in the rocks have been sealed. This fire is meant to harden the potion, but it can't be too warm."

The sharp chill compelled him to keep moving. He paced around the smithy, tracking other small changes they'd need to make, while Mila continued to nudge the fire along the rocks seams. Bare fingers showed from one hand. She kept the other clutched close to her chest, fingers tucked inside her sleeve. A wide fur hat framed the sides of her face and chin as she gently blew on the crackling flames.

Andrei stepped closer.

"It looks very good, Mila. Thank you."

"You're welcome."

Her easy acceptance of the compliment pleased him, though he wasn't sure why. The uneven surface of the hearth had smoothed out. She'd chunked rocks back into place, sealed them with what appeared to be a pale paste. When he touched it, it felt porous and hard.

She gave him an amused glance.

"Is your sword happy?"

"Very."

The truth of it became readily apparent. Flows of warmth warbled through his body. She tilted her head to the side, watched the fire inch along a turn at the top of a rock.

"You can't create a very hot fire tonight, but you can tomorrow."

Disappointment streaked through him. Not his own this time. That remained clear. He touched the sword.

"What is your hurry?" he murmured.

A flow of frustration followed.

Andrei had spent too long this afternoon hiding in his dwelling, working on a better scabbard from old leather pants. The scabbard was too ungainly, long. Like the sword, it hit everything, but it was better than the last one.

He eyed the smaller sheath that Mila wore on her back with jealousy.. After his discussion with Sacha, he couldn't stop thinking about villagers. Magic. The world outside the clan. Perhaps he had an interest in more.

There was little to do about it tonight. Eagerness to get started with the metal again made his fingers itchy, though he still didn't know what he'd do once he started. The instructions would arrive.

Mila set several larger sticks on top of her budding flame, then strategically laid several more. A lopsided rectangle grew from it. When she sprinkled dried twigs over the top, the fire spread. The wider fire would heat the whole hearth evenly, he presumed.

Ingenious.

An idea came to him as he spoke it. "We should gather more metal pieces," he said.

"We?"

Her voice echoed in the cave of rocks. A note of amusement lingered. "*We* should gather more metal pieces?"

His cheeks warmed.

"Only if you want to. I don't . . . I don't know how. Do you?"

She glanced back, smiled. "Of course I do, Andrei. We'll gather them together at the river while this potion settles."

"The river?"

"You didn't know?"

He shook his head. "No."

"Didn't you have a bag of metal ingots on the table yesterday? I thought I saw it earlier. They were glinting inside."

He turned, gazing at the table. The leather roll of tools, the hammer and anvil, hadn't budged. Where *were* the ingots?

Piles of gems had been there once also. They disappeared as well. This magic was so . . . unstable.

Insistence rose from the magic and the stirring it caused in his chest nearly carried him outside. He braced his legs against the sensation. Mila, unbothered by how strange this must seem, crawled farther into the hearth. Lines of fire zipped around the curlicues of rocks in lines of glowing crimson.

"There were small ingots," he said. "I don't know where they went."

She leaned back on her haunches. The fire crackled and tossed buttery light over her features. She fanned the flames.

"What *do* you know?"

He sighed. "Only that I need to search for more."

"There will be none here."

"The river, you said?"

"Yes, but I'm not sure where to show you that the villagers don't control. They will not fancy you pillaging their metals."

"No doubt the magic will take us to a good place."

He said this firmly, with more confidence than he should have, perhaps. He couldn't deny the rising instinct.

"I trust you."

She said it as she fed more sticks into the fire. A different type of warmth spread through him at her words. Is this what friends said to each other? Had he ever had a friend?

Mila stood up, brushed her hands off. She slid her glove back on. The friendly heat reached through the space, stealing the depth from the cold.

"I set a spell on it. The wood will burn more slowly than usual, which will keep the heat temperate as the potion sets. It'll also help the house warm up a very little. At the least, it'll keep the potion from cracking."

"Are you sleeping here?"

Mila recoiled. "No. I'm staying with Tikhon."

"Who is Tikhon?"

"My partner. We are trying to find a place to build our house together. It's been . . . difficult."

"Why?"

She said nothing further, closing the topic. Andrei gestured around with a limp rise of his hands. "You can."

"Can what?"

"Stay here, if you need to."

The swords sang in response, so loud he reached down and gripped it in his hand to quiet it. The exultation calmed.

A waterfall of hair tilted around her when she canted her head to the side.

"Why?"

"The swords want to protect you."

Surprise registered on her face.

"Come, let's go." He tightened his jacket more firmly around his waist. "I'm ready to finally see the river."

* * *

Snow crunched under Andrei's footsteps until Mila swerved around him, beckoned with a hand, and led the way along the stream, via a different path.

A far more arduous path.

"Isn't it harder this way?" he called, nose wrinkled at the ledge of snow she scaled so quickly. Broken tufts kept her path fresh. A lacy puff of breath curled out of reach.

"Mila?"

She ignored him.

With a grunt, he struggled in her wake. Why didn't the sword supply the metal this time? The wasted struggle meant time he could have been at the forge, building the fire. The mental equivalent of a *humph* issued from the sword.

Andrei acted like he hadn't noticed.

"How do you know where we're going? You said the villagers wouldn't like us getting their metal. I don't even know and the magic is . . . sort of tied to me somehow."

Over her shoulder she said, "A hunch!"

Mila moved like a moonlit shadow over the ground, able to read the snow as nimbly as a winter hare. She blithely avoided deeper spots prone to collapsing, navigating along firmer ridges that held weight better. Like a sprite, she danced along the night, dodging from moonbeam to moonbeam.

A pair of netted snowshoes appeared beneath his feet when he struggled through a deeper spot, near to the stream. Andrei stared at them for a moment, panting and sweaty under his layers, then shouted, "Thank you."

She waved from far ahead.

For an hour, they broke through the snow. For an hour, he contemplated why he *didn't* learn ancient magic, like Sacha, that would have incantations to make his life simpler. If he was going to tromp around outside clan lands, inexplicably searching for things that made little sense, it might as well be easy.

Finally, Mila stopped at the edge of the forest. A riverbank split the snow like a glittering maw. Dark, churlish waters tinkled past in a black ribbon against the white banks.

Andrei doubled over. "Where . . . are we?" he asked. Condensation formed below his nose, nearly re-freezing with each exhalation.

"At the river."

"Which one?"

"The small one."

His nose ached. The tips of his ears had long since lost sensation. The cold pinched his cheeks. Only his core felt warm from the blood thumping through. The clan lands received piles of snow, but the Sirilas magic cleared the paths for them to access the *maleesa*. He'd never had to work this hard to get anywhere.

Besides, trails carved through their land from the same traffic over many years. Like perpetual grooves in the ground. The lack of structure lent a wild tinge to the air.

"We're by my village." Mila swung around to face him. Clumps of hair had frozen together where the moisture from her breath accumulated.

"You live here?"

Her hand pointed the other direction, to the left.

Snow huts speckled the landscape. Lazy columns of smoke, too. The unbroken ground gave way to trampled paths, scooped-out sections. Blood stains around a fire pit, and shreds of reindeer hair like wisps. Winter mushrooms clung to the sides of the trees closest to the huts, most made of snow and ice. Gliding past all of them was the river.

"Why here?" he asked.

"The river holds the metal shards. It's how we villagers make our swords. Since I'm with you, no one will protest us being here. I'll claim it for myself with the villagers, if I must, then give it to you later. There are metal pieces here, but more other places. Smaller tributaries that have . . . different types."

"Of metal?"

She nodded. "Mmm."

Andrei straightened, startled by a sudden realization.

By Chthu . . .

Moonlight sliced through the water, illuminating a path through the inky shadows. Sparkles erupted from beneath the top, as if the moon pulled their iridescence from the ground. He stepped closer. Mila meandered away from the huts, farther up the bank.

He followed, fatigue forgotten.

A brilliant, shimmering display. So much metal lay down there.

She led him away from her sleepy village, on the side of the bank. Slippery portions led down the water in frozen landslides. He almost lost his footing several times. When she stopped, it must have been middlenight. The veracity of this unknown exploration filled him, a buoyant levity in his chest.

"You see it?" she asked.

A wide eddy stretched from them to the other side, black as pitch. The moon, hidden vaguely behind a cloud, offered no help.

"See what?"

"The river filled with metal."

"Yes."

"And?" she drawled. "Inside?"

"There are shards?"

Mila crouched at the river's edge. Splashes of water chewed at jagged parts of the bank, froze others. Ice crackled when she leaned forward and put her fingertips in the water. He reached out, a hand posed just above her jacket to grab her in case she fell.

He attempted to see past flashes of moonlight on the top. For hiding behind a cloud, the moonlight was quite vivid tonight.

No.

That wasn't only moonlight. The reflection of shiny substances in the water flickered deep within. He lowered next to her, balancing on a ledge of snow that didn't feel nearly strong enough to hold his weight. It held as he narrowed his gaze.

"Is that—"

"Yes."

Mila plunged a bare hand into the water, extracted a fistful of glimmering rock. She held it up, wet fingers filled with darkness.

"You see?"

Four small rocks dropped into his gloved hand. She wiped her fingers on her leather pants, tucked her fingers under her armpit. He felt her intense study as he turned each rock over and over and over, inspecting every side in the low light. His fingertips felt blunt and sharp edges, some porous, others smooth.

They reminded him of the nuts he hunted in the forest in the summer as a boy. The same size, about half his thumb. Instead of round, the shards lay in uneven angles on his palm. Set against the black rocks rested flecks of metal.

"How many of these are there?"

She lifted both arms. "As many as you want."

"But there's so little metal in each one."

"Per rock? Yes." She laughed. The bell-like sound rippled over the water. "Forgive me, I should have prepared you. It takes a lot of time to gather the metal for a sword. Were you . . . did you not know this?"

Andrei frowned. The cold nipped at his knuckles, the end of his fingers. The delicate puncture of the rocks into his palms felt dull. It should hurt more. The ebbing sensations meant he grew too cold. They'd stopped moving. His blood seemed to stagnate. Slush seeped into his boots, the leather protecting his knee.

"Let's harvest, then return."

A bag appeared in her hand. She held it out to him. "I don't know as much magic as witches in the other Networks, but I know enough to be functional. This empty bag was at the smithy. I assume we're supposed to fill it up?"

Andrei nodded. It felt right, even when everything about this should feel wrong. He didn't look forward to plunging his hand into the icy river, but he'd do it. Because it was right. Though uncomfortable. Dreadful, even.

Yet required.

Andrei split the bag, dropped the shards and rocks inside. Mila already reached into the stream for more.

Silently, they worked together. Minutes passed in the crash of hand into the water, the sloop of withdrawing fingers, and the tinkle of shards tumbling over each other into the bag. The bag froze as it filled, the corners dragging into the water.

Andrei couldn't feel his hands when he stood. A dizzy sensation moved through his mind as he leaned away from the bank.

"Walk," he said.

He meant to say: *we need to walk, return to the smithy, and defrost our hands. I can't return to the clan like this. They'll ask questions I'm not ready to answer.*

The rest wouldn't form.

Mila reached out, grabbed his sleeve.

"Hold on, Andrei. I'm going to take both of us back to the smithy. We're in no condition to trek back. Close your eyes. Transporting with the ancient magic is less nauseating that way."

* * *

Sunlight broke over the distant horizon by the time Andrei warmed completely. He lay in bed at his dwelling and stared at the ceiling. Thoughts of Mila, of snow lands, of glittering riverbeds in moonlight, cluttered every thought. He'd never seen such raw beauty nestled in rampant danger.

At every turn, open space.

No edges.

No walls.

He reached to his side. Three shards lay on the blanket at his hip, where he'd set them down before he slept. They drew him back, as if they couldn't bear to be parted from his touch.

Something began in them already.

Did the metal recognize him?

How would he extract enough from so many rocks?

The linen bag had been bursting last night. By daylight, it would likely be a disappointing amount of usable metal. Guidance followed, calm as a thought. He would need to get five more bags.

Five.

He already knew the answer, but asked anyway. "So many?"

No response, which seemed to serve as all the confirmation he needed. Andrei closed his eyes, exhausted beyond belief. He pressed a hand over his eyes, blocking the rising sun.

"Why is this the path? The materials appeared before now. You tricked me!"

The sword hummed, wordless tones sloshing in an empty vessel. It reminded him of a warm bath. Comforting, even if it held no answers.

"Why are you in such a hurry?"

Silence.

Finally, his quietest whisper.

"What are you?"

The reply came all at once.

Sarasam.

"Sarasam."

He spoke the letters slowly, allowing the sound to pirouette through his mind. The syllables twisted to the right contours. A deep sense of rightness flowed through him. Belonging. The sword had a name.

No, the magic seemed to insist. *All* the swords had a name.

"Sarasam."

The sword's mood brightened with each syllable. A satisfying answer that spurred greater questions. Like all the other queries that floated through his mind. The gentle tap of someone at his door reverberated through the overly warm dwelling.

"Andrei? Are you in there? I didn't see you at lastmeal yesterday. Is everything all right?"

Anastasia, he thought sleepily. Andrei turned onto his side, draped his arm over the sword, and fell back to sleep with the thought that he had never gone a full night without sleep before.

Chapter Fourteen

Oh, Hulu, we bargain for your favor.

*On your pyres, we burn these failed maleesa and ask for
your intercession on their path to the eternal grounds.
May they emerge better creatures on the other side.*

—Alfonso, Provider
Year 1400

Andrei frowned at the words on the scroll. A snort drew his
gaze higher, to a short, rotund witch with a protruding belly,
hairy arms, and a constantly runny nose. Andrei turned back
to the invitation.

If *this* was who Alek Popov chose as his messenger, the
Southern Network would face dark times.

"His Majesty wishes me to express his deepest delight at
inviting you to lastmeal, sir." The man bowed at the waist with
a poorly suppressed belch. "May I return with your acceptance
of the invitation?"

The words sounded garbled from lips slick with oil and

reeking of ipsum. Small flecks of food littered his beard. Clearly, Alek had attempted to force the man to memorize what to say, and he executed it sloppily.

The afternoon sun waned low in the sky, though it wasn't much after middlemeal. The days grew shorter. Soon, the solstice would arrive. The turning of the world, so that the *maleesa's* internal clocks would rest. A new birthing and larval stage would begin for the South Caves soon, which would set up the silk for next year's silk harvest.

Andrei shook his head. *Ira,* but he needed to focus.

"His Majesty has not included an hour." Andrei tugged on the paper, exposing more scroll. "When is this lastmeal?"

"It begins at four o'clock. The Council will gather at that time after closing a productive session with a feast in the name of the clan!"

The rest of the Network regarded hours in the day. The clan moved according to mealtimes, *maleesa* shifts, and available light. Daylight drove life in the winter, activity in the summer.

He'd have to find a clock.

Irritation clouded his judgment. For the last four nights, he'd spent at least an hour or two at the river, collecting rocks, memorizing the path, carting the frozen rocks back to the smithy, where Mila worked. The walls boasted fewer holes now and the smithy held more heat.

Slowly, progress inched along.

Always the metal sang.

Lastmeal with the High Priest would cut into his sword production schedule. A fact he didn't enjoy being irritated over. It should have given him relief, yet he felt only annoyance. The swords would complain.

A string of missives that the messenger had been ferrying back and forth all morning lay below the latest communication. Correspondence with Alek had occupied far too much of an already overpacked day.

He skimmed them from the beginning, starting with the one that arrived so unexpectedly.

Andrei,

I hope this letter finds you well.

Please accept my fondest gratitude for your saving grace and quick sword the other day. I am rarely astonished by raw talent, but you have done so for me.

The arctic baer tasted most delicious.

Have you considered my proposal about a greater friendship?

My Council Members have inquired, and I realized in all the excitement I had forgotten to ask your final thoughts.

—Alek

Nothing in the missive sounded like the High Priest. Without a doubt, someone else wrote the letter, or at least coached him on it.

Alek,

I have been considering your offer. I have questions.

—Andrei

Andrei,

Please, send your questions. I would be happy to relay any concerns to the Council.

Again, they wish only to see a single silk bug under your direction.

Send your availability to my messenger and I shall find a day that works for both of us. My entire Council is at your disposal.

—Alek

Alek,

I have no immediate availability.

—Andrei

Andrei,

My Council and I will expect you in eleven days.

We have scheduled a grand feast in your honor, during which you can display your silk bug to those gathered at Zamok Castle.

Would you be open to discussing training strategies while we eat? I'm most interested in your sword work and what the clan can do for defense.

—Alek

The messenger cleared his throat, drawing Andrei out of his perusal. Andrei closed the scroll, handed it back. Of course. Barring Andrei providing the High Priest with an adequate time, Alek forced one upon him.

"Tell him I will attend."

Surprise lifted the messenger's eyebrows. He scrambled to accept the scroll, stuttering as he attempted to grab it. The scroll bounced from hand to hand, then settled in his palm. He shoved it into a pocket in his jacket with a vague smile.

Andrei nodded to the door of the Meeting House.

The messenger left.

Andrei stared at the place where he'd stood. His brow furrowed in deep grooves. He'd made the wrong decision.

No, there had been no other options. Alek would brook no refusal. Now, Andrei risked a great insult if he didn't attend a feast at the castle. Eventually, he would have had to agree or else risk deepening tension between clan and Network.

Andrei lowered to a chair, rubbed a hand over his face. *Ira,* but he wanted nothing to do with this. The sword shifted, brushing along the edge of the chair. The movement was a quick jolt.

A reminder.

He had swords to forge.

Sacha's voice seemed to chatter from within his head, though she was nowhere to be seen. She wouldn't like this development. Would disagree, tell him he'd been a fool, but no fool refused the High Priest.

A knock on the Meeting House door startled him. The door pushed open. Sergei peered inside, saw him there, and pressed farther in.

Andrei stood.

"Sergei."

"Messenger again?"

Andrei nodded, reporting the contents of the letter. Sergei grunted. He leaned on a cane as he hobbled past and lowered into a chair near the fire.

"Wise decision to go." His brow furrowed. "It's not as steep a request as I might have expected, wanting to see the *maleesa*."

Andrei blinked.

"Sergei?"

"The *maleesa*," Sergei snapped. "Taking a single *maleesa* to show the Network isn't what I expected him to ask. I thought he'd have increased the expectation by now. Demanded a tour of the clan lands or something like that. If he's holding onto the original path, it's worth consideration."

Shock rendered him unable to reply. "You think I should bring a *maleesa* out of the clan?"

"Yes, because you should consider everything that crosses your path as a Guide." Sergei's tone iced over. "Clan prejudice can blind you, Andrei. We live here, in a carefully controlled world, that enables us to feed our children and care for ourselves. The magic makes us invisible to enemies and clears our snow and warms our bathwater and delivers our food when we can't eat in the dining area. The world isn't the same way outside our protected bubble. You must take *all* variables into account when you guide the clan."

"Would the magic allow me to take a *maleesa* outside of here?"

Sergei held his gaze.

"I wouldn't know."

The placid expression sent a dart of warning through Andrei. Sergei's lack of emotion, of outrage, startled him. He turned to the side, at a loss.

"The Gatherers have reported a lower thread count in one

pocket of *maleesa*," Andrei said. "I need to check on them, see if we haven't met the proper conditions. It's a cave that's been struggling to maintain."

Distraction with the minutiae of clan work lifted the stoic burden on the air. Clan business, he understood.

Sort of.

Sergei leaned back against the chair. "Is the worker competent with the magic?"

"Yes, but not experienced."

Thoughts of swords and smithy and the *clang* of anvil on metal rang through his head, robbing his concentration. Not on accident.

A reminder.

Sergei nodded. Weariness passed through him as he leaned his shoulder against the wall.

"Then go. Consider Alek's request and let me know what you decide. You are the Guide already, despite whether or not we have cast the vote. Time for you to step into those shoes and act like it."

* * *

"Do you know anything about the High Priest?"

Mila paused, a handful of goopy pitch spread across a sturdy chunk of bark. She stood on the other side of the smithy, stuffing pitch into the seams of boards, the cracks in the outer wall that bled heat like severed veins.

"Why are you asking about the High Priest?"

"I'm curious."

"The villagers try not to know about him."

"I didn't ask about the villagers."

She harrumphed.

Firelight brightened the room with warmth and dancing

colors. A bulging stack of firewood waited against the wall nearest the hearth. Mila must have spent all day gathering.

"It was easier than usual," she had said. "The sticks and logs and twigs found me."

Set in a half circle on the table were five bags chock full of rock, metallic shards, and pieces of ice. The smithy hadn't warmed enough to allow him to remove his coat, which meant ice still clung to the shards.

"No." Mila gave him her back, slapped pitch onto a groove. "I know nothing about Alek, nor do I wish to. He leaves most villagers alone, but only because his tax collectors keep dying when they try to find us, and South Guards fear our gods."

The wryness of her tone made Andrei chuckle.

Nearly a week had passed since he last held the hammer, pounded the metal against the anvil. The break from the unfinished sword brought all the imperfections to damning clarity.

He *really* didn't know what he was doing.

Fortunately, the sword remained patient. It heated in the fire, nestled in coals, while he chose a hammer. Not the widest, nor heaviest, yet not the smallest. A mid-size one.

Lack of sleep left Andrei in a fuzzy tunnel all day. He longed to rest his weary eyes, but the two swords wouldn't let him. They prodded him awake, demanding he return to the fire.

A buzz of anticipation from the sword kept him oriented. The blade didn't fear the shaping, the pounding, the required knocks against its thick form. Such a response startled Andrei.

Why wouldn't it fear the pain?

Tongs waited nearby as he piled more charcoal on the sword, tugged it back and forth through the flames. They spoke rarely, but having Mila present felt as easy as breathing. She held no expectations, no prejudice, no stoic irritation.

With Mila's friendship to contrast Anastasia's awkwardness, the fallacy of his betrothal appeared all the greater.

"The High Priest sent me several messages," he continued, needing to get it out of his mind. "He wants to meet with me at Zamok Castle."

Mila stilled.

"You told him no."

She voiced no question. He turned, studied her. In the firelight, she held a soft figure. As nimble and thin as ever—too thin, if he had an opinion on it—and gentled by the buttery light. Her face became an erratic toss of shadow against the far wall.

For someone who didn't care about the High Priest, she carried a lot of tension.

"I agreed to go."

She frowned, slapped more pitch onto the wall. It slopped over the top of a hole, dripped onto the ground. "There is no good you can expect from the High Priest."

"I know."

"He'll try to take the secrets of the clan."

"That's what he's doing."

Her head canted slightly. A shuffle of hair drifted to her shoulder like a supple wind.

"So why would you go?"

"Enemies close are far easier to study than enemies far," he murmured. "They want to see the *maleesa*."

The word slipped through his lips without a hitch.

"Mmmm."

Mila accepted the word without a blink or question, which likely meant she'd heard the word before.

From whom?

The terror of speaking sacred clan words outside the clan lands rendered him paralyzed. He swallowed through the sick feeling as Mila quietly stewed.

Would the Sirilas magic stop working now?

Would it punish him?

No. That made no sense. The magic had been unchanged —only a few issues in caves here and there that could be normal variations—for the past weeks he'd had this other magic. Whatever he did here didn't seem to affect the clan.

Would this?

"Sergei thinks I should consider it." He breezed through a light explanation of all the rest. The messages, the implications. The unpacking of his fears felt like releasing an infected wound.

In the silence, he sensed her attempts to understand. He gave her space to think it through. What would he have thought of such a report?

In the end, she snorted.

"Yes, you must go."

"I know."

"Will you take a *maleesa*?"

"I don't know."

Guilt for sharing it with her followed. She wasn't of the clan. Was it fair to the clan for him to share with her?

Was it fair to Mila?

Her past remained a lurid mystery. A question too big to ask, for it wasn't his place. Not even as her friend. Andrei reached for the heating sword, repositioned it deeper in the coals. He pumped the bellows several times, enjoying the illumination across the blade.

Instructions whispered to his mind. Vague pushes of instinct. Deeper into the fire. More color at the end of the blade, where it lay slightly crooked. His fingers itched to feel the flattening metal beneath the hammer. The hardened push and resistance of the new shape, a novel form.

He piled more charcoal on the fire.

"What do you really think of Alek's motivations?" Mila

asked, using an old rag to remove the pitch from the creases of her fingers.

"I think Sergei is correct. A Guide must consider all possibilities, lest prejudice blind him to the right path."

She said nothing.

"The event is in nine days. I have time to speak with Sacha, figure out all the possibilities."

Delight brightened her response. "Sacha?"

Andrei checked the sword, understood it needed two more minutes, and glanced back. She came up to his side, held reddened hands to the fire. When she tossed the rag inside, it hissed.

"My aunt Sacha."

"She's your aunt?" Her voice lifted with interest. She smiled with crooked bottom teeth. "Yes. Yes, I can see some resemblance."

He reared back. "You know Sacha?"

She laughed. "Who in the villages *doesn't* know Sacha? She comes all the time!"

No one but the clan should know Sacha, he thought. But that wasn't right either. The thought halted. His last conversation with his *tanta* revealed that Sacha had her own secrets. She'd admitted to learning magic outside the clan, reading the grimoire, and sneaking out at night as a girl.

A streak of jealousy shot through him as he pulled the sword from the fire. Did other clan members venture into the villages?

Did *they* practice the ancient magic forbidden to him?

With Sergei as her father, he doubted Anastasia would be as rebellious to Sergei's dictates as Sacha, but he didn't *know.* These days, what he didn't know overshadowed the little he thought he knew.

"Sacha is opinionated," he said as he rocked back to his feet, sizzling metal in hand. Mila held her hands to the flames.

"I know." Mila nodded emphatically. "She speaks her mind. Sometimes women in the villages don't do that. They're afraid of their husbands, even their sons."

Andrei frowned, set the blade on the anvil and grabbed the hammer. In between hits, he said, "No woman should be afraid."

"I agree."

"Are you afraid?"

"Now?"

"Yes. Of me."

She shook her head. "Not once."

"Of your partner?"

"Tikhon? Oh, no. He is gentle and kind."

"Will I meet him one day?"

"Of course."

Silence fell. The sword spoke to Andrei, reminding him of pressure, where to hammer, how to shape. An image of the next step lurked like a dream in the back of his mind. The goal.

Andrei fell into the motions.

All the cavorting to the river, the fire-building, the hammering, had strengthened his body. His energy flagged, but not so quickly as before. The burn of his arm felt more like a triumph than an irritation.

When the color ebbed, he inspected it from each angle. Width. Edges. Length. Not yet complete, but closer. The strange shape of the metal had smoothed. Back into the fire.

Again.

Again.

Again.

Mila left around middlenight. Driven by an impulse not his own, Andrei hit the metal until the magic told him to stop. Exhausted, he held it up. Through bleary eyes, he conducted his final inspection.

Width. Edges. Length.

Perfect.

Startled by the transformation, Andrei could only stare.

The sword settled with a sigh.

It is enough, it seemed to say.

He set it on the anvil for the heat to ebb. Sapped, he braced his hands on the table and leaned forward. His shoulders burned, forearms spasmed.

"What now?"

The intuition of the magic didn't flare. No stir, command, or information. Simply silence.

"Fine. I'm going to bed."

He reached to his hip, where Sarasam usually waited. His fingers found only fabric. It lay on the table, near the unfinished sword.

"Right now. Going to bed. Unless there's more . . . ?"

No response.

Another pause. He waited, but no further instructions came. Inquiries fell flat, like screaming into a blizzard. He reached for Sarasam. The sword flared to life, as if it had been sleeping. He half turned, glancing at the sword over his shoulder.

"Tomorrow?"

Another stir, this of promise. Anticipation. Quiet exhilaration.

Sarasam returned him to his dwelling where a cold room awaited. He hadn't been here all day. His stomach growled. No lastmeal sat on the table, as it always had.

No warm bath water.

Fear struck him for a moment, exacerbated by wild fatigue. Shivering and ravenous, he stripped off his clothes, scrubbed the sweat and grime free with cold water from a pitcher, chugged what little water remained, and dropped onto his lumpy mattress.

He fell into an instant sleep.

Chapter Fifteen

We believe that the Sirilas magic exists within the maleesa.

That to break the maleesa down into parts before it is dead, when the magic is still alive, would give you a palmful of barely alive magic. Some have postulated that you could ingest said magic and become a maleesa.

I scoff.

But integrating magic within the creature is no fallacy. It entwines.

Shrouds.

Overtakes.

There is no maleesa without the magic, as there is no magic without the maleesa.

My observations of maleesa larva that do not make it to the pupa stage of development have always been consistent. They are gray, lacking life. Hideous beyond even that of which we already know.

They're other.

Without.

To me, they are the maleesa without magic.

—Odessa, Reeler
Year 1292

Morning dawned slowly.

As always, the clan rose with the sun in the winter. Late rising required less food during the lean months, when they could huddle safely beneath their blankets for longer periods of time. Andrei dreaded the rising sun.

Despite little sleep, his mind had cleared. Bleary eyes guided him through his dwelling when he finally slipped from bed. Bitter cold air attacked. He trembled, teeth clattering, and yanked his clothes out from the foot of his bed.

"Can you make a fire?" he asked the Sirilas magic. Curiosity more than necessity drove him. The magic provided no food or warmth last night.

Had he finally unbalanced it?

Or did something else?

No response.

A deepening pit dwelt in Andrei's stomach as he quickly stepped into his boots, and pulled on his coat. Not even the memory of Sacha's voice telling him the Sirilas grimoire never prevented the use of outside magic could comfort him.

According to Sacha, he'd broken no rules. According to Sergei?

Well . . .

Fingers of guilt seemed to point at him from all directions. He hunched lower in his coat when he stepped outside. Anastasia approached.

Seeing him, her gaze dropped, darted up and down again. Set against the confident version of Mila he'd gotten used to, he'd forgotten how Anastasia appeared so . . . jumpy. Had he not noticed her nervous energy around him before? Interactions with Mila flowed with ease. Time with Anastasia felt like the hoar frost in comparison.

Prickly and unexpected.

Anastasia lifted her chin as she approached. "Andrei, I'm glad to see you're well."

"I slept hard." He gave a trying smile.

She nodded, kept moving. He fell into step beside her as they walked the same path to her cave. Weeks had passed since they strolled together. She peered ahead, though there wasn't much to see. A white skyline with occasional whips of snow curled up from the ground, then settled in languorous waves.

"How are you, Anastasia?"

"I'm well."

"I heard rumors of your handf—"

"It's been busy in the Creator's cave," she blurted. "The Weavers delivered several bolts of silk that were the wrong color. We've been sewing an order from the Northern Network for a gown and the panels were all wrong and it was a disaster and we're trying to . . . figure it out."

"I'm sorry to hear that. Do I need to speak with the Weavers?"

"I think so. That batch had been consistently producing the deep mauve that has been so popular in the Northern

Network. It came out a strange . . . green color. Something is wrong."

He frowned.

Maman's warning from weeks ago rippled back through his mind. *I'm telling you something is wrong with the maleesa. This batch . . . it feels different. The magic is out of balance.*

The lacking Sirilas magic from last night, this morning.

His throat thickened.

Clan concerns returned to the forefront of his mind. Sarasam lay quietly at his side, the magic apparently satisfied. For now.

Yet the Sirilas magic must not be, for it denied him and other parts of clan life experienced turmoil. Was there a balance to be had between the two magicks? Too late, he heard the silence. He forced himself back to the moment.

"Thank you for telling me."

Anastasia opened her mouth, closed it again. The words she didn't release hung between them. He didn't know how to dispel the ungainly sensation. Before Mila, Anastasia had been his only sort of . . . friend.

Yet, she wasn't even that.

They had so little in common. To hold a conversation with her was a laborious event. Without the *maleesa* or the clan, they might never speak. Her cave approached, so Andrei slowed.

"If something else occurs that I can help you fix, please let me know."

She nodded.

They stopped at the juncture. Anastasia hesitated, one gloved hand tapping the top of her thigh. "*Papan* said that the High Priest wants you to show a *maleesa* to the Southern Network Council."

He leaned back. Rarely did Sergei discuss clan business outside of the glacier walls, and less so with his family.

"Yes."

"That you agreed to attend a lastmeal?"

"Yes."

She swallowed. "Will, uh, you require your betrothed at that lastmeal?"

Stupidly, the thought had never occurred to him. "It would honor me to have you there."

Her teeth sank into her bottom lip. "Oh."

"Do you want to go?"

"I'm happy to support the clan."

Her rote words had a wooden feel.

"Did Sergei say anything else about it?"

She lifted her shoulder in a shrug. "Only that some clan members think it would be fine. Others disagree. Like Sacha," she added gently. "She thinks we need to stay open to negotiation, and told me to support you by discussing the opportunity with other witches."

Andrei braced himself.

"I see."

Anastasia cleared her throat. He regarded the top of her head—she wouldn't look at him—and wondered why Sergei didn't just show Alek the *maleesa* himself. Andrei held no real claim to the Guide of the Clan yet . . .

Anastasia's quivering voice drew his mind back. "I, uh . . . can we speak? Later. N-not here or right now because I'll be late to work. Perhaps at your dwelling before lastmeal? Somewhere a little more . . . private."

"Yes."

She dashed away.

Andrei stared after her retreating form. The question, *what did you want to discuss?* lingered on his lips. The call from another clan member drew his gaze away for a moment. He lifted a hand to wave.

When he looked back, she was gone.

* * *

The Reeler's Cave flowed in smooth planes of icy marble.

Waves of tan rock undulated back, spiraling into open recesses. Ceilings twice the height of a witch unfurled. Cave pearls—head-size round rocks that rolled away from the walls hundreds of years before the *maleesa* moved in—held up thin slabs where the Reelers worked. Soft pillows of silk topped the cave pearls for witches to sit upon, otherwise they'd be bone cold.

Candles, hidden by glass panes, flickered at intervals along the rock walls. The *maleesa* did not live here, so the temperature was not so strictly regulated. Andrei let the door whisper shut behind him as he stepped away from stairs that led down here.

Several eyes peered at him, then away.

"Ah, our Guide has arrived."

A witch named Janokov approached and clapped Andrei on the back. The *thud* between his shoulder blades would have knocked him forward—he'd done so in the past—but after working with Mila, and at the smithy, his body held upright.

Janokov laughed.

"Well, well. About time you put mass on those bones of yours, Andrei. Can you help us with our magical issue?"

"I just received your message." Andrei held up the slip of paper. "What's happened?"

"Can't see anything causing it, myself." Janokov led the way to the other side of the room. Barrels sculpted out of ice awaited. Slashes of paint formed runes on the wall, stating which cave and *maleesa* batch the barrels held.

Within the barrels lay millions of tiny threads, like discarded hair clippings. Some threads were long. Others were short, curled, or straight. Piles of the clogged threads curlicued together in a teeming mass.

At the table, a Reeler reached to the closest ice barrel, grabbed a tuft of threads, and put it in front of them. A silk pad, tacked down with sap, held the threads as the Reeler lifted a glass to his eye and inspected each one.

While he murmured magical spells, the threads unwound. He tugged here, pulled there. The threads loosened, falling into gossamer strands. After he separated each string, he stated another spell. The magic gathered the individual threads to be collected in a fist, then carefully laid flat.

All appeared balanced there.

Janokov led him past those Reelers, toward the end.

A young boy sat with a scrunched face, fists clenched. He radiated annoyance.

"He's been down here for three months now, and hasn't had a problem," Janokov said. "Reels great, gentle touch. The threads obeyed his command. Now? We can't get the magic to listen to him."

Andrei paused just behind the boy.

"Try it."

The boy huffed. Without looking up, he reached for a pinch of the threads. Andrei studied each step, his calm touch. Slow movements. He didn't sloppily toss the graceful thread around. Rough handling would cause breakages when the Reelers sent the thread to the Spinners. After they spun, magic fused the threads from each patch into one long coil. Breakages would interrupt the coil, thus production.

The boy spoke each spell with correct pronunciation, yet nothing happened. No softening of threads.

No gentle persuasion of derangement.

"Your execution is fine." Andrei glanced at Janokov. "Have *you* tried reeling?"

Janokov shook his head.

"No."

Andrei reached for the threads. Memory resurrected. He

remembered being a boy, working for an hour before and after school. Each clan child moved through the silk production stages as soon as they turned eight. The orderly world had been soothing.

Andrei lay his fingers on the cloth, so lightweight, yet sturdy. Like the swords, though decidedly different. Each magical path had power and demand. Reward, as well. One required fire, the other ice.

The Sirilas spell came quickly to his mind, though he hadn't used it in years. When he released it, the threads remained stagnant.

Janokov stepped back. "*Ira!*" he cried. "What does this mean?"

Nonplussed, Andrei motioned for Janokov to try.

He obeyed.

Nothing happened.

Andrei's breathing ratcheted higher; he forced it to calm. No, this couldn't be his fault also. This couldn't be a punishment for doing magic or working with the swords or a result of his lapse in concentration as Guide to the North Caves. . . could it?

Fear plagued him.

What if he'd missed a step? They would blame a bad batch on the Guide of the Caves in the end, for the Guide holds responsibility for all the *maleesa* and witches within. He educated, inspired, regulated, led.

Failed.

Janokov stared at the inert thread in astonishment. The boy glanced up, eyes wide with relief and shock.

"It's a bad batch of threads." Andrei shuffled further away, his throat tight. "Trace this barrel back to the Gatherers that brought it. Have them send word of which cave it originates in. We'll run checks on the *maleesa* there."

"Is it possible for an entire barrel to go bad?"

"Rare, but possible."

"Does it mean something?"

"It means that there is a sick *maleesa*, perhaps. Or simply a bad batch. It may mean nothing. Until we can look further into it, we won't know."

Janokov frowned. He reached over, plucked different threads from another barrel, and set them before the boy. He initiated the magic. The threads separated and loosened in his hand, lining together in the air as he gently worked to break them apart.

Confirmed bad batch.

A long breath escaped Janokov. "I'm relieved. I thought —" He stopped. Cleared his throat. "That is . . . I apologize. I'm never happy about wasted resources. Only it's not my pr—"

"No need." Andrei held up a hand to stave off platitudes he didn't want. They'd only make this worse. He had to get out of there first, then figure out what this meant so he could . . .

What?

Continue to cement his position as Guide of the Clan until he had to walk away from the swords?

Sarasam revolted, causing a wave of nausea to well up in his throat. No, he couldn't. The magic had somehow knitted itself into him. There was no separation anymore.

"Everything all right, Guide?"

Janokov peered at him through slotted eyes. The man had almost no lashes. His forehead was so flat that the folds of his eyes existed directly above them, lending a constantly irritated expression.

For now, his open brow revealed concern.

"Just thinking." Andrei waved a hand. "I will investigate this with the Gatherers. Thank you for bringing it to my attention."

Andrei turned to go. His chest felt as tight as stones crushed together. He could barely breathe the words out.

Another moment and—

Janokov's hand on his arm stopped him. Andrei glanced back, startled. In the clan, touch was a carefully regulated commodity. Janokov didn't release his grip, but nodded to the outer door.

"A word?"

Andrei hesitated, nodded. Outside, there would be more space to breathe and think. The Reelers worked in quiet contemplation at their back as they left. Together, they ascended the hard rock stairs and burst into the daylight.

Sunshine spilled over them as they jerked heavy fur coats over their arms and stepped into the chill. Janokov shoved his hands into his pockets. He stared at the empty vastness of the tundra.

"Forgive me, Guide, but you haven't seemed well the past several weeks."

"In what way?"

"All ways."

"An example would be helpful."

Janokov's nose ruffled as he faced Andrei. They were exactly the same height—neither of them very tall—with similar black hair. Janokov wore his in the traditional clannish braid, cut at his neckline. The weight of Andrei's knee-length braid tugged on him, threatening a headache after so much sleep loss.

"We've seen you less than ever before."

"I was present for all audits."

"One was late."

"Is that your concern?"

Andrei's tone gained an unusual edge. Normally soft-spoken, almost bullyable, such a firm response felt strange on his lips.

Janokov pressed his lips together, frowned.

You lead, Sergei once told him. *You show integrity, work hard like those you ask to work, and you also lead. They want you to be solid and firm, a decision maker.*

"What do you want from this line of questioning, Janokov?"

"Sacha says that the High Priest wants to share our way of life with the Network."

The pit in his stomach deepened.

"Sacha . . ."

"It's not just her. Sergei has been talking about opening up the clan. He said that you're working to form relationships and friendships with the Network." Janokov's gaze darted to his, nervous as a hare. "Is that . . . true?"

"When did Sergei say this?"

"When speaking with my *papan* last night." Janokov shifted. Wind blasted vents of cold air, brushing the thin hairs away from his brow. "They debated whether they should do it. He mentioned that the High Priest asked you to show the Council a *maleesa*."

Fury coursed through him. That wasn't Sergei's place! Well . . . perhaps it was. Considering that Andrei wasn't *yet* the Guide of the Clan, Sergei could do as he felt best. But stirring up questions?

Did the clan members need these details?

In the past, the Guides handled such issues so witches could support the clan, the *maleesa*. Do their work, work the plan. This most divisive issue would only distract and create imbalance.

Is that what happened here?

"I was not aware he mentioned this to anyone else," Andrei said carefully.

"So it's true? The High Priest wants you to take a *maleesa* into the Southern Network and show them?"

"Yes."

"And will you?"

Janokov's controlled expression could only hide fury or fear. A voice from behind spoke up.

"Andrei believes in the clan's sacredness above all else," Sacha said. "It has always been this way. Who else would have endured all of Sergei's rigid rules?"

Sacha stood across from them. A hood framed her face, where tendrils of hair escaped around her neck. Her firmly set gaze, hardened with simmering angst, bore into him.

"Sacha," Andrei drawled.

"Andrei, I'd like a word, please."

"I—"

As his *tanta*, he couldn't refuse her outright, yet he wouldn't let her charge over the conversation either. In the past, he'd allowed Sacha too much space to overtake everything.

Not anymore.

Sarasam stirred up, imparting courage.

"When I finish my discussion," he said firmly, "you may have a turn. You have interrupted a conversation that isn't yours to interrupt, and you may leave until I'm ready to speak to you."

She blinked.

Andrei kept her gaze. Never had he stood up to her in such a way, nor with such power. Janokov's lips parted, eyes wide.

Finally, Sacha shrugged.

Andrei turned to Janokov, relieved she hadn't challenged him again. "More details will come soon, Janokov. Please, do your best not to stir up rumors or gossip."

"You want me to keep quiet?"

"I didn't say that. You're a free witch. You can do and say

what you like. Stirring up falsehoods, however, I will not allow."

A hint of ferocity filtered through Janokov's once friendly eyes. "And what will you do to punish me, Guide?"

Andrei's jaw clenched. Janokov wanted to challenge him now? With Sarasam in her hidden scabbard down his leg, he felt less fear than ever before. Also, more reluctance.

Did he *really* want to defend his position as Guide to the Clan? More than questions, the desire not to be bullied around rose within.

Before he could respond, Sacha stepped forward. Fire flashed in her dark eyes.

"You'll be demoted, Janokov," she hissed. "If you stir up issues that disturb the magic, you'll face the same consequences as anyone else. You have two marks against you already. One more and you'll live in the outlying dwellings to hunt. You'll never feel the warmth of the caves again."

She waved a hand.

"Go back to work."

Janokov's upper lip curled over his teeth.

"Fine," he muttered. "But I'm not staying silent."

Andrei conceded with a nod, though he felt sick to his stomach. Sacha scowled at Janokov's back when he made the "Pft" sound, then disappeared into the cave.

"You undercut me, Sacha!" Andrei cried. "I looked like a weak Guide with you giving consequences over my head."

"We'll deal with that in a minute," she muttered. "For now, we have bigger issues to discuss. Go. The Spinner's Cave is empty while the Spinners are at middlemeal. We'll discuss them more in-depth there."

Chapter Sixteen

*Clan members grow weary of routine, particularly in
the winter months. When snow scuds the top of the ice
and wind is a lonely howl in our ears that never abates.*

*Entire weeks pass when clan members don't surface
from the caves. The magic takes us to our dwellings, back
to our work, when the cold is so bitter.*

*Those days, the groans and cracks of the glacier are the
only sounds. One feels that they might go mad.*

Yet, the maleesa require such sacrifice.

The clan offers it.

*In our souls, we all grow weary, yet our life force doesn't
extinguish. Why would we cease to do magic?*

*—Ivan, Overseer
Year 1302*

The last thing Andrei wanted to admit was relief that Sacha had shown up, helped him deal with Janokov.

Yet, it lingered in the recesses.

Problems with the *maleesa* he could face. Witches he could handle. Problematic witches with superiority complexes? He'd much rather be at the forge, with the swords.

Sacha sat him at a small, square table made of wood in the Spinners Cave. Between them lay a long, cylindrical rod. At the end of the rod, a handle. When a Spinner turned the handle, and executed the right magical spell, the threads that Reelers had carefully untangled and gathered together would fuse. They'd slide onto the rod, spooling in glimmering gray strands.

All *maleesa* strands were gray, until the finishing, when the final color revealed itself.

The Spinners had finished their spool before middlemeal in the main hall—an immense cavern beneath the glacier. All the caves interconnected below ground, allowing clan members to avoid the bitter cold snows in the depths of winter. Echoes reverberated constantly, as if the sounds that made them lived in the rock.

Sacha planted her hands on the table and leaned forward.

Andrei spoke first.

"I'm going to Zamok Castle, Sacha. I'm going to speak with the High Priest and the Council and you can't stop me."

Her mouth snapped closed. She recoiled. "Why would I stop you?" she cried. "Of course you should go—it would be good for you. That's not what I brought you here for."

He deflated. "Really?"

"Yes!"

"Then why?"

"Because you must go to Zamok with the right answer on your lips." Her brow lowered. "And no *maleesa* in your pocket."

"Sergei has different opinions."

"I know." Her chin lifted. "He's speaking with clan members about it, intentionally stirring up questions."

"Why?"

She scoffed. "I'm not his *fere-fil*. How would I know? I suggest you go find out."

Andrei gritted his teeth. Oh, he planned on it.

"What do you need, *tanta*?"

Sacha set her hands on her lap. She studied him for a moment, then burst out all at once.

"You don't know what you're getting into, going to the castle. You've never even left the clan lands."

"I have."

Her eyes widened. "What? When?"

"Recently."

"After we last spoke?"

"I'm not sure if it was before or after." He rubbed his head to stave off a headache growing there. "Time is blurry."

"Because of the swords?"

He groaned. Of course! He'd been a fool and told Sacha about the swords! He'd entirely forgotten.

"Yes, the swords."

She made a noise at the back of her throat. "Hmm. Well, I didn't come to tell you what to do, if you can believe that."

"No."

She blithely ignored that. "I came to give you some advice while you're there. How to . . . navigate the castle."

He hesitated. Now that he thought about it—because he hadn't really thought through his acceptance all that much— it might help to know what he was getting into. The Network had inexplicable customs.

"Yes, this seems wise."

Relieved, she let out a rolling breath. "First, they're going to use utensils, like knives."

"We use knives."

"But not forks."

"What are forks?"

"Smaller knives with two prongs, meant to pierce things. They also use spoons instead of drinking from bowls. Make sure that you never eat food with your fingers and you'll be fine. Watch those around you. It will help."

"That's not so bad."

"They're also going to be wearing different clothes. Don't look like them, just take your best silk shirt and cleanest leather pants. Wear the black silk shirts you love so much."

"Fine."

Sacha chewed on the inside of her cheek with a look of quiet contemplation, then said, "And if they ask you to dance, just say no. It's not a custom we adhere to and there's no time to teach you how to dance. Whenever you need an excuse, just say we don't do that, or something. They'll let most things slide."

"Sacha, how do you know all this?"

She waved that off. "Doesn't matter. Do you hear me?"

"Yes."

"They're going to be very kind, but you can't trust it. It's just an act to get you to do what they want."

"Which is to show them the *maleesa*?"

"Yes. Trust no one, Andrei."

The advice, even though extreme and harried and delivered too quickly, was sound, no matter what side one took. His troubled thoughts moved to the batch of bad threads. To the lacking warmth and food in what felt like a wavering Sirilas magic.

"I . . . may have brought trouble upon us."

"What do you mean?"

He gestured behind them. "There is a bad batch of threads."

"Oh."

Her surprise amplified the stress already buzzing in his chest. If Sacha, who seemed to take everything so easily, responded in such a way, all had reason to be concerned. He swallowed past the rising lump in his throat.

"I've been . . . experimenting with this sword magic."

"Still?"

"I can't get rid of it."

She shrugged. "Are your duties fulfilled? Have you finished the sword?"

"No."

"So finish it!"

"I can't! It impedes my clan duties. I get no sleep. My caves, my checks, have been fine. Within the windows of expectation, anyway."

"So?"

"The bad batch! What if I have broken something in the Sirilas magic by showing allegiance to another system? It's more than just common magic, Sacha. This magic is . . ."

. . . in my soul.

"It's different," he said instead.

"I use other magic."

"But you are not the future Guide and you are not sinking into another magic system that, for what I can tell, also requires allegiance. Both the Sirilas magic and this . . . other one . . . demand much. Eventually, I fear I cannot satisfy both."

Her lips lifted slightly as she considered, then shook her head. "A bad batch is a regrettable and rare thing, but it's not a sign from Chthu, Andrei. This other magic system found *you*, remember?"

"Yes, but I want it."

She blinked.

"You what?"

He leaned forward. "Sacha, I'm not sure I can part with this other magic. It has opened something inside me . . ." The vulnerable words wavered in the air. He sat back again, rubbed a hand over his face. "I've almost completed a full sword, and I can't wait to do another. There's a smithy that I've found, and Mila is a friend. I've never had a friend. The world is so big."

"Mila!"

Delight filled her voice. Andrei hushed her, eyes darting around the empty room. What if the Spinners came back early?

Sacha laughed.

"Oh, Mila is wonderful. No wonder you're gone and having more fun out there than here. Do you like her?"

"She's very nice."

"Also exquisite."

"Stop that," he snapped. "It's not like that between us. I'm betrothed, and so is she."

"Oh, are you?" Sacha yawned. She set an elbow on the table and peered at him with a peevish expression. "I hadn't noticed."

"Sacha!"

"What?" She lifted both arms. "You and Anastasia have as much fun as solid ice."

"Handfasting isn't about having fun. It's a marriage of convenience for the good of the clan. That's all it's ever to be. Both of us have accepted that fact."

"That," she drawled, "is not true. Handfasting can be so much more than a tool in which to serve other people." She leaned forward. "Andrei, don't you ever tire of giving up everything for the clan? Don't you ever want to do something *different*?"

The words struck the hollowed-out core inside him. The empty space he hadn't known existed. A separate version of himself, previously bound.

How to answer?

Words welled up in his throat. *Yes! Yes, I want more!*

But the greater part of him shrank back. The too-bright light, the disorganization that came with freedom. Was wildness worth the pain?

"I don't know, Sacha."

"Think about it. Meanwhile, make sure your clothes are pristine, and I'll talk to Anastasia about the utensils, the dresses, and how to speak to them. You'll be lucky if she says a single word the entire time," she muttered as she pushed to her feet.

Sacha twined her scarf back around her neck, then stopped in the doorway. The distant rustles of movement from the far hallways of the cave—which connected with the Reelers and the greater dining area—meant that the Spinners would return soon.

"By the way, with Janokov and the other witches? Just . . . make sure you're talking to them."

"What do you mean?"

"Sergei hasn't been that open of a Guide. He's too . . . process-oriented. He thinks he's taking a burden from the clan when he keeps business from them, but it's more of a hardship to not know. Lately, you haven't been around as much. Arguably, you weren't around a lot before that either, but that's not your fault. It's what Sergei taught you. Now, you need to decide if you want to lead like him."

Andrei frowned. How *else* would he lead? Sergei had been his trainer, his *fere-papan* for most of his life.

"Clan members are noticing your absence, so they're talking to me. I won't hold back what I say to them, Andrei, and I won't turn them away. Given the chance, I'd fight you to be Guide for the Clans if I thought I had one. Consider yourself warned. I will voice my opinions, and Sergei won't like that."

* * *

That evening, Andrei escaped to the sword.

The blade finished, the magic now showed him the guard, the pommel, and the tang. Two small jewels, oblong and pointy at one end, would need to embed in the guard and above the pommel. He didn't know how.

It still needed a pommel, too. In his mind's eye, he could see it. Carved into an easy design, with the jewel set above. It had a glow, but that made no sense. The curved blade at the end, sharp on one side, swooped on the other, lent an elegant feel.

The images filled his mind—he knew what the magic wanted, but not how to create it. He set aside the not knowing and stared at the five bags of rocks that had been patiently waiting.

"Metal," he said.

Sarasam agreed.

Mila chuckled.

Firelight filled the smithy, now warm enough to remove his coat in. Mila had pitched the walls, smoothed it out. No awkward lumps interrupted the flow of wood, and the heat held more firmly. The hearth, tight as a bowl, cradled the flames. Magic reinforced the window panes. During the day, she worked on the roof.

"How do I extract the shards from the rocks?"

Mila dumped one bag out. "Sort through the rock and shards, and then you have to use magic."

His eyes jerked up to hers.

"What?"

"Magic." She gestured around with a ruffle of fingers. "As we've been doing to make the smithy habitable. You're against it now?"

"No."

"Are you opposed to doing it yourself?"

His hesitation resulted in another chuckle. Mila straightened the rocks into a single layer on the top.

"Andrei, you're a funny witch. You'll tolerate other witches using magic to support your efforts, but you won't do it yourself?"

Stated that way, the situation sounded far more selfish than he thought. "That's not my intent."

She grinned. "I know, but it doesn't make it less true."

He scowled.

Mila laughed. Her hand swept over the loose, glinting shards. "You could try to extract the metal yourself, but it would take months to process all these. Besides, you might have different metals."

She plucked two pieces from the table that shone on one side, and remained black on the other. One held a deeper hue, like amber. The other a strict silver.

"See the color difference between these? The magic will sort them, too."

"How do you know it?"

"All villagers know this magic. It's as familiar to us as breathing. The earth has done much of your work already. See? The river has already cleaned them. Tonight, I say that we crush all five bags with magic, then use a spell to get rid of the rock. The metal remains behind. Then we'll know how much more we need. I expect at least six more bags."

Crush them with magic.

A thrill slipped through Andrei.

Contemplating magic use outside of the Sirilas grimoire was one thing. To watch *others* take part in it was another. Executing it himself was something else entirely. This swordmaking magic hadn't required incantations or spells at the beginning. He'd been a passive recipient.

To start ancient magical use would draw a line in the sand

he couldn't take back. Already, the Sirilas magic had stopped supporting him at his dwelling. No more waiting lastmeals, ready baths, made beds.

It meant *something*.

He couldn't cross that line yet. Not when the fate of the *maleesa,* the clan, hung in the balance.

"Do you want to do it?" Mila asked, oblivious to his darkening thoughts.

"I want it done."

She grinned. "But not by your hand."

"I'm not ready," he mumbled.

All hilarity dropped from her expression. Softness entered there. With a nod, she reached over, set her hand on top of his. "Then allow me to show it to you? Seeing it might help it not seem so frightening."

Lump in his throat, he nodded.

Mila reached for the next bag. "Empty them out, Andrei. We're going to make a delightful mess, crushing rocks, separating the metal, then cleaning it all back up again at the end."

Chapter Seventeen

*Entropy is real. The clan faces great struggles if they
don't take the deleterious effects of staunch routine into
account in their care for the maleesa.*

A wise Guide lets no one live too comfortably.

*Gleb, Guide to the Clan
Year 1298*

Gems scattered the top of the smithy table.

They were rough-hewn chunks, and some of them
required faceting and a sturdy polish. He had no idea what to
do with those. The magic had chiseled others from the hardened stone where they originated. Intoxicating, with their
depths of shadow and pools of vibrant color.

But why did the magic bring so many gems? The sword
required four—the same oblong sort of shape, like a stretched
oval with pointy ends. Two for each side, front and back, of
the guard and tang. He held those four, thin gems in his hand.
At some point, he'd set them into the sword.

Yet, no glowing, golden pommel lay in the gem pile.

Earlier collections of sapphires came and went without use. A diamond or emerald or garnet here and there. Did the magic want to show him what was possible?

Andrei regarded the jewels with his palms pressed to the tabletop, his body canted slightly over it as he considered. Candlelight bounced in a half circle around the jewels. A week had passed by as he pieced the guard and tang together, working in the depths of night. He'd messed up three times, had to start over.

The finished tang and guard now waited with the blade, but it had no pommel at the very end.

Mila showed him the magical process of separating rock from metal. Then he melted all the small pieces, formed the ingots, and listened to the inner guide that told him every next step.

Never beyond what he needed to know, never before he needed to know it.

By day, the Sirilas magic simmered in the background of his thoughts while he answered questions from Gatherers, audited care logs, met with Sergei, prepped for the lastmeal with Alek. He attempted to speak with Anastasia—she'd asked for time with him—but she blithely avoided private conversation.

He returned his thoughts to the smithy and sank his teeth into his lip.

"Yes, your blade is finished with hammering," he murmured to the expectant dark blade next to the gems. "We have heated you all up, quenched you in ice water, and you did not break by some miracle. But I don't think we can call you complete. How do I set the gems? What of the pommel I see in my head."

The unfinished sword protested, but mildly. Mere exclamations, like huffs of annoyance, more than true rebuttal.

Andrei rolled his eyes.

"I'm not sure how to use the gems. Also, the metal is . . . not beautiful. You are not yet strong. You could be stronger, I feel it."

Another irritated response.

"All right, all right. There *is* more. You attest to this as well. But how do I polish you? The whetstone and oil worked for sharpening . . ."

Andrei trailed away, his gaze drawn by an old shirt that he'd cut into pieces, then dipped in *yakuza* oil. Mila had ground the seeds with a mortar and pestle and a brown sheen stained the rag where the oil had been.

The sword spoke again. The emotions came more intensely now, like jagged pinpricks.

"I understand you want the decoration, but how? Where is the pommel?"

Andrei touched a hand to his head, where an image of the final sword lived. He understood then that the pommel would be a piece of amber that glowed with a subdued color. Clear throughout, without blemish, that he'd have to chisel, somehow.

"There is no amber here. You've given me diamonds, emeralds, rubies, and a lovely opal." He ran his finger over the top of a half-moon opal, smoothed and polished as if by expert hands. "But no amber."

The unfinished sword gave a *humph*.

"Why are you annoyed with me? I cannot go traipsing through the dark night to find a chunk of amber. And no," he added quickly, anticipating the next question, "I cannot come earlier when there is more light. The clan is already suspicious of me as it is. I may only come when I'm supposed to be in my dwelling."

Sarasam lay next to the finished blade, to which he had no name to assign yet. Would the magic give it to him? He assumed so, for he would never have presumed to name Sarasam.

If the sword had a body, he had a feeling it would have turned its back. Andrei straightened up when a clatter came to the door. The unfinished sword brightened with a familiar rush of bliss.

"Come in, Mila," he called before she could announce herself. The sturdy door swung open, admitting her thin eyes and wide smile.

"You're here earlier than I thought," she said.

"And still too late." He rubbed a hand over his face. The sleep-deprived burn of his eyes, the sensation of being able to sleep at any moment, felt all too familiar these days.

"Here." Mila tossed something to him. "I found this on the way in. Thought you might like it."

Andrei caught a smooth globe. He lifted his hand to peer at a perfectly preserved ball of amber, without blemish and clear throughout.

The unfinished sword cheered.

Andrei shook his head. He shouldn't be surprised, but he was. He held the future-pommel against the light. The color was as warm as he expected.

"Where did you find it?" he asked.

"In a tree trunk."

"In a trunk?"

"There was a hole." She set several bulky objects on the other side of the room, near a table she'd used for supplies.

"There was a hole?" he repeated with amusement.

She glanced up, saw his half smile, and her own widened. "There was a hole in the tree," she continued. A strand of hair slipped free from her braid. She reached up, tucked it behind her ear. "So naturally I put my hand inside to see what was there."

"What if it was an arctic baer?"

She rolled her eyes. "This was a small hole." Her hands joined to form a circumference the span of both his hands together. "This big. A nest for a squirrel or something. I found dried leaves and shells and the amber inside. A creature must have found it first."

He studied it with deepening curiosity. No, not a creature. The magic.

He marveled at all the intricate details the magic wove together. The swords resulted from a greater magic than had already been apparent.

Yet . . . it might be more superlative than just magic. All remained ethereal and vague behind certainty. He'd never pressed beyond clan credence before this magic entered his life. Everything spiraled into the unknown afterward.

"Thank you, Mila. The sword and I were just arguing about this exact piece of amber."

"What?"

He motioned to the sword. "It belongs to this sword."

"Oh."

He gave a half shrug. "I don't know anything else."

A chuckle followed.

"Is there more oil?" He peered into a clay bowl she'd left from the night before.

"Just what's in the bowl. Why?"

"I think I know what to do to finish this sword," he murmured. "And if I'm correct, it will require oil and . . . magic."

"*New* magic?"

He nodded distractedly, not wanting to think about it. When he picked the sword up, the weight felt appropriate. The range, the swing. With more experience, he could tailor the grip of a weapon—finger placement grooves, perhaps. But this sword? No. It didn't want the details.

It wanted the amber.

And . . .

Oil.

Insistence followed. A readiness to move, to do. The desire for action. Both swords had a jittery energy now, as if they danced on the balls of their feet. They wanted something to happen.

This . . . finish.

Would the magic end with this sword? He doubted it.

Mila bustled quietly in the background while Andrei studied the blade. The sound of spilling shards and rock followed. She'd harvested more from the river on the way here, he wagered. The first batch had been just enough. That's how this magic seemed to work. He had just enough of everything, but never too much.

"What will I do with you once you're done?" he murmured to the sword, flipping it over. "For whom are you made?"

The movement didn't feel as awkward or uncoordinated as before. Over the weeks, his fingers had become more nimble, his forearms sinewy. He wielded more than a feather these days, and the strength changed the way he stood.

A flow of harried energy, followed by an urge to pick up the amber, came next. He grabbed it, glanced at the bottom of the handle. It ended in a flat spot. An image of frozen sap came to mind. A giant hunk of it, wedged in the juncture of two branches on a tree.

"Sap?"

An impatient reply came next.

"But how do I make the sap stay? It will drip all over the amber and detach with the first swing."

No answer.

Of course.

He rolled his eyes, reached for his jacket. Mila glanced up —she'd long ago learned to tune his conversations with the swords out. Andrei slipped into his coat, then grabbed the handle of the nearest lamp.

"I'm hunting for sap."

Amused, she followed.

The cold radiated through the open sky, twice as bitter as anything he'd felt before. This might be the coldest night he'd ever experienced. He always had the novelty of a warm dwelling to shield him from a chill so bone-deep.

A soft glow drew his eyes back. Mila tromped behind him, following in his footprints. Candles floated above the snow to illuminate a path.

"Where is this sap?"

"On a tree?"

"Which tree?"

"That is the question."

He tilted his head back to canvas the area overhead, looking through branches set against a twinkling dark sky. The candles elevated. Seeing no break in the boughs nearest the ground, he kept going.

She motioned off to the right. "Over there," she said, her breath a fog in front of her. "I noticed some of the trees are damaged near the stream, probably from arctic baers. You can find more sap on a harmed tree."

He veered toward the gentle tinkling sound, lifting his feet high to wade through the fresh powder. He yawned, eyes watering. They turned to ice at the edges, crackling along his lashes.

"Have you always lived in the villages?" he asked.

"Many villages."

"These?"

"Others deeper into the Network. These for the longest."

He studied a tree. It was easier to ask her questions when they didn't have to look right at each other.

"Is that how you know so much about making dwellings

and the forest and magic?"

"When it's where you live, you must."

The underground caves, the *maleesa* magic, leadership of a sometimes unwilling clan. That was his world. He knew that well, because he must.

"Do you think we're born to a certain life?"

Thanks to Sacha, the question had been brewing inside for some time. Now that it escaped, he wondered if he should call it back. Mila thought it over, her gloved hand running over the snowy boughs of a nearby evergreen, before she stepped between two saplings.

"Yes, but we don't have to stay in it. We can't help the circumstances in which we're born."

"I suppose not."

"Why do you ask?"

He shook his head. "I don't know. I'm . . . thinking of a lot of things."

"Any reason?"

The drawl in her tone felt like an invitation. With all the pressure bearing down on him around the upcoming lastmeal with Network leadership, he loosened the worst of it.

"In two days, I'm eating lastmeal with the High Priest. I won't be able to work on the swords tomorrow because I have to prepare my clothes, my questions. My . . . words."

He skimmed over Sacha's warnings—wondered again how to figure out what a spoon did—and then thought of Anastasia. Darker gloom settled over him. If Sacha feared for him—though trained for leadership—how would Anastasia fare?

Mila's voice modulated carefully when she said, "Have you decided what to do yet?"

"No. The situation is odd because Sergei supports Alek's initiative to see the *maleesa*. Every day, he speaks more about it to me, to clan members. His opinion grows bolder. He wants me to take the *maleesa*."

"What does the clan think?"

"I can't tell. It's too divided."

Everyone had different ideas of what would be best for someone else. Andrei didn't know where—or how—to land. Somewhere in the middle of the extremes, most likely, where most modulation happened.

"Do you understand that you can't trust Alek?" she asked.

"Yes."

"Or the Council?"

"Yes."

"Or Sergei."

He stopped. Snow fell gracefully around his ankles as he turned around to face her, his errand for sap almost forgotten.

"What?"

Mila hesitated. "You can't trust him, Andrei. Not if he's advocating for someone outside of the Sirilas to see the *maleesa*. *Maman* says the rules are strong, like iron."

He startled.

She said *Maman*. *Maleesa*. Sirilas.

"How do you know?"

Confusion weakened his question. Her eyes widened into giant globes. She tossed a hand to her mouth, squeaked, and disappeared. Snow filtered up from the ground in a white spray in her wake.

"Mila?"

Where did she go?

With an exhalation, he turned away. The quiet forest ebbed and flowed around him, filled with black pools of shadows and the silent tones of trees. Rarely did he venture out here without Mila. There was safety in her company. Assurance in her presence.

Sarasam lay at his side, the only reassurance left.

Resigned, he pressed on.

Chapter Eighteen

If you test a maleesa, it will run away.

—Bogda, Threader
Year 1346

Sergei's head tilted to the side as he inspected Andrei. He shrugged.

"Looks fine."

Andrei tugged at the front of a brand-new leather vest. The softest, whitest rabbit's fur lined the inside. It buttoned from waist to neck. Etched designs in the dark leather swirled with images of arctic baers.

Underneath, a black silk shirt stretched to his wrists, fitted close to the skin in the clan's way. A thicker silk than usual, it would be slightly warmer in the winter chills, but not by much.

Boots, freshly scrubbed, clasped his feet, stretching over his pants all the way to his knees. The leather ties were new, freshly replaced.

Glacier walls surrounded them with a constant chill. The

planes of cerulean layers, compressed in lines of silver, cyan, and gray, reflected the torches and candlelight. Smoke curled to the top of the room. Water droplets raced down the wall, carried to the small canal that lined the edges, and whisked down to lower levels of the glacier to collect in barrels for wash-water.

Despite this constant force of change, this room never altered. The Sirilas magic maintained this exact size.

Sergei stood behind a desk of dark wood, pipe in between his teeth. He regarded several pieces of parchment as Andrei pulled a new fur-lined coat over his shoulders. The Creators, directed by Anastasia, sent the ensemble.

A mounting dread teemed in his gut. The moment to talk to Sergei about his decision for the clan had arrived. Until now, there had been no suitable time to open the difficult discussion. Sergei had been elusive, claiming ill health as he withdrew to allow Andrei the time to step into the role.

The *Praznick* loomed a month away.

Now that his chance had come, Andrei's voice turned to ash. He cleared his throat, but it didn't ease the discomfort.

"Sergei, about the *maleesa*..."

Sergei didn't bother looking up from the parchment. A stream of smoke billowed out of his mouth from around the pipe. He had one fingertip pressed into the desk while he read.

"Yes?"

Andrei drew in a breath, forcing his spine to straighten. He pulled his shoulders back, driven to greater confidence by the advice that Sergei had given him years ago.

No one can solve a problem when they're hunched over like a small child about to receive punishment.

The reminder made this situation all the more confusing.

"I believe you want me to take a *maleesa* tonight."

Sergei looked up.

"I will not take the *maleesa*. Not yet, anyway. I'm not committed to a path. The time to decide isn't right."

The statement broke most of the building tension. Sergei pulled the pipe from between his teeth. A pause several heartbeats long followed.

"Why not?"

"I haven't met the Council. I don't know their individual motivations. I know only what Alek has said. After tonight, I'll have more information. We will make a better decision for the clan once I see them face-to-face."

Sergei set the pipe down. "There's some wisdom in what you say. As there is wisdom in departing away from the *known* path."

For Sergei to oppose him was nothing new. He had often forced Andrei to account for his decisions and think out loud. A different glint appeared in Sergei's eyes.

Andrei continued. "To expose the *maleesa* when I haven't even met the Council Members would be foolish. You've taught me that the entire clan rests on my shoulders."

Sergei resembled Anastasia when he dropped into concentration like this. Thin lips. Intense bearing. She carried her mother's slighter stature and thin body, but her father's facial intensity.

"The decision is yours, Andrei."

"Do you approve?"

"I never said you needed my approval."

Irritation clouded Andrei's emotions. Sergei paused, allowing the quiet to roll between them.

"Then I'll press forward."

"You are to be the Guide to the Clans and this is your decision to make."

"I am not yet."

Sergei scoffed. "You're on the doorstep, Andrei."

"There is still time for the clan to complain and protest my ascension."

Sergei gave a lift of one shoulder. The move would have looked uncertain on anyone else, but appeared dismissive for him. There was an assertion of . . . something . . . in Sergei's response. A flippant regard, as if Andrei held more power than he thought, and should use the power.

"You don't have to give the Council what they really want, Andrei. Do you see that?"

"What do you mean?"

"They don't know what they don't know," Sergei cried, hands tossed into the air. "Not what a *maleesa* is or the name of our magic. They call them bugs, worms. We have a grimoire, and that's all they know. The glacier, the caves, the magic that hides and sustains and imprisons us is hidden. They don't *know*."

Andrei's breath suspended.

"You think I should lie?"

Sergei blew a sharp, irritated breath. "Pft! I think you should do what is right. What is that to you? As Guide to the Clan, you can't ask me these questions anymore. Decide and *do*. I know you don't enjoy going on your own and deciding alone, but you must do it. Yes, there's a chance you'll be wrong and you'll fail, but you'll fix it. I won't be here forever. Now is the time for you to grow."

Frustration grizzled his voice now. It struck Andrei all the way to the core.

You must do it.

I won't be here forever.

Now is the time for you to grow.

He'd followed for so long in Sergei's footsteps that he hadn't often stepped outside of them. In some ways, he desired such a release from the tether. In others, he never wanted the path to change.

"I see."

"Do you?"

Sergei's insistent question, so rapidly thrown out, brought his gaze back up. Andrei nodded.

"Yes, Sergei."

"You're a good witch, Andrei. You're wise and kind, but . . . if you are to guide, you must also be confident, even if you head into the dark."

"I know."

"Can you do that?"

Thoughts of the sword filtered through his mind. What did he know of established paths anymore? His whole life had become an unknown space. With confidence, Andrei's shoulders rolled back. "I can."

"Will you?"

"I will."

Something in his firm tone must have convinced Sergei, because he slumped against his desk. Weariness rippled through him.

"Sergei?"

Sergei passed a hand over his forehead. "Yes, I think we should take the High Priest's offer and open the clan to the Network more. Not in a nefarious way." He let out a breath. "But to get witches talking. Andrei, difficulties will come. I must see you navigate them on your own. The clan will divide over this. It will come back together."

Renewed annoyance swept through Andrei, then settled as quickly as it came. Amongst the prickling sensation was the deeper sense that Sergei was right.

"I see."

"Perhaps you do." Sergei gave a weak bob of his head. "Perhaps you finally do."

Sergei's face paled as the light waned. He lowered into a

chair and closed his eyes. When they opened again, he eyed Sarasam at Andrei's side.

"Good luck tonight, Andrei. I trust you will keep my daughter safe. Whatever you've been up to has changed you. Not for the worse. Without that sword and what you're capable of with it, I would never have let you go away from the clan lands with Anastasia. Go. Form your own opinions. Make your decisions. I'll be here when you return."

* * *

Anastasia wrung her silk gloves in between twisted fingers. She peered outside a small window, worry lines etched into her face.

Andrei kept his gaze straight ahead, but placed a hand on her forearm. She paused, stiffened.

"Can I do anything to ease your anxiety?" he asked.

She swallowed hard.

A gentle shake of her head followed.

Dark locks trailed around her shoulders, the strands curled around the bottom. The smell of *zandelia* flowers that populated the stream banks in the spring and summer drifted from her silk dress. Clan members often gathered them, pressed them, and put them into soap.

She wore a silk dress underneath a floor-length fur overcoat. Her skin had a brightness to it that meant she'd scrubbed all the cave dust free. He had done the same, but didn't enjoy the feeling of shucking the caves off.

If one were to wrap up a representation of the clan, the two of them would be as good as any. They wore their best silk, softest leather, cleanest garments.

Still, they'd never blend in.

Anastasia's nervousness filled the carriage as the hum of wooden wheels on dirt turned to the clatter of paved stones.

Hours of stilted conversation and awkward silence lay behind them as they approached Zamok Castle. The Sirilas magic had taken them to the Meeting House, then another distant spot where a carriage from Zamok met them.

At his side, Sarasam waited in the scabbard. He didn't know if he could have it at the castle. What if they said no? Would Sarasam allow them to be parted?

His conversation with Sergei reminded him of an animal bred in cages, now turned loose on the world. A thousand other lives rested in his hands, and all of them depended on the decisions he'd make today.

Decisions he didn't *want* to make.

None of this thrilled him. None of it felt as good as being at the smithy, with the metal and the swords.

A long, flat warming rock, strapped by thin ropes to the top of the carriage, had long since cooled. It shifted as the trotting horses slowed. Outside, the driver, bundled under very thick coats and furs, called out.

Andrei swept aside a drape meant to keep out the cold and sucked in a sharp breath. Lights glittered on the not-so-distant horizon, soaring impossibly far into the sky.

Though not quite the four o'clock hour Alek had referenced, night had fallen, leaving sunset a blush in the distant sky. Stars sparkled overhead, funneling his gaze straight to the warm windows of the castle.

Anastasia squeezed her eyes shut.

The drape fell back into place.

"Have you ever left the clan lands before?" he asked.

"No."

Hearing her voice gave some reassurance to the brittle air.

"Me either."

Sacha's advice sprinted through his mind. Forks. Utensils. Two Finishers he spoke to today mentioned napkins, not spilling soup from the spoon. After which they'd giggled, and he fought not to roll his eyes.

What did *they* know about spoons?

Within Anastasia's tangle of fingers, she clutched something. He peered at it, curious, until her fingers twitched. She swiped her thumb back and forth across the top in an unconscious, soothing gesture.

A gem.

She clasped a heart-shaped diamond with the softest bloom of pink. A hole drilled into the top looped a thin piece of silk. They had woven the ribbon from two different batches. A soft white, and a pearl gray.

The trinket disappeared when the driver called out a second time. Anastasia pulled her glove back on. The horses slowed.

"Are you afraid, Anastasia?"

Her head bobbed up and down on her neck. "Are you?"

Her squeak of a question surprised him, though not as much as his response.

"No."

A truly uncomfortable evening waited ahead of both of them. They had already endured hours in a carriage, a departure from everything they knew, and the company of someone they didn't know how to talk to. They still faced a castle full of foreign witches and strange customs and food they didn't eat. At the end, they'd return sleep deprived after another long carriage ride to the Meeting House.

He feared none of it.

Without realizing it, he had reached for Sarasam. The touch of metal against his fingers was reassurance without words.

"This is far outside your usual routine," she remarked drily, and he heard more courage in her voice. "I thought you hated it when your schedule changed."

"I did, once."

"Not now?"

Her curiosity amused him. He thought back to all they knew of each other. All the bland days they'd spent in each other's presence. The conversations that meant nothing.

It once felt safe. Structured. Routine.

Fake.

"Not now," he murmured. "I . . . think I had held too closely to my schedule in the past. It's insufferable, if you ask me."

"What makes you say this?" she asked with carefully modulated astonishment.

"Not sure. I just . . . I see it all so differently these days."

She fell silent.

"We'll make it out of here alive," he said, wanting to reassure the wide-eyed panic developing as the horses slowed. "Just follow my lead. You don't have to speak if you don't want to."

Her voice trembled.

"Thank you."

The door opened. A witch in a crisp uniform stood there. His black hair shone in torchlight, flickering at his back. He gave a half bow, a blue silk vest around a thick upper body.

"Guide to the Clan. You are most welcome."

A butler, perhaps?

He'd heard of these. A castle worker, meant to keep things running smoothly. Like a Guide to the Caves, only for a castle.

Andrei stepped out, stretched a hand for Anastasia. She accepted, but released it as soon as her feet touched the ground. The silk dress whispered over her boots and legs as the butler motioned them into the castle. The horses trotted away, stable bound.

The butler pointed to two wide doors that glimmered with an array of ice-blue gems.

"This way. His Majesty most eagerly awaits."

Anastasia stepped quickly to keep up with the butler's long strides. Andrei tipped his head as they passed under the doorway and gazed all the way up the front of Zamok Castle.

Like a glacier, it soared out of comprehension.

A dizzying maze of hallways, black-and-white floors, glittering candles, dangling chandeliers, and gaudy opulence led them to a wide open room. The sound of soft drums, barely pressed, trilled in the background.

At least thirty witches milled around a sprawling table set in the middle. A handful of them wore a uniform similar to the butler. Others swept by in more elegant gowns made of silk.

A woman in a bright pink dress with a shawl of golden silk around her shoulders drew Anastasia's attention. The sash covered pale, bare arms.

"Andrei!" called a booming voice. "Welcome."

In three strides, Alek separated himself from the crowd and headed toward them. Andrei held out an arm, accepted Alek's crushing grip, and motioned to Anastasia.

"This is my betrothed, daughter of Sergei. Anastasia, meet Alek, High Priest of the Southern Network."

Her solemn face was impossible to read as she curtsied for Alek. Her knees trembled when she rose again.

"A pleasure to meet you," Alek said with a bright smile. "Thank you for coming. I trust the carriage ride was no problem?"

"No, none."

He tilted his head to the side. "You really don't transport?"

"No, Your Majesty."

A glimmer of curiosity slipped through Alek, then faded. "Interesting." He swept an arm to the fire. "Let's get you warmed up first. The Council is all here, but I won't overwhelm you at once. We await a few more witches. This is quite informal, I assure you. A simple feast so the Council might better know and understand the Guide to the Clan."

"About the—"

"Later." Alek clapped him on the shoulder. "That's not as important as you being warm and comfortable. There's always time for business later."

Two witches stood near the fire already. Alek introduced them as Lena, a slight female witch similar to Anastasia in her calm bearing, and her husband, Nikolov. His hollow, thin cheeks led to a puffy mustache. He studied Andrei as they clasped hands.

"Call me Nikolov. I own and run the Hapduk mine, in the northwest mountains, near Gimsteinar, which I also own. I have been a Council Member for over twenty years now."

The words buzzed right past Andrei.

He knew nothing of mines, Gimsteinar, or mountains in the northwest, but he knew enough to sense that *this* witch was perhaps the most powerful in the room, second only to Alek. There was no accident about the fact that Alek brought him to Nikolov first.

The wisdom in Nikolov's creased eyes, the well-kept strands of hair, and the quiet exchange of a knowing look between Nikolov and the High Priest hinted at deeper intrigues.

Alliances, perhaps.

Andrei braced himself.

The night had truly begun.

Chapter Nineteen

I've never known a maleesa to hesitate.

Then again, I've never known them to do anything but show up in the world they're placed in, do the one thing they're certain of, and repeat that day after day until they die.

Still.

They never hesitate.

—Vlad, Creator
Year 1399

Overwhelm arrived in minutes.

While Nikolov spoke about Network exploits and great battles, Council Members leisurely strolled closer until they formed a half circle around Andrei. Alek stood to Nikolov's left, but slightly behind. With a smile, Lena tugged Anastasia into a circle of women occupying the area near the hearth, in the warmest part of the room.

A calm ambience lingered in the air. Paintings cluttered the walls—nearly every spot overtaken with images, jeweled designs, or marble busts. Former High Priests, Andrei assumed. None of the witches in the artwork had a clannish appearance: no thin eyes, dark black hair, or broad facial structure.

Of course not.

Candles dropped great beads of wax down their chunky stems, contributing to the stuffy feel of the room, which smelled like sweat. Music trilled from beyond, not close enough to distract. Servants and women and the men wore silk—so much silk.

Seeing their garments in the world set a strange sensation in his chest. Did all their work, their life force, come to this?

Nikolov held a glass with a thin layer of amber liquid in it. Gently, he swirled it as he spoke in his low-toned voice about art pieces visible in the room. The ipsum glided around the cup in delicate whirls.

The rest of the Council Members held more space, standing back. Male, all of them. No females amongst the leadership, which didn't surprise Andrei at all. The Network had never recognized women as a social power. Plenty of Guides to the Clan had been female in the past.

Andrei waited for the tightening of his gut. The fear of doing something wrong in a world so new, but it didn't come.

He remembered the swords.

The smithy.

The bitter nights in the wild open riverbed, with a chill so powerfully raw that each breath made his throat ache while he searched for metal. The flex of his powerful arms as they brought the hammer down to metal. The magic had chosen him, and that meant something.

He met Alek's sharp gaze without fear. The too-bright candor in his eyes turned a little sour at the edges.

"So," Nikolov drawled. "You are to be the Guide to the Clan from now on."

"I officially step into the role during our annual celebration."

"The *Praznick*."

Andrei assented with a nod.

"When is that?"

"Soon."

Nikolov nodded, as if that information made sense to him in some other context. A few grunts issued from those in a half circle. Alek kept a bright gaze on Andrei.

"And you're eager for this appointment?" Nikolov asked.

"Yes."

"It's a high honor, we hear, to gain any sort of political power amongst the clan. A hard won event you should be proud of."

A smoothness infused Nikolov's response. It sounded as if it were an unnatural state for him. He delicately raised his glass, murmured, *"Saltov,"* and sipped. Those around him did the same. Andrei's fingers tightened around his own glass, which Alek had placed into his hand a short while ago.

He pretended to drink. The liquid lingered on his lips like metal beads. Within Nikolov's comment lay something. A searching. *It's a high honor, we hear, to gain any sort of political power.*

A question masked by praise.

Someone else spoke. A dusty old man with a voice like grating rocks. "We would like to support your ascension to Guide to the Clan. Is anyone allowed to attend the *Praznick* from the Network?"

"No, I'm afraid not."

"That's disappointing."

"Do you have the power to overturn that rule as the Guide?" Alek asked.

Andrei hesitated. Again, the searching. The questions. His heart raced with the implications. If he didn't answer, he'd stir up greater prejudice against the clan. If he gave away too much, they'd learn more.

Neither would he lie.

"Our clan," he said slowly, "isn't ruled by a single witch. We vote. Allow all members to have a say, to speak as required or desired. I am not a leader so much as a guide. Someone with specific experience chosen to help witches solve their own problems."

"So . . ." Alek drawled, "that's a no."

An expression of annoyance flitted over Nikolov's face, but disappeared as quickly as it came.

"A no," Andrei said.

"Do you enjoy life in the ice?" asked another Council Member.

In the ice rang through his mind with quiet emphasis. Another distinct question, hidden behind a pleasant enough voice. They wanted to know if the clan *lived in the ice*. He realized, with a start, that the magic of Sarasam brought his awareness to the nuance.

"My clan has always appreciated the cold."

"Indeed." Alek motioned to a butler, who carried a large plate of food. "The ice is in our veins. We love the ice!"

The butler veered closer, a silver platter perched on strong fingertips. Small eggs, cut in half, the yolks taken out and stuffed with something fluffy and red and built in a twirling tower. Several witches plucked them free with fingers and popped them into their fat lips.

So they ate with their fingers too.

They asked deeper questions. Andrei fielded them carefully, with vague details and a noncommittal smile. Each minute that passed heightened the tight smiles, the nervous fidgets. Butlers brought more ipsum. The fire crackled. Trilling laughs came from the women, who surrounded Anastasia with their own fixed smiles.

"Do you feel the clan recognizes your value as a leader?" asked a stoop-shouldered man with a neatly trimmed beard.

"Yes."

"You mentioned training?"

"We have mentors." Andrei's throat burned for water, but he didn't dare ask. Would it be rude?

"How old are you, Andrei?" asked another witch who introduced himself as Ivan. His voice had a reverberating tone. Crystal clear curiosity came from him. Andrei sensed no malice in his dark eyes.

"Thirty."

Maxim nodded. "Young, to be a Guide."

"I have been prepared for it since I was twelve. It is my path in the clan."

Another nod, this one more curious than before.

"Your fiancée," said another, motioning with a pointed hand toward the gaggle of women near the fire. "She is the daughter of the current Guide, no?"

"She is the eldest daughter of Sergei."

"Sergei," the witch repeated. "That is right."

Nikolov's gaze tapered as Council Members continued to pepper Andrei with banal, yet loaded, questions. The evasion became a game. All of them played it with fixed smiles, rote words, and inflexible tones. A conversation in which they discussed much and said little. If this is what they desired, he could achieve it easily enough.

Perhaps some discomforts weren't as encompassing as supposed.

In the background, servants carried platters, bowls, goblets to the table. Utensils, glasses, and plates glimmered under the influence of thousands of candles that hung over the top. A plane of glass, kept there by a magical spell, prevented wax from dripping on the food.

For the better part of two hours, the controlling share of the conversation remained in their hands. Instinct told him to take over from here. When the smell of roasted meat lay thick on the air, and more food cluttered a long table on the other side of the room, Andrei caught Nikolov's eye.

"You want to know more about the silk trade," he said, breaking apart several smaller, quieter conversations. He stood almost in the middle of a circle now, like a rabbit nearly ensnared by arctic baers.

The Council paused.

Silence replaced the chatter and bustle of life as all eyes returned to him. He almost regretted asking it, but prevented himself the trouble.

A slow affirmation came from Nikolov as a nod. Alek moved somewhere behind Nikolov, but said nothing. Until that moment, Andrei didn't realize that he'd all but forgotten the High Priest.

"Yes," Nikolov said. "We have questions."

"Why?"

The single word question stirred up snorts, snuffles, shifting bodies. He might not be aware of the Network culture at large, but he knew how to read witches.

Nervousness followed.

"The silk trade," Nikolov said, "is the most elusive part of life in the Southern Network. Most of us are simply curious. We've lived here all our lives, we serve our witches, and we raise our families. The Network openly scrutinized all of them to ensure they pay their taxes and do well for the economy."

"So do we."

"The implication wasn't given otherwise." Nikolov's smile didn't quite reach his eyes.

"Is there a problem with allowing us to continue as we have lived before under new leadership?"

"Problem?" Nikolov echoed with strained control. "No, of course not. Opportunity? Yes. We are interested in doing things better than our former High Priest. With the silk trade contributing so much to our economy through the taxes you pay, we see a place for improvement in relationships."

The word *we* lingered in the air.

Alek remained silent.

"The clan is interested in peace with our neighbors. We work hard not to intrude on the lives of others."

The words came to Andrei with rote, informed precision. They sounded bland, though true. Attempts to drive more force had little effect. Did he bear the same glazed expression as all of them?

The attempt at caring?

While he truly wanted to protect the clan, the sensation that he didn't belong here hadn't left him.

By sheer willpower, he stopped himself from touching Sarasam. It had become an unconscious tick that revealed far too much.

"It's impressive that the clan works so hard not to disturb witches, but it creates a sense of isolation."

Nikolov spoke with a slightly imploring tone. It had explorative notes in it, as if softening the previously harsh conversation.

"Isolation is perception," Andrei countered.

Nikolov lifted an eyebrow, then seemed to concede with a slight shrug. "Perhaps. Perhaps not. Please, don't assign us ill will preemptively. We are not here to intrude on your life, Andrei. We are simply here to enhance and strengthen relationships through openness.

"We have business owners in this room and in the Network—gem miners, ice blockers, trappers—that strive to keep their work and taxes transparent. Many of those business owners simply want the same from the silk trade, which is a powerful presence in our economy. Do you feel that is too much to ask?"

His tongue felt thick in this throat. No. On paper, it wouldn't be. But the inner Sacha voice rose in his mind like a shrieking rabbit.

"Transparency," he finally managed, "needs definition. I have brought nothing to reveal to you tonight. If that's disappointing, I understand. I am here, however, to discuss better relationships and building trust."

A flicker of something—amusement, resignation, perhaps—appeared in Nikolov's eyes. It disappeared as he released a tilted smile. Whispers shuffled through the rest of the Council at Andrei's pronouncement. Disappointment?

The *ting* of a little bell ringing in the distance drew their attention.

"Spoken," Nikolov murmured, "like a clannish leader. Come, the food has finally arrived. Let's set aside business for now and enjoy the fare."

Alek barked a few commands to nearby servants. Council Members filtered to chairs at the table. As if silently commanded, the women dispersed with laughs, quiet smiles. One of them looped an arm around Anastasia's waist—she'd never appeared more uncomfortable in her life—and escorted her back to Andrei's side.

Anastasia stood next to him, stiff as an ice pillar, while the woman retreated to Nikolov.

Andrei shuffled toward a spot indicated by Nikolov. Anastasia trailed at his side. Two cards displaying their names sat in the middle of the table, closest to the hearth and away from the windows, which radiated from the cold.

"How are you?" Andrei asked quietly.

"Fine."

"Can you endure the lastmeal?"

"Don't insult me."

Her snappish tone startled him. Hadn't she been the frightened mouse in the carriage on the way here?

He sealed his lips. Other women reached for their husband's arms, trailing at their side to specific spots on the long table. Anastasia made no such move, for which he was grateful. They settled at the table where rising voices created a low cacophony, loosened from the ipsum.

By the time the feast dwindled down, slurred voices and bloodshot eyes littered the room. Most Council Members kept their wits, but the rest disintegrated into sodden piles of ipsum. Amongst them, Alek leaned back in his giant chair—larger than all the rest—and snored. Sapphires glimmered in a dark halo around him.

Andrei couldn't swallow down the foul taste in his throat.

Sergei sent him to Zamok Castle to have a taste of Network life and experience making tough decisions for the clan while under duress. Not to mention see how political requests culminated.

Now?

He wanted nothing to do with it.

As Andrei and Anastasia stood from the table, a voice came from just behind his left shoulder. "Allow me to escort you to your carriage, Andrei?"

Nikolov stood back there, alert, with a high brow and inquisitive gaze. No signs of ipsum lingered in his face.

"Thank you."

Anastasia, who hadn't uttered a word since they sat down, slowly stood. Her gaze roved over the table, the wives cluttered in corners, speaking to themselves, and she turned to follow. Servants appeared with their coats.

Nikolov began to walk. Andrei, Anastasia, and the servants followed.

"Thank you for your generosity in having us tonight," Andrei said, willingly dropping into the words that he'd practiced for the last couple of days. Words so highly regarded in the clan. "We're grateful recipients of your abundance."

"You are most welcome. We appreciate you coming." He lifted an eyebrow, his mustache rising with it. "We understand that your appearance here is a sort of allowance and cooperation. I have asked Sergei to attend several such meetings."

"You have?"

"He attended years ago and never returned."

Andrei set that information aside for later.

"Alek is a young High Priest," Nikolov said as they turned a corner. His voice had the careful intonations of someone aware that servants and women listened in, as if he were afraid to impart too much information.

"He is how old?"

"Twenty-five."

Andrei almost swallowed his own tongue. He'd known that Alex was young, but not *that* young.

"I've taken him under my wing," Nikolov continued. He spoke with a slightly weary tone, and he walked slower. An almost-imperceptible limp appeared in his left leg as they turned yet another corner through the maze of the castle. Bright blue pennants hung overhead with an embroidered, snarling, white arctic baer.

"The clan believes that the wiser witches teach the younger."

Nikolov laughed. "Yes, that's what we have."

Darker undertones made it immediately apparent what

Nikolov was trying to say. Alek might be the High Priest in name, but not in true power. A puppet, at best.

The wide, double doors at the front of Zamok Castle appeared ahead, at the end of the hallway. Nikolov stopped, then looked to the servants and tilted his head. On the silent command, they continued filtering past to wait at the door. Anastasia paused. When Nikolov said nothing, Andrei turned to her.

"Please, I will meet you in the carriage."

Jaw clenched, she sent Nikolov an icy look, curtsied, and walked away. Nikolov eyed her as she faded. Once out of earshot, he turned back to Andrei.

"You will hear again from Alek. If you don't mind, please tolerate his interference. Teach him how to lead. He needs the feedback and help. But understand that he does not lead this Network."

An icy chill crept down Andrei's spine.

"*I* run this Network," Nikolov continued. "Alek came to you not to satisfy the Council, but to satisfy me. I've dedicated nearly all of my life to serving the South, and I'll spend the rest of it ensuring its stability. Alek is an ornament. He sits on the chair while I run the rest. The South is on the way to the best position we've ever been in. We exceed the Central Network in economic strength, and the Eastern Network has stopped harassing us since I put Alek on the throne and Guards on the borders. We will continue our prosperity, and I will do everything to ensure that happens."

Nikolov leaned closer, his breath a foul space between them. It smelled of sweet grapes and something fetid.

"Remain in isolation if you like. Harbor your secrets if you must. But know, Andrei, that I will protect the Southern Network. There will not be an economic power beyond our reach. You are not above the rest of us, no matter what magic your witches harbor.

"At one point, the clan will answer for the privileges and their debts. That point comes soon. Consider whether you want to create silk or bloodshed while you guide your witches, for those are the only choices you will have."

The filthy threat hummed between them. Andrei said nothing. His body felt like a glass vase, ready to shatter. He didn't move. Didn't breathe. To nudge himself in either direction would be a toppling disaster.

Nikolov straightened up. "I believe we understand one another. Travel safe, *Guide*."

With that, he turned away. The torches on the nearby wall were crackling, emitting a greasy smell, as Andrei recovered his breath. He turned, headed for the doors, and gratefully left Zamok Castle behind.

Chapter Twenty

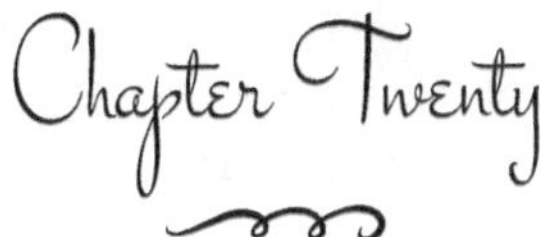

Weary, o weary, is the maleesa who spins too much.

Whose threads become life.

*Life is threads, little maleesa. You are not the weaver,
the finisher, of your work. Others will come to sew the
strands of your fate. It is not for you to decide.*

Toil wisely, little creature.

There is magic in you.

—Ludmila, Cook
Year 1405

Anastasia stared straight ahead.

He expected her to close her eyes, rest. Lines of exhaustion
tugged her face down. Now that they'd left, she seemed to
dismantle. Every minute that swept them closer to the clan
relaxed her shoulders a little more. Her hands lay limp on her

lap, her coat pulled tight. Warm rocks lay at their feet and over-head, exuding the heat that filled the carriage.

The rocking of the carriage sent Andrei swaying to and fro. The motion might have been soothing, if he'd not been so rankled. Lights and opulence continued to dazzle him, though he kept his eyes closed. Like fireworks in the night, the glamor of Zamok Castle flashed too brightly.

He longed for a quiet cave, the sighs of life.

Andrei opened his eyes—it didn't help when he closed them—and thought of the smithy.

The time crept ever closer toward middlenight. It would be well past that before they returned to the Meeting House and the Sirilas magic swept them to their dwellings. With any luck, Anastasia wouldn't speak and he could think through what had just happened.

"Baers, all of them," she muttered. "Bloodthirsty, power-hungry baers."

Ah, so much for silence.

The pronouncement came out of her with a firm judgment he'd never heard before. She continued without looking at him, ferocity in her voice.

"They treat women like servants."

"I saw that."

She sent him a scathing look.

"What? Why are you looking at me like that?" he asked.

At his shocked question, Anastasia recoiled. Had that been the first time he'd ever questioned her? Stood up to something while in her presence? Normally, he ignored such displays. Let go of his frustration or questions or annoyance because it kept the peace.

Asking felt infinitely better.

"You acted no differently," she muttered.

"When did I order you around? I tried to keep track of you all night, but you turned your back to me."

"You didn't order me around."

"Did I fail you somehow?"

She paused. Her shoulders slumped. "No."

"Did I disrespect your position as my betrothed?"

Her chin lowered. "No."

"Then why are you angry? Anastasia, help me understand. Please?"

"I don't want to be here."

The words burst out of her all at once, pressured by what sounded like a sob. Her hands come to her face. She cried into them.

"I hate everything about Zamok Castle and I never want to come back. I never want to take another carriage ride and I don't want to be the wife of the Guide to the Clan. This was too much. I hated it."

Something inside him curled up. *I don't want to be the wife of the Guide of the Clan.* A prickling sensation, almost like pain, followed. While they held little romantic regard for each other, Andrei still couldn't fathom his life without Anastasia. She'd been a quiet presence, an expectation constantly there. Rote. Routine.

But there.

"I don't want to be handfasted," she continued, tears on her cheeks. Her eyes squeezed shut, her fists pressed into her forehead. "*Papan* will not let me refuse you."

"It is your right," he whispered.

"I cannot!" she wailed. "*For the good of the clan, Anastasia. We need stability. Andrei needs help.* It isn't fair."

In her words, Andrei heard Sergei.

"He cannot deny you your right by clan standards," Andrei said. His voice was so quiet he could barely hear it over the clattering wheels.

She scoffed with the same annoyance she'd expressed toward the Southern Network witches.

"And what kind of witch would I be if I were to refuse a stable, kind man who would do me no harm, provide for the clan in the highest possible way, and ensure the safety of my future?"

At that, Andrei hesitated. Indeed, the clan would view it that way. They would see it through the angle of privilege. They might pride themselves on giving the woman the power to walk away, but their judgmental tongues would still wag.

"You want something else?"

"Passion."

The word wrenched out of quivering lips.

"I want love, Andrei. Romance. To feel adoration for the man that I handfast. I want to feel as if our souls are knit, not as if my soul is safe."

Such a wild notion wasn't unheard of. Anastasia had grown up with a more romantic side. Particularly in her early teenage years, when the time they spent together was the most awkward and stilted. In her older years she had lost some of that desperate quality, and the two of them had settled into something like the bland interactions they shared now.

Other thoughts occurred to him. The heart-shaped gem in her hand before they arrived at Zamok. The day she pushed off the handfasting yet again, and her joyous relief when he'd agreed. Her constant irritation with him otherwise.

Ira, but how long had she hated the sight of him?

"Who is it?" he asked quietly, so low she might not have heard.

The answering sobs told him all he needed to know. For nearly a full minute, she cried.

Finally, she said, "He's a villager."

Andrei held a breath. He waited for some kind of pain. Or the jolt of frustration and annoyance that usually came with an unexpected change in his plans. Their betrothal had lasted over a decade. Surely, some issuance of irritation might follow.

None arose.

Instead, he felt relief. He thought of the smithy. Of Sarasam. The clutches and beginnings of a life of swordmaking. These days, his mental gaze drove forward toward the smithy more than it ever looked at the clan past. Without Anastasia, that life would be fathoms easier to grasp. A witch for whom the magic had not allowed him to explain.

He lifted his hand, set it on her back. The shuddering sobs slowed.

"Tell me about him."

She straightened, stared at him in watery disbelief. "You .. . you're not angry?"

"No."

His hand fell away. Slowly, she turned so that her knees faced the middle of the carriage. He could see her expression better, though not well. A creaking sound, then a jolt, jostled them from side to side.

"He's in the fishing village." She swallowed, wiped the tears from her cheeks. They replaced, but she didn't seem to notice. "I met him two years ago while helping to bring fish from the streams for food."

"Why were you at the streams?"

She shrugged. "*Papan* asked for some help, and we were awaiting fresh silk at the cave."

Such a responsibility, shared to someone who rarely had it, wasn't unheard of. Some Guides had witches routinely swap trades—as long as they weren't in direct care of the *maleesa*— to remember and comprehend the views of the other witches.

"We became friends. He was gone all of last winter. I didn't know where. I was worried about him. I . . . couldn't find him."

Vague reminisces from last winter replayed through his mind. She had been distracted, even sullen. A little more depressed than usual. Rarely could he pull much more than a pathetic smile from her, but it had been even more difficult then.

Her voice lifted. "Then he came back."

"Where had he gone?"

"On his *mizziya*."

The word rattled through Andrei's brain. Many non-clannish Southern Network witches believed in proving themselves before breaking away on their own. Men and women ventured into the great white wild to survive, to build their home, to establish a life, a reputation. They would take their talents and live away from their parents and village, forging a path elsewhere, before the village would welcome them back. Most lasted a month or two.

"A whole winter?" Andrei clarified.

"On his own," she echoed, her voice stilted with prolonged astonishment. "When I found out, I could barely believe it. Then I saw him again and . . . *haniye.*"

Haniye.

The word exhaled like a precious thing. The slope of the sounds curled around itself and back again.

Haniye.

The word replayed through his mind again and again, the meaning striking deeper each time.

Stirred my soul.

"That is when you knew?" he asked.

Her hand reached up to her breastbone, curled there as if she could capture her heart, lock it inside. Anastasia let out a long breath.

"That is when I knew that there was more to this life than the clan. Than routine. Than structure and . . ." She paused, cast him a sidelong glance, and finished on a barren, ". . . safety."

"What does he feel for you?"

"The same. He'd do anything for me."

"And both of you want to be together?"

"There is only the clan that prevents us."

"The clan?"

Anastasia sighed. "Forgive me, Andrei, for you've never given me reason for such treachery, but I would have left you the moment I saw him again if all the clan didn't hold such great judgment or condemnation. I am afraid you've endured the weight of my rage, my frustration, and . . . that hasn't been fair."

She ended as softly as she began, and another cry peeped out of her. Her head hung in her hands, her shoulders bowed as they trembled.

Andrei looked away to give her a moment to grapple with her deep emotions. How long she must have hidden her tears for them to come so strongly now! He couldn't help a stab of jealousy, though he couldn't pinpoint why. It had nothing to do with this other man.

Everything to do with options.

His thoughts ran ahead of him, already rattled from such a long night with the Council Members. Of all nights to discover the truth, this was the best one. The night she could be certain whether she would or would not want to be the wife of the Guide to the Clans would be *this* night. Arguably, there would be similar nights.

More of this life would come to the Guide to the Clans. Expectations. Some travel. Discomfort.

Ira, but did discomfort follow *everything*?

Her misery, her frustration, her irritation. All of it made sense. The desire to not be near or with him more than she must, her avoidance of his touch. No, there was no surprise that she didn't want him.

He let out a long breath.

"I would never ask you to join in a handfasting that would tie you to something you don't want, Anastasia."

"I know."

"Nor would I maintain a facade and prevent you from happiness. Or . . . passion."

Her gaze lifted.

"You have been speaking to another woman in the forest, haven't you?"

His breath caught. He hesitated, then nodded. "She is a friend, only. Betrothed to another man. She's helping me with . . . a few things."

"Mila."

"You know her?"

"Many do."

The frown that pulled her lips down surprised him, but he didn't want to ask what it meant. Didn't want to know what she thought.

"You haven't been the same lately," she murmured. "What is it you're doing out there? Where have you been? You went from a rigid, unbroken schedule to never being around. At least you still wear your favorite black silk shirts all the time."

Andrei chuckled. Yes, at least that had remained stable. The skin between her eyebrows, normally so smooth, had wrinkled.

"Everything about you was predictable and . . . boring, if I may say it. Now . . ."

She trailed away.

He leaned back, laughed. Taken from her perspective, she was blatantly correct. The amusement ran deep. Would she believe it if he told her?

"Yes," he murmured. "That's true. It has been vague and strange. I apologize. Something else . . . found me."

"Are you happy with this *something else*?"

He paused, searched in his soul. Found the pieces that he hadn't known were missing until Sarasam, the smithy, and the magic spiraled through his future and plans.

"I am," he said lightly. "I am happy."

"You weren't before."

"I was content."

"There's a lot of space between those."

"So I'm learning."

A pause, then a desperate whisper that felt stark in the cooling night. The tears had dried on her face. She scrubbed their paths away, sniffling.

"What do we do, Andrei?"

"I'm not sure."

She stiffened. He held up a hand.

"We will figure this out."

"But—"

"There is a way to prevent the judgment of the clan from your decision. If you can wait a year to handfast your villager, that would be sufficient time for us to call off our engagement, recover quietly, and for you to find and fall in love with him without question. Clan members will talk about him being a villager, but other clan members have married outside the clan. It won't be the biggest scandal."

Her mouth opened, then closed.

"Why would you do this?"

He chuckled, imagining the Andrei of only a few months ago. How stiff he might have been. Horrified by the shifting circumstances. Terrified, perhaps, by the prospect of change and unexpected deviation and . . .

His right hand reached to his side, felt Sarasam.

"Because," he finally whispered, "no one should have to live a life they don't want to, when perhaps we're made for something else. You would only end up hating me in the end, and I don't desire that for either of us."

She reached over, put a hand on his arm. He looked at her tiny fingers, wrapped around his forearm, so petite and warm and surprisingly heavy. It was the first time he recalled her touching him.

"Thank you, Andrei."

He lifted his eyes, nodded.

"Be happy, Anastasia."

Tears filled her eyes.

"I will."

* * *

Mila didn't appear at the smithy the next day.

Nor the next.

Nikolov's threat circled his dreams like an arctic baer ready to attack. Clearly, the Southern Network had their mind set on the silk trade. They would bring more demands. Bigger ones.

Andrei had no qualms over denying them. The Sirilas magic would protect the clan. It always had.

Or, so he hoped.

His fear questioned what they would do next. Nikolov's hunger for power wouldn't be satisfied until the silk trade thrived under his control.

Instinct drove Andrei to stroll through the forest, dig into the snow at a specific juncture of trees, and uncover several strangely porous stones. He'd seen them before in the forest as a boy. Some of them, only the size of his thumb, called to him.

He packed his pockets full, brought them home, dropped them on the table, and proceeded to polish the blade. The repetitive, back-and-forth motions opened his thoughts to breathe. He cycled through the night at Zamok Castle, the implications, until he understood it from every angle.

Urged on by the power of the restless sword, he obeyed each nudge. When he set the sap-covered amber ball against the bottom of the tang, magic issued in the air. A wash of light consumed the new pommel. Sap liquefied, melted, and wrapped in a thin line all the way around the amber. Etched designs appeared in the sap, carved through the amber until it had a new shape, then faded. A tightening of the design seemed to indicate it hardened, though kept its luminous hue.

He placed the sword hilt on top of a flat rock in the hearth, which crackled with cheery flames. The amber adhered on top at a gentle angle while he waited.

He hoped for Mila to return while smoke curled off the sap. Blue light emitted from the pommel every few seconds, like bursts of magic. Waves of happiness emanated from the sword, as if it could shed joy. When a final pop, and settling, occurred, Andrei grabbed the blade and brought it out of the fire.

Middlenight surrounded the smithy in quiet shades of darkness as he ran his hands over the metal, letting his fingertips trail the delicate swirls, then back. Never had he felt as happy as this.

The sword cooed in his mind. A gentle sound that thrilled to his touch. He should go back to his dwelling and sleep, but couldn't bring himself to do it. Anticipation lay in the air.

A sense of something about to happen.

The fire sneezed a burst of citrus glitter into the hearth as he straightened up, set the sword on the table. Magic had fused the amber to the bottom of the tang. A string of leather and the blade would be finished, perhaps.

Though . . .

The sword rocked back and forth, clattering on the wood. He frowned, reaching for it. An explosion of light shot through the room. With a cry, he threw one arm in the air and wheeled back.

The light continued as he spun around to find the sword on fire with bright green flames. The jade hues faded to pink, then cerise, blue, and a buttery orange. Light seared the sword, racing fast in sweeping lines down the blade.

Andrei staggered to the table as the magical fire faded, then extinguished.

A new name entered his mind.

Mangana.

"Mangana."

Ashes of its former self riddled the table. The sword gleamed with a pristine polish. Finely sharpened edges maintained their integrity all the way to where the guard and tang fused together with greater density. No heat remained in the blade.

When he withdrew it from the table, Mangana sang. Compared to earlier, the voice was brighter, easier to find, less peevish. No more irritation. Nothing but joyous rapture. Elation, tinted with eagerness.

Then . . . hunger.

Power reverberated from Mangana all the way up Andrei's arm. It radiated through him to shake his chest, restarting a shocked heart. A firm, feminine whisper came from without. Not from the sword. It wasn't the sword that spoke to him—they didn't use words. Only thoughts. Basic emotions, like sliding into the mind of a toddler that couldn't articulate.

A voice from . . . somewhere.

You are the Ensis.

"Ensis."

You are the Ensis.

Andrei contemplated that, feeling a rush of heat to his toes.

"What do I do with you now?" Andrei asked, flipping it over. Mangana replied instantly. If the sword had been insistent before, it was utterly demanding now.

Mila.

"Mila? But—"

Before he could say another word, the magic whisked Andrei away.

* * *

A house built of snow stood in his path.

A foot trail carved into the ice swept away from the icehouse, closer to the river. It curved into the trees at one juncture, then to the east at another. Smudges of smoke rising from the forest meant that he'd come to a village.

Shuffling sounded from inside.

The icy, aquamarine facade resembled a thick lacquer. Not unlike the glacier where the clan lived and worked. Rivulets hardened into it that had once raced down the side, now frozen to the surface. His fingers ran down their trails. He thought of silk.

"Mila?"

The sound of his own voice, slightly choked, startled him. The shuffling sounds stopped. A hesitant pause filled the air, one he couldn't hope to read. Last he'd seen Mila, she'd mentioned the *maleesa*, then disappeared.

Andrei swallowed, stifled by the quiet of the surrounding air.

"Mila, I . . . finished the sword, and it chose you. It insists that it's yours and brought me to you."

And how will I get back to the smithy? he thought, then dismissed it.

Mangana surged with excitement. A wordless chatter streamed through Andrei's mind. The emotions slipped by too quickly to understand.

No sound from within.

He gazed around. Cold nipped at the tip of his ears, his nose. Mangana had been so excited that the sword didn't give Andrei time to grab his coat. With a shiver, Andrei set

Mangana in the snow, right outside the door, in the same tip-down position where he'd found Sarasam.

When no attempt to speak with him issued, he stepped back. The magic would have brought him to the right place—he didn't doubt that this was where Mila lived. He missed his friend, however.

"It's yours," he said firmly.

To Mangana, he bid a silent farewell.

Gratitude surged from the sword, but distractedly. It had only space and heart for Mila now.

Andrei stepped back in the snow. One moment, he stared at the sparkling river. The next at the smithy.

With a relieved sigh, he ducked back inside.

Chapter Twenty-One

The "halfway point" is the moment at which all Caretakers hold their breath.

The larva has become a pupa and rests within the thinly veiled husk that separates them from their living space.

The hideous, gangly creature from before, at once hairy and bulbous, has disappeared within and must eventually emerge.

Most larva give up. They die. They fall asleep. This batch, I count 1,000 dead amongst the 100 living. I know this, for they turn gray, brittle, and fall apart at my touch. The ones that fight survive.

It's difficult to become something new.

—Ivan, Overseer
Year 1302

The soft shuffles of *Maman's* feet reminded Andrei of a steady spring wind. Her inaudible murmur when she spoke to the *maleesa* was as comforting as a steady hand on the shoulder. Andrei stood in the doorway to her cave, eyes closed, and listened.

"You are not as quiet as you think, Andrei."

Her back faced him, covered by a long silk dress that swept her legs, where her boots rose to the knee. An affectionate cadence lived in her comment.

Chuckling to himself, Andrei stepped farther into the cave. "No, *Maman*. I wasn't trying to sneak up on you."

She sent a twinkling smile over her shoulder. She stood near the edge of a rock wall of ice, just shorter than her waist. On the other side of the protective wall, crystal clear like a pane of glass, lay holes and cubbies that populated into the thousands.

Within each hole and cubby lay dried grasses, pulled from the tundra in the height of summer and carefully treated with magic, then twisted and twined into the flat shape that the *maleesa* preferred to hibernate on.

"How far into their transformation are they now?" he asked, standing at her side.

"Just began, really. Some of them are finishing their pupal screen."

"Hmm."

"The *Praznick maleesa* is doing well. It hibernated right after you last visited."

Andrei didn't count the days. Already a week had passed since Nikolov threatened him at the Network lastmeal. Life raced by.

Maman eyed him. "Why are you so tired?"

"I am always tired, *Maman*."

"That isn't good!"

"I know."

"So sleep more."

He laughed, a delirious sound. Another sword was already in progress. He'd just smelted the metals he harvested from the river to form the final ingot. The momentum of the magic forbade him to stop.

A familiar tightening in his throat followed. No, he still couldn't tell *Maman* about the Ensis magic. Not yet, anyway. Redirection would be his best strategy.

"Why does it take so long for the *maleesa* to transform, do you think?" He leaned closer to their cubbies. He'd also worked as a Caretaker for several years, when he was eighteen. The quiet days, calm hours, clashed against the sizzling fire, smoke, and metal *ting* of his life in the smithy.

Both had their own catharsis.

"They take what they take, Andrei." A light note of exasperation riddled *Maman's* voice. "Pft. It's only a few weeks. No one hurried you along, and you're *still* a transforming creature."

He managed a smile.

At her feet lay a basket filled with broken and bent twigs. She held one in her hand. With the Sirilas magic, the twig elongated. Green buds formed junctures in the middle and sprouted outward. A dozen tiny leaves appeared as the twig faded away.

Eventually, the leaves collected in her awaiting hand, and the stick disappeared entirely.

"So few?" he asked.

Each twig normally produced a handful of fat leaves, enough to set ten *maleesa* up for meals for the next day. Only five or six thin, brittle leaves filled her palm.

"Told you," she muttered.

He frowned.

"So, you survived your time with the High Priest last week."

"I did."

"I'm relieved."

"Me too. I'm sorry I haven't come to see you since then."

Maman opened her palm. Leaves swept out, as if borne on a wind, and scattered. Several of them settled right onto the green *maleesa* beds. Others angled deeper into the burrows.

She waved his apology off.

"You're almost the Guide to the Clan. You're busy. I'm here, where I always am. Tell me, *fil,* is there something bothering you?"

Andrei swallowed hard. His thoughts swirled around the Ensis magic. Anastasia, Mila, the next sword. He held so much in his mind it left no room for the rest. All his life, Sergei and the clan had told him what to think about and how to think about it. Now it all was suspended on the edge of a sword, ready to break.

"Just . . . thinking."

It was a half-truth, one that *Maman* must have expected, because she grunted and turned back to the *maleesa.*

"Thinking about what?"

"Gossip around the clan says that some members are upset that I didn't show the *maleesa* to the High Priest."

She scoffed. "The foolish ones, maybe. You were correct in not doing so, Andrei."

"I know, but that doesn't make this easy."

"No, the best things never are. Clan members will always gossip. You do something right? It annoys them. If you do something wrong? It annoys them. You already know this."

"I do." He nodded. "But I still don't like it."

She turned to face him. "Most clan members are grateful you kept our secrets. Our culture and way of life rests on them, and the magic is already out of balance. Now, tell me what else is on your mind. I can see the thoughts swirling in there, Andrei."

"Anastasia."

Maman went oddly still.

"I'm breaking off our betrothal. She's meant for another that is not me." He leaned his elbows onto the glassy ice pane that separated them from touching the *maleesa* directly. "We would have been miserable."

Maman relaxed her tense shoulders.

"I'm not surprised."

After a week without seeing her or dodging the awkward burden that dissolving their agreement created, Andrei wasn't either. No gaping hole remained in his life, only the mild irritation of who he used to be.

Had he been so insufferable?

Yes.

"In hindsight, I'm not surprised either. Later today, there will be news that our betrothal has broken off. I wanted you to know the truth before I went to her *maman* and made it official."

"Ah. You'll save her pride in the clan?"

"Within the hour."

His nose wrinkled. By tradition of the clan, all engagement and handfasting business went through the mother of the female. If bartering must happen, the mother worked directly with the potential partner, for who would care more for her than her *maman?*

Sergei would already be at work. Anastasia as well. It wouldn't be long before the news ripped through the clan. *Maman* deserved better than whatever gossip would reach her first.

Besides, he might need her help to allay other, more nefarious, rumors.

Andrei cleared his throat, continued.

"With the *Praznick* coming up, I desire my days to be open and not encumbered by the care of anyone else."

Except the swords, he added silently.

"Other Guides have refused to handfast, Andrei. You are not obligated to take a partner, and not even one that is female, if you wish."

"I know."

Her hand lifted, settled on the middle of his back, near the spine. The steady weight was reassurance without words.

"You are a good witch, my *fil.*"

A dozen replies surfaced. Would *Maman* say the same thing if she knew of his depth of loyalty to the Ensis magic? Would she understand if he also forged his own path, split away from expectation?

"You're not disappointed?"

She laughed a little. "Anastasia is a good witch, but the two of you were never close the way we hoped. I'm . . . relieved that you've taken the obligation from your shoulders. If you are sad, I am sad with you."

"Not *that* sad."

The tips of her fingers scratched a design into his skin. Soft as a baby bird wing, and rhythmic, like she did when he was a little boy. He wanted to curl around the sensation, but her hand dropped away.

After a serene silence, *Maman* gestured to the *maleesa* with a tilt of her head.

"This is the most critical point of their life."

"Mmm."

"Aside from the very end, right before they can spin, this is the phase in which most *maleesa* are likely to die. Transformation is powerful, though exhausting. Many of them won't make it. There are two thousand in this batch. I expect only three hundred to emerge. I will sweep up the rest of the bodies and send them back to Hulu."

Sadness lingered in her voice. Andrei couldn't help but marvel at the Caretakers ability to love the *maleesa* through this disgusting stage, when they were little more than bundles of antennae and hair, and needy, at that.

"They're split in half right now. Half one, half the other. There is no going back or forward, only waiting. They aren't sure the pain of change is worth it. Soon, they'll have to decide. It's a miracle, isn't it?"

Andrei turned to meet her gaze. Wisdom and love and compassion lay in the folds.

"Do you think that any *maleesa* really thinks this much about it, *Maman*? Do you believe they aren't just another bug enduring what they must?"

Maman only smiled.

Flakes of metal glimmered in the bottom of a long wooden trough, shimmering against the candlelight, later that night. Rocks and shards cluttered the bottom, warming quickly in the bath after he dumped them out of the frozen bags.

While all lay in uproar at the clan—those sharp-as-knives gossiping tongues over whether Andrei should have taken a *maleesa* to the Network—the smithy lay in silence.

He stood at the edge of the worktable, hands braced on the wood. He had no idea how to get to the next step of his new blade. As before, he knew only what was in front of him, not the finished design. This new blade was more complicated as well. The tip was wider than the base and it had no guard, just a very long tang. Would that be easier? More difficult?

More metal upfront, surely.

Which led him to his current conundrum.

Last time he'd harvested metal from the river, Mila had done the separation of shards from rocks. He didn't know how to extract this metal. And the more he worried over the strange shape, the less work he completed. The magic became restless with any wait, so he set aside the questions.

Sarasam whispered at his side. Idle pieces of emotion that drifted through his mind here and there, like a gentle chatter of someone humming in the background. Feeling her presence in his mind made this dark house, creaking in the wind, not so big.

A voice interrupted his reverie.

"I'm sorry."

His head jerked up.

Mila stood across the way, just inside the door. A single coat wrapped around her, dropping from her shoulders to the floor. She wore a long pair of boots made of softer, newer fur. They covered her feet in a sleeve without laces, like a house slipper. Her hair trailed around her face in soft strands.

In her hands, she held Mangana.

Her knuckles were white, blanched against the dark night. Yet she held it with an effortless ease that testified to a lifetime of experience.

Andrei inspected the sword with a little pride. Could he claim all that much ownership over it? Not really. He'd beaten it into shape, but the magic had transformed it into the sparkling wonder.

A bundle of nerves sat in his throat now that he saw her. Almost ten days had passed since she left unexpectedly. He'd been worried about her.

Worried about *them*.

Not knowing what to say, he asked, "You're well?"

"Yes."

"The sword?"

She smiled and her eyes nearly disappeared. "My better half, I suppose you could say. It shocked me when I heard you that night."

He chuckled.

The sentiment sounded just right.

Her mirth dropped. "I shouldn't have avoided you, Andrei. That was a cowardly thing to do. If I can help it, I'm never a coward. I just . . . I wasn't ready to talk about my past."

The last of their previous conversation twirled through his mind. *You can't trust him, Andrei. Not if he's advocating for someone outside of the Sirilas to see the maleesa. Maman says the rules are strong, like iron.*

How do you know?

His astonishment over her knowledge of clannish rules had long since faded. How could a non-clan member know such details? Clearly, the world didn't operate the way he once thought it did, and he became more used to that notion every day.

The villages along the river weren't exactly clannish, but they were friends with the clan. The members of each interacted openly and in harmony. Anastasia was proof of that. Arguably, the river villagers knew more about the clan than anyone, and even that wasn't much. They still shouldn't know as much as Mila had expressed.

"We don't have to talk about it, Mila. I'm just happy to see you again. I missed you."

Her eyes widened. "Really?"

He shrugged. "If you don't want to explain how you know so much about the clan, I won't force you. I understand. Some of us . . . hold secrets."

The breath that escaped him sounded more like a sigh. Every day, the burden of the Ensis magic, of his life in the smithy set against life in the clan, weighed more heavily on his shoulders.

He had no judgment on Mila.

"Mangana chose you," he said. "It let me know it belonged to you, then the magic brought me to your hut. It's . . . it's all I know."

A rueful twitch of her smile lifted both edges of her lips. "There isn't much you *do* know, Andrei."

At that, he laughed.

She brightened, then sobered. "You're my friend."

"You're my friend, Mila."

"I tell my friends things. You can ask questions. I trust you."

He tilted an eyebrow.

She nodded, earnest.

"What village are you from?" he asked.

"A smaller village, down the river." Her head jerked to the south. "But I have family across all the tundras, so I'm welcome to any village on this arm of the river. Some of them, in different areas, would not be so welcoming."

Not a surprise. The villages which populated the riverbanks here were notoriously interrelated.

Andrei felt a pang of jealousy. Mila was born into a world that encouraged movement, exploration. Like most witches in this part of the world, she probably had an expansive family, with lots of cousins and aunties and uncles.

He saw the same glacier, the same snow.

The thought felt like a loose marble in his head. Before now, he appreciated the steadiness of his life. The known expectations, the path ahead.

"Do you have any brothers and sisters?"

"Ten."

"So many?"

"Not all of them are at home." She shrugged. "I know a few of them, as I'm one of the youngest. My parents are quite old."

"Still alive?"

"Yes."

"Impressive."

"*Papan* was clannish."

He paused. "Really?"

She didn't quite meet his gaze. "They exiled him for choosing *Maman*. The Guide to the Clan was a rather strict witch."

"Not Sergei."

She shook her head. "The one before him."

Sergei's predecessor, a woman named Ingva, had been just as strict as Sergei. More so, perhaps.

"I'm sorry. Sergei does not exile for marrying outside the clan now."

"My parents almost died many times," she said. "*Papan* struggled to live outside the clan for most of my early years. It has . . . left a sour taste in my mouth regarding the clan, of which he tells me many stories."

"I understand."

"But you and Sacha have proven my beliefs wrong. Good witches live in the clan. I'm sorry I judged you."

"No apology necessary, Mila."

Her tone became carefully musing, as if she wanted to step out, but not too far. "What about you?"

"I have three sisters, but all of them died before I met them. *Papan* died years ago, when I was young. His heart stopped at work one day. He was a Guard for the clan."

She frowned. "I'm sorry."

"Me too."

"How old were your sisters when they died?"

"Small children. Babies."

Not a surprising end for children in this part of the world. Sad, but true. Not even the protection of the clan and the caves could guarantee life in the coldest climate. Mila's gaze drooped.

"I'm sorry, Andrei."

"*Maman* calls me her *chudo*."

She smiled in her quiet way. "A miracle, indeed. I want to

have children. Tikhon does as well. We want lots of them, like my *maman*. Quiet homes are empty homes."

"When will I meet the elusive Tikhon?"

She laughed. "He has asked me the same question! I will bring him to meet you one day, when he's not so busy finding a place for us to live. He thinks you're not real."

"He's not jealous that you spend time with another man?"

She recoiled. "No! Our trust is absolute."

Handfasting, the tradition of many parts of Alkarra to bind oneself to another witch through words, held less importance with the river villages than the clan. In the villages, witches simply chose each other. The act of moving into another house or building one together signified a commitment. Rarely was such a bond broken.

Life required life.

In the wilds of a frozen tundra like this, romantic love, like what Anastasia had fallen into, existed as a mere fairytale. Most grounded witches, like Mila, recognized necessity over desire.

Andrei thought only of swords.

"Is he going to ask you to live with him soon?"

"Eventually. He's finding our home along the river, preparing it. It will be one more summer before it's ready to hold us safely through the winter. When I finish with the smithy, I'll chink and build our home."

"Will he let you?"

Mila nodded.

"Why do you help me?"

She hesitated, met his gaze, then looked away. "Because," she finally said, her words low, "it called to me."

His heart stirred.

So . . . someone else *did* understand.

Mila stepped closer, gesturing to the glimmering shards below the surface of the water.

"You've been harvesting?"

The question marked the end of their discussion, and he was glad.

A snort followed. "Something like that. I'm not as good as you were at picking out the rocks with the most metal in them."

He didn't mention that he'd fallen into the freezing river, came up sputtering and glacially cold. That Sarasam had to whisk him back to the smithy before he died.

"You need to use magic to call the best rocks to you. And split the rock from the metal," she added.

"Yes."

She lifted a single eyebrow. Her hand hovered over the top of the water. "Do you want me to do it again?"

Deeper questions lined that one. In her hands, Mangana shortened, changed, shifted down, until it fit into a smaller knife sheath at her side. He watched with growing interest.

"I've never done magic outside of our clan magic." His voice sounded hoarse. "I'm . . . I'm not entirely sure it's wise for me to do so."

"It is."

Her quick reassurance, so easily spoken, stirred a little amusement.

"I command Sirilas magic all the time. Every day. But it is allowed magic. The magic that my position in my clan requires."

"There is so much more out there."

"If the judgment from the clan gods falls upon my head?"

Her thin-lined eyebrows rose slightly. "Do you believe that's what happens?"

"It's what I have been told. All my life, they said—"

"I didn't ask that." Her sharp voice startled him. "I asked if you believed that was true."

"No. I don't think I do."

He used to believe in things that seemed so much smaller

than his beliefs now. This new version of the world appeared inflated. Bigger than he'd ever expected. Wider, too, like distorted mirrors pulled from silver.

He craved more. More magic, more ability, more ease of life. To travel to and from the smithy on his own. Though the Ensis magic had given no sign, he sensed it wouldn't ferry him around forever. Deeper acquisition of skills and knowledge was a necessity to be independent.

He touched his fingertips to his temple. "Magic is here. If our mind hasn't surrendered, and doesn't believe it is possible, it will never work."

After a pause, she said with amusement, "Sounds like something only you can fix."

He chuckled, but the truth lay bare. At the clan, the Sirilas magic continued to behave in erratic patterns, but he no longer believed it had anything to do with *his* magical use. It must be something else as yet undiscovered.

If there was an imbalance in the clan, it was a problem with the clan, not him. For Sergei to imply that the sole burden lay on his shoulders had been wrong. Sacha did other magic. Anastasia went to the villages. He released those ideas, eager to open a fresh path.

Yet, two options remained present.

The swords.

The clan.

Two puzzle pieces that would never fit together.

Filled with resolve, Andrei said, "Teach me?"

The query sounded like a cracking tree in the silent night. He motioned to the rocks with a nod.

Mila smiled.

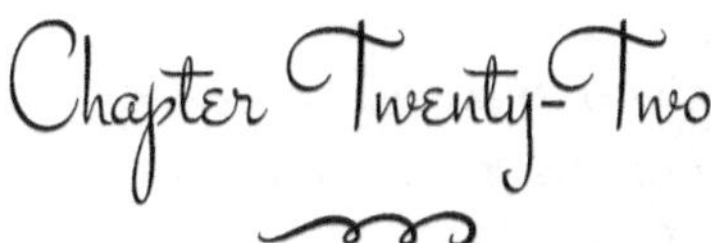

Chapter Twenty-Two

Maleesa must transform. In fact, one could argue that their purpose in life is to be transformed from one thing to the next. The cycle is fairly simple.

Egg.

Larva.

Pupa.

(This takes six months.)

Adult.

(This lasts for about three years.)

When they weaken, and death is clearly near, eggs form within the maleesa.

(No impregnation—which isn't understood. Clan scholars believe this to be part of a magical influence.)

Death comes.

The new eggs hatch from within the body of their dead parent, feed upon them, and grow strong enough to transition to their larval form.

In a sense, maleesa are . . . cannibalistic.

—Alyona, Caretaker
Year 1324

Sergei peered at him.

Andrei met the hard stare.

Nine days had passed since Zamok castle, and two days since the broken betrothal. Sergei had disappeared for all of it. Claims of ill health kept him shuttered away in his home. Neither his wife nor Anastasia spoke of him to anyone.

Andrei had run the clan as any Guide should. No one questioned it except him—and maybe Sacha.

Seeing Sergei confirmed that all was not well with the Guide to the Clan. His tapered eyes were bloodshot, his hair askew at the back. Wrinkles in his shirt showed a restless night. He didn't smoke his pipe, which he often did after troublesome sleep.

"Nikolov."

Sergei's statement was issued almost as a question, but not quite. He ran his fingers down his mustache, peering past Andrei. He leaned forward, the legs of his chair clomping against the floor.

"Yes, I have met Nikolov and never wanted to repeat the experience. I am not surprised that he's Alek's advisor. Or puppeteer, if you will. The man is too young and stupid to run the Network on his own."

"Intelligence isn't a requirement," Andrei said idly. "Not when you can beat a High Priest by sheer brute strength and claim the throne."

Sergei cast him an annoyed glance. "Don't be a fool, Andrei. It takes strategy and calculation to access the ruling High Priest *to* kill him. You think the former one didn't have protections and Guards and everything else in place?"

Andrei opened his mouth to reply. *What about the Vyzov Bitvay?* he wanted to ask. Of course anyone could access the High Priest to issue the *Vyzov Bitvay* challenge. Realizing the moot point of arguing with such a tired old man, Andrei stopped. Sergei's foul humor put him in the mood for a fight. Andrei wouldn't line himself up as the first target.

Sergei reached for his tobacco bag.

"Nikolov is too old to defend himself, but too strategic to release an opportunity to use Alek to his advantage. Alek must know, on some level, that he could never be High Priest without someone else calling the shots. So, no. I'm not surprised."

Wispy, short leaves dropped to the top of Sergei's parchment, sprinkling it with shards of light green and gray. Andrei watched him gently pick the fallen pieces up, set them inside the pipe. Sergei muttered to himself, simple sounds that had no distinct meaning.

Soon enough, Sergei would tire.

The bluster storm only lasted a few more moments before the next question came.

"So? What will you do about it now?"

Andrei blinked, arrested by a moment of pure panic. *Which path will you take?* For a moment, he thought Sergei might understand that two distinctly different, but not all that dissimilar, magicks tugged at him. The time where he'd have to choose one over the other rapidly approached, and he stood paralyzed in the middle.

Two days ago, he'd broken Sergei's cardinal rule for the Guide of the Clan, and used outside magic with Mila. No judgment fell on the clan in his name yet. No wrathful god rebuked him with brimstone and agony.

In fact, he slept better than ever.

A beat before it would have been too late, Andrei remembered Sergei asked him about the showing the *maleesa* to the Southern Network, not the magicks that demanded.

"Nothing. I have no plans to do anything with the *maleesa*."

Sergei's brow lifted. "What?"

"I will do nothing. I want to see the situation as it unfolds. We can assume what they might do all day, but it only wastes our time. I went to their lastmeal as requested. If Alek or Nikolov have a move to make, then they will soon."

"You've thoroughly considered this course of action?"

"I've been thinking of almost nothing else. Nikolov's implication is that, should we not cooperate, there will be physical retaliation and bloodshed against the clan."

"Guardians?"

"He was more subtle rather than using direct inferences."

Sergei grunted.

"It becomes a question of trust in the magic," Andrei continued, grateful to air his thoughts. This situation was reminiscent of the past ten years of his life. To stand with Sergei, map out how to think about a problem. Whatever path he chose, he would miss his former *fere-papan*.

"Do you trust the Sirilas magic to protect the clan?"

Andrei hesitated. "I want to say yes. That we have nothing to fear, that all will be well, but . . ."

"But it's difficult to do that as the Guide, because you are the one that bears the responsibility if the magic does not work?"

"Yes, Sergei. And there's little doubt that *something* is wrong with the magic. Small things fail daily, and nothing seems to right it."

Color leached from Sergei's face as he leaned back in his chair, balancing it on the two hind legs. Today, more than before, he looked every bit his age. Previously, Sergei had energy and optimism in spades. He used to bound through the clan with his relentless zeal. The muted variation of the same witch was a shocking antithesis.

"Magic is as magic does, Andrei. If a path that creates more certainty or safety—even if it requires change—presents itself, then as a leader, I would be more likely to take that path."

"There is no certainty in revealing the *maleesa* or our life to the Network."

Darkness entered Sergei's tone. "There is certainty in their Guardian force. In the clash of weapons, the spray of blood. Will you take the lives of clan members on your shoulders?"

Astonishment filtered through him. "You still believe I should show the *maleesa* after what Nikolov said?"

"I believe in the might and power of the Southern Network Guardian force, and that we face a difficult problem. Nikolov is a complicated, power-hungry man."

A hardening sensation filled Andrei's gut as he perceived what the Guide implied, but would never say outright. Sergei didn't believe the Sirilas magic could protect the clan.

The truth should have surprised him, but somehow it didn't. He wanted to ask Sergei why, but couldn't bring himself to do it. Mila had warned him against trusting Sergei, something at which he'd scoffed.

Now, he couldn't help but wonder.

"You give your life to the magic," Sergei murmured. "And you think . . ."

The chair legs returned to the ground with a *thunk*.

"The decision is yours, Andrei. But heed my advice. When they offer a peace branch, only a fool turns his back. Particularly a peace branch that has so little requirement on our part."

Unable to conjure words for more, Andrei nodded. Sergei stood, walked over to the fireplace. He plucked a shard of burning wood and straightened again. The smoldering piece he set against his pipe and puffed.

"Sergei, about Ana—"

Sergei cut him off with a sharp back-and-forth. "No, Andrei. This is a matter not discussed in these rooms."

Relieved—also quite annoyed—Andrei slipped out of Sergei's office. Closing the door behind him gave a physical sensation of release. Ghosts from their discussion chased him out of the glacier, out toward the clan lands.

He stepped into an empty world. Snow scuffed the horizon, driven by an abrasive wind that ground against his skin. The magic hid the clan, hid their life.

Could their subterranean secrets remain hidden from Alkarra forever?

* * *

The *clink* of plates, the plop of wet food falling into bowls, and the gentle buzz of conversation drew Andrei from his deepening thoughts.

Whispers abounded from clan members milling in the dining area around him. Obligation compelled him to eat with the clan for middlemeal today, just to stay visible after the announcement of his broken betrothal.

He tried not to listen to the conjectures and questions that rose in whispers. Didn't care what the clan members said.

She doesn't want children.
He's too committed to his position. Doesn't even want a wife!
Things went terribly.
I heard he hit her.

None of them were true, which gave him steady reassurance. With any luck, the rumors would fade. Anastasia, who had been lying low since it happened, would venture back into real life again soon.

She'd recover, marry the witch she loved.

And he'd . . . something.

The thick cerulean walls of the ice formed an oval around the room. Wooden tables, chairs, and plates littered the open space. The gentle motion of bodies streaming in and out, the steady cadence of voices chattering here and there, had a soothing effect.

Smells of wild onions and mushrooms thickened the air with their steep scents. Clan members harvested them in the fall and preserved them in the ice for months. They filled his soup bowl with their translucent skins, bumpy shapes in a dark brown broth.

He sat alone along the periphery. Cool air radiated from the frozen wall, so he kept his coat on. The warm stew heated him from the inside out as he lifted his bowl and slurped.

The moment he set it down, Sacha glared at him.

"We need to talk."

He sighed.

"Sacha—"

Her low voice continued, intense as it had ever been. "I know what happened in Zamok Castle and that you've been avoiding me."

"I haven't avoided you. *You* haven't been here. This morning, Katya said you've been sick."

Her nose lifted. She sniffled, and when she spoke, her voice had a rasp. "I have been sick, but I'm feeling better. We need to talk about the lastmeal at Zamok Castle. I have a few opinions on what it means."

"How do you know what happened at Zamok?"

She waved a hand. "Doesn't matter."

"No, it *does* matter."

"I'm not explaining it here. We should talk somewhere else. For once, I think you did something wise in coming here today. Show up, let them see your face, see that you aren't brokenhearted over Anastasia."

"Should I be?"

She rolled her eyes. "No. Love is a joke. Listen, we need to talk about Alek and Nikolov and the threat he made against us."

His eyes nearly bugged out.

How did she know about Nikolov?

"Sacha!"

"We don't have time for you to scold me," she hissed. "I have to be back at work in ten minutes. They're going to approach you again."

"How do you know?"

"It's not that hard to figure out!" she cried. "Their demands will be steeper this time. Nikolov thinks he has a hook in you. Whatever they ask, tell them no, Andrei. They're trying to put you on a slippery slope—one where you can't deny them their requests. They'll make it impossible to refuse. You'll have to betray the clan and our lives will be lost. Do you see that?"

"I don't think it's that dramatic."

"Not yet! They will subject us to their rule, Andrei." Her expression hardened. "I read history books. It's very clear. No Network witch has ever felt that clan witches were worth anything. It's not about to change. Not with someone like Nikolov calling the shots."

Andrei had another sip of his stew, but his appetite had

fled. The conversation with Sergei stirred back up in his mind, like restless leaves. He set the bowl down. The taste of onions filled his mouth in a disorienting way.

"It's not just a question of whether they'll subject us to their rules," he said, so quietly she had to lean closer to hear. Her hair fell over her shoulders, drifting around her face. "It's a question of whether the Sirilas magic can protect us from Nikolov, from Alek, and the Guardians. The sheer . . . might . . . that they wield."

Indignation crossed her scrunched face. "What question is there?"

"Sacha, you should have seen the Guardians at the castle. There is wealth and power that we cannot match. Our magic is . . . weakening. It's not balanced."

"I saw the castle, you fool," she snapped. "I was *there*."

"Where?"

"*Ira!*" she cried. "You're an idiot. How have you made it this far to almost be our leader? I went with you to the South."

"I didn't—"

"No, you didn't see me. I was invisible. I rode on the top of the carriage the whole time. Why do you think I've been sick?"

He shuddered. The night had been so cold. How had she not frozen?

As if she read his mind, she rolled her eyes. "Yes, it was extremely cold and if I ever had to do it again, I might not. I was . . . anyway. It was worth the discomfort to learn what I learned. I had the advantage of moving around the room, listening to *all* conversations."

"The Guardians didn't detect you?"

She shrugged. "I guess not. I used an invisibility spell, but one taught to me by the villagers. They may not have known it, or everyone was so distracted by fawning over you they didn't think about it. Clan witches don't do outside magic, remember?" she quipped with a snarky undertone. "They completely underestimate us in every regard. It was my chance to take advantage of that and learn something. So I did."

Andrei pushed aside his nearly empty bowl. Curiosity had him now.

"What else did you hear?"

The first sign of uncertainty flashed through her eyes. "Not much in the way of concrete plans. They're idiots, but they're not fools enough to speak their plans to harm us out loud while the future Guide to the Clan stands in the room."

"Perhaps because there are no plans?"

"Chthu help me! When did you get so stupid?"

"Sacha—"

"Of course they mean to harm us. Don't you see what's happening? Nikolov controls two of the most prosperous gem mines in the Southern Network. I may not have heard the plans from their lips, but I snuck into Nikolov's office."

"You did what?"

A smug expression followed. "Just that. I saw his ledgers. His two mines? They aren't doing that well, Andrei. I know what the clan pays in taxes to the Southern Network every year —I've been present for the audits. We pay far more taxes than he does. That means the silk trade is, arguably, the most powerful trade in the Southern Network. Of course Nikolov doesn't like that!"

Irritation filled him with a heady, prickling sensation. "When?" he demanded. "When did you listen to the audits? Those are between the accountants, the Guide, and the Southern Network emissaries."

"By Chthu, Andrei, how are you this obtuse? I work in the glacier and I've been using outside magic since I was a small girl! How do you think I know so much about the clan? Why do you think I care *this* much?"

Wordlessly, he could only sputter. The implications were

clear—she'd been spying on clan business. Listening to the audits, the reports, and who-knew-what-else? It at once infuriated him—what a breach of privacy!—and impressed him.

Brilliant.

Indeed, Andrei had played right into Southern Network expectations as a straight-laced Guide to the Clan that wouldn't use outside magic, thus be easier to dupe. They saw him as a fool. His loyal nature to the magic would make him an easy target amongst witches like Alek.

Sacha blithely avoided such inevitability by taking risks he'd only just discovered. As if it were in her nature to find the edge and walk it. She folded her arms in front of her, then pressed them into the table. She stared at him with such intensity he almost couldn't meet her gaze.

"Report me to Sergei for exile, if you must, but I'll fight it. I'll drag you down with me if I have to, Andrei. I won't be swayed."

With a resigned sigh, he muttered, "I won't report you."

She eased off.

"These fools in power in the Southern Network are wily. We must be wily too. Nikolov wants to break us and take over. The fastest way to do that is to break our trust in the current Guide, and to learn as much as they can about the *maleesa.* That's what he's doing, Andrei. This isn't a peacekeeping mission. It's a masquerade."

The black sludge of fear slopped around his gut, made all the worse by the very-real panic in her usually calm gaze.

"Nikolov would send the might of his armies," he said.

"Let him."

"Could the Sirilas magic withstand it?"

"Of course."

She said it so quickly, with such confidence, he could only stare. Sacha drew in a dragging breath, as if she strove for patience. Several witches bustled past, calling greetings to

Sacha, then to him as an afterthought. Their cool gazes lingered on him, but clearly warmed when they looked at Sacha.

Odd.

"The Sirilas magic is here to protect the *maleesa* and protect us," she said firmly. "Why do you doubt?"

Because it isn't a part of me like the Ensis magic. Because I'll have to choose and I don't know what I want anymore.

"Sergei doubts the Sirilas."

She didn't bat an eye. No shock. No dropped jaw. The truth of it didn't slam her in the stomach the same way it did to him.

"Of course he does."

"Why not?"

"He hasn't believed in it for years. Why do you think he leans so much on structure? On rules? He's a frightened man at his core, Andrei."

"The burden of the clan is heavy."

"Doesn't have to be. We're a family. We share the burden." She reached out, tapped him lightly in the middle of the forehead with a finger. "Don't get it into that brain that you bear the weight of the clan as Guide, or something stupid like that. You have your clan to hold you up. Only a witch like Sergei would make you think it all rested on you."

Andrei didn't know what to say. The spot where she'd thumped him with her finger ached, but he wouldn't reach up and rub it. A concession too far.

"Regarding Alek and Nikolov, deal with this *now*, Andrei. Don't wait. Stand your ground. Don't cower before bullies. If you cower, they will return. The moment the bully appears, you must teach them how to treat you. You establish what you will and will not tolerate. The same is true for Sergei."

"I won't deal with Nikolov now."

"Why not?"

"I'm going to see their next move. They've established their hostility. Now we can buy ourselves time to let this play out. The *Praznick* is in twenty-one days. If we can get through that, it will be easier to deal with this on the other side when the clan can pull back together under new leadership."

The words sat in his throat like a leaden weight. Sacha rolled her eyes, but thankfully didn't fight the point.

"In all my years, and all the threats against us, no outside force has been able to defeat the Sirilas. Not if you trust the magic."

Sacha stood. Her overall mien had calmed, but she held her scorching glare.

"I'm here if you need any help."

With that, she spun and headed toward the entrance. The rest of the dining area had settled into quiet, with only the occasional creak of ice or distant closing of a door. The clan did most things quietly, which left little space for errant noises, lest it disturb the *maleesa*.

Today, the silence rang louder than the protests, the doubts, and the questions. It swelled, filling him from the inside out.

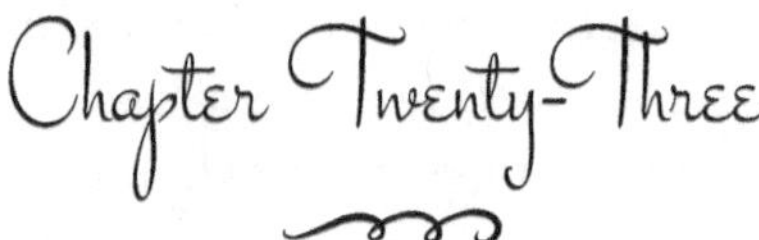

Chapter Twenty-Three

Though they have wings, the maleesa will never fly.

—Odessa, Reeler
Year 1294

A message found Andrei at the smithy over a week later.

It hovered in front of him, a sharply folded rectangle that dangled just within reach. He gazed at it, hammer poised over the blade, and paused. The tip of the sword—much wider than Mangana—lay on the anvil.

Startled by the unexpected arrival of the envelope, Andrei fumbled with the hammer. It clattered onto the sword with a painful noise. He winced.

Muttering under his breath, he set aside the hammer and grabbed the parchment. By the light of the fire, he flipped it open.

Alek's handwriting filled the inside.

Andrei,

I hope this letter finds you well. Nikolov and I have been discussing you and your health lately. It's been several weeks since we spoke to you at the castle, and we're curious about how you're doing.

Do you have any news or updates for us?

—Alek Popov
High Priest of the Southern Network

Andrei pitched it into the fire. The flames took it, and the parchment curled away, lost to ashes, in moments.

After a moment of deliberation, he used the magic Mila had been teaching him and summoned a piece of parchment from the glacier. It lay on the table while he plucked a long stem of charcoal from a cool portion of the hearth.

High Priest,

All is well in the clan.

I will have an answer for you and your Council after the clan votes me into position as Guide to the Clan.

Andrei

For now, he would watch the *Praznick maleesa* slowly transform.

The white days of winter stuttered by with blizzard winds. The clan eked closer to a warmer life as the crest of the bitter chill slipped past during the *Praznick* celebration, then headed toward warmer seasons.

He would watch, wait, guide, and bladesmith.

In the meantime?
Nothing more.

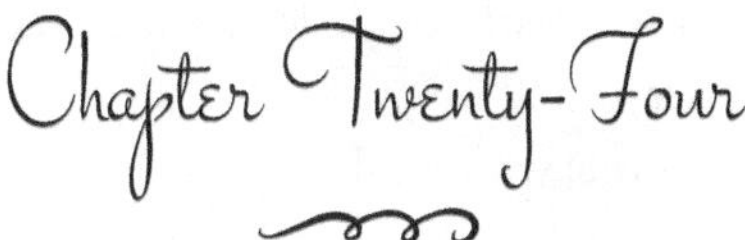

Chapter Twenty-Four

Clan members like to think we have been set apart—are special—because Hulu bestowed the Sirilas magic upon us.

Here is the truth: all have a debt to Hulu and the maleesa and the Sirilas magic. I try not to think about it.

—Varvara, Accountant
Year 1398

The routine of working in the glacier, returning to his dwelling, building a fire, and waiting for the clan to settle before he left for the smithy left Andrei wrung out.

Loss of sleep, greater physical activity, and less cozy comforts at his dwelling compounded into weary days. At night, however, he yearned for the bladesmithing. Sank into it. Breathed the metallic scents, felt the fire on his skin.

"Pay attention!"

The sharp command came a second after a stinging blow to his arm. Mila's feet danced through the snow, away from him as fast as an arctic baer. Andrei grunted, lifted Sarasam, and blocked a second attempt from Mangana. He ducked, fell, and paused when the cool kiss of ice pressed his back. Mila set her blade to his neck.

Sarasam gave a metaphorical eye roll.

Mila grinned.

The ease of using Sarasam to save the High Priest against the arctic baer had faded. His attempts to understand swords had been awkward and clunky, though they improved every day. Sarasam's occasionally snarky sensations certainly didn't help.

Mangana disappeared from sight as Mila stepped back, hand held out. Sweaty despite the cold, Andrei accepted. She helped to pull him to his feet from the trampled drift. He doubled over, hands on his knees, and panted.

"You win. Again."

"One day you'll stop expecting anything else."

He chuckled.

Mila reached for a square wooden box, wrapped with leather and furs, that she carried her water in. Hanging arctic baer claws swung around a jutting lip. She pulled a piece of wood out of the top and let water dribble into her mouth. When she finished, she passed it to him.

"Here."

He drank, the water warmed by a spell. It sank all the way into his stomach in a refreshing burst. She nodded toward the smithy and he turned that way. Though sweating, the cold would freeze them faster for it. They couldn't linger. Clouds puffed up on the horizon and winds swept closer. The precursor of darkness that hailed an incoming blizzard built in the sky now. He sniffed. The scent of snow lay heavy in the air.

"Tell me the incantation again?" he asked.

Carefully, Mila repeated words from the ancient language. He scooped up a palmful of snow as he walked, repeating it. The flakes melted to water in his palm, steaming lightly.

"Magic to keep water warm. So easy."

"Easy can be lifesaving," she said.

"How much water does it work on?"

She shrugged. "I've tried it on a frozen barrel before. Took a while, and I was very, very tired afterward, but it eventually worked."

A low fire lit the hearth when they returned to the smithy. Andrei stepped over, stacked more logs on top. Mila peeled her coat off, set it on a peg near the hearth, and tugged at her shirt. Lines of sweat barely showed under her arms. Her shirt would need to dry out before she ventured into the woods.

Mila leaned back against the table, arms folded over her chest. The planes of her face smoothed out.

"What sword are you working on now?" she asked.

Andrei used a poker to rearrange the burning logs. Flames sprouted higher at the jostling, as if they protested being woken up.

"The same."

"Still giving you problems?"

"It . . . feels off."

"You altered the metal, didn't you?"

Andrei frowned. "Not like that. I added less charcoal to the melted mixture before it became an ingot. I wanted more, but . . . it wouldn't let me."

"You should try bones."

He reared back. "What?"

"Bones. It works. The witches of my village use the blackened bones of our ancestors to forge our swords. It keeps them with us forever."

Andrei pondered that, still troubled by her question. The sword had taken up too much of his time, but no amount of his own impatience hurried the process along. In the meantime, the Ensis magic must be in a hurry as well, because the sword nagged him hourly.

Other sword images swirled like an eddy in his mind. A different sword, this one smaller. The metallic beginnings of a long sword with an integral guard and tang. No apparent pommel—perhaps added later. Simple, small, nimble. It desired attention *now*, as if in a hurry.

"There is another. I don't know its name or when I'll start it, but I've seen the first stage. Hopefully, soon."

"When do you receive their names?"

"At the end? At least, I did with Mangana. I saw your sword as it ended up from the beginning, though. Mangana was different. This one? The magic is retracting from what it initially represented as. I can't make sense of it."

"Does your Ensis require staunch obedience also?"

"Not that I can tell."

The thought that yet another magical system required rigid discipleship made his stomach curl. A surprising response.

When had he ever questioned his obedience to magic? He had always accepted his position in the clan. His lot in life. Yet the magic of the ancients, the simple daily magic that Mila was teaching him, required no such devotion. The power existed. He drew on it.

No ardor necessary.

Andrei shook his head. Those thoughts wouldn't help. He continued to bounce between two magicks, and both of them desired more than he wanted to give. The Ensis magic brought him to life, yet he owed everything to the Sirilas.

"I think I need to work on another sword. There's another

one that keeps coming to my mind. I haven't had two at the same time before."

Mila brightened.

"Let's get going! You mentioned a metallic design along the interior? I'll get the metal ready to smelt. I grabbed some more rocks for you."

Andrei chuckled as she rushed for the bag of rock they had yet to sift through, and extract the metal from. Mila loved the process of the work. The movement from one stage to the next.

With a bright fire dancing in the hearth now, Andrei stood. As he joined her at the table, a form appeared outside. He froze, eyes wide, and lifted a hand. Sarasam zipped to his palm, the metal hilt gleaming.

At the flash of light, Mila glanced up. He tilted his head to the window, which had frosted at the corners.

"Anastasia."

Mila tilted her head. "Your previous betrothed?"

He nodded, throat thick. Why was Anastasia here? She stumbled around, looking right at the house, then beyond. As if . . . she couldn't see it. He frowned. A chord of fear struck him.

Had something happened to *Maman*? He set aside Sarasam, rushed around the table, and headed to the door. Mila remained behind, but her attention was at the window as he jerked a coat on and hurried outside. The wind increased, picking up from the east. Whorls of snow twirled over the ground, then raced past.

A cry from Anastasia's lips found his ears.

"Andrei?"

He stepped around a tree in the path. Anastasia whipped round, eyes wide. Seeing him there, she relaxed.

"There you are."

"How did you find me?"

"I don't know! I just . . . I knew I needed to find you. The Sirilas brought me to this spot. Is your place here?"

Ignoring that, he said, "What's wrong?"

"You've almost missed the welcoming party of Anatov and Katya's first baby. The clan has gathered in the dining area. There is . . . discontent that you're not there. Sacha is speaking with clan members. She's brought up . . ."

Her lips sealed, eyes wide.

"The *maleesa* question?"

Her shoulders bowed. "Yes. I normally wouldn't interfere with whatever it is you do out here . . . but I'm concerned. This should be a joyous event for them, and Janokov has soured it. Sacha has him mollified, but only because she's keeping him and the others that follow him busy with a debate."

"Your father?"

"He's sick. Besides," she added quietly, "he would only make it worse. Most of the clan members present are frightened of letting the Network know anything about the Sirilas magic, and he thinks it should happen. Not all clan members are frightened. Some are attempting to debate back from the other side. I just . . . this isn't the time or place. You are the Guide. If you want to be voted into position at the *Praznick* in four days, this needs to be fixed before it becomes a bigger problem."

A traitorous thought followed. *What if I don't want to be voted in?*

"Thank you, Anastasia. This was a kind gesture to me. I'll come now and try to subdue the discontent."

She softened.

"You have done as much for me, and more. I'm happy to be your friend, Andrei."

With that, the magic took her back to the clan lands.

Resignation, perhaps a little fear, swept through him. The Sirilas magic knew he was here. Of course it did. It must have known before now.

What did that mean?

And what did he face back at the clan? He didn't want to go, but it couldn't be helped. The third sword flittered back through his mind, eager to start. Within an hour, Mila would be halfway through the extraction process . . .

Andrei shook his head.

No. From the issues in the clan, he couldn't just walk away. No matter how much he wanted to.

* * *

The utter absence of life met him when he returned to clan lands.

An incoming blizzard covered the moon, casting darkness on the world. Not a flicker of torchlight or candle or starlight revealed a path. Nothing but frozen, open tundra that howled under brittle winds.

Guided by memorized paths and instinct, Andrei headed toward the glacier. Snow flurries dropped in a busy wall the moment he touched the icy door and the magic opened it for him.

The smell of charred meat and spices and crackling fat gently assaulted his nose. His stomach growled. After two hours of practice with Mila, he felt ravenous.

Two clan members sat in the middle of the dining hall. Chairs filled with witches ringed around them, putting them dead center, near tables piled with food. Offerings from clan members burdened another table, right next to the couple. Rattles, a chair that moved in a rocking back-and-forth, diapers. Thick clothes and blankets passed from one family to the next.

A tiny head of black hair was just visible from a tight swaddle in its father's arms. Anatov smiled at those bringing gifts. Clan members spoke quietly with Katya, who had a blanket wrapped around her shoulders.

The clan officially welcomed new lives two weeks after birth, to allow the child and family time to heal, to adapt to a new life pattern. Anatov and Katya appeared tired, but bright-eyed.

Immediately, Andrei made his way over to the couple. On the farther side of the dining hall, away from the happy murmurs and gift-giving, built a darker storm. Clan members with scowls, hardened edges, stood in a cluster around Sacha and Janokov, who stood in the middle.

A debate, indeed.

Long winter nights, when the *maleesa* were hibernating or tucked into sleep, depending on their cycle, had to pass somehow. The lacking light and unvarying routine would drive one mad if such schedules didn't alter at least a little so the clan would gather for debates to entertain, open the mind, and discuss new purviews.

With the winds of change threatening clan life, this sort of debate wasn't unheard of, yet wouldn't leave anyone feeling better.

Surprise, perhaps relief, registered on Katya's expression when Andrei stepped closer. Too late, he realized he brought no gift. Panic slipped through him, cold as winter's breath.

Without thinking of *where* he stood, he put his hand in a pocket and used one of Mila's summoning spells. When he withdrew it, a small gem from the smithy sat in his palm. A pale, pink little thing, the size of his fingertip.

He held it out.

"A beautiful child deserves beautiful things to look at. May it be a talisman of luck for her on her journey into clan life."

Katya's eyes widened as she accepted. Anatov's face stiffened like a glacier plane. His head barely shifted when he nodded an acknowledgment, brittle as it was. Anatov's gaze cast down to the sparkling gem in his wife's palm, then away.

"Thank you," she said.

Her lack of using his title didn't slip by him.

Anatov's trenchant expression urged Andrei to slip away, allowing the remaining stragglers space to congratulate the happy couple.

Anastasia had come for him none-too-soon. The gem would have been a delightful surprise under other circumstances, when the caves yielded so little color and so few lovely things.

He turned toward the wall near which the debate was taking place. The urge to leave it alone—let the clan members debate whatever they want—nearly compelled him to leave. Was it really his place to tell them what to think about an issue?

No.

He didn't really want to answer their questions, either. He'd come, at least, and fulfilled his initial obligation. Several clan members could witness that, even if he didn't stay. Not that any of them had surged forward to speak with him.

If he left now, there would still be time to help Mila with the metal extraction . . .

He nearly gave into the almost-irresistible pull back to the forge, forced it away by sheer willpower. Andrei pointed his feet to the other side of the space. Obligation took him the rest of the way to the debating crowd.

Hot, embittered words met him once he stopped a few paces back. Janokov stood before another clan member, Yurina. Both faces were flushed, stances tight. No violence lay in the air. Nothing but a thrumming tension, like something about to explode.

Sacha stood amid them.

"To expose the *maleesa*?" Janokov cried. "There must be other ways to find peace with our neighbors."

Yurina scoffed, hand waving. "That we haven't tried? You forget, Janokov, that I work in the glacier. I review and audit everything. I see the books, the notations from former Guides. There is no other witch that has a picture of the clan like I do—save only Sergei. We've tried everything. The Southern Network will continue to put pressure on us, and who can blame them? We have secrets that control their economy."

Janokov waved that off with a gruff shake of his head. "Let them feel endangered. It's no less than they deserve after their treatment of us. The Sirilas magic has been active and working for one-and-a-half centuries now."

"Exactly! One hundred and fifty years."

An uproar occurred from behind Janokov. Swelling voices lifted behind Yurina in response. Feet shuffled, ushering witches farther apart. Only Sacha stood in what had been the middle.

"Silence!" she cried.

The sound of her sharp voice cut through the rising cacophony. Her glare sliced through the crowd, quieting those that might take advantage of the silence to say something. The whole dining hall seemed to obey. Movements and exclamations from near the baby also stopped.

"We're here to debate, not to create more anger. There is uncertainty in the clan, but there has always been."

Sacha's head twisted to the right and left, stopping when she saw Andrei. A flash of something slipped through her gaze. He didn't move. She looked right at him, voice unyielding as she said, "But our Guide will lead us right."

The rest of the group, catching her stalled review, turned to see Andrei standing there. A mixture of relief and irritation filled the faces of those present.

He couldn't decide which was worse.

"All I know," Janokov said, loud enough that the words rippled to the rest of the dining hall, "is that the *Praznick* is four days away. If we're going to vote for a new Guide—one that *actually* cares—we better find someone worthy. Because I don't see any candidates put forward here that have proven their loyalty enough for my vote. Color me surprised that Andrei even showed up to welcome a new clan member."

Grumbling assent followed.

Annoyed growls from Yurina's side, too.

Andrei had reluctant followers and hot-headed opponents. A less-than-optimal start to his tenure as a Guide. Before he could speak, the crowd began to disperse on their own. They filtered to other parts of the dining hall, but the convivial air had faded. The lack of energy that they left behind made the room ring in a hollow way.

Andrei let them shuffle past, ignoring him, until all had left save Sacha. She stood with hands on her hips, an unreadable expression on her face.

"Anastasia?" she asked quietly.

Andrei nodded.

Her disappointment was a palpable thing, riding on the air as she studied him. Regret that he hadn't remembered that the event was tonight on his own filled him with a leaden weight.

Sacha lifted her chin.

"Meet me at your dwelling. We need to talk."

* * *

A tepidly warm room met Andrei when he returned to his dwelling.

Though Sirilas magic obeyed his query to take him there, it hadn't kept the place warm. Just enough heat remained inside so that nothing formed frost, but not much more.

Andrei shivered, kneeled to light a fire. No need to ask the magic for help. The Sirilas didn't execute those simple spells for him anymore. While a weak flame grew to a burgeoning fire, he pulled Sarasam from her scabbard, set her on the table. The glimpse of her gleaming blade made him think of the next sword, and he fell into swirling thoughts.

By the time a *thud* on his door drew him out of his reverie, the fire crackled with energy. He stepped to the door, opened it.

"Come in, Sacha."

Sacha glared at him as she stalked inside, dropped parchments on his table, and whirled around.

"Are you ready to talk?"

"Yes."

"You look distracted. Thinking about swords again?"

"Always."

She blew a raspberry and threw her hands in the air. "Do you even care, Andrei? I hate that I have to ask, but here we are."

He started to reply, but his mouth had turned to a desert. His tongue stuck to the top. He didn't know what to say. Finally, he scraped out, "Of course I care about the clan, Sacha."

"More than the swords?"

He stared at her.

How could he answer that question when he didn't know?

"Leva reported ten *maleesa* survived Cave Four's pupal stage. She came into the glacier in a panic today because she couldn't find you and she didn't know what to do."

Andrei racked his mind, startled to recall that his last check showed Cave Four waiting on two thousand *maleesa* in their pupal stage.

"Ten?"

Her stiff nod was her only response at first.

This morning he'd slept later than usual, then spent most of the afternoon catching up on accountant requests before they paid the taxes for the summer silk trade profits, which left him in the glacier longer than usual today.

Sacha leaned closer, hands planted on the table between them.

"If you don't convince the clan that *you* will be the best Guide, then the vote will be a no or an impasse for the first time in almost a century. Sergei will remain the Guide unless, by some horrifying miracle, they vote someone else into the position. If Sergei remains Guide, he will give the Network information about the *maleesa*. All of our magic could fall apart. Can you live with yourself, in your smithy, exiled from the clan, if that happens?"

Her words echoed deep in his breast, bouncing in the cavernous place where his adoration of obedience used to live. Could he love both magicks?

Yes.

Could he serve them both?

No.

By some extent, both magicks had found him. Both gave him the opportunity for growth and creation and change. Both magicks had something to offer, for neither were good nor bad.

A question pulsed in the back of his mind, hot and thrumming and demanding answers. Which magic was the *right* one? He had hoped time would prove the answer, but so far, time had only provided greater pressure.

His lack of immediate response seemed to annoy her further, but she said nothing. Instead, she motioned to the piles of parchments on the table. Her tone modulated, losing the reprimanding sharpness.

"That's not all I came for. I've discovered something else you need to see."

Curling papers, held together by shape, awaited on the table. He spread them open, planting one hand on either side. The papers were brittle, a weak batch scraped too thin, though it was new.

A ledger.

The drawn boxes were familiar enough. He'd seen these before. Accountings for silk sold, sorted by buyer, with total amounts paid. A column for taxes, final costs, total received, populated at the end.

There were empty boxes, more than one might expect, because not all Networks paid in gold. Some used trade items, such as mushrooms, gems, currency, or geese. Accountants like Sacha that helped run the clannish trade had interesting exchange stories.

"What is it?"

Sacha tapped a finger at the top of the page. "Everything looks fine here. No mistakes."

She shuffled to a bottom layer and pulled it out. Their vague familiarity meant that Andrei had already perused these ledgers before a meeting with all Accountants weeks ago.

"See this?" She slapped a second ledger. "It's the next day. Same sort of deal. Everything looks right to you?"

"Yes."

"Then here."

The last page at the bottom of the paper displayed the words *Accounting Totals*. The final totals of goods brought into the clan, the taxes paid, and the leftover funds totaled three columns.

Andrei's gaze bounced around.

"I only know a little about this," he said, lifting his eyes to meet hers. "Sergei hasn't trained me that much on it. I wouldn't be able to tell just by looking at it if something was really amiss."

She frowned. "I know. I only noticed the issue because Katya had her baby, and I'm filling in while she cares for her."

Andrei lifted an eyebrow.

She smirked.

"Sergei may not like my outspoken opinions, but he recognizes my skill with numbers. Anyway, I didn't realize it, but Katya hasn't been doing the final totals on the accounts. Sergei has."

"What does that mean?"

"That *no one* but Sergei knows our final numbers."

Andrei frowned. "How is that possible?"

"Easy!" she cried. "Katya receives the ledgers after all the other Guides have everything filled out and ready to go. She gives the ledger to Sergei for the last check. All the rest of us? We're checking that all the other information is correct, not that it's *final*."

"All right."

"So I went to the Storage Rooms to check the totals. Katya didn't know what was actually in those rooms, and I wanted to calculate what we have against what we *should*. It didn't match. According to the ledgers, we should have fifty percent more currency and trade goods."

A terrible sensation dropped into his belly.

"Fifty percent?"

She nodded.

"You mean Sergei has been lying?"

She slammed a fist onto the ledger with a growl. "It's the only explanation! But it gets worse. Not only do we have less than expected, I'm not sure if he paid the taxes *for the last five years.*"

Andrei sifted through that slowly. Her eyes widened, hand flapped, as if to say, *do you finally understand?*

"Perhaps you saw the Storage Rooms after the distribution of tax payments? It might have looked empty because Sergei paid."

"No, the accountings aren't marked as paid."

He frowned. "I see. What accusation are you making?"

"None." She swallowed, held up a finger. "Yet. Until I can figure out if Sergei has paid the taxes or not, it's all conjecture. If the taxes owed to the Southern Network have been paid, then the situation is bleak, but not tragic. If we have not paid the taxes . . ."

She trailed away.

"How long has it been like this?"

A shrug followed.

"I only found out today. I was going to speak with you after going to Katya's celebration. It could be as long as five years, might only be as little as a few months."

Andrei drew in a breath, his thoughts settling as he sifted through recollections of Sergei. In all the time that he'd trained with Sergei, the reports and number scrolls had been taken care of by other witches. Rarely did Sergei mention such details.

For this purpose, perhaps?

"Can you talk to Katya?"

"Without drawing suspicion?"

"Yes."

Sacha pushed her lips to one side of her face, then nodded. "Not as easily as just going to the Southern Network and stealing into their tax reports to see what *has* been paid."

"What?"

She smiled slyly. "It's not as hard as you think."

His breath caught in his chest before he let it back out with a shake of his head. What was there to say? Sacha would do what Sacha wanted. Not to mention the fact that it *would* be more effective to have outside proof supporting such a claim.

"Do you trust the Southern Network accounts more than ours? They might also be lying."

At that, Sacha's serious mien returned. "I don't know." Her sober expression caused a deepening pit of concern. "But I have to try. If Sergei has been hiding something or creating false financial information, we must know. And we must know *before* you become the Guide. He may try to pin it on you."

"He wouldn't."

She scoffed.

"Believe that if you must, but Sergei will always protect himself first, no matter how much he cares for the clan. The *Praznick* is soon, Andrei. You realize this?"

"I'm aware."

"Are you prepared?"

"Yes."

"Have you told Alek the answer for letting them see a maleesa is unequivocally no?"

"No."

"No?"

"I haven't given him an answer."

"But—"

"I'm buying time."

"For what?"

"For me to be the Guide."

Sacha opened her mouth to protest, then stopped. Her lips sealed in a moment of silence. Clearly, she wanted to rebut, but the logic of stasis seemed to follow.

"That will only last for so long, Andrei."

"We'll see."

"We will. When I come back with more information from Katya and the Southern Network ledgers. I have a bad feeling that Sergei is up to something—which would explain why he's supporting such a foolish idea of letting the High Priest see a *maleesa*."

Renewed determination filled her tone now.

"Don't get yourself killed, Sacha."

A look of revulsion crossed her face. "You insult me. I'll be back with more information by tomorrow. In the meantime, act like nothing is different. If Sergei *is* up to something, the last thing we should do is alert him."

Chapter Twenty-Five

Oh, maleesa.

I give my soul to you. In the repetition of my days, I offer at the pyre. Quiet spirit within. Hands do the same work, feet trod the same path.

Caves, dwelling.

Ice, companion.

For you.

For magic.

For the clan.

—Tavish, Spinner
Year 1417

Andrei's muscles tightened as he slammed the hammer onto the blade. It gave way beneath the mallet just a little. He sensed the shift, more than saw it. A spray of fire flared beneath the sword, then faded.

The burgeoning creation continued in solitude. A low-toned, dark presence lived in Andrei's mind. Not evil, but not happy either. The giddiness of the other blades didn't exist in this one. A far more solemn shroud filled it.

Andrei shoved it back into the fire. He'd avoided working on this sword by creating another one. The small sword, lighter and nimble and simple. Taravaren, it called itself, when Andrei finished.

His back and arms ached, but in an enjoyable way. Wiry sinews had overtaken his chest. His shoulders thickened with muscle. Instead of ink stains, he hid burn marks, soot, and charcoal.

While he worked, he thought of the audits. The clan had stopped whispering over the broken betrothal. Anastasia waved, and gave a cordial nod when she saw him. Their lack of drama around the decision gave the clan little to gossip over, and the topic had faded into the wind.

The clan resisted change. No shifts, questions, or instability. They wanted everything predictable and easy.

He snorted.

Nothing was predictable and easy.

Or maybe it could be. Maybe that's why Sergei appeared so tired. Had years of abiding by the rules, living within the box, experiencing nothing but routine and precision led Sergei to failing health?

To treachery against the clan?

His thoughts ran to Sacha. She'd disappeared yesterday, worked at the glacier as usual today, then left early, claiming a headache.

Don't be foolish out there, he thought to her.

Andrei stirred the fire when a knock came from the door. Mila had already come and gone. She'd finished the pitch on the roof, tested him on a few new incantations, then left without explanation, as usual. No one had found him in the smithy or knew he lived here.

Driven by curiosity, he pulled open the door.

A witch stood there, teeth chattering. He trembled, arms clasped around his chest. Frozen icicles formed along his shoulders, and dripped down hair near his ears.

"P-p-please," he gasped in the common language. "W-w-w-warmth."

A swell of emotion from the other side of the room startled him. Taravaren sent waves of giddiness into the room, stirring up Sarasam. The two swords sang in a melody that could only mean one thing.

Andrei pulled the door open.

"Come in."

The witch stumbled inside, tripping over his own feet. His pants had nearly frozen solid. Andrei shut the door against a wind that blew in a blizzard from the east.

"L-l-lost. F-f-frozen."

Andrei grabbed the stiff coat sleeves and tugged him next to the fire. A flurry of movement and haphazard speech followed for the next twenty minutes. Andrei stripped the near-frozen man of clothes, nudged him closer to the hearth, and wrapped him in his warmest furs.

Agonized teeth chattering and moans filled the air for an hour after. Cup after cup of warm tea disappeared down the man's throat.

Eventually, the shivering subsided. The warmth of the greedy fire filled the room, and permeated his frozen bones. Andrei crouched next to the hearth, the new blade set aside and already cool.

"Finnigan."

Andrei glanced up, out of thoughts. The witch regarded him. He had closely set eyes, light blue, and yellow hair that lay loose around his shoulders. He had hacked it off, and it drifted around his ears in uneven wet strands.

"I'm Finnigan."

"Andrei."

"You know the common language?"

Andrei nodded, and didn't explain that it had been a requirement from a young age. No Guide could do his job when he couldn't speak to others in the Network.

Finnigan lacked the rougher voice structure of a Southern Network witch, and he was far more fair-haired. His name indicated he was from a different part of Alkarra, but Andrei couldn't fathom where. He also didn't care. He set aside his mild irritation at stopping work to realize he was starving.

"Hungry?"

Finnigan nodded, but wearily.

"I have food if you want some."

"I've already asked so much. In a few minutes, I'll be ready to transport away again, thanks to your hospitality. I was . . . too far frozen. It's like I couldn't transport when I tried, and I did try."

Andrei waved that off. If the balance of hospitality was on this witch's mind, he definitely wasn't a Southern Network witch. A villager, perhaps. They tended to pay attention to debts. Gratifying in a part of the world where resources weren't plentiful.

The smithy was silent for several moments while Andrei gathered a frozen fish and clay jar of seal blubber. Finnigan, seeming to clue into his surroundings for the first time, tilted his head back to study the soaring ceiling.

Sarasam glimmered on the wall just over the hearth, set in a place of honor in the exact middle. Taravaren lay just next to

Sarasam. She resurrected in Andrei's mind with a subtle push, an explosion of excitement.

Finnigan wasn't the owner of Taravaren, but . . . he was here for Taravaren. Andrei paused, halfway through shoving green herbs into a pot, and waited.

"Deliverer?" he murmured, gaze locked on Taravaren.

The sword thrilled and revealed a witch in Andrei's mind. A young man, probably only fifteen. His name was Fingal, and he looked like his father with ruddy cheeks and a cheeky smile.

Fingal.

The name sent further warmth through Andrei, given by Taravaren. Sarasam, pleased for her friend, chattered happily in her fathomless way. He couldn't imagine life without their prattling in the back of his mind.

Andrei turned back to the pot.

"I'll have some soup soon." He slipped on a coat to step outside. A wooden box waited close to the stoop, filled with rock-hard meat. Normally, it simmered in the cauldron, shoved to the back of the fire to avoid burning all night. In his haste to get back to the sword, he'd forgotten to start a meal.

Finnigan said nothing after Andrei returned. A confirmatory zip of delight from Taravaren confirmed his hunch.

"Your son is Fingal."

Finnigan stilled.

"What?"

The statement, he realized, should have come about a little less suspiciously. Andrei kept his back to Finnigan to give him space.

"I know about your son," Andrei continued, a little hastily, "because I am a swordmaker. These swords know and choose their own witches. I have just finished a sword and I believe you are here to deliver it to its master, Fingal."

The words *I am a swordmaker* rang through the air. The first time he'd uttered it, owned it. They settled in his chest with the same reassurance he felt every time the magic guided him.

I am a swordmaker.

The more he spoke, the more it made sense in his mind. Facets of the Ensis magic came together for him to better understand.

"There are deliverers for each sword. Someone must come, take the sword to the master. The master shouldn't see me—not with gifting. I don't know why. It's a rule of the magic. I don't know all the rules, as the magic breaks them often enough. So, you are here."

The tension in the air didn't alter. Andrei turned around, aware of just how difficult it was to soften an already awkward situation. Finnigan blinked at him, expression like glass. His fingers had tightened into curled fists.

"How do you know my son?"

"The magic."

"Of what?"

"The swords. I am Ensis, the swordmaker called Andrei." He gestured to the little sword, gleaming so brightly in the happy firelight near Sarasam. "That sword is Taravaren. It wants to go home to its master, Fingal. You came here to deliver it. I just finished. The timing is no accident."

Finnigan frowned. "I didn't come here. I transported on accide—"

Some of the color drained from his face.

"Oh."

Andrei reached for Taravaren. Now that Finnigan had warmed up, and some color restored to his face, he'd be able to transport to wherever he called home.

Perhaps Finnigan had been transporting somewhere else and the magic pulled him here. The stuttering words seemed to suggest the possibility. The certainty of the magic when he had this thought felt right above others.

Andrei pulled Taravaren free from her hooks and extended her to Finnigan. Her shiny metal was a luster to behold. She was lean, nimble. Finnigan hesitated, then wrapped his hand around it.

"My son is quite small. My wife expects he will never be a normal size—not tall and strapping like his brothers. The boys in our town tease him relentlessly. He gets in fights he can never win. He comes home bloodied and bruised and desperate to be safe. I've never been so scared for a child of mine. But a sword would give him confidence. Power. Because . . ."

Finnigan trailed away. A sheen of moisture appeared in his eyes.

"This sword will be perfect."

The emotion in Finnigan's voice struck Andrei at the core. Andrei affected as smooth an expression as he could, though Finnigan's relief deeply moved him.

"I know." Andrei nodded. "It's an excellent sword."

"How is this possible? A sword like this must cost—"

"No."

Finnigan reared back, started by the force behind Andrei's tone. Andrei could hardly believe it, or the swelling of darkness, inside of him.

"I cannot accept payment for these swords. Never."

"Why?"

"I don't know."

"Then . . . how do you make these?"

Sweat. Time. Blood. Guidance.

"Magic," he said.

Finnigan studied the blade a third time, and met Andrei's gaze over the top. Taravaren rejoiced, and the darkness that had come as a warning against payment dissipated.

"Magic? It must be powerful magic."

"A new magic system, I think. Or maybe old. Maybe it has

been before and is only coming back now? I don't know." The words made him chuckle. "In fact, I know almost nothing except this: that sword is for Fingal. Taravaren is eager to see her master. If I were you, I wouldn't dawdle here longer than you must. She's annoyingly insistent."

Finnigan, still astonished, only nodded distractedly. He ran his hands over her planes and surfaces with a deep reverence that reassured Andrei. Taravaren would go to a suitable home, a welcoming master. Many swords, such as Taravaren, must move through his life. He'd learn to say goodbye to all of them.

Except Sarasam.

Minutes later, Finnigan had left. Sarasam's wordless chatter ended as soon as Finnigan was gone. The hole that had been Taravaren rang in the quiet. Gone. Taravaren would not return—he felt that in his bones.

It wasn't supposed to.

Andrei regarded Sarasam.

"The magic has little to do with the swords, doesn't it?"

Sarasam gave no response, but in her silence, he sensed a smile.

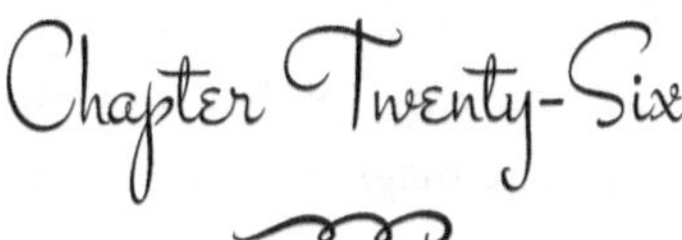

Chapter Twenty-Six

*There is no correlation between wing color and thread
color, no matter how hard you seek for it.*

It's magic, controlled by Hulu.

—Odessa
Year 1295

The next evening, while awaiting news from Sacha for a
second day, Andrei frowned at his new blade.

Yesterday, as he pounded out the piece, still insufferably
not right, it demanded to be so. Every time he attempted to
start over, to convince it to have some other composition, it
resisted. The shape of the blade happened astonishingly fast.
Less than half the time of the other two, which also made little
sense.

Why the hurry?

Finally, he gave in.

The sword, so strange in its feel—oddly brittle, though it

stood solid enough—wanted what it wanted. Fighting had proven useless.

"It's not right! Maybe the mixture of charcoal in the metal is fine, but there should have been more. I know there should have been more. Too little will weaken it. I put in too little."

How he understood this, he didn't question. The magic, certainly. Why would the magic tell him to make a weak metal on purpose?

No response from the sword.

"Why are you so confusing?" he muttered.

He stopped ranting to the magic of his annoyance—it didn't do any good—and just kept going.

"You're confused again."

Mila's accusation came from the other side of the room. She knelt on the floor, river rocks clustered around her. Mila had stacked them in front of the hearth for most of the day, with the warm fire attended, so the ice would melt off of them.

Despite his protests, she didn't seem to mind working at night, like him.

Now, she stacked the rocks in a wall-like formation in the middle of the smithy. She'd mumbled something about a hearth-like structure—but different. Long, so that he could access it from any side. He could have the fire on one end, or the whole thing, which would allow for several swords to heat.

He learned long ago to let Mila's ideas unwind without interruption.

"I'm not confused." He lowered the ingot back into the fire, then released the tongs and set them aside. The bottom smoked lightly. "I'm trying to figure out why this sword is off."

And ignore the fact that the Praznick will happen soon.

"Not enough bone. I told you to add more."

"I couldn't. The magic didn't want me to."

She lifted her brow in silent opposition, but didn't remove

her focus. Two rocks scraped together as she attempted to set one on top. A bowl of gray paste rested on her right. She used a piece of sturdy bark to scoop it, set it on the rock, and stabilize the next rock on top.

Buschye, she called it.

Andrei crouched next to the fire, and watched the yellow color slowly deepen. The gentle sounds of the night descended, and starlight was just visible from beyond the trees. Mila hummed quietly.

The smithy, his blade-forging world, would have been so much lonelier without her at his side. Far less functional, too. Her ability to make things happen, to work quickly, had changed the smithy entirely.

Andrei reached for the poker, and heaped some more coals on top of the blade. The quiet *whoosh* of the bellows flared the heat to greater fire.

He welcomed the warm air that followed.

A message appeared in front of him on a piece of parchment. The sloppy words appeared hastily written.

Meet me at the glacier.
—Sergei

Andrei frowned. Sergei had been unreachable all day. Andrei had tried to find him several times. With Sacha claiming illness and refusing to answer his missives, and Sergei nowhere to be found, Andrei had been the one planning for the *Praznick* with the kitchens most of the day.

He straightened.

"Take the sword out of the fire for me, will you?"

Mila didn't look up. "Yes."

"I need to go back. I don't think I'll return tonight."

She waved a hand a moment before he used one of the ancient spells to take him back to the clannish lands.

"Hulu bless you," she said.

* * *

Sergei tapped his pipe against his teeth with a gentle *click, click, click.* His pallor hadn't improved much, despite the extensive rest.

"I think," Sergei drawled, "that the Guards don't need to be present in uniform at the *Praznick.*"

"Why not?"

"It's the *Praznick.* Why do we need to be so paranoid? Let them have the night off to celebrate with their clan."

Andrei frowned, unable to puzzle through the justification. The Guards took rotations through the years to cover the *Praznick.* Arguably, the most important time to have Guards was then, when the entire clan assembled as one within the glacier.

Sergei leaned over his desk. Ribs jutted beneath his white silk shirt, and he breathed heavy. A yellow color glowed from his skin. No smoke curled from his pipe, but he kept it clutched in his hands.

"Just give the command," Sergei said irritably. "Now, we assume the vote will go through because it will."

"Sergei, I believe—"

"Doesn't matter. The vote must go through, and it will. You've been acting as the Guide for the last month, anyway."

"There is discontent."

"There is always discontent. Allow me one last piece of advice? When you're the Guide, you have to look beyond the now. To what could happen, what will happen, and what has happened. Working with the *maleesa* is the straightforward part of our life, because you live in the moment. It's here and now. They vote Guides into position because someone has to look at everything."

"Yes, Sergei."

"Keep that in mind. What you do as the Guide is in the now. Seeing the past only as it's represented on parchment. We don't have all the answers and we don't know everything! So do the best you can and hope that something works out. . ."

Vigor filled Sergei, so powerful it might have been panic. He thumped a fist on the desk, eyes teary.

"It's never enough, Andrei. Sometimes, you must settle into knowing you weren't enough and hope that Hulu understands the heart and the mind."

"Sergei—"

"No, no further questions. That's all I have to say." Sergei waved a hand, dropped back into the chair. It squeaked, sliding back with an obnoxious, grating sound. "Go."

Hesitating for only a moment, Andrei obeyed. He stepped into the hallway, which ran down the length of the glacier until it disappeared into darker recesses. They rarely used those rooms unless the clan had truly grand prosperity. Just outside the door, he paused.

The rantings of a frenetic mind?

Had Sergei lost his sanity?

A choked, strangled cry came from down the hall. "Future Guide! Future Guide!" Pila, a woman that helped the Accountants, waved both arms. She stumbled, nearly choking on her words. "Oh, Andrei! Andrei!"

"What is it?"

"An arctic baer!"

"Where?"

Her voice issued in a mere squeak. "In the clannish lands!"

He blinked. The sentence made little sense. The Sirilas always protected the clannish lands from outside invaders, even the furry type. Animals never trespassed past the glacier because an invisible, magical barrier separated the worlds.

Arctic baers would often prowl just beyond the clan lands, but nothing passed within.

"You're certain?"

"It's outside. I saw it with my own eyes. They sent me in here to find help."

"Has it hurt anyone?"

"Not yet, but it's prowling around. Clan members are trying to hide. It chased the little Petrov girl! There are no Guards in sight."

"Take me there, please?" he called.

The Sirilas ignored him.

Andrei rushed toward her, panic making his heart pound. The woven carpet that prevented him from falling on the icy floors squeaked under his footfalls.

Together, they rushed outside.

Screams and cries came from not far away. Andrei hurried closer, hand at his side. Sarasam had woken up with a vengeance, streaming promises of protection. With its righteous wrath in his mind, he felt no fear.

An arctic baer stood on its back legs. Even from here, Andrei could see that it towered over his height. The pristinely white fur on top glowed. The depth of yellow tinge on the belly, the hunch at its shoulders, and the wider-set face, meant this would be a male. Territorial. Hungry, too, if the loose fur meant anything.

An irascible one, at that.

Giant claws jutted from paws the size of Andrei's head. He yanked Sarasam from a hidden sheath at his hip where it lay, no larger than a small knife. The magic Mila taught him unfolded; Sarasam elongated and widened as he approached the baer.

All clan members scuttled back, out of the baer's way. The baer dropped with a thud, the black-tipped nose and open lips panting.

Andrei stepped closer.

Sarasam calmed, opening a space in his mind. He no longer heard the frightened cries of the clan members that hustled away from the baer.

Most arctic baers lived in the ground. When winter first showed, they dug out giant burrows that didn't collapse only because of the frozen ground. In summer, the baers roamed. This giant baer must not have an underground burrow. He would be too big, perhaps, which explained his bedraggled, scarred appearance. Nowhere to hide left him open to elements and exposure and timberwolves.

Andrei spoke, a low chant of ancient clannish blessings, quiet in melody. The baer snarled at him, but didn't close in. Sarasam gleamed in the sunlight as he held it out.

Confidence, thanks to Mila's lessons, returned. He knew what to do with Sarasam. He just didn't always execute it well.

"I hope," he murmured to the sword, "that I can be enough for you."

A steady stream of warmth ran through his mind. Taking it as affirmation, Andrei shifted to the left, closer to the edge of the clan lands. Perhaps the baer would follow. If he could get it out of the magic, Sergei could go to the Sirilas grimoire and find the spell to strengthen the boundary again.

Sergei's exhausted face, barely open eyes, replayed back through his mind. His dismissal of Andrei had left no space for a return to Sergei for help. Andrei needed someone else to help him fix this mess.

Over his shoulder, Andrei called, "Pila?"

A terrified squeak replied.

"Yes?"

"Find Sacha. Tell her to locate the Sirilas grimoire and reinforce the boundary. I'll get the baer out of here."

A scuffle of sound meant she'd left, but he didn't turn

around to ensure it. Instead, he kept a steady gaze on the baer and hoped Pila could find Sacha.

Increasing murmurs came from behind him. More clan members, he presumed.

He took another step.

The baer swung to face him, then jumped on his front paws, up and down. The aggressive action meant it felt threatened. A pre-attack ritual. Andrei stepped toward the clan boundary a few more paces.

The baer followed.

"Come, big baer," he sang under his breath, moving steadily closer.

The baer charged, then skidded to a stop. Shocked gasps littered the clan members not far away. Only Sarasam kept Andrei from tripping over his own feet. He kept himself planted, strengthened by the blade.

"That's right," he drawled. "Keep coming."

The baer false charged again, covering the space Andrei had backed up. Andrei continued to move away. Slowly, they slipped the right direction. Farther from the clan, at any rate.

If Pila could just find Sacha . . .

The baer charged. This time, it didn't stop. Andrei felt the *thud* of paws on the ground as it closed in. He held Sarasam higher, but he didn't want to strike. There was no integrity in killing a starving baer. He wanted only to divert it to preserve life.

As the baer closed in, Andrei swept to the side with a spell Mila taught him. He moved far enough the baer wouldn't reach him, but kept himself in his line of sight. The baer skidded on the ice with a growl, turning to chase.

Andrei transported a little farther away.

The baer followed.

Sarasam flashed as he turned and ran, drawing the baer farther from the clan. The thud of footsteps at his back

meant the baer followed. The boundary lurked just ahead . .
.

Ten more steps . . .

A roar, then a swipe across his back, toppled Andrei.

He plummeted, head over feet, into the snow. An instinctual spell transported him away from the baer's broad claws, but not by much. He gasped, reaching for Sarasam, who had fallen out of his reach. Another spell brought it back to his palms as the baer reared up overhead.

Andrei rolled onto his back.

The baer slammed both front legs into the spot where he'd just lain. Ignoring the pulsing pain across his spine, Andrei hurried to his feet. He lifted the sword in front of him to counter a slashing paw. Sarasam clashed with long, black nails. Blood sprayed into the air from a pierced paw.

The baer roared.

A putrid scent issued from its mouth as Andrei scuttled over the boundary line. Movement caught his gaze. Sacha stood in the open space between Andrei and the clan. Her mouth moved rapidly as she read from a book in her hands. Pila stood at her side, hopping from one foot to another.

Andrei dodged another paw swipe with a transportation spell, drawing the baer out of clan lands. Blood lust dilated its eyes. Andrei tripped, scrambled back to his feet. Unused to the ancient spells, he tired quickly. The next transportation spell sent agony through his shoulders.

The baer sprinted across the invisible boundary, toward Andrei.

Pila shrieked.

"Come on!" Andrei shouted when the baer attempted to look back over its shoulder. Half the clan had assembled to watch. "Over here!"

The baer hesitated. Andrei ripped his coat off. Blood slaked down his back, spraying with the desperate movements.

The baer spun, hesitated, then charged. Andrei held the transportation spell at the edge of his mind. The depths of his reserve drained.

He had one opportunity left.

The boundary had better hold.

With a growl, the baer approached. At the last possible second, Andrei loosed the magic. Dark transportation magic swept him away. He landed on his back, inside clan lands, with an agonizing thud.

The baer spun. An enraged roar tore through the air as it charged yet again.

Andrei watched through glazed pain, breath held. Ten steps and it would reach the boundary. It would stop from the magic or cross and eat him for lastmeal. Spittle dripped from giant incisors, shockingly fast despite its behemoth size, as it crossed the boundary.

The Sirilas failed.

A hard paw slammed into Andrei's hip. He felt hot breath on his neck. With a shout, Andrei swung Sarasam high. The blade arced through the air, ringing through his mind with a bloodthirsty song.

Sarasam collided with something firm, then sank.

Deep, deep into flesh.

Blood spurted.

The baer squalled, then stopped in an eerie calm.

Andrei froze, barely able to breathe. Curved talons pressed against the sensitive skin near his eye. The claws didn't move. His back stung with pain and sticky heat when he risked a look.

Blood chugged from the white fur around Sarasam. He lodged the sword in the baer's neck. Sarasam had entered the brain. The lifeless body stared at Andrei with wide, glossy eyes. No breath in the giant ribs.

Andrei, flat on the snow, could only stare.

Silence simmered across the clan lands. He reached out a trembling hand, pressed his fingertips to the wound.

Sarasam was silent but he felt a mix of uncertain emotions. It's regret matched his. Though a sword, it never desired violence. It rose to the occasion to combat it, but didn't yearn for the chance.

By clan custom, the paws belonged to him. He could sever them in the butchering process—for the clan would eat the meat this baer provided—but he wouldn't.

This wasn't why he made swords.

"I'm sorry." He pressed his palm to the baer's head. "I'm sorry it ended like this."

A reckoning would have to come. From the Sirilas, but also him. He had a sword, and he used outside magic, in front of the entire clan. Such inevitability swirled through his mind, lost in the shock of what had just happened.

Running feet came from behind him. Sacha's breathless voice called out as she skidded to a stop.

"Andrei!"

She dropped to her knees at his side. The sticky heat at his back intensified. The world canted around him, oddly out of place, when Sacha gasped. A tingling sensation swept him away, to the comfort of a sleepy darkness.

Chapter Twenty-Seven

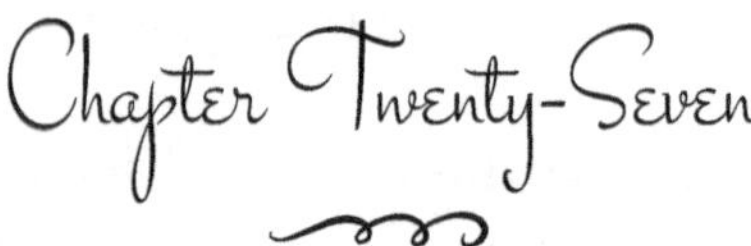

*The path of the maleesa is decided. They have accepted,
or else they wouldn't have survived their birthing process.*

Why do we fight and tear our own wings?

—Odessa, Caretaker
Year 1296

Pain escorted Andrei out of the fuzzy refuge of sleep, where torment didn't remain. He winced, feeling a hard surface on his stomach. Unyielding, but warm. One at a time, his eyes opened. A blurry picture coalesced.

Candles, shadows. Whispers. Moving bodies.

Maman's voice in the haze.

"Andrei?"

He swallowed, licked dry lips. Pressure on his stomach meant he lay there, instead of his back. Why?

"Yes, *Maman*."

"Are you in pain?"

"Yes," he croaked. Flashes of memory served. He wished

they hadn't. The arctic baer, Sarasam. Panic bolted through him. He planted his hands, pushed up. "Sarasam!"

Sacha's voice replied. "I have it."

A glint of metal against the candle light appeared near the wall, close to her voice. Misery tore through his back as he lowered down. *Maman* clucked her disapproval. Her cool hand pressed to the spot where his neck met his back.

"Stop jarring the wounds, *fil*. You'll interrupt my healing. The Sirilas magic works on your wounds now. You received them to save the clan, so it is healing faster than usual. Go to sleep. Avoid the pain. We will be here."

Grateful for the permission, he obeyed.

* * *

"They think the arctic baer was a sign from Chthu."

The wry words, spoken from Sacha's lips the next morning, made Andrei scowl. He sat on a stool near the smithy hearth. Mila fed logs and twigs into tender flames that grew in greedy licks, consuming each piece.

Andrei moved his shoulders, the discomfort palpable. New, pink flesh covered his back where the baer had slashed him with its claw. A mild fever had consumed him through the night, but burned off. The wound should have required weeks to heal, but the Sirilas magic had conjured a miracle.

He ran a hand over his face. The movement made him wince. Though healed farther in a single night than he could have achieved in two weeks, he wouldn't fully recover for several more days.

"The clan will be afraid of me now."

Sacha didn't disagree. He winced, uncertain if the pain was from the wound or reality.

"It . . . doesn't paint a simple picture," she finally said. "You used outside magic. The Sirilas grimoire failed us twice.

The clan remembers you saving the High Priest, but thought it was a fluke. Now, you'll need to explain Sarasam. You may have done a heroic thing, but you did it in a way that conjured questions at the wrong time to have questions. The *Praznick* is tomorrow."

He swallowed, but the tension remained in his throat. "I know."

The moment *Maman* had released him from her dwelling, he walked to his own and transported away from inside. The pressure of the magic had been agony. Transporting while hurt was not a fun thing, but it had been better than sitting in his dwelling.

His nose ruffled.

He just wanted to get away.

Andrei dropped his head into his hands. "I know that the *Praznick* is tomorrow. Please, don't remind me." He expected Mila to crack a joke. *At least you finally know something*, but she didn't. Her pervasive silence lent weight to the already tense air.

Fortunately, Sarasam remained quiet. Eager, but not bothersome. Sacha frowned at the floor. She leaned against the wall, where fresh firewood dripped water and smoke curled off the wet logs. Mila had restocked them. She said little, sent worried gazes to his back, and worked on her project in the middle of the room. He felt her concern like a tether. A comfort in a tempestuous time.

"What of the taxes?" he asked.

Sacha scowled. "It's not as easy as I expected to break into their tax records, but I believe I've found a way."

"Sacha . . ."

"No." She held up a hand. "We have to know, Andrei. I'll figure it out."

"Did you speak with Katya?"

"No. They aren't taking visitors after the welcoming ceremony, just to prevent the baby from further chances to be sick. In the meantime, some of the clan members say that Hulu has forsaken you. I caught two witches attempting to suggest such a thing to your *maman* this morning."

He tensed.

Sacha waved him off with a roll of her eyes. "My sister is fierce. She took care of them."

Andrei turned back to the heat of the flames. The difficult sword lay on the table. He built up the fire to heat it to prepare for its quench, the final stage. The part that broke the weak swords and strengthened the toughest. He had no hope for it to survive, what with the strange mixtures the magic insisted he give it. Yet, at the same time, everything felt tied into this sword.

He had to make it work, and it had to work now.

He didn't understand why.

Sacha pushed away from the wall. "I'm glad you're doing better, Andrei, but heed me when I advise you to be at the *Praznick*. Your disappearance would cement suspicion. The clan is grateful, but the clan is scared. The magic that protects us has failed and the blame will rest on you now that they've seen evidence of your outside magic."

Andrei scowled. "No more than you."

"I know their suspicions aren't true," she said gently, "but they don't."

"I don't want to go back, nor attend the *Praznick*, no matter what the outcome."

Admitting the words cost him something. The hope in Sacha's face crumbled. Her expression slackened.

"I see."

He ran a hand over his face, through his hair. She didn't see. She couldn't possibly *see*.

"Fine." He sighed, an aggravated sound. "I'll . . . try to come back in the morning and be visible during the day. I'll be present for the *Praznick,* I swear it. First, I must quench the sword. I won't return until it's finished."

"I'll do what I can about the taxes."

She reached for the door, gave Mila a smile that disappeared too quickly, and stepped outside. Andrei stared at the doorway with a heavy frown. Mila straightened, gray paste on her hands and river rock around her legs.

"She means well."

"I know she does," he mumbled. "But she's not good at it."

Mila chuckled, turned back to her work. Andrei stared out, lost in a haze of thought, while the fire built itself ever hotter.

Chapter Twenty-Eight

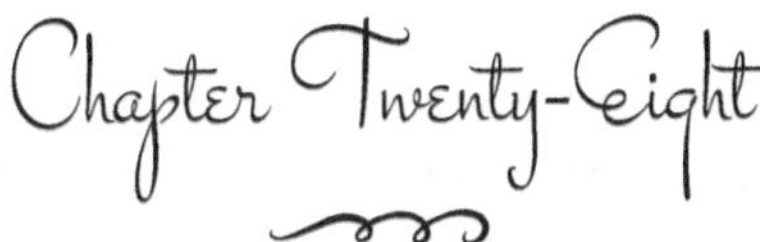

Where is the intersection of magic and life for these creatures?

Where soul meets flesh.

—Daria, Seller
Year 1357

"Well," *Maman* sighed. "The *maleesa* has lasted most of the way through the pupal stage. The only thing left is the wings. Arguably, the part where most of them die. This is when they decide."

Together, Andrei and *Maman* peered into the glass case, viewing the *maleesa* of honor for the *Praznick* that evening.

"Will the wings bud in time for the ceremony?"

"Hulu knows, my *fil.*"

Andrei studied the *maleesa* through the thin veil in which it protected itself. A fallacy. The *maleesa* put up a worthless shield against the world that could descend on it. The Andrei of old would have *something* to say about the bug. He could only conjure the truth.

It is no sword.

Could he not even appreciate the beauty of a magical creature anymore?

If the *maleesa* survived the emergence of its wings this evening, and spun the silk threads before the sun rose after the ceremony, it would foretell fortune and prosperity for the clan for the next year. If it died, didn't spin any thread, or the thread was brittle and broken, it would foretell hard days ahead.

"The beauty comes from the struggle," *Maman* said. She straightened, her hair sweeping the edge of the glass panes. "With any luck, we won't have to sneak a different *maleesa* in here before the clan finds out that the *Praznick maleesa* has died. That happened one year, you know."

"No. When?"

She waved a hand. "Years ago. Clan members panicked when word spread, but Sacha and I smuggled another one in. We showed the clan the rumors were false. They attempted to track down the origin of the rumor for days and never found it. I'd thrown it in the fire."

A wink seemed to tease him. Andrei could only stare.

Was everything about his old life a lie? All the false perceptions. What he thought had been steady and true had also been . . . not real and loose. No stable ground actually existed. Not even routine and structure, because it hovered on rocky ground.

He managed a weak smile for *Maman's* sake, but only barely. She put a warm hand on his shoulder and gave a soft squeeze.

"Andrei?"

"Nothing," he said quickly, anticipating her question. "Nothing is wrong. I'm just thinking."

"About the *Praznick*?"

"About everything."

The words sat on the tip of his tongue. *I don't want to be the Guide. More than the clan lands, I want to make swords.*

He couldn't say them.

The Ensis had required his secret-keeping, and he had done so. The thought of telling *Maman* about his new magic bound up his throat, which only surfaced more questions.

Why Mila, why Sacha, but not *Maman*?

If there was any witch he thought it would be foolish to trust with such a secret, Sacha would be the one. Mila, her quiet life, the way she excelled with everything he couldn't do, made more sense. She fit at the smithy. Her strengths countered all the things he didn't know.

But Sacha?

Maman would understand. He could feel it in his bones. Yet, he obeyed the magic. In most regards, he had no choice. It simply wouldn't allow him to speak.

"Come." He stood, hand held out. "I'll escort you to your dwelling to get ready. We only have a few hours."

She finished wrapping a scarf around her neck while he blew out the remaining candles. The banked fire in the corner continued to burn, emitting a gentle orange-and-red glow. The night clan member would arrive soon to check the temperature. *Maman* left the record scroll with the other notes, near an inkpot and a feather.

Together, they stepped into the brittle evening air. After tonight, an elongation of light would gradually occur.

"So," *Maman* said with a sprightly voice. "About—"

Something hard struck him on the back. Andrei made a sound in his throat and whirled around. A collection of torches and clan members gathered close to the *maleesa* caves, as if they had been waiting. Fifteen witches clustered under and around the torches. Enough light allowed him to see facial expressions. The hostility was unmatched.

He stepped in front of *Maman*.

"Go," he breathed.

She hesitated, but he gave her another nudge. Seeing the amassing group—more witches joined from different paths every second—she obeyed without a sound. Instead of scuttling to her dwelling, she split down a different path.

Hopefully to find Sergei.

Sacha.

Anyone.

"What do you want?" he called.

Janokov led the group. He shifted uneasily from one foot to another, regarding Andrei from beneath a lowered hood. Their breaths billowed in front of them, whisked away by a vague wind.

"Rumors have been circulating," Janokov cried. "Rumors that you have a career and interest outside of the clan. With swords. That you've been leaving for long periods of time to work away from here. You are up for vote this night and we deserve the truth!"

Janokov held onto a torch lit with an old, discarded swath of silk soaked in potions to keep it burning. It snapped and crackled, emitting occasional sparks. The stunning effect lent an aggression to their irate expressions.

So, the situation was worse than Andrei expected. Any fear the clan may have had of him had already turned to malice in the space of a day. They stood before him for an accounting.

Andrei held up a hand. The clan already knew or had puzzled a few details together about the swordmaking. He couldn't hide it. He'd stopped the arctic baer, but revealed his entire hand.

"You deserve the truth, but not like this. Not as an ambush."

"When?" Janokov demanded. "Before the *Praznick?*"

Andrei opened his mouth, not at all sure what would come out, when a body appeared in front of him.

Sergei.

He stood tall, straight, but thin as a stick. He leaned on a cane for support. His knees trembled.

"Andrei is your future Guide," he called through a wheeze. "If you have a problem with it, you may go through the proper channels to request an audience. Or you make your wishes known tonight, at the *Praznick*, with the final vote. Under no Guide is violence and threatening allowed. He will answer whatever questions you may have afterward."

Several clan members shrank back. In Sergei's presence, the light from the torches dimmed. One extinguished, as if a wind had swept through, though nothing moved at all.

His sallow appearance and hollow cheeks didn't lessen the ferocity of his voice. Janokov slinked back, eyes downcast. His lips pursed together, but he didn't open them to speak again. Those at his back followed.

"Follow me, Andrei," Sergei said. "To the Meeting House."

Andrei followed.

* * *

Sergei positioned himself in front of the fire, in an empty chair. Andrei stood off to the side. He could meet Sergei's eyes this way, though Sergei hadn't been eager to meet his.

Tension hummed between them, fraught with their last encounter in Sergei's office. The increasing heat and passion in Sergei's voice lingered with Andrei now.

"Put your sword on the table, Andrei."

Andrei hesitated. Sarasam lay in its scabbard, waiting at his side, silent. The only certainty he had these days.

"The Sirilas grimoire won't allow another witch to have a weapon in the same room as the Guide. You know this."

Reluctantly, Andrei obeyed. Was that true? He'd been in the same room as Sergei with Sarasam before. The day they met Alek. In fact, every day since he received Sarasam, he'd carried it with him.

He set Sarasam on the table to his right. Firelight flickered off its surface. Sergei's hand rested on the curved arm of the chair, worn to a smooth polish over the years. His fingers drummed on it.

"Your *maman* is fine. I saw to it myself."

"Thank you, Sergei."

"You killed a baer yesterday."

The statement left nothing to say, and Andrei wondered for whose benefit he uttered it. Surely not Andrei's.

Unsure of what Sergei expected, he said, "Yes."

"You had to."

"I didn't like it, but the Sirilas did nothing."

Sergei hid a wince, but not very well. "There will be many things you must do that you won't like. They might seem distasteful to you, even brutal. Perhaps . . . unnecessary. But they'll be a requirement. It's part of accepting how the world turns. Whether you liked it or not, the lesson was a good one."

The distant tone of his voice made Andrei wonder if they spoke about the same thing.

Sergei leaned forward, used his cane to poke at a fire. Flames sprang to life out of a low bed of coals. He must have been working here, because the room felt warm.

"Janokov," Andrei said. "He only wanted answers. I will—"

A hand rose, silencing him. "I know what Janokov said. I know what Janokov thinks. He's stirred up a mob of witches and came at you, and everything worked out fine."

Wearily, Andrei sat down. No, that wasn't entirely it, but it wasn't a wrong summation, either.

"We don't have a lot of time," Sergei continued. "The *Praznick* starts soon. There are things you and I must discuss."

A glance outside confirmed. Daylight dropped toward the horizon, a promise of the upcoming night. The *Praznick* began when night descended and all light fled on the shortest day of the year.

"Tell me, Andrei, about Janokov's accusations. He mentioned swords, didn't he?"

"What about them?"

"Are they true?"

Andrei halted, but the Ensis magic didn't prevent him. "Yes, the rumors are true."

"There are other swords?"

"Several."

"Yours?"

"No."

Sergei's face didn't alter. Not a snuffle of surprise or lift of thin eyebrows. He stared into the flames, hands propped on top of his cane. Andrei wanted to engage with his own line of questioning.

Did you pay the taxes?

Why don't the books add up to the storage room?

What are you hiding?

Sergei spoke first. "The sword you brought here before, when Alek first visited, was not just a distraction, then."

"No, Sergei. The sword is much more than a distraction."

The hours at the anvil, in front of the fire, flame under metal, sparks at his hands, whirled through his body. He felt the smithy in his blood. The pull of the magic. The encompassing, overwhelming feeling of being plunged into something he couldn't stop.

"There is a house?" Sergei asked.

"Yes."

"Is that where you have been going?"

"Yes."

"Tell me about swordmaking."

The reply stopped in Andrei's throat. Swirls of anxiety and doubt spiraled from Sarasam. Its uneasiness amplified his own. Andrei swallowed, his throat unlocking enough to say, "I cannot."

For the first time, Sergei looked into his eyes. His brow dropped.

"You cannot explain?"

"No."

"Why?"

Andrei shook his head. Several heartbeats passed before Sergei leaned back, eyebrows canted together.

"That's disappointing."

Andrei felt suspended in air as Sergei studied him for a protracted length of time. Finally, Sergei turned away. With a shove of his stick, he pushed a log higher into the building flames. A spray of cinders erupted in the chimney.

"You are to become the Guide tonight, if the clan will still vote for you. According to what I've heard from clan members, there are still supporters out there. You have a chance."

The words didn't bring as much relief as they should have. Nothing but confusion. This had been the day he once looked forward to with the stoic certainty of someone that knew his place in the world and had accepted it.

Now?

He knew less than ever.

Sacha had given no report of any findings, which meant he had no proof against Sergei that he could use to defend himself. Nor did he have any hope that the Ensis magic would allow him to explain swordmaking. He would stand before his clan as a leader or be exiled as a traitor.

No middle ground.

The only truth that Andrei could be certain of was that a choice awaited. Which life did he want? The Sirilas magic, or the Ensis?

No matter what he chose, he disappointed someone. Down one path lay certainty, leadership, and decisiveness. Comfort and family, too. Belonging to the witches that he'd known all his life.

The other path?

He couldn't even name what might await him, except for the swords. Always the swords. Unknown paths. Probably desperation. Hunger. Uncertainty. Grappling for survival away from the clan, and lonely days where he might see no one.

But also the swords, and they would be worth it.

Sergei continued.

"The vote will happen at the beginning of the *Praznick* this year, though we normally wait until the end. Sufficient reasons to nudge the timeline sooner exist, I believe. It'll be my last act as Guide. I hope."

A nervous tremor rocked Sergei's voice. For the first time since all of this began, Andrei realized he wasn't the only witch deeply affected by whatever events would occur over the next several hours.

Sergei had invested as much—if not more—than Andrei into this process.

"If they don't vote for you as Guide, you'll leave the clan lands. It will ruin your life and cause a fracture in our stability. I can't guarantee that you could return as more than a visitor, though I know the outer clan support villages would accept your help."

Sergei tacked the last on with a glance his way. Andrei

pretended not to notice the silent, searching question in his words.

What did Sergei expect from him?

Sergei reached up, smoothed the tips of his fingers down the sides of his mustache. The silky strands already lay flat against his skin.

"Of course, all of this can go away," he added affably. "You need only to declare yourself allegiant to the Sirilas magic in front of the clan. Renounce any other magic, any other path. It would satisfy Janokov and those in the clan that are afraid you've created this issue if you renounce it at the *Praznick*."

Andrei's mouth turned to ash.

"Renounce?"

Sergei lifted a brow. "The Sirilas magic has given you everything, hasn't it? Your life. Your comfort. Care for your *maman*, healing for a wound that might have killed you otherwise. Is there really a decision here, Andrei? Swords or clan?"

The chiding in his tone, filled with disappointment, cut deep. Sergei had been like a *papan* to him for years. To end their mentorship in this way . . .

"Loyalty to the Sirilas magic isn't much to ask, Andrei. And it is something that I will ask of you tonight. If you don't renounce the other magic and take your place as Guide, then I'll take drastic measures."

A dark sensation stole over Andrei. What could *drastic measures* possibly mean? He resisted the urge to step back. Sarasam stirred to life with a nudge of concern.

"Drastic?" he croaked.

Sergei opened his hand. "Imagine if one of your swords went to our enemies. How would you ever live with yourself again? Your blade spilling the blood of a clan member. Such would destroy the Sirilas magic. The clan. How would you justify such a thing?"

Andrei's breath held. He tried to work through the shock such an idea mustered, but he couldn't find the willpower.

In fact, he'd never thought of it before.

What if?

"Could you promise not to give swords to an enemy? Or to outfit them only for clan members?"

Andrei shook his head. His body plunged to a new chill. He thought of Finnigan, the deliverer. Of the way the swords spoke in Andrei's mind. They made the decisions, and he followed. This wasn't his magic to control.

"You see that this is a problem, Andrei?"

Reluctantly, he nodded.

Indeed, how hadn't he seen it before?

"The clan believes this new sword is a curse from Chthu. Now that they know you do outside magic of some kind, trust is broken. We must fix it, Andrei. We must. And we must fix it tonight. Renouncing all other magic and re-adhering to the Sirilas is the only way to do it."

Sergei stood slowly. His bones trembled under the effort, but the shaky effect didn't diminish his powerful glare, determined jaw, pressed lips.

"You will be Guide, Andrei, and you will guide us into a friendly and prosperous relationship with the Southern Network. You will restore balance to the magic and erase old debts. I have ensured that there are clan members to possibly guarantee the vote swings in your favor. They must act as I've requested, and I think they will. Then you can restore balance, clean up the clan that has become so divided."

"You divided it!" Andrei cried. "You were the one who wanted to show the *maleesa* to the High Priest."

Sergei ducked his head for a moment. His voice was low when he said, "No, that's not it. I don't want to show the *maleesa* to the Network. There are . . . other things at play here."

The dark fear continued, rolling down Andrei's back now. It crackled along his spine in warning. He sucked in a sharp breath.

"What?"

Outside, thudding boots approached. Their reverberations drew his gaze toward the door. Sergei didn't move, locked into place. His body shook so much now that his cane bounced on the ground, clattering like old teeth.

"Sergei?"

The heavy tread stopped, and became a foreboding bang on the wooden door. Before Andrei could summon the power to say a word, the door flew open. Alek advanced inside, Nikolov at his side. The grim expression on Alek's face illuminated as he stepped in.

One side of his mouth canted up.

"Ah, Sergei. So you brought him, as we agreed. Very good, very good. Well . . ." Alek gazed around pleasantly. "Shall we begin? I believe we have a *Praznick* to watch."

Chapter Twenty-Nine

The final phase of transformation is a violent, thrashing
thing.

The maleesa must fight their own home, their own body,
to allow their wings to emerge. It must shed the pupal
veil that held the changing larva. The old layers set
aside. No more wrinkled, hairy skin.

Yet, so many fail.

Most do not have the strength, after all they have been
through, to complete their transformation at the end.

Of this batch of three hundred, only six have emerged.

The others have shriveled. Some stop halfway out.
Wings torn, antennae smashed, body too tired to press
forward. They curl up on the lip of freedom, and die.

I will cast their tired bodies into the embers for Hulu to

accept again, and will pray that Chthu does not intervene.

It is a prayer that other maleesa might fight harder.

—Mirella, Overseer
Year 1409

Alek's fixed smile brought him farther into the Meeting House. "Andrei, how nice it is to see you!" he cried.

Andrei ignored him to study Nikolov instead. The older man stepped in with a great cloak made of furs billowing behind. Nikolov's glittering stare met Andrei's. The glacial chill that entered Andrei's blood had a worrisome slant.

"Mind stepping aside?" Nikolov asked.

Before Andrei could speak, the cold iron of a manacle clasped around one wrist. He sucked in a sharp breath, glanced over as a second one grabbed his other wrist. The feeling of something hooking his belly button and jerking him back followed.

He slammed into the rock wall next to the hearth. His teeth jarred painfully. The back of his head throbbed where it had slammed into a smooth river rock above the fire. Pain reverberated down his neck, shot through his temples.

Alek stopped right in front of him, a maniacal glint in his eyes. "We'd just like to make sure you don't leave before we're done here," he drawled.

Anchored to the wall next to the hearth, where heat crawled through the river rock to warm his back, Andrei couldn't move. Invisible, magical bonds held him fast. He didn't struggle against the magic. There was no purpose, and he had a sense that Alek *wanted* him to fight.

Sarasam remained on the table. Neither of them seemed to notice it.

"Andrei," Nikolov said, his deep voice barreling ahead of him. Sergei appeared small against the broad boards of his chair. "You have come here to talk with Sergei about what is best for the clan, have you not?"

Alek snickered, stepping away. His heavy boots shed snow all over the floor. It melted in puddles that reflected the torchlight. Andrei kept his focus on the melting flakes. Shock rendered him almost useless.

Sergei.

Alek.

Nikolov.

Something came together in hazy lines. Clearly, Sergei had . . . some form of alliance or relationship with them. Otherwise, he would never have allowed them to walk into this room uninvited. This was clannish land, even if used for negotiation with the Network.

Only one thing became blatantly clear: betrayal.

Sarasam keened. He ignored it, tried to make room for him to think about what to do next. Nothing occurred to him.

"It just so happens," Nikolov continued, unbothered by the silence, "that Alek and I have also come to discuss what is best for the future of the clan. Do you have any idea what that might be?"

Nikolov stopped next to Sergei's chair, gaze fixated on Andrei. Andrei said nothing. With the side of his boot, Nikolov kicked Sergei's cane, which propped against the wall. Sergei gritted his teeth, said nothing as he righted the stick.

Nikolov shifted until he stood in front of Andrei. A stunning smack to the side of Andrei's face jerked him out of his stare. The spiral of terror that he felt for the clan dissipated in the brazen show of violence. Andrei attempted to right his mind after the blow.

"You will answer me!"

Nikolov's shout rippled through the room. All at once, the Ensis magic hit him like a falling star in the gut. It activated, swelling inside his body. The sword at the smithy streamed through his mind, giddy. Whirling.

Delighted.

A deliverer had come.

Andrei lifted his head. Felt how the Ensis magic responded to their presence and knew that he had to give the sword up.

To Alek.

Acid rose to the back of his throat. He panted now, bound by the magic and frozen to the spot, except for his head. The spell allowed him to look up and to the left and right.

Mila had taught him enough ancient magic to overpower this spell, but they wouldn't know that. They'd assume that, as Guide, he adhered to the expectations Sergei set and not use outside magic. Something he would continue to use to their advantage.

The truth might be his only hope.

Nikolov grunted.

"Alek and I will attend the *Praznick* tonight. Call it repayment of a debt, if you will. Sergei hasn't mentioned this? Sergei, you decrepit old bat. Just how *much* have you hidden?"

Nikolov ripped the cane from the wall, then used it to tilt Andrei's chin a little higher. Forced to look at him, Andrei met his level gaze. His cheek throbbed, but he ignored it.

"We will view your bugs, your clan, and your ways. Then we will leave. No one will be any wiser for us being there, and then all will be forgiven. For now."

Forgiven.

The word rang through Andrei's head. Even if he wanted to, he wouldn't have been able to ask his questions. Nikolov had wrapped his throat in a tingling magic that prevented speech.

Nikolov turned to face Sergei. The old man had shrunk

further into the chair, curling into himself like a dead *maleesa,* fallen from the thin veil that had once been its entire world.

"Won't it, Sergei? Erased, like so much smoke. All the mistakes, the lies, the fear. Gone in a single night. All those years of stress and angst and hiding come to nothing but a *Praznick.*"

Sergei whimpered.

Alek laughed. "Ice and taxes, Sergei. That's all anyone can be certain of in the Southern Network. Isn't it?"

"Ice, taxes, and silk," Nikolov purred. "We're here, Andrei, for the secrets of the silk trade. We won't leave until I am satisfied, and then all the debt that Sergei has built over the last ten years of not paying taxes to the Network will be . . . gone."

Andrei's gut twisted. His gaze shot to Sergei. His head hung too low to see his eyes.

"What," Nikolov said to Andrei through gritted teeth, "do you have to say for your clan, Guide? You have inherited a great debt, and we have given you a way out of it. Will you oppose our presence and lose your life? Or will you accept that we will be at the *Praznick* tonight to get what we came here for?"

Alek removed the magic from around Andrei's throat. Andrei managed a derisive half-smile. "Welcome to the clannish lands, High Priest, Council Member. I believe I have a sword for you."

* * *

Silence hung in the room.

Alek stepped closer, regarding Andrei with deep suspicion.

"A sword?"

The snap of the fire behind them interrupted the hanging

astonishment. Whatever Nikolov expected Andrei to say, *that* hadn't been it.

Andrei held Alek's gaze. He could almost see the memory replay through Alek's mind. The arctic baer that attacked. Andrei's adept skill with the sword. The sense of jealousy that had permeated the air when a mere clannish witch had saved the High Priest.

Alek's jolly attitude toward Andrei afterward had been all show, as Alek radiated rampant antipathy now. The High Priest had lost his calculated exterior for a far more rash one. Behind the wall of violence that always lurked beneath the surface of Alek's gaze, Andrei saw it.

Curiosity.

"The sword," Andrei said, just to keep the power in the conversation, "is just finished."

A lie.

Sort of.

He had quenched the sword to strengthen it, but it still didn't feel right. There had been too much slag. Too much uncertainty hovering around the metal. It felt thin as he pounded it out, but it hadn't split. No fractures appeared during the quench, either. He wouldn't have known what to do if they had.

Nikolov barked something to Alek in an unfamiliar language. Not *Yazika,* nor the common tongue. The words, low-toned, were difficult to make out behind his husky voice. Andrei didn't need to know what Nikolov said. The way he held his shoulders, the slight tilt of his head, revealed Nikolov's agenda. He didn't trust Andrei, didn't want Alek to take the sword.

Alek's gaze swung back to Andrei.

"Where is the sword?"

"Allow me to move my right hand and it will come."

Another pause.

Finally, the magic retreated from Andrei's right arm and shoulder, bleeding away like a second skin peeling free. Andrei held out his palm, and the desired sword appeared.

A dark feeling swelled within when metal touched fingertips. He didn't summon the sword, didn't want to hand it over, but the Ensis magic worked through him now. He was no master of swords.

He was a *servant* of swords.

Alek wrenched it from Andrei's grasp. The sword exulted. He wanted to ask its name, but he sensed it wouldn't tell him. It didn't *want* a name. Once the sword left Andrei's touch, it faded from his mind. Just like Mangana and Taravaren. He could still hear the strange, swirling thoughts, but not so loudly.

This had gone wrong. Technically, he sensed he was supposed to give the sword to a deliverer, but Alek stood right here. Andrei had been the deliverer for Mila, yet he could have sworn the swordmaker *didn't* deliver the swords.

He felt a frisson of frustration because of the lack of clarity. The Ensis magic made no *sense* when the rules moved and shifted. The Sirilas magic had a map. A path.

Alek inspected the nameless sword from several paces away at first. His presence in the smithy would have felt like petting a cat the wrong way. Irritating. Wrong by so many means. At least the sword came here.

Alek's head tipped back as he held the sword overhead. Andrei hadn't polished it yet, so the black exterior held no luster, which created a ghastly thing. Sharp, too. The slice of it whistling through the air sent a shiver through the room.

"Very nice," Alek murmured.

"Though not polished, it should be functional. Deadly, if not beautiful. It's . . . asking for you."

"The sword speaks?"

"To me."

"Will it speak to me?"

"No, I don't think so."

Nikolov lifted an irritated eyebrow. Alek's brow rose, his light eyebrows illuminated by the weak sunset slanting through the windows. He touched the cool metal with the tips of his fingers. A note of reverence entered his voice.

"The length?"

"It's shorter than a standard long sword, with the angle up at the top. The handle is . . . quite long, but it seems to balance well enough. There is no guard."

"What advantage does it give?"

Andrei searched for an answer. "I believe," he said, for it was all the magic would allow him to say, "that's what you will discover as you use it. If anything, it's one of a kind."

Interest illuminated Alek's gaze. He grunted, swung the weapon around. It glinted vaguely as it whirled through the air. While Alek mumbled to himself, attempting different sword routines, Nikolov turned back to Sergei and Andrei.

"Now that we're done with *that*, there is one hour until full sunset. We have a few things to discuss, then we'll return. Stay here. South Guards surround this place, so attempting to leave will only result in your death at a most unfortunate time."

Nikolov stepped back outside. Alek cackled, slapped Andrei on the cheek, and joined Nikolov in the cold with his new sword at his side.

It never ceases to amaze me how hard the maleesa would fight during their transformative process to survive. At the end of such rigor and trial, they did nothing but spin.

Spin, spin.

As if they were perfectly content to fulfill their life mission, then die.

—Boris, Gatherer
Year 1370

The moment they left, Andrei called for Sarasam.
"Sarasam!"
Nothing.
No movement.
Not a sound in his head.
Sergei, Nikolov, and Alek spiraled through his mind like a braided song. The depth of betrayal that Sergei had given into

became more and more apparent. Sacha had been correct. Sergei didn't pay the taxes after all, and Nikolov and Alek used such a truth to leverage against Sergei. They'd receive what they most wanted.

The silk trade.

But why?

With the questions bubbled fury.

Terror.

"Sarasam!"

No reply.

His right arm remained free of the magic. He extended it, but the sword gave no movement. No nudge. As if the magic had never existed. As if he'd dreamed all of this into being.

Why would the Ensis magic abandon him now?

"They will be back," Sergei said hoarsely. "If you attempt to break free, the clan will suffer. They have enough trials coming their way. We shouldn't add to them."

Sergei's mournful words, spoken like a defeated animal, shocked Andrei out of his rage. He tried to flex his other hand, break whatever invisible bonds held him there, but it was futile.

He couldn't escape with brawn.

He could with magic.

The gradual darkening of the world increased his actions. Right now, clan members would gather around the feast. *Maman* and Sacha should have crossed the ice already, the *maleesa* and its cage hovering between them, protected by the Sirilas magic.

Laughing children. Plentiful food. The ice-lacquered walls inside the glacier sweating from the warmth of so many bodies. In its weakened state, would the Sirilas magic maintain the integrity of the ice walls?

Sergei peered at Andrei from his wooden chair. Andrei ignored the silent plea for understanding in the man's searching gaze. Betrayal burned too deep to consider atonement, like captured fire in his bones.

Finally, he could bear it no longer.

"Why, Sergei?"

The Guide dropped his gaze to the floor. He swallowed, throat bobbing.

"I . . . felt I had no choice."

"What happened?"

"There were back taxes when I first began as Guide. Not much. Enough that we could compensate in a year with steady profits. Not unusual, according to the books. Other Guides had played with tax payments and repayments. But then . . ."

He trailed away for a moment, lost in other thoughts. With a shake of his head, he pulled out of them.

"Then came the difficulties. Under producing caves. Poorly positioned Guides to the Caves. The sickness that swept through from the villages to here? Your *Maman* spoke of them? The year was so cold that we couldn't maintain firewood for the *maleesa* and had to merge into fewer caves, which bled our production and profits."

"Not even the magic?"

Sergei shrugged.

Maman had told stories of the difficult times, a clump of six years when the clan continued to weather trial after trial. Losing his sisters had been part of those horrendous times. Eventually, the clan seemed to right themselves. Catch up.

Or had they?

"I made a deal with Leonid, the former High Priest, to pay taxes on installments. He took free silk for silence about the debt. I felt it would get us through the rough time, but it only hurt us in the long run. For I gave up silk and received only his silence. I thought he could consider the silk compensation for some of the debt, but the next year came and our total owed was greater with interest. Leonid had duped me."

Sergei slouched into the chair, head tilted back. He didn't move far. Nikolov must have strapped him to the chair with magic, because his legs didn't shift.

"A silencing agreement?" Andrei asked.

"If that's what you want to call it. He seemed pleased enough to forget about us in exchange for the silk that made his wife happy."

"Then he died," Andrei murmured, licking his lips. The picture coalesced. "And Alek and Nikolov took over."

A stark whisper confirmed. "Yes. We have been making payment on the back taxes for years, but it's pebbles against a rockslide."

Quiet drenched the room. Further explanation wasn't necessary. Nikolov used the bargaining power of owed taxes to navigate a way into the silk trade.

"You couldn't be honest with the clan?"

"There would have been fear in a time already rife with devastation. The production of silk had been declining, so were sales. It . . . seemed like the best option at the time. You know how sensitive the clan is to change. They fear the slightest deviation . . ."

"Yet you taught me total honesty and transparency!"

"Yes," Sergei said with feeling, "so that you would never experience what I have. The guilt. The terror. I've lived with the fear of the High Priest calling in our debt all my life."

"Is that why you sent me to the castle?"

"You needed to go and see their life. Comprehend their power and how small we are before them."

"So that I'd give in to what Nikolov wants?"

"You needed to understand, Andrei. We have locked you into the clan for so long that you lacked proper perspective."

The fury didn't abate with this deeper explanation. It intensified. Sergei had lied, made assumptions, all this time guided the clan on a rocky, false path. What trust could they have in *any* leader?

Andrei shook his head. "No, I refuse to believe that Nikolov is so much stronger than us. I refuse to believe that we have so little power. We have the Sirilas grimoire. It will protect the *maleesa*."

"For a long time, I believed that as well."

The melancholy echo of Sergei's voice only made the tension worse.

"You don't believe it now?"

Sergei scoffed. A light sound, more breath than bitterness. "No, I don't."

Andrei's heart squeezed too tightly. No wonder the magic had been failing. The broken balance, indeed. Secrets. Debts. A Guide to the Clan who didn't truly believe in the magic. Had Sergei even maintained the perimeter spells for their protection?

How could the clan possibly weather this?

"If you had just said *something*," Andrei insisted, desperate for this to make sense. "There would have been collaboration with other clan members. A sharing of the burden and the result. No wonder the *maleesa* have been dying! The magic wavering. The most basic tenants of the Sirilas magic, the clannish family, has been fading for years. You never said a word!"

"I know."

The bitterness of such a response stung deep. Andrei's upper lip curled in disgust. Was all of their time together, Sergei's careful imparting of knowledge, a waste? Sergei stared at the wall like a lost old man. A glazed expression of shock filled his face, as if he felt the full weight of his decisions.

"Perhaps," Sergei allowed quietly, "there may have been a better way to act. Alas, I did not take it. Here we are."

A slight lessening of the angst loosened in Andrei's chest. Despite his rage, he couldn't help his history with the old man.

Whatever Sergei did or didn't do, he wasn't a malicious witch like Nikolov.

Misguided and frightened, but not nefarious.

"What now?" Andrei asked. "We need to do something."

Agitation coursed through him. He pictured the dining hall, where the *Praznick* celebration would take place. The hundreds of clannish workers packed inside. The merry laughter, bright gazes, flushed cheeks, the scents of spices in the air.

Above it all, the *maleesa*.

"Nikolov and Alek will view the *Praznick*." Sergei's shoulders lifted. "They say that alone will satisfy the debt. They will clear it for you to start fresh and the clan will never need to know it happened."

"It's a lie, Sergei. Alek and Nikolov will not just observe and leave. You must know this."

"Of course it is a lie, but there is no other way. I had to take the risk and hope we could bargain out of an enormous debt one step at a time."

"The *Praznick* starts in minutes! They'll be here for you soon."

Sergei nodded.

"It cannot be, Sergei. We can't just give up!"

Sergei closed his eyes. His pale expression, like bleached bones, lost all color. He leaned back, as if he couldn't maintain another moment of speech. Of reality. Andrei gazed around. They had to escape.

"I've tried," Sergei rasped. "There is no way out. They have us imprisoned here until the *Praznick* begins."

"There's always a way out," he muttered, thinking of Mila. Sacha.

If they had any hope of stopping the High Priest and Nikolov before they flooded the clan with South Guards, they must get a hold of Sacha.

With any luck, she already knew what was happening.

A plan to overwhelm the magic that pinned him to the wall with something from the ancient spells that Mila taught him ran through his mind. Then, he'd transport himself, though still clumsy with that ancient spell, to find Sacha.

Sergei would have to figure something out . . .

"Sergei, I—"

The door slammed open from outside, admitting Alek and Nikolov. The same villainous gleam remained in the High Priest's face, amplified in the minutes that passed. A finalization of their plans, no doubt. Perhaps preparation and amassing of their South Guards. Andrei froze. The spells shuttered out of his mind.

Nikolov crossed the room with crisp steps, and stopped in front of Sergei.

Sergei stared at the floor.

Silently, Andrei attempted to command Sarasam. He opened his fingers—barely able to move them—but she didn't budge from the table. He tried to call Sirilas magic down, but nothing happened.

A stalemate.

A locked path.

Nothing to aid them now. Emptiness rang through him. No sensations or knowing filled him up inside. Not a single thought that tugged at his attention or prodding annoyance from swords who knew more than him.

The *nothing* frightened him the most.

Where were the magicks?

Had both forsaken him?

Sarasam!

The magic didn't respond.

"Come, Sergei," Nikolov said briskly. He must have released the magic, because Sergei's hand lifted. He rubbed the muscles in his wrist, wincing. Alek stood at the window. The setting sun cast him in a darker profile.

"Better get going."

Nikolov plucked at Sergei's sleeve, forcing him to stand. "The *Praznick* is about to start, according to you. There's a vote to cast and a debt to have repaid."

"Please," Andrei cried. "Don't do this."

Nikolov acted as if he hadn't spoken. "As a reminder to you both, Sergei will escort me and Alek to the *Praznick*. As planned, Alek and I will be invisible. Any alteration in plan, Sergei, and I'll run a sword through your gut, then take over the clan. Andrei, you will stay here until Alek returns for you. Once the vote finishes and we observe the secrets, our agreement ends."

Sergei's pallid expression didn't improve as Nikolov put a hand on his shoulder. Alek crossed the room, put his hand on Nikolov's back.

Nikolov kicked Sergei.

"Let's go, Guide."

Sergei closed his eyes. A shout built in Andrei's throat. *Don't do it. Take him somewhere else. Save the clan!* It wouldn't have mattered. If Sergei had the strength to kill Nikolov, the debt would have persisted. Alek, still in power, would wreak havoc on the clan.

Still pressed to the wall, Andrei could only watch as all three disappeared.

* * *

The room rang with emptiness.

For the first few breaths, Andrei could only watch the dampening light. The growing shadows. The sun had almost set in the distant sky. Sergei would make his way through the dining hall by now, with Nikolov and Alek trailing him. The crowd would part, whispers of excitement follow.

Andrei shook his head.

With a push of magical power, he attempted to break the spells that bound him. His body trembled, but nothing gave way. Finally, a transportation spell—though difficult and awkward and taxing—took him to the other side of the room.

He gazed around, slightly disoriented at the brief, but intense, struggle of the competing magic. With no further spells, the power within him calmed. Shackles remained around his hand. The spell that Mila had taught him to separate metal from rocks sent a giant crack through one. A fifth issuance broke both down entirely. Lucky that it should work.

He left the pieces to clatter on the floor.

Clearly, neither Nikolov, Alek, nor Sergei expected him to be capable of magic, which bought him a tiny advantage. The vote wouldn't take long. Clan members wrote *yes* or *no* on a slip of parchment, which the magic sorted into different piles. Twenty minutes, perhaps more.

The shift of a shadow on the porch prevented Andrei from crossing the room to touch Sarasam. He remained back, crouched in a darkened hallway, and stared at the table.

"Sarasam."

Nothing.

The hope that Sarasam hadn't responded to him because of Sergei quickly melted away. Anxiety built in his chest like a welling blizzard. Dark. Swirling. A storm unto itself.

"What have I done wrong?"

No response, not even a surge of emotion. No general sensation to guide him toward what he should do next.

"I can't leave the clan!" he hissed. "I can't just let them fall apart while I go make swords in the woods, and Alek and Nikolov make slaves of the witches. I won't do it. You can't ask it of me."

Andrei ran a hand over his face. The feel of his calloused palms against his skin felt like a shock.

How far had he deviated from who he had once been?

This far.

"What of *Maman*?" he snapped. "Of Sacha and Anastasia? There are witches I care about. The Ensis magic is . . . selfish."

He swallowed back other budding words, far darker. No, that wasn't entirely fair. It might be selfish of Andrei to desire the Ensis magic so exclusively, but not the magic. Magic was magic, unalterably.

"I won't . . . won't even be a good Guide . . . but I can't just abandon them. I want . . ."

Andrei leaned back against the wall. His hair shifted over his shoulder, sweeping along the wood in a limp braid. He closed his eyes.

What did he want?

The smithy ran through his mind, like a wavering image on a hot day. The feel of the metal in his hand. Crisp heat reaching for his skin. Charcoal briquettes, the smell of oil, the sensation of hammer hitting metal.

"I want to be Ensis."

He gazed over to Sarasam, hoping to feel a stirring of life deep inside. An answer to the questions he blasted into . . . nothing. A quick glance outside revealed that the South Guard hadn't moved. His back faced the Meeting House.

"But I can't."

His shoulders bowed. He tested the words out, attempting to see if a sign would come from either magic. The Sirilas, which said nothing but gave much. Or the Ensis, which said much, but gave less and less.

He paused, waited with held breath for a stirring.

A sound.

A sign.

The air had paused. Each lick of fire dimmed with every passing second. The sun sank all the way beneath the earth, pulling the light with it.

"I didn't think I could be a good swordmaker either." He lifted his chin, peered back at the Guard, who stood in stoic silence. Soon, he'd notice Andrei wasn't where he had been. Andrei could transport elsewhere, but he didn't want to leave Sarasam behind.

His annoyance hardened into resolve.

"Fine. Clearly, I'll have to get out of this myself. You won't tell me what to do for once? You'll let me flounder when I need you the most? I'll . . . "

Words lodged in his throat.

Find my path.

In fact, he faced what he feared the most: lack of certainty. Unknown. The great miasma of what *could* happen and all it meant. The future jealously hoarded a void of darkness that swirled in a giant mystery that he'd rather not approach. An *uncomfortable* place. One rife with indecision, uncertainty, lack of solid ground.

Was the unknown really as frightening as all of that?

"Haven't I, though?"

The words, spoken from his mouth, took him by surprise.

"Haven't I found my own way before? Haven't I endured change?"

Two metaphorical paths existed at his feet: the path of the Ensis and the path of the Sirilas. Neither would tell him what to do. Both faded to the darkness of the unknown because not even the rigidity of the Sirilas was infallible.

Sergei remained proof.

Sergei, so strict to the magic, hadn't wavered at first. Yet troubles came anyway. He lost his path and clung to a different darkness, despite the Sirilas.

"No guarantees," Andrei murmured. He'd been a fool. All of that safety and structure was a fallacy, in some regard. Ahead of him waited the actual path. The one in between the two he thought were the only ones.

Wildness.

Obscurity.

Terror and discomfort. Cold and isolation. Perhaps a lot of not knowing, but doing anyway.

He'd already done that.

Maybe the magicks hadn't left him. Maybe they just expected him to decide already. Hulu knew he loved to hesitate. Both magicks had revealed themselves and let him know what was possible. They lay ready at *his* feet for a decision.

Finally, the knowing returned. The certainty that he was on the right track. With renewed determination, he stepped back. A shuffling sound from the porch preceded a shout of, "Oi!"

Sarasam remained on the table, unwilling to come to his side, as the door slammed open. Too late. He couldn't grab Sarasam and arrive at the clan in time.

Andrei left the Meeting House, bound for clan lands.

Chapter Thirty-One

*The Praznick, o holy of holidays. We come together to
praise you, the maleesa, the Sirilas that sustains us.
Thanks to Hulu, we live in the coldest of climes. Glaciers
are our habitation, yet warm blood slides through our
veins. Meat in our bellies. Life, our soul.*

Maleesa, we are unworthy.

Sirilas, we are unworthy.

*Oh, Praznick, remind us of why we are here. For
maleesa.*

For clan.

*—Lari, Guide to the Clan
Year 1287*

A warm closet in the midst of the glacier surrounded Andrei.
Furs brushed up against each arm, tickling the back of his

neck. A band of light fell from a crack in the door that dropped into the enclosure, admitting the gentle sounds of gathering witches in the distance.

Well, he landed right where he wanted to.

Nikolov would be invisible, but right next to Sergei, no doubt. Perhaps at his back. Certainly within immediate reaching distance, should Sergei do or say something wrong.

Alek remained the true wildcard.

Unlikely that he'd stay in one spot. Alek would roam and wander, at least initially, to gather as much information as possible. Would he stay by the main doors, perhaps? A back entrance?

They wanted the *maleesa* the most, though they didn't know what the *maleesa* were. Alek would have likely canvassed the room by now and moved to a position that gave him fastest access to secrets.

Which meant Andrei would need to go somewhere . . . different.

The thought that they might have brought South Guards flitted through his mind, then back out. Nikolov and Alek had nothing kind planned for the clan, but they wouldn't be ready for total domination yet. Too many unknown places here to risk South Guards.

Given *this* access to the clan, they'd likely be confident to gain deeper ground later.

Or so he hoped.

Someone walked by, talking quickly. Another laughed. They disappeared around a corner. Moments later, Andrei stepped into the hallway.

Empty.

The Sirilas magic should have done something by now. Alerted clan members of Nikolov and Alek's presence. Stirred up alarms, difficulties, barriers to the strangers, but nothing had happened. The extent of how off-balance the magic had gone as a result of Sergei's betrayal shocked him. Or, most likely, Sergei hadn't renewed the protective magic from the Sirilas grimoire.

He hurried down the hallway, heading to the left. The main entrance to the *Praznick* would be to the right, through the double doors. The fewer witches that saw him, the better.

Sergei's voice rippled down the hallway as Andrei slinked along.

"As you cast your votes," he called, "please keep in mind the betterment of the clan. The years of training that have already taken place. You may not always agree with your Guide or what they say, but we are not here to vote on a popularity contest. Will this Guide keep the clan safe? That is the question you should answer."

Andrei stopped just outside a side door, behind the table where *Maman* would have left the *maleesa*. His heart cantered in his chest like a running timberwolf, thudding through his ears so he could hear almost nothing else.

Standing here without Sarasam felt wrong, like he'd torn a piece of his body out and expected it to work the same. He pressed his back to the wall, closed his eyes. Sergei's voice continued to ring through the closed glacier.

"I give Andrei the full power of my approval, notwithstanding recent rumors. These are rumors he will gladly dispel. I have already spoken with him on this matter. I feel he has the wellbeing of the clan at the forefront of his mind, and we can work any questions out together afterward."

A voice called from the back.

"What about the request from the High Priest? Will Andrei show the *maleesa* to the Network?"

Silence fell.

Andrei reached back, held himself against the chilly wall.

Oh, how bitter this irony.

"That," Sergei said with a shaky breath, "is Andrei's

choice, not mine. He is the future Guide to the Clan. Only you can ensure this. The bumps we experience now may have also resulted from my—"

Sergei's voice broke.

"—failing health," he continued in a wobbly tone. "The magic will return to balance, as it always does. Do you trust the magic?"

A foolish question to end on. Of course the clan trusted the magic, but they didn't trust the leaders. At least, they shouldn't. Andrei pulled in a deep breath. This wouldn't be as difficult if there had been more than one candidate, but no one else had stepped forward . . .

Now, he told himself. *The time to declare yourself as Guide or Ensis is now.*

For neither magic told him what to do, though he didn't know himself what he'd say.

A deep, dragging breath gave him the power to reach for the doorknob that would admit him inside. The wooden knob felt cool on his palm as he wrapped his fingers around it.

"No!"

A hand grabbed his wrist, flung it back. He whirled around to find Sacha standing there.

With a frantic shake of her head, she motioned for him to follow. Sounds came from within as the vote began. Shuffling footsteps, murmuring voices. Pencils and paper would soar around the room—if the Sirilas magic was active enough, anyway—and into awaiting hands.

Sacha hurried down the hall, glancing back every few steps to ensure he followed. He slowed as they neared the main entrance. With a sharp gesture from her hands, she pointed to her side.

He stepped up.

"Sacha—"

A closing motion of her fingers followed. He shut his

mouth. She peered around the doors, pointed inside. There, across the way, and in front of the door he would have slipped through, stood . . .

. . . no one.

Only the *maleesa* table, which had the usual adornments. Ice blocks built on top of each other, one layer at a time, until they reached a single block on the zenith at the top. They glimmered in aquamarine and sapphire hues, glittering from the thousands of candles that stood around the room to shed light.

Torches led the way down the middle of the room to the top, where Sergei stood. In the roving light, he appeared paler than ever. Anastasia, her *maman*, and two of Sergei's sons stood behind them. A space to Sergei's left remained empty. Nikolov likely occupied that area, no doubt hidden by a spell.

Andrei's fists tightened. He peered around the edge of the doorway only, but it could be enough. Nikolov may see him. Alek might. Alek would know that he'd left soon, which meant he should—

Papers soared through the air all at once, funneling into a woven basket close to Sergei. One at a time, the pieces peeled into different piles, whisked together by the Sirilas magic. No one would know which pile represented the *yes* and which represented the *no*. Both appeared to hold an equal number of votes.

As a candidate, he would be exempt from the vote. All clan members that helped run the *Praznick*, like Sacha, would have voted before the festivities began. Andrei's fingers twitched.

The reverberating silence that followed rivaled anything Andrei had heard in his thirty years.

Sergei glanced down as a single paper popped into the air, then sank with a sigh into his awaiting palm. He stared at it for a moment before lifting his head.

Andrei held his breath.

"The clan has voted," Sergei said shakily. "Andrei Kuzmin, you are the Guide to the Clan."

* * *

Sacha gasped.

Andrei paled.

He slipped back into the hallway, fully out of sight. His chest expanded with air, but it felt like nothing entered. All thoughts drained from his body, moving like water out of a sieve.

Guide to the Clan.

The expected path of his life.

A growing rustle of shocked whispers followed. They should have churned his stomach, but they didn't.

Because he already knew. As he'd known it all along, but couldn't put into words until this very moment when the decision had to be made. He knew what he wanted to do.

When he considered the future path he most wanted, only a few things appeared obvious.

The smithy.

His friends.

The Ensis magic.

The rest remained unknown. A buried adventure awaiting discovery, which was just the way he wanted it.

Growing ripples and exclamations expanded around the dining hall and echoed into the hall where he stood. Sacha gave him a wide-eyed stare, hands hanging limp at her side. By this time, Alek would be frantically looking for him back at the Meeting House.

Maybe Alek had already returned and reported Andrei missing.

Who knew?

It didn't matter.

Andrei knew his path. He'd act despite the questions and uncertainty.

"Sacha?"

"Andrei, I—"

"Go in with me?"

"What?"

"Follow me inside. I need to speak to the clan, and I want you to be there."

A moment of hesitation preceded her nod. She faded, and he breathed a little easier without the weight of the questions she bore in her eyes. With a deep breath for courage, he stepped into the room.

Rugs lay all over the floor in a patchwork design, preventing witches from slipping on the packed ice as they congregated. He stepped on one, felt the confidence beneath his feet.

This step.

Then the next one.

Clan members had clustered toward the front and middle of the room, naturally veering away from the ice and closer to the torches in the middle. Heads whipped around as he strode past, headed straight to the *Praznick maleesa* table.

Shocked exclamations bounced from the high ceiling. Water sluiced down the sides, carried over to small trenches that whisked the water out.

Like the glacier, there was truly no stasis in life. He'd chased a dream when he thought everything would remain the same. In a life without growth, fear would rule him.

Once at the table, Andrei stopped. He turned, met Sergei's horrified stare, his wide eyes. The punishment must be far more frightening than Sergei expected.

With a slight nod, Andrei spun to face the clan. He cupped his hands around his mouth and called out.

"Clan, may I speak?"

Those around him calmed first. Several clan members whispered behind them, and the room quietened by degree. A few gasps littered the crowd. Elbows to the ribs. Harried whispers.

Andrei called again.

"Clan! Give me your ears."

The second time carried to the end of the room. One at a time, all clan members faced him. He slipped to the side, climbed up several blocks of ice, and stood on a table near to the *Praznick maleesa*.

The stare of every clan member rested on him. Expectant and hopeful, with a mixture of fear and scorn. Perhaps not the worst combination on so important a day.

Andrei glanced at Sergei, who had lowered into a chair, eyes large as saucers. He shook so hard the hand resting on his knee bounced. Andrei forced himself to look away from his mentor—his previous *fere-papan*.

He set Nikolov out of his mind.

He'd deal with them next.

"Thank you, clan. I have come to give my official answer to your vote."

Residual sounds died completely, leaving only the drip and gentle hustle of water going down the small streams and out of the room. Power filled him. The presence of a magic he chose, a life he craved.

"I am Andrei, and I am Ensis."

He held out a hand.

Sarasam appeared.

The moment he touched its grip, felt the cool leather in his palm, the knowing brightened through him. Joy broke next. The sense of rightness he'd sought on his own, but only found after he'd trusted himself.

Sarasam's beaming relief illuminated him like a light. A

known thing. The guide in his darkness. It responded because he had *finally* decided. His chosen path remained clear, if not shrouded.

"I stand before you as Andrei, the Swordmaker." He lifted Sarasam higher. "These creations are my future, my path. The magic found me, and I listened, and with the Ensis magic I will remain. You will find me in the forest, creating more swords. The swords tell me what they want, and they know their owner. If their owner is in the clan, so be it. If not? So be it. The decision is not mine.

"That might mean I will give the swords to our enemies. If the clan cannot accept this, I understand. You may exile me, but I choose the swords. It's my path, the one I want. I have no guarantees or promises to give you, except that I love all of you. I want to be part of you, as I always have."

As if the clan could take no more surprises, not a single sound issued. Andrei gripped Sarasam all the tighter.

"I am not meant to be your Guide."

He pointed to the piles of votes—nearly the same size—with Sarasam's tip.

"You made that known today. I will not go into a position without the full trust of my clan, and half of you don't want me here. All of us have seen the truth over the last few months. You may have selected me because I trained to take you into the future, but that doesn't make me right for it."

A sigh, like a ripple of relief, swelled through part of the room.

"There is a witch who will guide you into safety. One witch that knows the clan, the struggles, and the management better than myself and Sergei. One witch that has constantly protected you from the grasping hands of the High Priest, and you weren't even aware of it."

He turned, pointed Sarasam to Sacha. "One witch who will give her whole heart to this clan: Sacha."

A cry came from the back of the room.

Then another.

Whoops and cheers followed. Sacha stepped forward. Her lips hung open as she stared at him in a shocked, silent question.

Andrei smiled.

"It was never supposed to be me," he said, so only she could hear. "Always you."

Questions, concerns, and support charged through the crowd. Clan members chattered. Others surged forward, arms lifted. Andrei raised his free hand until the exclamations calmed.

"Please! Please, we will cast a second vote, me against Sacha, when I have finished explaining. First—"

Another voice called from the front of the room.

Alek.

"First, we reveal the silk bugs!"

His words rippled across the room, carried on a spell that drowned out all other sounds. He stood behind Sergei, holding the old Guide to his chest. The sword Andrei had given him pressed to Sergei's throat.

Sergei, nearly limp, didn't fight back. He hung in the High Priest's arms, defeated. Sarasam warmed in Andrei's grip. Confidence slipped through him. He was in the right spot.

He knew this.

"This is your High Priest," Andrei called, pointing to Alek. "He and Council Member Nikolov have forced their way in here today to see the creatures from which our magic is derived."

"Why stop at creatures?" Alek cried with a terse smile. "Why not just hand over your grimoire, eh? We can make all of this go away so much faster if you give it to us."

A subtle shifting rippled through the crowd. Children pushed back. Mothers screened each, shuffling the youngest out the back doors. Men stepped closer. No Guards were visible, but the calmness of the crowd meant . . . something.

"Andrei," Sacha said with a tug on his pant leg. "Andrei, I must—"

"Who will provide the book and save your clan?" Alek cried. "If I don't have the grimoire in my hands in the next thirty seconds, Sergei will die. If I don't have it within a minute, Andrei will die. Another minute after that? Sacha will die."

Behind Sergei, Anastasia's brother grabbed her arm, tugged her to safety away from Alek. Sergei's wife stumbled with them, reaching for her husband with a muted cry. Andrei leaped off the ice blocks near the *maleesa* and strode closer to Alek.

Sacha hurried behind him.

"Andrei!"

No one moved.

"Now!" Alek screamed. He lifted the sword, tilting it against the pulse in Sergei's neck. Sergei winced, turned away. His face fractured into a painful grimace. Blood bloomed across his skin, dripping down the blade.

Horror gripped Andrei.

His blade.

Sergei may have betrayed the clan, but he didn't deserve this. He was no Nikolov, no Alek.

There was only one way to stop Alek, and the answer came from a long-lost recollection. The first time he met Alek.

The challenger declares the Vyzov Bitvay, he had said. *Then the time and the place. Gaining a Network is as simple as that.*

At his decision, Sarasam warmed.

I'm not good enough for this, Andrei thought. *Mila trained me a little, but not enough. The magic hasn't been helping. I—*

Sarasam gave no words, but her plea remained clear. *Trust me.*

"High Priest!" Andrei called, racing closer. "I issue the *Vyzov Bitvay!* We fight for the Network right now, right here, in front of the clan."

The High Priest locked his jaw, nose scrunched. Annoyance rippled through the tense muscles of his cheek. The clan held its collected breath. Unable to deny him, Alek shoved Sergei onto the ground with a growl. Sergei collapsed.

Alek whipped the blade back with a snarl. His lip pulled over his teeth.

"Then let us fight."

Chapter Thirty-Two

Oh, maleesa.
Your days are short.
Your nights are long.
Wings of porcelain blue,
Hearts of needle depth.
Our lives wheel around yours.
You do not know.
We die.
You die.
And hope Hulu listens.

—Tavish, Spinner
Year 1453

Alek sneered at him from the other side of the dining hall.

Witches had parted to the edges and formed an open oval. Children continued to scamper out the doors, hiding in the hallways. Mothers followed, though reluctantly. Andrei's gut twisted with dread. He didn't relish drawing blood.

Yet, he loved his clan more.

Alek lifted his new sword when they met in the middle of the oval. Alek reached his blade forward. Following his lead, Andrei did the same. Alek touched his blade, retreated with a silent snarl.

Andrei brought Sarasam in front of him. The scattered lessons with Mila moved through him like living memories. Each muscle in his leg tightened to plant him more firmly against the woven rug. His now-powerful arms held Sarasam as close as instinct. Rote motions whirred through his mind, ready to act.

He was no match for the High Priest, a witch trained to fight for his life since he was born.

Yet, Andrei stepped forward anyway.

The path would appear, this he knew.

Alek feinted with a slash. Andrei dodged, twirled out of the way. He lifted Sarasam as he spun, heard and felt the clash of metal on metal, and regained planted feet. Alek feinted again, this time a different way.

A test, Andrei sensed. Alek attempted to suss out weak spots in his defense, in the way he moved. He wanted to learn *how* Andrei used the sword to defend, where he whirled first. It would take less than a minute for Alek to see the truth.

Andrei knew almost nothing about sword fighting. Andrei fumbled in a parry, then faked a trip when he tried to drive forward. Hints of a smile appeared on Alek's face, buried in concentration.

A growl came from behind.

"Finish him!"

Nikolov.

Several clan members whirled around, attempting to find out where the voice issued from. Like a true coward, Nikolov had yet to reveal himself.

Alek's nostrils widened with irritation. He said nothing, but executed another slash, another shuffle forward with quick, dancing feet. After too long toying with him, the High Priest slipped into full drive. He came at Andrei with stunning speed and near-perfect footwork.

Andrei hurried back. The rug ruffled between them and Alek tripped. He righted, but his attack spun wide. Andrei countered with ease, pressing what little advantage he held.

The High Priest sprang back to guard faster than expected. Andrei rushed, but Alek laughed him off. Alek side-stepped into a hole in his defense Andrei hadn't noticed, nearly gaining a chunk of Andrei's shoulder in the meantime. At the last minute, Andrei crouched. The sword whistled past his ear as it swung by.

Heat filled his body. Like the Ensis magic in the beginning, at the forge, when he first accepted it. Andrei turned his body to the magic.

To the moment.

Smaller openings in Alek's offense became more apparent. Alek favored his right side. Andrei forced him to spin left. He moved too quickly, over-corrected, and Andrei slashed at his ribs. A rent tore in Alek's clothes.

He growled.

Andrei advanced, but stepped off when Alek countered too quickly, coming with certain force. He ducked, the blow swung just above his head, and straightened. Alek regained his footing.

They stood across from each other, panting.

Alek held the sword with both hands, the wide blade and heavier weight allowing for a stronger swing. His arms vibrated with tension. Sweat already dotted his upper brow. Andrei lifted Sarasam.

"You're in a difficult position, High Priest," he muttered. "If you want to remain High Priest, you must kill me. But I will not die tonight. If you attempt to surrender the fight, the Network is mine."

"Look who knows so much about their Network now. You and your ugly sword. You're as fallible to death as any other clan member."

Andrei laughed, stepped to the side.

Alek followed, his left foot crossing behind his right as they circled. Alek feinted again, but Andrei didn't twitch. The High Priest held his body differently when he meant to attack. One couldn't entirely fake inertia, and all the bluster in his movements would tire him.

Alek stepped forward, twirling his step—and his torso—slightly to the right to remove himself from Andrei's immediate attack.

Sarasam cut through the air, singing. Alek lurched back, just shy of scraping his chest open with the tip of her blade. Andrei swung up, Alek dodged, and they settled at the edge of the circle.

"You could have just left, Andrei. I didn't care who became Guide. Why didn't you stay away? Live in your woods?"

Andrei swung, but Alek caught him at the same spot. The swords clanged together, preventing the blow from landing on his neck. Andrei whirled, removing his sword. Alek hit his blade on the other side, disorienting Andrei.

The room spun as Andrei attempted to right himself.

"I will not abandon my clan."

"They will abandon you after this, I have little doubt." Alek grinned, beckoned him with a tilt of his head. Andrei feinted, Alek parried.

"Your clan will hate you and Sergei," Alek sang, licking his lips. He swung the sword, testing the distance between them. Andrei didn't take the bait to attack, but waited. Sarasam cautioned him to be patient.

To be calm.

"We're going to take your grimoire, then use your magic

elsewhere. If your clan members want to help us, we'll take them. They'll make livable wages, should they be cooperative, of course."

Alek slashed, but Andrei didn't flinch. The air stirred as the sword swung by, far too wide, eclipsing the High Priest.

Andrei tensed to move, but Sarasam cautioned him to hold. Something welled up inside. Knowing, again. The same flow of sensation that happened when the magic first manifested, though it didn't always make sense.

"The clan will be ours!" Alek cried, drunk with laughter. "Nikolov will be happy. I will remain High Priest, and the Network will continue in prosperity under my name. No one else. You will die tonight, Andrei, in your pathetic attempt to save your clan. I, for one, cannot wait."

Alek attacked again with renewed vigor. Each clash rang harder, each step more aggressive. The High Priest pressed closer, faster , until clan members scattered and Andrei skittered back against a wall of ice. He collapsed it. Shards shattered at his back, breaking into stunning fractals that scattered on the ground.

Andrei rolled out of the way as Alek's sword slammed into the ice.

Then he heard it.

A *ping*.

His head jerked up. Andrei sprang back to his feet, crouched low. Alek ripped the sword from the ground and whirled to face him again. Alek hadn't heard the crack of metal. Didn't know that his sword—weakly made from the beginning—had just broken.

The magic surged within him. Sarasam, in her voiceless way, spurred him to act.

Now.

Andrei swung.

He carried all his force into the upward movement. Tensed

his weight bearing leg, moved his torso, and loosed all his heart into a single swing. Alek brought his sword down at the same time. The two met in the middle.

The nameless sword shattered.

Pain rippled through Andrei's hands, into his wrists, through his arms. It made his teeth chatter, shook his body. He held onto Sarasam, through the change in inertia, and brought her around.

Alek's sword crumbled to the floor.

Dying sounds issued from it. Exultation. Relief. Joy. The sword, brittle and imperfectly structured, had been made for this moment. A one-fight sword. A sacrificial gift. It had been imperfect from the beginning, yet perfect for its purpose.

This had been the reason for the divergence of the magicks. The Ensis magic hadn't come as competition for the Sirilas, but as protection.

From the moment Sarasam dropped into the snow at his feet, everything made sense.

Shock glazed Alek's expression as he stared at the jagged hilt. Andrei sprang on top of the High Priest, crashed with him to the floor, and kneeled on his chest. Sarasam hovered at the High Priest's heart. Alek groaned, then froze.

Andrei sank Sarasam's tip into his clothes until he felt the unyielding pressure of a breastbone.

Alek held his breath.

So the room could hear, Andrei cried, "Give me your vow this instant, High Priest. You forgive all tax debt to the clan, and we will forgive the hostilities toward our witches from the former High Priest. You and Council Member Nikolov will submit to a memory potion of our making. The potion will ensure that you can never find the glacier again. If you don't, I will kill you now and take over the Southern Network myself."

An interminable silence passed.

Alek studied him, malevolence in the hard angles of his frown. His left arm tensed.

Andrei pushed harder.

"Fine!" Alek shouted. "I submit. I will vow to forgive the tax debt this instant, and will submit to the potion."

"Council Member Nikolov must take it as well or the vow has failed and your life is forfeit."

"Agreed," he muttered.

Sacha appeared at Andrei's side. She grabbed the High Priest's hand, put it on Andrei's shoulder. Andrei kept his gaze locked on Alek, who scowled back. Heat moved through Andrei's arm, slipped into his blood, as Sacha repeated the vow, sealing it with magic.

Both agreed.

The moment the incantation finished, Andrei backed away. He crouched, Sarasam held out, while the High Priest stood. Clan members inched forward, several Guards at the front. They wore regular clothes, not their typical blue silk that set them apart from others for quick identification.

Sacha motioned to them with a tilt of her head.

"Escort him to the Meeting House until the potion is prepared and given. Do not take your hands off of him or else he will be able to transport. Keep three witches holding him at all times, and put him in manacles." She smirked at Alek. "He might be strong, but not even the High Priest could transport three other adult witches with him if he were to try to escape."

Alek bared his teeth.

She patted his cheek.

The Guards ushered him away. A crash came from behind. The room turned to see Nikolov standing at the offering table, where the Sirilas book lay open. He clutched it, eyes wide with madness.

"It's mine, Alek! The grimoire is mine!"

Two witches appeared from invisibility, tackled him. The

book flew into the air, then settled with a thunk on the ground. Andrei gasped, rushed forward, but Sacha grabbed his shoulder and held him back. She waved a hand.

"Don't worry about that. It's a fake book. An accounting grimoire with really terrible magic. So is the bug, by the way."

The *maleesa* home had appeared, the glass dome carefully suspended in the air above the table. Inside lay a creature—decidedly *not* a *maleesa*—along the bottom seam.

"But—"

"I figured something was up," she said blithely, folding her arms across her middle. "I just didn't know what. Thought we'd play it safe, just in case Sergei had plans. I told the clan that something might happen, so the Guards hid in plain clothes, just in case. Well, I was right!"

The glee in which she said the words brought a slow, hesitant laugh from him. He let it roll out until she threw her arms around him. Tears thickened her voice as she said, "Oh, Andrei. Thank you for saving the clan."

Sarasam purred contentedly at his side as he slipped it back into the scabbard. Slowly, the day unwound. The loosening tension slipped free. He let it go, slumped into a nearby chair, and hung his head in his hands.

The clan bustled to life around him with exclamations, cries, and shouts. The cacophony grew. Sacha responded. She stood on a block of ice and called out orders. He let it happen. All he wanted was his smithy.

Sarasam issued a quiet agreement at his side.

Chapter Thirty-Three

Spring snowmelt pattered on the eaves outside.

Slush dripped from high boughs, sluffing ice and water onto the roof of the smithy. A dollop landed on the back of Andrei's neck, slid down his shoulder blades. Andrei hooted, danced away until it cleared, and rushed inside.

Firewood clattered to the ground as he dropped it in a pile near the fire, eager to be rid of it. The prickling bark dug into his forearms. He should wear a coat, but the gradual warming air felt too delicious to ignore. The dark tides of winter faded, giving way to life again.

As it should be.

Heat billowed through the smithy, almost too warm now that constant blizzards didn't threaten from the west. Thanks to the construction of the building, the air funneled higher, then out a vent at the top that, with a spell, he could open as needed.

Mila's ingenious invention—a long hearth that ran through the middle of the room—currently housed two fires, one on each end. Unfinished swords lay on the table, awaiting fires hot enough to heat their blades. Moving from one to the other proved easier than he expected.

Now that he didn't have to run off anywhere.

Andrei moved quietly around the smithy, conscious of the four swords that perched on the wall above the hearth. Sarasam, in the place of honor, at the very bottom. She hummed contentedly these days, surrounded by other swords. They came and went at regular intervals now. Deliverers arrived at least once a week, then faded. They never came back.

He wished them well, off to their own grand adventures.

The sound of a bird call came from the door. He glanced up, smiled. Mila crowded the doorway, bags of rock shards in her hands. She beamed as she hustled inside, set them on the table.

"I assume you need these?"

"Always."

A man stood behind her, hovering in the doorway. He was a broad-shouldered witch with a trim beard, a loose coat of furs, and firm hands. He eyed Andrei, showing no suspicion or wariness. Mila swept a hand toward him.

"Andrei, this is Tikhon, my partner."

The man nodded once, a quick greeting.

Andrei responded in kind. "Good to finally meet you, Tikhon. I've heard only good things. Your dwelling is ready?"

Mila brightened. "Ready and almost warm. We moved in yesterday. I'm finishing up the hearth later this week while he sets the rest of the roof. There's room to grow when we need it in the fall."

She set a hand on her belly.

"No!" he cried, attempting to picture Mila as a mother. Filling her home, wherever they found it, with all the children she'd always wanted. Andrei grinned, laughing.

Mila's hand lingered on her belly, then swept away. Andrei waved Tikhon into the room. He entered, cast his gaze around. Mila set the rock bags on the table.

"That's not the best part, Andrei! You didn't even *ask* where our dwelling is."

"Where is it?"

She pointed. He pivoted, following the direction. It pointed to . . . the creek.

"What?"

"We're neighbors!"

"No!"

"Just down the stream," Tikhon said with a little shrug. "This is a pleasant area and Mila wants to help with the swords."

"But it's nowhere near the river villages. At least, not close enough to be convenient."

Mila sent Tikhon a sly glance.

"We are where we want to be, convenient or not. Besides, we always have magic to use to see them, don't we?"

While she invited him to a lastmeal to welcome their family to their new dwelling, Andrei stepped away from the swords. Tikhon warmed into the conversation gradually. He interrupted at intervals, mostly to tease Mila. Andrei laughed every so often, usually with Tikhon, as Mila protested loudly.

"Sacha wants the clan to interact more regularly with the villagers," she continued like a happy bird. "My *Maman* is interested in what that might mean. There's also rumors that Sacha has scheduled a meeting with the entire Council and the High Priest. Can you imagine facing Alek again after how she bested him? Sacha is fearless!"

While she continued to prattle about fortifying their

house with a different pitch than she used here, Andrei eased into work again. Two swords moved in and out of the flames as he shaped them, discussed metallic conformations with Tikhon, and let the friendly *ting, ting, ting* of hammer on metal fill the air.

That evening, he would return to the clan to see *Maman* for their weekly lastmeal. His clan family would greet him, as they always had. The Sirilas magic often provided his favorite meal as the world crept back into balance.

Far away, in what would amount to days of walking from any desirable land, lay a quiet valley with a glacier. The glacier was hidden from those who wanted to see it, revealed to those chosen to see it.

Near it lurked a family.

Nay, a clan.

Andrei's clan.

Acknowledgments

First and foremost, a *hearty* thank you to author Jonathon Smidt, who walked me through so much of the blacksmith and blade forging process with humor and serious skill. He's only one reason this book was *so much fun* to write.

A second *huge* thanks to Jenny Zemanek, who not only designs the most beautiful covers on this planet but also the lovely sword drawings that helped so much of this come to life.

THE SWORDMAKER was a book that, frankly, I dreaded for a while. My idea summed up with the words *lotsamagicinoneplaceOMG* and executing that kind of vision is always interesting.

It involved a lot more online videos about metal and forging than I ever expected, walking around my neighbors yard while talking to a blacksmith on the phone and taking copious notes as my dogs played, and staring at the wall, attempting to imagine just what limits magic had in this snowy clime.

To my KCW team, you are the wind beneath my wings. Thank you for all that you do for me. Sam, Jenny, Mike, Kerri, Kaley, Evan, Laila, Louise, Debbie, Kim, Carol. Your skills, talents, and brains even out all the Katie-Math that tries to take us down, so thank you from the bottom of my heart.

To my CWKites and readers—may this story sweep you away as it did for me for many years to come.

MUAH!

ANDREI, THE SWORDMAKER

The first Andrei is most frequently known as Andrei of 1447, which is the year the Ensis magic appeared.

Andrei of 1447 established the Ensis magic when it came to Alkarra, in the Southern Network, for what is believed to be the first time.

For reasons unknown, but assumed to be sheer organizational ease, the magic has insisted that all swordmakers in the Ensis magic bear the name, and the mantle, of Andrei. Some have been named Andrei since birth, others have changed their name.

You will find each Andrei referred to according to the year the mantle passed to their care.

TYPES OF METAL

There are many types of metal available for the Ensis to use, and more developed all the time. The most common metals that the Ensis will use is *utug*, found in the riverbeds and earth of the Southern Network.

- 1. *Utug*—A metal found in Southern Network riverbeds. Typically fortified with charcoal, blackened bones, or other strengtheners such as black diamond dust. When *utug* is mixed with charcoal, it creates steel.
- 2. *Guta* steel—Charcoal and *utug*. This is the most common variety of basic sword composition.
- 3. *Omgrarian* steel—Formed when *utug* is mixed with black diamond dust for a stronger blade that is resistant to specific types of magic. This mixture was discovered by the Andrei of Year 1543, during the year 1551.
- 4. *Hipuka* steel—*utug* mixed with blackened bones. This creates exceptionally versatile swords able to bend ninety degrees without cracking or breaking. The mixture is attributed to the Andrei of Year 1447.
- 5. *Orgon* steel—*utug* mixed with charcoal from a dragonian flame. The residual dragon's breath creates a sword that will bounce to life with flames when it finds its master. This new mixture is attributed to the Andrei of Year 1603. This was discovered in the year 1613.

Other types of metal exist that various Andrei's have used throughout the years, but the above mixtures are the most hearty and popular.

TYPES OF SWORDS

While some Andreis have been more creative than others, most Andrei swords fall under the same basic categories as seen below. Though mostly a swordmaker, Andrei has created some daggers, knives, and other sharp weapons as instructed by the magic.

- **Cutlass**—Contains a wide tip with a tapering width near the tang.
- **Dae**—The curved blade creates greater steel.
- **Long sword**—This sword is the most popular sword amongst Andrei creations. It tends to be as long as an entire arm, and requires a certain height to be safely wielded. These are typically the weight of a thick book. To be used with a shield.
- **Machete**—The width of this sword from tang to tip is most often used to stave off incoming blighters. Too heavy for fencing-type defense.
- **Rounded tip**—The tip has a rounded edge. Typically more successful when used from a horse, a magical carpet, or a dragon.
- **Sharp tip**—The tip is quite sharp and comes to a thin point. Typically more successful when used at close range, such as a Mactos.
- **Short sword**—This type of sword is used for close combat, or those with shorter height and arm span.

TOOLS

While not exclusive, these are the tools that most Andrei's have used throughout the years. The tools—as well as the layout of the smithy—has altered under each Andrei. As the mantle passes, the smithy, tools, and types of swords may also change.

Presumably, the Ensis magic approves of these variations.

- Anvil
- Bellows
- Charcoal
- Chisel
- Clamp
- Firewood
- Hammer (varying sizes according to use)
- Hard-bristled brush
- Hearth
- Post vise
- Tongs

THE SWORD MAKING PROCESS

As a general guide, the following process is how most Andrei's have started their swordmaking journey. With growth, each Andrei may develop different systems to speed up and slow these processes down. Some Andrei's have involved family members—if allowed and trusted by the Ensis magic—to help with things such as metal collection, bone burning, etc.

No Andrei sword is allowed in the hands of another witch until it's deliverer shows up.

Finding the Metal

- Locate *utug* in a riverbed.
- Separate it from the rock through a grinding, magical process. (The incantations are not specific to the *Ensis* magic, but those are available as well.

There is no grimoire, so listen to the inner knowing.)

- Filter it through mesh to get rid of the rock and dust.
- Collect the *utug* metal together.
- Weigh out a specific amount of ground charcoal or other additives (depends on the amount of *utug*. This will be given as part of the knowing.) Melt the *utug*, add charcoal, glass, sand, or whatever you have been instructed. Always combine the glass and sand, as it will absorb impurities.
- Melt together. This will take several hours. To achieve the desired heat, you'll need to use the correct bellows and more firewood than you might expect.
- Pour into the rectangular cast and allow to cool. This forms the steel ingot.

Forging the Blade

- Allow the ingot cool. Remove slag with a hard-bristled brush, if any. Inspect for issues.
- Reheat to a bright orange color. The exact shade to watch for will be given by the magic, so remain calm and in tune with the inner knowing. The temperature of the ingot will vary depending on the individual sword. The sword will inform when to stop, where to apply more heat, etc.
- Hammer the sword into the desired length. This will be difficult at first and requires some precision. Remember, it's difficult to pull out of mistakes. It should require about half a day of work. The sword may not want this completed all

at once, or it may demand to be finished in one day. This will be given with the knowing.

** Note for swords with Orgon steel: As you hammer the blade, you will see multitudinous sparks of differing colors issue from beneath. They will settle into the flame color that the sword will burn when the blade completes. Wear protective leather to avoid catching on fire.*

** Note for swords with Omgrarian steel: Though the black diamond dust makes these swords almost unbreakable, you must treat the entire hammering process with great delicacy. The black diamond dust doesn't activate until the final quenching. Expect to work an Omgrarian steel sword double the amount of time.*

Setting the Inlay

- Once you have finished the blade and it appears to your satisfaction, carve out the desired inlay, such as a name, a symbol, whatever is given to you in the moment.
- Be aware that carving into a metal blade can introduce weakness, cracks, or break your blade. Listen to the knowing when you consider depth and width. The less you try to forge it yourself, the more the magic will guide.
- Curl and straighten and hammer the metal to fit into this shape.
- Put the sword with the inlaid metal into the fire to treat it with heat. Watch the color and listen to your inner knowing. It will guide you. If the letters

bubble, fear not. Some of the metal will melt off of the top.

- Allow it to cool.
- The result will be hidden until after the polish.
- If you haven't set the guard yet, now is the time to do so. If your sword contains an integral guard, proceed to the next step.

Quenching

- When you have completed the sword to your satisfaction, it's time for the final stage. Put the sword back into the fire—make sure the entire blade is heated evenly. Pile charcoal on top. If the blade instructs, keep it moving in the flames. Use the bellows to generate enough heat.

Note: for swords forged with Orgon steel, the flames will need to reach a precariously high temperature. Do not do this alone. You will need a second witch to assist with the bellows. The magical properties of this steel create heat that is nigh unbearable. If it is not hot enough—dragonfire hot, to be precise—the blade will break.

- When it glows a consistent, dull orange, dunk the entire sword into cold water or oil.

Note for Guta steel swords: Water is preferable over oil with this chemical and magical composition. This steel is used for swords that have extremely loyal masters, but do not lead very exciting lives. It's a more basic composition, and the oil serves its lower-magical threshold more thoroughly.

- During the quenching process, listen for a loud sound, particularly within the first ten seconds. If there is a loud sound, the sword is broken. (You will hear it almost immediately.)

Polishing

- When the sword has cooled from the quench and you've had a large glass of water, it's time to finish your sword. First, take a coarse-grained stone and begin to polish. The location of these stones will be given to you as the sword is ready. Each metal will require a different level of grit.
- As you smooth the stone over the metal, drop to a finer-grit stone to make the metal really start to shine. By the end, you should be able to catch the light with it, smear away all blemishes.

** Note for Orgon steel blades: due to the violent and intense nature of the dragon flames, Orgon blades will require a specific, more acidic potion during the final polishing. The ingredients will be given to you. You will need dragon egg dust, which contributes to the rarity of these swords.*

- Expect hours to days of polishing with the stones, potions, and rags. Having the polishing potion available around the fourth hour of polishing (whether those hours are spread out or cumulative) will be helpful. The ingredients and steps for making it will be given to you when the sword is ready.

**Note for swords with Hipuka steel: the blackened bones*

will create a slight opalescent sheen and luster to the final sword, after the quench. The properties of the bones will emerge at this stage, and you'll begin to understand whether the sword will be sharp, strong, or bendable.

- Once the polish is finished and the metal gleams, putting a light layer of an acid on the inlay will reveal the letters / symbol.
- At the end, *yakuza* oil will most benefit the metal, and really create a brilliant shine.

SWORDMAKING TERMS

Bastard sword: hand-and-a-half sword. Longer and broader than others, but not as long or broad as a two-hander. A witch could wield this sword two-handed or one-handed. These have a thicker blade, because they wield one handed or two and will switch their fighting style with it. Parrying, heavy on blocking.

Bellows: This tool stokes the flames higher by blowing the air into the coals. With the magic, these sometimes won't be needed. Two or more are required for Orgon blades.

Casting: The process of melting certain melts down to a liquid state so they can be changed in form to something else, such as a guard, pommel, or tang.

Flux: The sand that keeps the metal from sticking to the molds.

Forge welding: When two pieces of metal are heated up to the proper temperature, then fused into each other.

Fuller: The indentation in the center of the sword. It allows for longer, wider blades, but without more metal. This allows the sword to stay light, adds flexibility, and reduces weight because it pushes more metal out to the edge of the blade. It's often aesthetically pleasing, as well.

Guard: The cross section at the bottom of the blade, near the tang.

Ingot: Single piece of metal that will eventually become the blade/sword.

Inlay: The name or design on a sword.

Omgrarian steel: *Utug* metal mixed with charcoal to form a harder steel.

Pommel: Sits at the bottom of the tang, the very end of the sword. Can be used to grip and maneuver.

Post vise: a free-standing clamping tool.

Quench: When the forged weapon is in its desired shape, it's superheated, then dipped into water or oil to strengthen the metallic bonds. The blade is evenly heated to a specific temperature, then rapidly cooled in oil or water for a short amount of time (typically 30 seconds to 1 minute.)
    Also known as the heat-treating process. This makes or breaks a weapon (literally).

Reins: The part of the tongs that do the gripping.

Slag: Impurities found in the metal that can weaken a sword. These are non-metallic.

Smelting: The process heating of the metal.

Tang: The part of the sword that is covered by the handle material. (Often leather-wrapped at the end.) An integral sword means the tang and pommel and guard and blade are forged together.

Tang slot: Where the tang meets the guard.

Tongs: A tool used in bladesmithing. They need to be long enough that a swordmaker doesn't have to be close to the fire.

Two hander: A type of heavier blade that requires two hands to use it. These have a longer handle, which means a longer tang, and they're thicker.

***Utug*:** The most dominant type of metal found in the Southern Network. Typically binds to rocks and is found in riverbeds in small pieces.

Taravaren

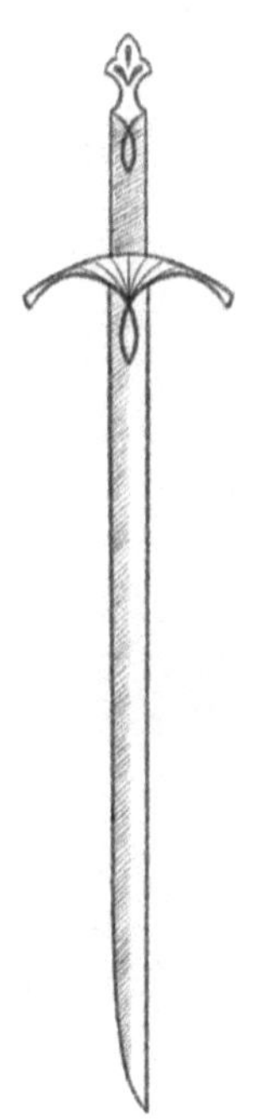

The Unnamed Sword

The Dragonmaster Trilogy

FLAME

Chronicles of the Dragonmasters (short story collection)

FLIGHT

The Ronan Scrolls (novella)

FREEDOM

The Dragonmaster Trilogy Collection

The Sisterwitches Series

The Sisterwitches Book 1

The Sisterwitches Book 2

The Network Series

Mildred's Resistance (prequel)

Miss Mabel's School for Girls

Alkarra Awakening

The High Priest's Daughter

War of the Networks

The Network Series Complete Collection

The Isadora Interviews (novella)

Short Stories from Miss Mabel's

Short Stories from the Network Series

Hazel (short story)

The Network Saga Suggested Reading Order

1. The Parting (novella #1)

2. The Lost Magic (full-length novel)

3. The Lamplighter's Daughter (novella #2)

4. Merrick (novella #3)

5. The Rise of the Demigods (full-length novel)

6. Priscilla (novella #4)

7. Viveet (novella #5)

8. Prana (novella #6)

9. Derek (novella #7)

10. The Forgotten Gods (full-length novel)

11. The Returning (novella #8)

12. Regina (novella #9)

13. Leda (novella #10)

14. The Sister (prequel to WOTG #1)

15. The School (prequel to WOTG #2)

16. The Council (prequel to WOTG #3)

17. The Goddess (prequel to WOTG #4)

18. War of the Gods (full-length novel)

19. The Finales (a collection of novellas)

20. Marten (novella #11)

The Historical Collection

The High Priestess

The Swordmaker

The Advocate

About the Author

Katie Cross is ALL ABOUT writing epic magic and wild places. Creating new fantasy worlds is her jam.

When she's not hiking or chasing her two littles through the Montana mountains, you can find her curled up reading a book or arguing with her husband over the best kind of sushi.

Visit her at www.katiecrossbooks.com for free short stories, extra savings on all her books (and some you can't buy on the retailers), and so much more.